T0116125

EILEEN CHANG

Half a Lifelong Romance

Eileen Chang (1920–1995), a novelist, essayist, and screen-writer, was born into an elite family in Shanghai. In 1941, while the city was under Japanese occupation, she began to publish the stories and essays that established her reputation in the literary world. She left China in 1952 to escape the influence of the Communist Party, settling in the United States in 1955. She continued to write novels, stories, essays, and screenplays for Hong Kong films. In the 1970s, her works became immensely popular throughout the Chinese-speaking world. Despite her growing fame, Chang grew more and more reclusive, and was found dead in her Los Angeles apartment in 1995. Her works continue to be translated into English. A film adaptation of her novella *Lust, Caution*, directed by Ang Lee, was released in 2007.

Karen S. Kingsbury taught and studied in Sichuan and Taiwan for nearly two decades, and is currently Professor of International Studies at Chatham University, where she teaches East Asian studies and world literature. She lives near Pittsburgh, Pennsylvania.

Half a Lifelong Romance

A Novel

EILEEN CHANG

Anchor Books
A Division of Penguin Random House LLC
New York

FIRST ANCHOR BOOKS EDITION, MARCH 2016

Introduction and translation copyright © 2014 by Karen S. Kingsbury

All rights reserved. Published in the United States by Anchor Books, a division of Penguin Random House LLC, New York, and distributed in Canada by Random House of Canada, a division of Penguin Random House Canada Ltd., Toronto. Originally published in China as *Shiba chun* by Eileen Chang (writing as Liang Jing) by Yibao, Shanghai, in 1951. Subsequently published in slightly different form in Taiwan as *Bansheng yuan* by Crown Publishing Co., Ltd., Taipei, in 1969. Copyright © 1969 by Crown Publishing Co., Ltd. This English translation originally published in paperback in Great Britain by Penguin Modern Classics, a division of Penguin Random House Ltd., London, in 2014.

Anchor Books and colophon are registered trademarks of Penguin Random House LLC.

The Cataloging-in-Publication data is on file at the Library of Congress.

Anchor Books Trade Paperback ISBN: 978-0-307-38754-7
eBook ISBN: 978-0-375-42525-7

www.anchorbooks.com

147028622

Contents

Introduction

Half a Lifelong Romance (Bansheng yuan) is, by almost any count, Eileen Chang's most popular novel, and the Chang tale most frequently adapted by others for stage and screen. And yet the author herself, despite her bilingual prowess, never produced an English version. This translation offers English-speaking readers a chance to explore, for the first time, this deeply felt, fully mature fictional world, created by a stellar writer—one of twentieth-century China's most accomplished and revered artists—during the long mid-life period when she was at the height of her powers.

Originally entitled *Eighteen Springs (Shiba chun)*, the story was published first in serial form, starting in March of 1950, in a Shanghai magazine sponsored by the newly ascendant Communist Party. Reissued in single-volume format the following year, the story became the author's first full-length novel. Eighteen years later, however, Chang released a significantly revised and retitled text that has to be considered the authorized version (and therefore is the basis for this translation). By that time, she had not only fled the People's Republic of China and moved to the United States, but married and outlived her second husband, Ferdinand Reyher, and written three other novels, each of which she published in English and in Chinese. Surely those experiences are part of the reason why *Half a Lifelong Romance* is more somber, but also more consistent and thematically complete, than *Eighteen Springs*. In any case, the later version of the novel soon attracted a steady, often devoted readership, especially among young people in Taiwan and Hong Kong. In the ten years following Chang's death in 1995, the story was retold repeatedly, in Hong Kong, China and Taiwan, via film, television serial and even musical stage show. Some productions followed the tale's earlier version, others the later; in either case they were part of the late twentieth-century groundswell of admiration for Chang's work, after her years of relative obscurity.

The only specific historical reference in the story is the 1937 Battle of Shanghai, a three-month struggle between Chinese and Japanese armies that is waged in the background of Chapter 15. At that point, Gu Manzhen, the female protagonist, is in her thirties; Eileen Chang was in fact sixteen when the bombardment began. Like most of her novel's characters, Chang escaped direct harm even though she was living in a war zone. She did, however, in this same period, suffer from domestic violence: beaten by her father for supposed insubordination, she was imprisoned in her room for half a year, until finally she escaped to her mother's apartment, through the connivance of a maid who took pity on the girl, now seriously ill.

Five years after that episode, at which point the Japanese invasion of Hong Kong had ended her university studies there, Chang returned to Shanghai and started supporting herself by writing. Her primary publishers were literary magazines that had to please middlebrow Chinese readers without displeasing the Japanese occupiers or their puppet-government supporters. Chang excelled in the seemingly narrow vein created by these pressures, turning it into an opportunity to plumb personal and cultural psychology, often by recounting, directly or indirectly, family dramas like her own. Then, in the late 1940s, after the Japanese and then the Nationalists had been defeated, the Communist Party created literary outlets like *Yibao*, a progressive but not strictly doctrinaire magazine aimed at a broad swathe of urban readers, and Chang tried her hand at writing under this new set of conditions. In March 1950, six months after Mao Zedong proclaimed the People's Republic, she began serial publication of this story in *Yibao*, under a pen name.

As indicated by its title, *Eighteen Springs* narrates eighteen years of its characters' lives, and the single volume, when it came out, was divided into eighteen chapters. The beginning and middle chapters of *Eighteen Springs* are almost identical to the corresponding chapters in *Half a Lifelong Romance*, and, as readers will see, the tale does begin with a sense of hopefulness, especially in the figure of Gu Manzhen, a charming young woman who is determined, after her father's early death, to support her large family through respectable, if poorly paid, clerical work. Shen Shijun, a young engineer at the textile mill where she works, finds her fortitude both graceful and inspiring—like many a sensitive young man, as described in early twentieth-century Chinese literature, he is the product of a conservative, emotionally complicated household and tends to be diffident and unsure of himself. Even in this first draft, however, Chang fleshed out these potentially flat characters by repeatedly setting up parallel yet differing events—two women's problems with shoes, for instance; or the varying reception accorded to Shijun on his visits to Manzhen's family—in order to reveal shades of difference in the various characters' personalities. Throughout the novel, the reader is invited to note the many possible permutations of a given social situation, and what those variations can suggest. Similarly, the repeated use of seeming happenstance—in order to drive characters apart or throw them together—is a technique she uses to produce a foreshortened glimpse of the patterns, both psychological and sociological, that shape an individual's responses to the vicissitudes of life. Her text also regularly employs certain set phrases that operate, in some senses, like stage directions, which gives the most ordinary conversations a distinctly theatrical tone. She also employs, in creative and deliberate ways, the culturally ingrained habit of using family rank and role designations—elder sister, grandmother, daughter-in-law, etc.—rather than personal names. All of these techniques of story manipulation can be found in the grand old classics of Chinese fiction (e.g., *Dream of the Red Chamber*) that she had been reading, and imitating, since youth, and Chang took to heart the example they set for using these techniques to deepen a story's psychological and thematic context.

But the ending of *Eighteen Springs* is a different matter altogether: it is set at a political rally in the northeastern city of Shenyang, shortly after the Communist liberation of Shanghai. The main characters (except the ones cast as villains) have made the patriotic decision to join the effort to rebuild the country. They also have shed their bourgeois ways and improved their attitudes and morals, all of which is conducive to a full and proper appreciation of revolutionary vigor and style. To top it all off, each of them has found, or returned to, the right romantic partner. Not surprisingly, Chang completely retracted this forced ending when she returned to the story nearly two decades after its first appearance, readying it for publication under her own name. She also reworked several scenes and events, modified some of the characters and reduced the plotline to fourteen years. The story now runs from 1931 to 1945, which eliminates any need to mention either the Communists or Chiang Kai-shek, since the period of open warfare between them (the Chinese Civil War) has scarcely begun. The novel can thus persist in its primary strategy of relegating to the background any major historical events or massive forms of public upheaval, in order to keep its emphasis on the personal, the psychological and the sensory—all those private dimensions of life that Chang took as her central subject matter.

Changing the title was a key element in this process, because the new title made clear the lingering, retrospective angle of the novel's position vis-à-vis time. Those connotations are hard to capture succinctly in English. A more explicit rendering of *bansheng yuan* might be "fated to share only half a lifetime." Perhaps the best way to see the long, yearning shadow that the phrase casts is to recall its association with older stories like the eighteenth-century memoir by Shen Fu, *Six Chapters from a Floating Life*, in which the writer looks back across time, vividly recalling early happiness shared with a beloved wife, who then succumbed to a premature death. The phrase evokes both lifelong attachment and sudden sundering.

Through all these varied methods Chang achieved a novel both consistent and complete, an illustration of the strength attainable through pain, rupture, and disappointment. And yet, despite this achievement, she never re-wrote it in English. It is true that by 1969 she had grown discouraged by the poor sales of her English novels (*The Rice-sprout Song*, *Naked Earth* and, closest to her heart, *Rouge of the North*), and the frustration of dealing with audiences whose views of China were all too often framed by reductionist Oriental and Cold War ideologies. Still, given this novel's strong dramatic structure and its clearly drawn yet internally complex and appealing characters, it should have been a good candidate for translation by its author. Two factors help explain why Eileen Chang chose not to do that. First, her tale directly transposes several elements of *H. M. Pulham, Esquire*, a 1940 novel in the office-romance genre by a now fairly obscure Pulitzer winner, John P. Marquand (1893–1960).* The general profile of the male protagonist, the pairing of two city-types (read New York for Shanghai and Boston for Nanjing), the patterning of two crucial sub-plots, and even some of the story details and dialogue twists have been transposed from Marquand's world to Chang's. While Chang did not hide her indebtedness to Marquand— and expressed her appreciation to him when they crossed paths in Hong Kong—neither did she advertise the fact that she had made this adaptation. After she moved to the US, she must have become especially aware of the criticism she could face if her exercise in transposition were viewed as plagiarism, or as a form of creative failure. Looking carefully at the two novels today, it is hard to see anything but a fascinating set of linked, overlapping, but still distinctly different texts. But in the 1970s and '80s, Chang could not count on readers taking that view.

Related to the Marquand issue, is another, perhaps even more compelling reason for Chang's decision not to work through this material again in English. There is, in fact, a major game-changing deviation in her use of Marquand's novel. Marvin Myles, the Marquand character who most closely corresponds to Chang's Gu Manzhen, is always viewed in that novel from the idealizing perspective of her lover, which is to say, as an object who has no needs of her own, except to return his tender gaze. When Marquand's novel was turned into a 1941 film directed by King Vidor, Hedy Lamarr's strong acting brought new vibrancy to the role, but could not change the basic plot. If, as seems likely, the film played in Shanghai and Eileen

---

* See Chuan Chih Kao's careful study of these questions in *Zhang Ailing xue* (Taipei: Maitian, 2003): 279–95; and Carole Hang Fung Hoyan's very useful "Hualiyuan zhong de ailing nushen" in Lin Xingqian, ed., *Zhang Ailing: wenxue, dianying, wutai* (Hong Kong: Oxford UP, 2007): 128–59.

Chang saw it there, Lamarr's performance may have inspired her to develop the character more fully. In any case, it is clear that Gu Manzhen, unlike Marvin Myles, has a stature, a background and a harrowing, deepening set of experiences that make her the primary actor in a significantly expanded plot. This way of reworking of Marquand's materials is quite different from the technical transpositions that shift the story from one setting to another. Through the character of Manzhen, Chang often can be seen delving deep into her own experience of personal trauma and domestic abuse, in some passages using sensory or emotional details that appear also in her more directly autobiographical writings. This is not to say that Manzhen's experience is Eileen Chang's, but that Manzhen is a vehicle through which the author—and we as readers—trace the patterns that can take us from naiveté, through trauma, and beyond. And while this is not the place to examine Eileen Chang's English prose style in detail, it should not be surprising to learn that her English versions often tame and contain her Chinese texts, trading greater decorum for less verve and pungency. In the case of this particular tale, she may not have been willing to tone it down.

Note on Romanization

Readers familiar with standard systems for Romanizing Chinese will discover that this translation uses a mix of conventions. This decision is based on a desire to make things easier for readers not familiar with those systems, and on the belief that a hybrid approach suits this novel in particular, due to its multilayered composition history in Chinese and its author's multifaceted interactions with English. Thus, for instance, the "x" and "c" that can be so forbidding have been converted to an older form: "hs" and "ts," respectively. The "zh," however, has been left alone (it may help to think of it as a softened "j" like the middle consonant in "pleasure"). Similarly, the syllable "shi" should be pronounced with a softened "r" at the end, as in "sure."

Note of thanks:

For lifelong friendship and early encouragement to undertake this project, I am grateful to Peter Yang and Jasmine Huang; for the opportunity to do this at all, LuAnn Walther; and for useful questions and attentive reading, Jessica Harrison and Elisabeth Merriman.

1

He and Manzhen had met . . . a long time ago. Working it out, he realized it had been fourteen years since then. Quite a shock! It made him feel, suddenly, very old.

Time does fly for the middle-aged: a decade whips by in the blink of an eye, a flick of the fingertips. When you're still young, even three or four years, maybe five, can seem an entire lifetime. That's all they'd had, from meeting to parting—just a few years together. But in that brief span, they'd had a full measure: all the joy and the sorrow that comes with (as the old saying has it) "birth, old age, illness, death."

She'd asked him, back then, when he'd first started liking her. "The moment I first saw you," he'd replied, of course. His feelings were running so high then, he'd have believed anything. He was certain he was not lying. But in fact, the moment when he first saw her was not all that clear in his mind.

It was Shuhui, his best friend from engineering college, who met her first. Shuhui, who'd graduated before him and found work in a factory office, had then found him a position, as a trainee, in the same factory. Manzhen worked in that office, at a desk next to Shuhui's, so he must have passed her several times on his way to see Shuhui, but nothing stuck in his mind. Probably because he was fresh out of college, shy around girls, too awkward to take a good look.

He was on his way to becoming a fully trained engineer, which meant he was on the shop floor all day long, with the manual workers; as soon as he'd grasped one thing, he was sent off to learn another. The work was hard, but the experience invaluable. It paid almost nothing, but fortunately his family wasn't relying on him. They lived in another city, and he was boarding with Shuhui's family in Shanghai.

That was the first time Shijun had spent New Year's away from home. He'd never enjoyed the holiday; something unpleasant always happened then, in his family. They'd wait for his father to come home and lead the ceremony, then have a family meal. But his father would always be late, held back by this or the other, over at the concubine's place. His mother did not usually argue about this, but at New Year's she had to say something: "A family should act like a family." The master of the house was supposed to be at home, leading the proceedings, if only for the ancestors' sake.

The problem was that festivities were being held at the other place too. This concubine had been with his father for many years. She'd borne him several children, and her house was livelier, filled with family: it had become his father's chief residence. He rarely went back to his first wife's home. When he did, he was received like a visiting dignitary, most of the time. But maybe because the holiday made her feel her lot in life, Shijun's mother just had to clash with her husband at New Year's. A woman her age, and there she'd be, in tears. It had been that way every year since Shijun was little. Hence his gladness at being somewhere other than at home, well away from all that unpleasantness.

And yet, when it came time to bid the old year adieu, with everyone gathering at dusk for the holiday meal while random bursts of firecracker noise filled the streets, he still felt the weight of worries he couldn't quite figure out.

He joined Shuhui's family for the New Year's Eve dinner, then invited his friend to see a film with him. The cinema ran a late show during the holiday break, and they stayed to the end of the double bill. Watching midnight movies on New Year's Eve was a peculiar experience: all that seasonal jollity, with a twinge of loneliness in the middle.

The factory had only a three-day holiday, but their usual lunch place took five days off. He and Shuhui went there, on their first day back, but the doors were shut. They turned around and headed back through streets strewn with the red-paper shells of burnt-out fire-crackers. When they passed a half-open restaurant, Shuhui suggested going in. The owners had not yet held their New Year's opening ceremony, with blessings from the God of Wealth, so the shop front was still half blocked by shutters, and the interior was dim. There wasn't much business so close to the holiday, but a young woman in an old gray sheepskin coat sat at a table facing the door. She had a teacup and chopsticks and was waiting for her food to come. To pass the time, she was rubbing her red-gloved fingers in slow circles, two fingers running down the opposite forefinger, along the inside of the thumb, then back again.

"Oh, Miss Gu! You're here too!" Shuhui called out, the moment he saw her. He started to sit down at her table, then saw Shijun hanging back. "We're all co-workers, you know—haven't you met before? This is Shen Shijun, this is Gu Manzhen."

She had a round face that seemed squarish inside the roundness—not four-cornered, but distinct, well defined. Her hair was ruffled and loose, falling over her shoulders in a casual style. Shijun wasn't in the habit of assessing a girl on some sort of beauty scale; he simply liked the way she looked. She thrust her hands into her coat pockets and smiled. The two young men pulled out a bench, only to find that the red-painted seat was black with grime. Shijun didn't care; he was grimy too, from working on machinery. But Shuhui, trim and tidy in a business suit, gave it a sharp look before sitting down.

The waiter came over, bringing two teacups that he held with his fingers stuck inside them. Shuhui noticed, and frowned. "This place is no good at all—so dirty!" The waiter poured the tea, and they each ordered a meal. Shuhui had an idea. "Hey there," he called to the waiter, "bring us some paper so we can wipe the chopsticks clean." But the waiter was already out of earshot.

"Wash them in the tea," Manzhen suggested. "I don't think you'll want this tea anyway." She swished his chopsticks around in the tea, dried them with a single firm shake, and balanced them across his teacup. Then she reached over to do the same for Shijun.

"Oh—you're too kind!" Shijun protested, with a half-bow of

thanks. After she'd washed his chopsticks, he took them from her and thanked her again.

Manzhen kept her gaze lowered, never looking at them directly, but she smiled quietly. After he'd taken the chopsticks from her, Shijun put them down again. Then he saw his mistake: he'd put them on the table, which could seem ungrateful, or even impatient, as if he thought her overly fussy. Quickly, he picked up the chopsticks and, following her lead, balanced them across his teacup. He lined them up precisely. Of course, once the chopsticks had touched the table they were dirty again, so now he was just trying to cover up his error. A wave of embarrassment swept over him. To hide his confusion, he picked up his soup spoon and swished it in the tea.

At this point the waiter brought their food. They each had a bowl of clam soup. Shijun took a spoonful and remarked, "Clams at New Year—I'll bet it's for good luck. They're *yuan bao*, little lumps that look like a stack of coins."

"Clams are money mounds," Shuhui agreed, "and so are taro cakes, and flour-wrapped dumplings, and egg-wrapped dumplings too. Even fresh fruit and tea eggs can be money mounds—apparently we Chinese are obsessed with money, since everywhere we look we see *yuan bao*."

"Oh, but it goes even further than that," Manzhen said. "There's a kind of caterpillar called a 'bag worm' that drops from the ceiling in a fat little roll, and people in the north like to call it a 'coin-string worm.' How's that for being money-crazy?"

"Miss Gu, are you from the north?" Shijun asked.

Manzhen shook her head and smiled. "My mother is a northerner."

"Well then, you're a half-northerner."

"Our usual lunch place does northern-style food," Shuhui said. "It's just across from here—have you tried it? It's good."

"I haven't been there," said Manzhen.

"Let's all go there tomorrow. This place is no good. So dirty!"

After that, the three of them ate lunch together on a daily basis. They'd order three dishes and a soup, definitely better than three set meals. Or they'd stand on the street side by side, and eat roasted taro straight from the vendor's cart. But even after their acquaintance had deepened, Shuhui and Manzhen stuck to shop talk. Theirs was simply a workplace friendship, it seemed. Shuhui didn't talk about her after work; he would at most mention her in passing.

Once, when he and Shijun were commenting on the various tensions among their colleagues, Shijun said, "You're lucky. The two of you in that office get along so well."

"Yeah," said Shuhui, offhandedly. "Manzhen is great. She doesn't play games."

Shijun let it go at that. If he seemed too interested in her, Shuhui would tease him.

But then, while they were chatting about something else, Shuhui suddenly said, "Manzhen was talking about you today."

Shijun was startled. It took him a moment to follow this up, and find out what she'd said.

"She wanted to know why I do all the talking—meaning that you can't get a word in edgeways," explained Shuhui. "I told her that lots of people think I'm unfair to you. Even my mother thinks that! But really, it's just a matter of personality. You're like the 'straight man' in a comedy."

"What?"

"You know, the one who's always getting smacked on the head with a folded fan." Shuhui couldn't help laughing at his own remark. "I know you don't mind my teasing. That's one of your good points. That's something we have in common—I'm not the type who dishes it out but can't take it."

Once Shuhui started talking about himself, there was no end to it. Maybe it's just that a man who is smart and good-looking is bound to be a bit of a narcissist too. Shuhui plunged into a stream of self-analysis, examining the finer points of his own personality. Meanwhile, Shijun could only wonder, in silence, what could have made Manzhen start talking about *him*.

Their factory was on the edge of town, where half-developed streets gave way to empty lots and open fields. Spring had come, dusting the fields with green, even though the air was chilly.

One day, at the noon break, Shijun washed himself quickly and went to the office to meet up with Shuhui, just as he usually did. But Shuhui wasn't there; Manzhen sat alone at her desk, straightening some papers. She was wearing a blue-and-red-checked scarf, even while indoors; it went well with her dark blue tunic-type gown, very much the outfit of a genteel young woman. The blue gown had been through the wash many times and a whitish nap stood out on the worn material. The effect was gentle and refined, like the soft blue cover of a cloth-bound book.

"Where's Shuhui?" Shijun asked.

Manzhen tipped her head in the direction of the manager's office. "He waits till five minutes before break time," she said in an undertone, "then calls you in for something terribly important. That's how bosses are, I suppose."

Shijun grinned and nodded. Perching on Shuhui's desk, he reached over to the wall calendar and flipped through the pages while he waited. "I'm looking for the first day of spring on the lunar calendar."

"Oh, it's started already."

"Then why is it still so cold?" He went on lifting the pages. "They've cut down on printing costs, no color here except the red on Sundays. I like the old calendars better, the ones we had when I was little, with Sundays in red and Saturdays in green. We tore off a page each day till finally we got to Saturday. Just seeing that bright green made us happy."

"Yes, yes—and when we were in school, Saturday was happier than Sunday. Sunday was printed in red, but that only heightened the image of a beautifully fading sunset."

Just then, Shuhui came in. As soon as he saw Manzhen, he called out, "Hey, didn't I say you two should go ahead?"

"What's the rush?" she asked.

"After we eat, we should find a good place to take pictures. I've borrowed a camera."

"But it's so cold. We'll have ruddy noses and eyes—that won't make a good picture."

Shuhui pursed his lips in Shijun's direction. "It's for him, you know. His mother wrote to him and asked him to send her a picture. For matchmaking purposes, I would imagine."

Shijun blushed. "What? No, it's just my mother worrying about me. She's afraid I'm getting thin, won't believe me when I say I'm fine. She wants to see for herself."

Shuhui looked him over carefully. "Well, you might not be thin, but you are dirty. If she sees you like this, she'll think you've turned into a coal miner, and then she *will* worry."

Shijun looked down at the workman's outfit that he always wore.

"Wipe your clothes with a handkerchief," Manzhen said. "I've got one here."

"Oh—no, that's fine," Shijun said quickly. "It's machine oil. It'll never wash out of your handkerchief." He took a crumpled wad of paper from the wastebasket and wiped his trousers with it.

"That won't do," Manzhen said, opening a drawer and taking out a neatly folded handkerchief. She dipped it in Shuhui's water cup, and handed it to Shijun. He had to take it. One swipe, and a black splotch spread across the snow-white handkerchief. He winced.

Shuhui stood by the window looking at the sky. "It looks like the sun's not going to stay out today. The pictures might not come out." As he spoke, he took a comb from his trouser pocket and smoothed his hair, using the window as a mirror. Then, craning his neck, he adjusted his tie. Manzhen, watching this little display of vanity, had to stifle a laugh. Shuhui gave himself a wink, then turned and prodded Shijun: "Aren't you ready yet?"

"There's a spot on your face," Manzhen told Shijun. "No, it's over here—" She pointed to her own face to show him where it was. "And here's another." She took a little mirror from her handbag and passed it to him.

"Listen, Manzhen," Shuhui said, "do you have any lipstick? Give him some of that too." Laughing at his own joke, he took the mirror from Shijun and used it to give himself another once-over.

They went to lunch, each slurping down a bowl of noodles, to save time. Then they headed to the edge of town. Shuhui said the empty fields were too plain, and remembered two willow trees, very picturesque, not much further on. But they walked a long way without finding any trees. Shijun noticed that Manzhen was having trouble keeping up. "Let's slow down," he said. Shuhui slackened his pace, but the weather was not conducive to mere strolling. The cold drove them onward, and they hurried despite themselves. Soon they were walking at a brisk pace. The wind blew into their faces, hoarsening their breath and chopping any conversation to pieces.

Manzhen, pulling her hair down to shield her head, looked at them and smiled. "Aren't your ears freezing?"

"Yes, of course," Shuhui said.

"I think I'd be sick with a cold all winter long, if I were a man."

But the willow trees were covered in golden leaf-buds, one tender wisp after another. They took quite a few pictures. Shijun snapped one of Shuhui and Manzhen standing next to each other. The wind flipped up the edge of Manzhen's light gray sheepskin coat; she held her hand across the corner of her mouth, and the red woolen gloves turned her face a pure, pale white.

The sun had no strength that day; the sky darkened before they could finish the first roll of film. They hurried back, but still got caught by streaks of springtime snow dissolving into cold rain. When they passed a little shop, Manzhen saw oil-paper umbrellas hanging inside, and wanted one. Trying them out, she discovered that some were solid blue or green, and others had a pattern. She looked at one that had a swirl of purple grapes and another in a solid color, and couldn't make up her mind. Shuhui said women were always like that, when they went shopping. Shijun smiled and said he thought the plainer one was better. She bought it right away.

"Don't you think the price should be lower here, out on the edge of town?" Shuhui said. "Are they cheating us?"

Manzhen pointed with the umbrella at the shopkeeper's guarantee posted on the wall. "Look—it says right here: 'We do not cheat children or the elderly.'"

Shuhui laughed. "You're not a child, and you're not old—they haven't promised not to cheat *you*!"

They went back on to the street. "Oh dear," Manzhen said, "I've lost one of my gloves."

"It must be in the shop," Shuhui said.

They went back in, but the shopkeeper hadn't seen it. "Just now, when I counted out the money, I didn't have it on," Manzhen said. "I must have lost it when we were taking the pictures."

"Let's go back and look," Shijun said.

But the lunch break was over, and they had to get back to work.

"Oh, it's not important. It's just a glove!" Manzhen spoke lightly, but in fact she was upset. Sometimes she focused so hard on little things she was almost small-minded. But Shijun, when he looked back at it all, treasured this trait of hers. Manzhen was the kind of person who, once something came into her possession, cherished it till it became, in her eyes, the best thing ever. He knew, because he'd once been hers.

It continued raining after they'd returned from the edge of town to the factory. At five o'clock, when they left work, the sky was already darkening. But a vague urge arose in Shijun, and sent him back to the city's outskirts through the rain. The muddy banks of the rice paddies were treacherous; his feet slipped as he made his way along the dykes. There was a little tiled tomb, the size of a kennel, lying low on the edge of a field. They hadn't noticed it in the daytime; seeing it now, in the dusky rain, gave him an eerie feeling. It was perfectly quiet all around, except for the wailing bark of a dog. He passed no one and saw only one other person, across the canal, carrying a lantern and a big, apricot-orange umbrella.

After a long walk, he finally found the willows. Using a flashlight, he spotted the trees from a distance, then a red glove on the ground nearby. At first it made him happy: holding the beam steady, he walked over and picked it up. But once the glove was in his hand, he paused. What would he say when he gave it to her tomorrow? Wasn't he behaving rather oddly? Walking all this way in the rain, to get a glove for her. Well, he'd owed it to her: if it hadn't been for the photographs that he needed, she wouldn't have lost the glove. But that line of reasoning sounded flimsy, even to him. So—what should he do? He wished he hadn't come, but now that he had, and the glove was in his hand, he couldn't toss it back onto the ground. He brushed off some mud that had stuck to the wool, and shoved it into his pocket. He'd have to return it to her. He couldn't hold on to it secretly—that would be the height of ridiculousness.

The next day at noon he went to the upper-story office. As luck would have it, Shuhui had been called again into the manager's office. Shijun pulled the mud-flecked glove from his pocket. He could have made small talk, but didn't. He just put the glove on her desk. The blank look on his face showed frustration at the mess he'd got himself into. If he had foreseen how awkward this would be, he never would have done it.

"What?" Manzhen stiffened with surprise, then picked up the glove and examined it. "Oh! You didn't go back there again, did you? Such a long way—and it was raining—"

Shuhui came in. Manzhen could see that Shijun didn't want a discussion. She crumpled the glove in her hand, then casually stuffed it into a coat pocket. Her motions were artfully smooth, but her cheeks were turning red. She could tell that something was wrong; her face was so hot it burned, and when the wave of heat passed, coolness swept over her skin like a little breeze—which only showed how red she had been a moment before. Not something she herself could see, but it had to be visible to others. That was a nerve-racking thought; she blushed all over again.

Even though she'd got flustered for no reason, she quickly regained her composure. Her behavior towards Shijun, over lunch, was perfectly normal.

In the spring, the temperature rose and fell quickly, and lots of people, Manzhen included, came down with colds. She phoned in one day, and asked Shuhui to submit her request for sick leave.

"Do you think we should go and see her?" Shijun asked, after he and Shuhui had returned home that evening.

"Err . . . She probably is quite sick. She wasn't feeling well yesterday."

"Do you have her home address?"

"Yes," Shuhui said, with a puzzled look, "but I've never been there. You've known her a long time too now, and you've never heard anything about her family—right? She hasn't got an ounce of mystery about her, and yet there is something mysterious about this."

Shijun balked. Was it because Shuhui had said Manzhen was ordinary, without an ounce of mystery, or because he'd implied there *was* some mystery, something she had to hide? Hard to tell, but either way he found it irritating. "What's so mysterious about it?" he shot back. "Maybe they're a big family, and their house is too small for guests. Or maybe they're old-fashioned, the kind of family that doesn't want a daughter making friends on her own—in which case she can't very well invite us round to her place."

Shuhui nodded. "Well, we'll have to go, even if they don't want us to. I need some documents that are locked in her desk drawer, and for that I'll need her keys."

"Well then, let's go. But . . . isn't it rather late?"

Down in the kitchen, preparations for dinner were already underway; the crackling sound of the wok reached the upper floor. Just as Shuhui was looking at his watch, his mother called from the kitchen, "Shuhui! Somebody here to see you!"

Shuhui ran downstairs. It was a little boy he'd never seen before. Shuhui was surprised, but the boy dangled a set of keys in front of him. "My sister asked me to bring you these. They're the keys to her desk."

"Ah!" said Shuhui, smiling. "Are you Manzhen's little brother? How's she doing? Is she feeling better?"

"She says she's getting better and she'll be back at work soon."

He couldn't have been more than eight years old, but apparently he was used to running errands. He turned away, intent on leaving the moment his message had been delivered, undeterred even by the sweet snacks that Shuhui's mother was offering him.

Shuhui tossed the keys around in his hand, looking at Shijun, now at the foot of the stairs. "It looks like she didn't want us to go looking for her, so she sent the keys here."

"Why are you so suspicious today?"

"I'm not being suspicious. Look at the way that boy acted—apparently he's been told not to talk to people outside the family. Hmm. Maybe he's not her brother."

Shijun was getting impatient. "Well, he looks a lot like her!"

"Maybe he's her son?"

Shijun thought Shuhui unbelievable, impossible to deal with.

Shuhui saw that Shijun wasn't going to respond. "Well," he said, "when a woman takes a job, she always goes by 'Miss So-and-so,' no matter what her marital status."

"True," said Shijun. "But, come on . . . she's very young, you can tell that by looking at her."

"A woman's age . . ." Shuhui was shaking his head. "Very hard to tell."

When Shuhui talked about "women," he put on the air of a man who has had lots of experience. But Shijun had heard all his opinions on this topic, back when they first entered college, and knew for a fact that Shuhui had had only one girlfriend in college, a classmate of theirs, Yao Peizhen. When Shuhui talked about "women," all those "women" were another way of saying "Yao Peizhen." He might, of course, have other women in his life now. But that was hardly the point, since he was simply talking for talking's sake—without a breath of malice, to be sure. All of this was plain to Shijun and yet he found the chatter excruciating. In all their years together, he'd never been so angry with his friend.

That evening, Shijun stayed away from Shuhui, giving as his excuse the need to write a letter home. Shuhui saw him sitting in the lamplight, staring at the writing paper. Must be family problems, he thought.

2

Manzhen recovered quickly from her illness and came back to work. The day she returned, Shuhui had another lunch date; a colleague was paying off a bet by treating him to a Western-style meal. That left Manzhen and Shijun to go to lunch on their own. Shuhui's absence made things very quiet; he'd always been the center of their little group. Now you could even hear the dishes clinking on the table.

Business was slow in this small restaurant. The woman at the cashier's desk had time to kill, and kept glancing over at them. Or maybe that was just Shijun's imagination; he was feeling others' eyes today. The woman seemed to be the owner. Her hair was done in a permanent wave with a wispy fringe at the front, and she was knitting a bright red sweater. The weather had warmed up; her light blue dress was short-sleeved, made of summer-weight cotton. The red knitting yarn brought out the lusciousness of her plump white arms. Encircling her forearm was a green bracelet, made of heat-processed artificial jade.

"It's warm today," Shijun said with a smile.

"Yes, it's hot already." Manzhen took off her coat.

"I saw your younger brother when he came the other day."

"That was my youngest brother."

"How many brothers and sisters do you have?"

"Five. There are six of us, including me."

"Are you the oldest?"

"No, I'm the second oldest."

"I thought you'd be the oldest."

"Why?"

"Because you act like a big sister, always taking care of others."

Manzhen smiled. There were scorch marks on the tabletop, left by hot teacups, and she traced the thin white circles with her finger. "I think you must be an only son."

"Ah—so you think I'm spoiled, used to getting my own way?"

Manzhen didn't answer directly. "If you do have siblings, they're all sisters, not brothers."

"Well, you're wrong," Shijun said with a smile. "I did have an older brother, but he passed away."

He told her about his family. Besides his father and mother, he had only a sister-in-law and a nephew. Even though he'd spent his whole childhood in Nanking, it wasn't his family's original home town. He asked where her family was from, and she said they were from Liu An, in Anhui Province.

"That's a tea-growing region," he said. "Have you ever been there?"

"Just once, the year we buried my father."

"Oh, your father has already passed away?"

"He died the year I turned fourteen."

Then he sensed quite palpably that she was holding back some secret. Shijun did not for a moment believe Manzhen had anything to hide, but when that silence fell, he had to admit there was something she wasn't sharing. Since she wasn't telling, he didn't want to ask. And, really, he'd rather not know. It felt as if Shuhui's wild guesses might be right after all—it felt, as if possible, even worse than that. And yet she looked so pure and sweet. He didn't know what to think.

Pretending to a calm he didn't feel, he picked up his chopsticks and started to eat. The food tasted like wood. He picked up the ketchup, intending to pour out a little, but ketchup stays in the bottle, then comes out in a spurt. He blinked, and there it was—a big red mess slathered all over the food. The woman at the cashier's desk was glaring at them, her eyes no longer kind.

Manzhen hadn't noticed any of this. She seemed to be debating with herself, trying to decide how much to tell him. After a long silence, her smile returned and she began to speak.

"My father worked in a bookstore. That little salary of his had to support our whole family, including my grandmother. When my father died, we had nowhere to turn. We children were too young to understand—except for my older sister, who was already grown up by then. She's been supporting us ever since."

Shijun could see where this was leading.

"My sister hadn't finished secondary school," Manzhen continued. "What kind of job could she get? Even if she did get a job, it wouldn't pay much. Not enough to support a family. Her only choice was to become a taxi-dancer."

"There's nothing wrong with that," Shijun said. "There's more than one kind of taxi-dancer. It all depends on the girl."

Manzhen paused. Then she smiled and said, "Yes, some girls do stay clean. But a girl can't do that *and* support a big family!"

There was nothing Shijun could say to this.

"In any case, once you go down that path, it's a downhill slope, unless you're good at the game. My sister—she's not that type. She's a person with a loyal heart, really."

Shijun heard her voice growing husky, but he couldn't think of anything comforting to say. All he could do was smile and murmur, "Don't be sad."

Manzhen picked through the rice with her chopsticks, her head bent low as she plucked out the wild seeds, one by one.

Several moments passed, then suddenly she said, "Don't tell Shuhui."

"OK." He hadn't planned to tell Shuhui anyway. What would he say, what reason could he give, if Shuhui wondered why Manzhen had told him her secret? Shuhui had known her longer, but she'd not shared it with him.

Manzhen had by now realized this, and the obvious discrepancy made her blush. "I've been meaning to tell Shuhui, but some-how . . . I just haven't."

Shijun nodded. "You shouldn't worry about telling him. He's sure to understand. Your sister is sacrificing herself for the sake of the family—she doesn't have a choice in the matter."

When Manzhen returned home that day, she felt sad and empty.

She'd always avoided discussing her family with others; now she'd broken her own taboo, by telling Shijun so much of their story. Her family lived in a set of rooms that had been rented for them by a man who kept her sister Manlu as a mistress. When that relationship had ended, Manlu recast herself as a second-tier escort, a more respectable occupation, closer to decency, but with a reduced income. She was always pleased if people mistook her for a simple taxi-dancer.

When Manzhen walked into the house, her youngest brother, Jiemin, was playing with a shuttlecock, keeping it in the air with little kicks. "Hey Sis, Ma's back!" he called out. Their mother had gone to their home town for Tomb-sweeping Day, to visit the family graves. Manzhen was happy to hear that her mother had returned. She went through a door at the rear, followed by her brother, still kicking his shuttlecock. Ah Bao, the maid, was in the kitchen opening a bottle of beer, and two tall glasses stood on the table. Manzhen turned and frowned at her brother. "Careful! Don't go breaking things in here! You'd better take that outside."

There had to be a guest, since Ah Bao was opening beer. And Manlu's door had to be open, judging from the crackly tune wafting into the kitchen from her radio. Manzhen went to the doorway and, without stepping out of the kitchen, tried to peer into her sister's room.

"There's no one, really," Ah Bao told her. "Mr. Wang hasn't come yet. There's just his friend, a Mr. Zhu. He's been here quite a while already."

"You know him," Jiemin piped up. "He's the one who looks like a rat—and then, when he smiles, looks like a cat."

Manzhen had to laugh. "You silly boy! How can the same person look like a rat *and* a cat?" She went out of the kitchen, walked quickly past Manlu's room, and headed up the stairs.

It turned out that Manlu wasn't in her room. She was in the stairwell, talking on the phone. Her voice was just as rough on the ears as that radio song: saccharine screeches that made the room and the crockery shiver. "So—are you coming or not? If you don't, you'll be sorry!" Her hips twisted back and forth, pushing against the phone book that dangled beneath the wall-mounted phone. Her apple-green silk cheongsam was fairly new, but there was a darkened area at the waistline, a sweat stain left by a dance partner's hand. It was a bit unnerving, that hand-shaped mark jumping out from the cloth. Her hair was rumpled, still undone, but she'd put on that stage makeup of hers: blocks of bright red and solid black, with blue eyeshadow. It looked pretty from a distance—up close it was rather scary. Squeezing past her on the narrow stairway, Manzhen felt her senses flooding, dread creeping over her. She could scarcely believe this was her own sister.

Manlu was still talking into the telephone. "Old Zhu is here, waiting for you—been waiting for hours!. . . Shit!. . . Since when does he rate?. . . Thanks, but no thanks. I don't need any of your fixing up. Not in this lifetime—or any other." She laughed. It was a laugh she'd started using recently, a loud, expansive laugh, as if someone were tickling her. And yet that laugh had nothing attractive in it. It was old and empty; Manzhen hated the sound.

She hurried upstairs, into a different world altogether. Her mother was sitting in the main room surrounded by traveling gear: a net-covered basket, a cloth-wrapped bundle and a roll of bedding. She was going through her things, telling Granny her travel stories. Manzhen stepped forward and greeted her mother. Mrs. Gu gave a warm reply, then looked searchingly at her daughter's face. Apparently she had something to say—but then didn't. It felt rather odd.

"Manzhen caught a cold the other day," her grandmother said. "She had to stay in bed for two whole days."

"Oh, no wonder she's so thin." Manzhen's mother smiled at her again. She smiled so hard her eyes crinkled up.

Manzhen asked about the journey to the family graves. Her mother sighed, and told her that all the trees had been chopped down. No one from the family had checked on things these past few years, and the grave-keeper wasn't doing his job. Mrs. Gu grumbled on for some time, then remembered something else. She turned to Granny. "Mother, aren't you always wishing you could get some home-town cooking? I brought some tea leaves back with me, and also some pudding cakes, sesame cakes, and pan-fried rice noodles." She rummaged through the basket and got the food out. "Didn't all the children, when they were little, love these pan-fried noodles?"

Granny said she'd get an airtight container for the cakes and went into the next room. As soon as she had gone, Mrs. Gu went to the desk and started moving things around, tidying up. "While I was gone and you were sick, the children made a mess in here." There were several small photographs stuck under the glass desk-top, photos taken on Manzhen's little trip to the city's outskirts. One of them showed her standing next to Shuhui, and another was of Shuhui on his own. The one with Shijun wasn't on display—she'd tucked that one away, out of sight. Her mother bent over to look at the photos. "Where did you take these?" she asked. "And who is this?" She pointed to Shuhui. She was pretending to be nonchalant, all the while keeping a close eye on her daughter, ready to catch any change of expression.

Manzhen finally understood why her mother had been smiling at her so meaningfully. She must have spotted the photos and, even though they were just ordinary snaps, for her they'd inspired high hopes. It's so amusing to watch parents scheme over their children . . . and sad, too.

Manzhen simply smiled and said, "That's a colleague from work. His name is Hsu Shuhui."

Seeing her daughter's calm face, Mrs. Gu couldn't figure out what was going on. She had to let it go.

"Does Manlu know you are home?" Manzhen asked.

Her mother nodded. "She was here a moment ago, but then a guest came and she had to go downstairs." She paused. "Has that Mr. Wang come yet?"

"I don't think so," said Manzhen. "But the man that's here runs around with him."

Her mother sighed. "These fellows she's seeing, they're no good at all. But then again, the whole world's going to pot—that's the real problem."

She could see that the quality of her daughter's clients was slipping, but it didn't occur to her that Manlu herself was sliding down the scale. Manzhen, realizing this, fell silent.

Mrs. Gu ladled out several bowls of rice noodles, added hot water to each, and gave one to her mother-in-law. "What happened to Jiemin?" she asked. "He was here a moment ago, asking for something to eat."

"He's playing downstairs," Manzhen said. She went out to the stairway, and saw him on the bottom step; he was craning his head and shoulders over the railing, trying to peer into Manlu's room. That made Manzhen nervous.

"Oi!" she whispered. "What are you doing?"

"I kicked my shuttlecock into her room."

"Then go and tell Ah Bao. Ask her to get it next time she goes in."

They were whispering back and forth when the guest suddenly emerged from Manlu's room. It was that Mr. Zhu—his name, in full, was Zhu Hongtsai. He was tall and lean, with thin shoulders and a thin neck, all clothed in a traditional long gown. He stood in the doorway with his hands on his hips, nodded at Manzhen and greeted her as "Second Young Miss." So he knew she was Manlu's younger sister—that meant he had noticed her before. It wasn't the first time Manzhen had seen him, either, but now she had Jiemin's quip in mind: the man who looked like a rat, then a cat. His expression at that moment was serious, his eyes small, mouth tight and sharp, altogether rat-like. She almost giggled out loud. She stifled the laugh, but her face, when she returned his nod, was lit with a suppressed smile. Zhu Hongtsai had no idea why she was so pleased to see him. She was smiling at him, so he smiled back, and then he did, quite suddenly, look like a cat. Manzhen almost erupted with laughter. Fighting to hold it back, she turned and ran up the stairs. From Zhu Hongtsai's point of view, this attack of shyness was most beguiling. He stood at the foot of the steps, starry-eyed with delight.

When he went back into Manlu's room, he asked, "Does Second Young Miss have a boyfriend?"

"And why, exactly, would you be asking about this?"

"Oh, don't get me wrong! All I mean is, I could find a boyfriend for her, if she hasn't got one."

"One of your friends!" Manlu snorted. "Right, and which of them is any good?"

"Goodness, goodness, why are you so worked up today? You aren't angry at Wang, are you?"

"You just tell me, straight out. Is Wang messing around with that Fei Na girl?"

"How would I know? You haven't managed to haul him in here, so how could I find out?"

Manlu, ignoring him entirely, stabbed her cigarette out. "Some taste he's got!" she muttered to herself. "Fei Na with her puffy lips and baggy eyes, and those legs like a Japanese's. She doesn't even have a neck. People say white skin hides a hundred flaws, but the saying should be: '*Youth* hides a hundred flaws.'" She flounced over to the dressing table, grabbed a mirror and studied her appearance, adding a few more touches. The makeup on her face required constant attention.

She was cold-shouldering him but he wouldn't take the hint. He saw a photo album on the table, pulled it over, and flipped through the pages. There was a four-inch-square portrait of a round-faced young girl with her hair done up in two short braids.

"When was this picture of your sister taken?" he asked pleasantly. "Here she is, still in braids!"

Manlu glanced at the album. "That's not my sister," she retorted.

"Then who is it?"

Manlu said nothing at first. Then she laughed sarcastically. "You really have no idea who it is? I can't believe I've changed so . . . so drastically!" Her voice faltered at the end, dipping almost into a sob.

Hongtsai suddenly understood. "Oh—it's you?" He took a careful look at her, then at the picture, studying it closely. "Yes! Now that you've said it, it does look like you."

He was talking off the top of his head, but for her it had a cutting edge. In lieu of a reply, she traced the outline of her mouth with lipstick, working slowly. Her breath escaped through parted lips and the handheld mirror misted over. She got impatient, scrabbled at the mirror with hard, fast fingers, then resumed the lipstick work.

Hongtsai, who'd been studying the photograph all the while, lobbed a question at her: "Is your sister still in school?"

Manlu grunted vaguely.

"You know . . . she's got the looks—if she wanted to try this kind of thing, she'd be a big success."

Manlu slammed the mirror down and roared at him, "None of that, do you hear? This may be the road I've taken, but that doesn't mean my whole family is doing the same. What's all this poking your nose into people's private lives just so you can sneer at them!"

"What's the matter with you today?" Hongtsai said amiably. "Getting all riled up for nothing. Must be my unlucky day, coming here when you're in a bad mood."

Manlu gave him a sideways glance, and picked up her mirror again. Hongtsai sidled up to her, shamelessly close. "Why are you getting all dolled up?" he teased in a low voice. "Going somewhere?"

Manlu didn't pull away. She turned and gave him a big smile. "Oh, my . . . where indeed? Is that an invitation I'm hearing?"

Hongtsai had a close-up view of Manlu's stage makeup, the same view Manzhen had seen a short while earlier. Great splashes of vivid color: hot-pink cheeks and crow-black eyeliner. But Hongtsai didn't find it repulsive—to him, it was alluring. It just goes to show that the same thing can look very different, to different people.

Hongtsai took her out for dinner, then hung around in her room till the middle of the night. Manlu was used to having late-night snacks, so Ah Bao heated up some steamed dumplings in an oiled wok and took them in to her. Manlu heard someone walking around upstairs—her mother, no doubt, whom she hadn't had a chance to see for quite a while. She threw on a black silk dressing gown embroidered with yellow dragons, took her plate of dumplings and went upstairs.

Manlu gave her mother a fried dumpling and took a bite of hers. Then she stepped swiftly towards the lamp, squinting at the dumpling to see what was wrong: the meat filling was bright red. "Damn, this meat is raw!" But when she looked again, she saw that even the white-flour pastry was red. It was lipstick from her own mouth.

Manlu looked towards Manzhen's bed—Manzhen slept in the same room as her mother—and whispered, "Is she asleep?"

"Oh, yes. She went to bed early so she could get up early."

"Second Sister is all grown up now. It's not good for her to be liv-

21

ing with me. It gets people gossiping. If only she had someone suitable—then she could get married right away. That would take care of it."

Her mother was on the point of telling her about the good-looking young man in the photos, but even she felt that Manzhen and her older sister were worlds apart. Best not to spill the beans by talking to Manlu; she'd wait till she could speak with Manzhen, and hear it from the girl herself.

Anyway, Manzhen's marriage was not her main concern right now. "She's still young, another few years won't matter for her. It's you I'm worried about."

Manlu's face stiffened. "Don't you go managing things for me."

"How could I do that? I'm just saying it's a problem, that's all. You're not a young girl anymore—this kind of work won't last. It's not something you can do your whole life! You have to think ahead."

"I have to live one day at a time. Looking ahead only makes me want to curl up and die."

"Oh dear," said her mother, "how can you say that?" A wave of shame swept over her. She pulled out a handkerchief and wiped the tears from her eyes. "It's all my fault. If it weren't for me and the younger children, you wouldn't be in this awful situation. But maybe I can help you find a way out. The little ones are growing up fast, they'll be out on their own soon—"

Manlu, fired up with impatience, cut her off. "They're growing up, don't need me anymore, so now you're ashamed of having me around—that's why you want me to get married! OK, fine—but who do you think will marry me now?"

When Mrs. Gu heard her daughter talking back, locking horns with her own mother, she got so angry that words failed her. It was several moments before she could speak. "What are you saying, child?" she finally retorted. "Here am I trying to help you, and you're lashing out at me!"

They both fell silent, and the breaths of the sleepers in the next room wafted in. Granny snored, as older people often do.

Mrs. Gu grew wistful. "When I went back this time, I heard that Zhang Yujin is doing well. He's the head of the county hospital now." She winced slightly when she mentioned Yujin. It had been a long time since she'd spoken of him to Manlu.

Manlu had once been engaged. The year she turned seventeen, two relatives came to Shanghai, fleeing the turmoil that plagued their rural home town. This Mrs. Zhang and her son were Granny's kin, so they stayed with her. Mrs. Zhang took such a liking to Manlu that she wanted her as her daughter-in-law. Her son's name was Yujin. Neither he nor Manlu had any objections. They both seemed happy with the plan, and the engagement was quickly arranged. Later, when Mrs. Zhang returned to the countryside, Yujin stayed behind in Shanghai, and moved into his college dormitory. He and Manlu kept up a regular correspondence, and often saw each other. But when Manlu's father died and she became a taxi-dancer, the engagement was broken off; it was the bride's side that suggested it.

When her mother suddenly brought up Zhang Yujin's name, Manlu seemed not to hear, she was so silent. Her mother looked at her, all the while holding back something else she wanted to say. Then she said it anyway: "I hear he's not married yet."

Manlu broke out in laughter. "And so what? You think he still wants me? Ma, you are so mixed up! Are you still dreaming about him?" The vehemence of this outburst lifted Manlu to her feet. She scraped her chair back, thrust her feet into her slippers, and went downstairs. Her slippers made a scratching noise as she scuffed across the floor.

Granny stopped snoring. "What's going on?" she asked from next door.

"Nothing."

"Why aren't you asleep yet?"

"I'm going to bed right now." Mrs. Gu put her needlework away and got herself ready.

Before getting into bed, she fumbled around, searching for something in the dark. Manzhen had to call out from her bed, "Ma, your slippers are on the trunk behind the door. I put them up there so they wouldn't get dirty when we swept the floor."

"Oh dear—you're not asleep yet?"

"I woke up some time ago."

"Your sister and I woke you up with our talking, didn't we?"

"No, I slept a lot when I was sick, and I'm not sleepy tonight."

Her mother put the slippers next to the bed, turned off the light, and got under the covers. In the adjoining room, the sound of Granny's snoring rose and fell. Mrs. Gu sighed in the dark. "You heard what happened," she said to her daughter. "All I did was urge her to find someone to marry. A bit of good advice like that, and she lost her temper with me."

Manzhen was quiet for a long time. "Ma," she said, finally, "don't say that kind of thing to her anymore. It's not easy for her to get married now."

But, as often will happen, that which is least expected comes to pass. Less than a fortnight later, there came word of Manlu's impending marriage. It came from Manlu's maid, Ah Bao. A clear division ran through the household, with little contact between the two floors, so Ah Bao was Mrs. Gu's main source of news about her daughter. That was how she heard that Manlu was going to marry Zhu Hong-tsai. Ah Bao said Mr. Zhu was a trader in stocks and bonds, but worked only on deals arranged by his friend Mr. Wang. He didn't have much money of his own.

Mrs. Gu decided not to say anything about it, and pretend she hadn't heard. She didn't want another unpleasant conversation, like the night she'd tried to show her concern for her daughter. But then one day, when Manzhen came home from work, her mother quietly said, "I talked to her about it."

"Oh? I thought you said you weren't going to."

"Well, then I was afraid she might be reacting to what I said, running off and grabbing anyone she could find. It's not that I'm being choosy, but since she has been with other men, several in fact, and it's always come to nothing, I don't want her to be taken advantage of again. If this Mr. Zhu doesn't have any money, what's the point, for her? And does he have another woman? It's hard to believe that a man of thirty or forty doesn't have another wife somewhere."

Mrs. Gu paused, looked down, and started picking at her sleeves.

Finding a few loose threads, she carefully plucked them with her fingers.

"What did she say?" Manzhen asked.

"Well," Mrs. Gu replied, with excruciating slowness, "she says he has a wife in the countryside, whom he never sees. He's always lived on his own in Shanghai, and his friends think he should set up a household here. If he and Manlu do get married, he won't treat her like a secondary wife. She thinks she can trust him on this point—or, at least, that she can manage him. He isn't rich, but he has enough money to support us—"

Manzhen had kept silent up to this point, but now she had to break in. "Ma, from now on I'll support the family. What was the point of Manlu's paying my school fees for all those years, if I can't take her place now?"

"That's very good of you," her mother said, "but how is that possible, on that small salary of yours? Of course we can cut back on our living costs, but the little ones still have to go to school—where will their tuition fees come from?"

"Ma, don't worry, something will turn up. I'll look for more work. After Manlu has moved out, we won't need a servant, and the extra rooms can be rented out. We'll have to scrimp a bit, but that doesn't matter."

Her mother was nodding her head. "Yes, that's a good idea. Even if money is tight, we'll be happier. The truth is, spending your sister's money has never felt right to me. I couldn't let myself think about it." Now her voice was breaking. "It bothered me so much."

"Ma!" Manzhen forced herself to smile. "Why are you going on about all this? Things are going to be good for Manlu now, aren't they?"

"Of course we have to look on the bright side. She's supposed to be getting married soon, and that's wonderful. But what I'm trying to say is, whether or not he has money isn't so important. Seeing as he's got a wife already, how likely is it that he and Manlu, with that quick temper of hers, will really settle down? That's why I'm worried about Mr. Zhu."

"Well, don't go saying anything to her!"

"If I don't raise this with her, she'll soon be saying all I cared about was the money."

Meanwhile, downstairs, the two parties concerned were holding their own talks about the wedding ceremony. Manlu wanted a full, formal wedding, but Zhu Hongtsai wouldn't go along with this: it made him nervous. Manlu got angry. The two of them had been sitting side by side, but now she stood up. "Let's be clear about this—I'm not marrying you for your money! And yet you can't give me even this little sign of respect!"

She plopped down on a sofa and, as she often did, curled her legs up under her. She was wearing purple felt slippers lined with white rabbit fur, and when she leaned over sideways to stroke the fur, it looked like she was petting a cat. She sat there stroking her slippers, her face a study in dark moodiness.

Hongtsai didn't dare look at her. He scratched his head and said, "Of course I know you're making a sincere promise to me. But all that fuss and bother—who needs it? Why should it matter to us?"

"Maybe it doesn't matter to *you*, but it matters to *me*! A once-in-a-lifetime event, and your idea is to invite a dozen people, set up two banquet tables, and call it a day?"

"Well, of course we need a memento of the occasion. How about this? We'll go to a photographer's studio, have him take some wedding photos—"

"Who would want one of *those* photos? That's a ten-dollar package deal. They'll lend you the wedding outfit, veil and bouquet included, right there at the studio. Ten dollars for the whole thing. How can you be so cheap?"

"I'm not trying to save money, I just think a big do would be too flamboyant."

This made Manlu even angrier. "What do you mean, 'too flamboyant'? Are you saying you're embarrassed to stand up next to me at a formal wedding? You're afraid your friends will laugh at you for marrying a girl with a bad reputation! That's your problem, isn't it?"

She had put her finger on it, but that only meant he had to change tack in the argument. "That's quite enough of these blind suspicions! That's not it at all. Surely you know there are laws against bigamy!"

Manlu turned her head sharply. "Well, that's a problem that disappears if that village woman of yours doesn't say anything. Didn't you say she's got no hold over you?"

"She won't dare say anything, but her family might."

"If that's what's worrying you, why not make this easy on yourself? We can forget everything we've said, and you're free to go. Just don't ever show your face here again!"

That softened him up. His hands clasped behind his back, he paced the floor. "OK, OK, we'll do it your way. Have I met all your terms now? If so, we're done!" He thrust his fist into the palm of the other hand.

Hilarity broke out across Manlu's face. "We're not talking business here!"

When her face lit up, both of them felt their spirits lifting. They each felt they'd given more than they'd taken, thus getting the raw end of the deal, but nonetheless a sense of bliss flowed over it all.

When Manzhen came home the next day, Ah Bao met her at the door and invited her into her older sister's room. The whole family was gathered there, along with Zhu Hongtsai, who stuck close to Mrs. Gu, addressing her as "Ma." As soon as he saw Manzhen, he said, "Second Young Lady, I should call you 'Second Sister' now." He was wearing a business suit. It was the first time he'd worn Western-style clothing, but he looked very much at ease, thumbs stuck in trouser pockets, collar unbuttoned to show the gold chain at his neck. When he called Manzhen "Second Sister," she smiled and nodded, but did not address him, in turn, as "Brother-in-law." Hongtsai had been eager to see her, but now that she'd appeared he came over all awkward, and couldn't think of anything to say.

The furniture in Manlu's room was the best in the house. Hongtsai went to one of the wardrobes and rapped his knuckles on it.

"This furniture is very good. I took her to half a dozen furniture-makers today, and she couldn't find anything she liked. The truth is, if you compare what we saw today to this set here, it's clear that the stuff on the market is overpriced."

This did not please Manlu, but before she could say anything, Mrs. Gu, anxious to tamp down any sign of discord between daughter and son-in-law, spoke up: "Well, now, you two don't need to go out and buy new bedroom furniture. You should take this set, and try to make do with it. It's the least I can do, since I don't have another wedding present for you."

"Oh, Ma, that's not necessary!" Hongtsai protested with a smile.

Manlu stayed calm. "We can think about it later. There's no rush about the furniture—we haven't found a house yet."

"After you've moved out, I plan to rent out the downstairs rooms, and there won't be any place to keep this furniture. Go ahead and take it now."

Manlu was startled. "But you should let this whole place go. As soon as we've found something bigger, we'll all move in together."

"Oh, let's not do that. It's so noisy, what with all the children. You two should get a place by yourselves, something nice and simple—and quiet. Wouldn't that be better?"

Manlu already suspected her mother of wanting to put a little distance between them, in order to improve prospects for her younger children. Since this was probably why her mother didn't want to move in with her, she didn't press the matter. But Hongtsai knew nothing of this. Manlu had told him she wanted her family to live together with them, three generations under one roof, all in his care, so he felt he should urge Mrs. Gu to agree.

"Oh, it'll be much better if we all live together. That's the right way to do things. I'm not at all sure that Manlu can keep house. If you're there, Ma, the house will be yours to run."

"She's going to be at home all day long, with lots of time on her hands. She'll have to learn how to manage a house. If there's anything she can't do right now, she'll pick it up, with practice."

Granny broke into the conversation. "You shouldn't think that Manlu doesn't know how to get by," she said to Hongtsai. "When she was little, her mother let me take her to a fortune-teller, and the fortune-teller said she'd be a good-luck charm for her husband! Even if she married a beggar, he'd become the head of a company. And you, Mr. Zhu, are already well off, so that means you soon will be very wealthy."

This pleased Hongtsai no end. Cheerfully wagging his head, he walked up to Manlu, then leaned over and peered into her face. "Is that really what the fortune-teller said? Well then, if I don't get stinking rich, I guess I know who's to blame!"

Manlu gave him a shove. "Look at you!" She frowned. "What a way to behave!"

Hongtsai laughed delightedly and stepped away. He turned to Mrs. Gu. "Your daughter has seen just about everything, but this is something new: now she gets to be the bride. We're going to play it to the hilt, make it a really big do. We'll ask Second Sister to be the bridesmaid, and Youngest Sister to hold the wedding train. Everyone will get new clothes."

Manzhen thought Hongtsai's speeches utterly disgusting. Everything the man said was insipid, his whole manner repulsive. She stole a look at Manlu's face and saw embarrassment written there. It looked as though she feared her family would laugh at her for choosing a man like this to wed. When Manzhen saw that her sister was embarrassed, her own heart ached.

3

Manzhen, Shuhui, and Shijun were once again lunching together when the talk turned to the birthday banquet for Mr. Ye, a senior manager at their factory. Everyone at the factory was contributing to a fund to buy him a set of commemorative rice bowls—two hundred, specially inscribed for the occasion.

"Here you go," Shijun said, handing some cash to Shuhui. "Here's the money you put in the kitty for me."

"Aren't you coming to the banquet tonight?"

"I don't think so." Shijun frowned. "The truth is, I get bored at social events."

"You ought to socialize more," Shuhui urged. "It's part of having a job. You have to show up, or people will get upset."

"I know. But the crowd tonight will be so big, chances are no one will notice."

This was just like Shijun, and Shuhui knew it. The most easygoing person you'd ever met—until he put his foot down. Once he'd made a stand, he wouldn't budge. Shuhui urged him to reconsider, but it was hopeless. Manzhen stayed out of it.

After they'd returned home that night, and relaxed for a bit, Shuhui left for the party. Suddenly, Shijun realized that Manzhen would be at the party too. Without a moment's further thought, he opened the window and leaned out, intending to catch Shuhui when he stepped into the alley and ask him to wait. The minutes passed, and still no sign of Shuhui—apparently he'd reached the main street already. Darkness thickened in the alley and the spring night air was moist on his face; it was warmer out there. The cold crept under his skin as he sat in the house, and the little lamplit room looked small, bare and unkempt. The lonely chill of a guest room, a feeling he knew all too well, suddenly became unbearable—he wanted to get out. He wanted to see Manzhen. After one brief moment of wrestling with himself, he was on his feet, heading down the alley, then out to the street, into a pedicab, and off to the restaurant.

The birthday banquet for Mr. Ye was on the restaurant's upper floor, and a writing-table with ink, brush and guest-book had been placed at the top of the stairs. When Shijun saw that, he had to grin. Here he'd been thinking that no one could keep track of the guests—it was a good thing he'd changed his mind and put in an appearance.

He dipped the writing-brush in the ink. He seldom used a brush, and wasn't sure of the technique: he held the brush over the paper, then paused. Just then, someone reached from behind, grabbed the brush and pulled it sideways, streaking his wrist with ink. He turned—and when he saw it was Manzhen, surprise turned to amazement. She'd never played tricks on him before.

"Shuhui's looking for you," she said. "Hurry now!"

She threw the brush onto the table and sped away as Shijun trailed behind, still feeling stunned. They were in a large hall, with room for a dozen banqueting tables. Mr. Ye's friends and relatives were all there, along with the factory employees, so it took a bit of looking to find Shuhui. Manzhen led Shijun to the glass door that opened on to the balcony and stopped there. Shijun peered out—and saw no one on the balcony. "What's going on with Shuhui?" he asked.

Manzhen looked a little embarrassed. "He's not really looking for you. But there's a good reason for all this and I'll tell you what it is. I will, I promise . . . in just a minute . . ."

Whatever it was she wanted to say, it apparently was daunting; she was gabbling away without saying anything in particular. Shijun's apprehensions rose. When Manzhen saw the strange look on his face, she blushed. And that perfectly reasonable explanation only got harder to produce, the longer she delayed.

Just then, another colleague came by and held the guest-book out to Shijun. "Hey—you forgot to sign it!" Shijun took a fountain pen from his pocket and quickly wrote his name. The man took the book away, and Manzhen kicked at the floor.

"Blast!"

"What?" Shijun was puzzled.

Manzhen looked around in all directions, then went onto the balcony. Shijun followed.

"I've signed it for you already!" She was laughing and frowning at the same time. "I heard you say you weren't coming. Everyone else is here, and I didn't want you to be the only one missing."

Shijun didn't know what to say. "Thanks" was beside the point, somehow. He smiled at her, a little too intensely. To avoid his gaze, Manzhen turned and faced outward, over the balcony. This restaurant was an old, Western-style building, well lit on both floors. Out here on the balcony, the surging din of the upper-story hall faded away, and instead they heard sounds coming from the lower floor: the rhythmic chant of drinking games, the sultry voice of a singing-girl, the scraping melody of a *huqin*, the one-string fiddle. Manzhen looked at him, over her shoulder. "You said you weren't coming tonight," she said with a smile. "What made you change your mind?"

She was the reason, but he couldn't tell her that. He smiled back, searching for something to say. "Well, since you and Shuhui were both coming, I thought I should too."

They leaned against the railing, one facing in, the other facing out. The moon above was long and oval like a pure white lotus-seed, filling the air with misty luminescence. On the balcony itself, the moonlight was swallowed up in the light of the lamps. But Manzhen's forearm, resting on the railing's outer edge and bathed in the lunar glow, gleamed white. She was wearing her usual dress, a simple, dark blue gown, over which she'd buttoned a short-sleeved cardigan, pale green with pearl buttons. Shijun took a careful look: it was the same outfit she'd worn to work.

"You didn't go home after work, did you? Came straight here instead?"

"So I did. And what are you implying? That this blue uniform of mine isn't good enough for a birthday banquet?"

Some colleagues called out to them, "Hello there, you two—aren't you coming in to eat? Or do you need a special invitation?" Manzhen went in quickly, followed by Shijun. Seating had not been assigned, due to the size of the crowd, and once a table was full, the food was brought to it. People shied away from the high-ranking places, of course, and Manzhen and Shijun were confronted with only two remaining empty seats—the places of honor at that particular table. Because they were the last to arrive, they had no choice. Shijun had a strange feeling, sitting there next to Manzhen: wasn't this where the bride and groom would be placed at a wedding banquet? He stole a glance at her. She might have been thinking the same thing, for she seemed embarrassed, and said nothing to him throughout the entire meal.

When the banquet was over and everyone went scurrying around saying goodbye, Shijun offered to see her home. This would be the first time he'd gone to her house, and even though Manzhen had said nothing about it, the unspoken agreement was that he'd leave her at the alley entrance, not on the doorstep. Since he didn't plan to go in, this seeing-home business was dull indeed; if they'd been on a tram or bus, they could have chatted a bit, but instead they rode in separate pedicabs, which gave them no chance to talk. And yet he wanted to, and got real pleasure from doing so.

Manzhen's cab, which was in front, stopped at the entrance to her alleyway. Believing her house to be off limits, not open to visitors, and wanting to respect her family's wishes, Shijun quickly paid the fare, said goodbye and turned to walk away.

"I'd invite you in," she said, "but the house is all topsy-turvy right now. My sister's getting married."

Shijun stood stock-still. "Your sister's getting married?"

"Uh-huh." Even in the dim lights of the street lamps, he could see her face shining with happiness. Shijun too was elated. As someone privy to the situation, he saw at once what this meant: Manzhen would no longer be stuck in an awkward situation, and her sister would have a proper home of her own.

After a moment's silence, he asked, "Your new brother-in-law—who is he?"

"His family name is Zhu, the 'Zhu' that means 'good wishes.' He's an investor."

Manzhen suddenly remembered that her mother had gone earlier with Manlu to set up the new house, and might come back at any moment. If they happened to return right now, they'd find her standing at the alley entrance talking to a young man. It wasn't a serious offense, but still they would grill her about it.

"Well, it's getting late," she said, ending the conversation. "I'd better go in now."

"See you later," Shijun said, and headed off. After he'd passed a few houses, he turned and looked over his shoulder. She was still standing there. When he glanced back, she broke out of her daze, and walked away. Then it was Shijun who stood and stared into space.

Back at the factory, Shijun heard nothing further about the wedding, but it occupied his thinking a good deal. Spending time with Manzhen would be a lot easier once her sister was married. He could even go to her house; the ban on visitors would surely be lifted.

A week or so later, Manzhen suddenly told him and Shuhui that her family had a room to rent, because her sister was getting married. She asked them to let her know if they heard of anyone looking for a place.

Shijun threw himself into the search for a tenant. A few days later, he brought a Mr. Wu, the friend of a friend, to see the room. It was the first time he'd entered the little alley, which held an air of mystery for him because he'd been avoiding it. The alley was in a busy commercial district, and the street from which it branched off was full of shops. During business hours, the wood-panel shutters were taken out of the shop-door frames and propped up along the alley walls. A group of women had gathered at the communal tap to wash rice and do laundry; the cement in that whole area was slick with water. One young woman was even washing her feet. She stood there with a knee and two elbows raised, rinsing her foot in the splashing water. Her toenails were painted with Cutex nail polish, in a shocking shade of red. Shijun wondered if this might be the maid who had waited on Manzhen's sister.

The Gu family lived at No. 5, and there was a "Room for Rent" sign posted near the back entrance to the building stairwell. No one answered his knock, and since the door wasn't barred, Shijun pushed against it. A little boy who had been playing in the alley, sitting on a pedicab and ringing its foot-bell, jumped down, ran over and blocked Shijun's path. "Who are you looking for?" he demanded.

Shijun recognized him as Manzhen's little brother, the one who had brought the keys to Shuhui's house, but the boy didn't know who Shijun was. Shijun smiled and nodded at him. "Is your sister at home?" he asked.

But Shijun was fumbling over his words, and Jiemin thought he was one of Manlu's former customers. He had sharp eyes for such a little boy, due to his family circumstances. The hostility he felt towards the men who came to see his oldest sister had been brewing a long time. Now he stood his ground, tall and self-righteous, and shouted at Shijun, "She's not here! She got married!"

"No, no," Shijun said pleasantly. "I don't mean your oldest sister. I mean the next oldest one."

Jiemin was taken aback; none of Manzhen's friends had ever come to the house. He still thought these two men were looking for a good time. "What do you want with her?" He glared at them.

The boy's open animosity, in front of Mr. Wu, was making things hard for Shijun. "I work with her at the factory," he said with a smile. "We've come to look at the room that's for rent."

Jiemin looked him over carefully, then finally turned, ran inside and shouted, "Ma! Someone's here to see the room!" The fact that he called his mother, not his sister, showed that he still had his guard up. Shijun had not realized that trying to pay Manzhen a visit would be so difficult.

Manzhen's mother came out to greet them, and invited them in. Shijun replied politely, and asked if Manzhen were at home.

"Yes, I'll ask Jiemin to call her. What's your name, please?"

"My family name is Shen."

"Ah—Mr. Shen, you must be one of her colleagues, right?" She studied his face. Was this the young man she'd seen in the photographs? No, unfortunately, he wasn't.

The downstairs rooms were really a small suite: one large and one small, both empty now. The bare floor, coated with dust, spread out in all directions. An empty room is big, yet small—four-cornered and taut, like a box. Trying to imagine Manzhen's sister living here, and what that life had been like, already seemed futile.

Jiemin went upstairs to find Manzhen, and several minutes passed before she came down. She'd been changing her clothes, putting on the new dress she'd got for her sister's wedding. It was a short-sleeved pink dress, with tiny polka dots of deep blue. She'd never worn bright, attractive colors before, not with her sister's friends traipsing in and out. Her plain blue tunic-dress helped keep expenses down, and was a form of self-protection. Now that need for caution was gone. For Shijun, it was as if she'd suddenly stepped out of sackcloth mourning. She filled his gaze with light.

Shijun introduced Mr. Wu. The prospective tenant said he thought west-facing rooms might be too hot in the summer, but he'd think it over and get back to them. He still had other places to see, so he said goodbye and left. After he'd gone, Manzhen invited Shijun upstairs. On their way up the steps, they passed a long line of black cloth shoes set out on the windowsill. Children's shoes, adults' shoes: all had been through the winter and were being aired now. The late spring sunshine was warm and buoyant, and a patch of light blue sky showed through the window.

They went into the upstairs room where Granny and several of the children slept. There were two big beds and a smaller iron-frame bed. Manzhen led Shijun to a square table next to the window, and they sat down. They hadn't seen anyone on their way in, and even Manzhen's mother seemed to have disappeared, but he could hear half-whispered talk and an occasional cough in the next-door room: the whole family must be gathered in there, too shy to come out.

A maid brought tea, and indeed it was the same girl he'd seen washing her feet in the alley, the one with the painted toenails. Apparently she was the last trace, in this house, of Manzhen's older sister. Her bare feet were now thrust into a pair of worn-out shoes, the white leather broken through in places; she wore a printed-fabric dress and a hair-clip with a pink-jade inset. She gave him a big smile when she brought the tea, and poured him a cup with flattering courtesy. Then she closed the door when she went out—which made Shijun uneasy. He couldn't believe that Manzhen's mother and grandmother would take kindly to the two of them sitting there with the door closed. Still, all he did was turn a little awkward; Manzhen, reacting to something else, was greatly embarrassed. She thought he had noticed what a smooth show Ah Bao could put on, after all that time in her sister's service.

Manzhen got up, opened the door and sat down again. "That friend you brought—did he think the rooms were too expensive?"

"Oh, I don't think so. Shuhui's family lives in a pair of rooms that they rent for about the same price, and their rooms aren't as big and bright as yours."

"Do you and Shuhui share a room?"

"Yes."

Jiemin came in with two bowls of soup, boiled eggs in a sweet broth. The portions were a bit unusual—two eggs in the guest's bowl, one egg in the other. Manzhen saw her mother's hand at work. Her little brother stomped across the room and set the bowls on the table. He would not smile, would not look at them; he simply turned and headed out. Manzhen tried to speak to him, but he would not turn around.

"He's usually good with people," she said with a smile. "I don't know what's got into him, why he's suddenly so shy."

Shijun knew very well what was going on, but felt no need to explain. He just smiled back and said, "You needn't have gone to so much trouble, fixing food like this."

"Oh, it's just plain, countrified stuff! Eat only as much as you like—it's nothing special."

Shijun started on his soup. "What does your family have for breakfast?" he asked.

"Rice porridge. How about you?"

"Shuhui's family has rice porridge too, but it's a bit of a problem.

Shuhui's father loves to have people over, so they often have dinner guests, lots of them. That means Shuhui's mother has to work extra hard late into the evening, then get up at the crack of dawn to make porridge. I hate causing her so much trouble, so I usually have breakfast on my way to work. I stop at a street stall and get fried dough wrapped in flatbread."

Manzhen nodded. "There are always a few snags like that, when you live in someone else's house."

"It's a good place to live, actually. Shuhui's parents treat me like family. Otherwise, I'd feel I'd overstayed my welcome, living there so long."

"How long has it been since you last went home?"

"Almost a year."

"Do you get homesick?"

"No—going home isn't much fun. When I get enough money, I'd like to bring my mother to live here. She and my father don't get along. They're always fighting about one thing or another."

"Oh . . ."

"They've had some big fights because of me."

"What about?"

"My father owns a leather-goods shop, and he has some other businesses as well. My older brother, after he'd finished his studies, was the one who stayed there. He was helping my father, getting ready to take over when the time came. But then he passed away. My father wanted me to take his place, but I'm not interested in business. I like engineering. My father got upset, and refused to support me. After I got into college, it was my mother who helped me, by sneaking out the money from her housekeeping."

So he knew what it was to be hard up. When Manzhen was in school, she too had to cope with financial pressures: the two of them had gone through something similar, in that respect.

"I'd like to ask you a favor," she said, "but since you're still new here, you probably don't know many people in Shanghai."

"What's the favor?"

"If you hear of anyone who's looking for a part-time typist, let me know. I'd like to work another couple of hours after closing time at the factory. Or maybe a tutoring job—that would be good."

Shijun looked at her a moment. "Wouldn't it be too tiring?"

"Oh, no. My job isn't very demanding. Working another hour or two would be no problem."

Shijun knew that Manzhen's financial burdens had increased after her sister's marriage. Even if her friends had been able to help her out, she wouldn't have let them. The only thing he could do was help her find some work. But he looked for quite a while without success. Then one day she gave him new instructions: "Earlier I said I wanted a job that started after six o'clock, but now I need something I can do after dinnertime."

"After dinner? That's too late, isn't it?"

"I've already found a job that lasts until dinnertime."

"What? You can't do this! Rushing around from job to job all day long—you'll wear yourself out, and then you'll get sick! TB is a real danger at your age, don't you know that?"

"'At *your* age'?" Manzhen repeated with a smile. "The way you say that makes *you* sound positively ancient!"

A short time later, she found a second extra job. She was busy all through the summer, and though she did grow thin, she always had plenty of energy.

At holiday time, Shijun always bought presents for Shuhui's parents, to thank them for their hospitality. When Mid-Autumn Festival came around, he asked Manzhen to help him choose the gifts. He gave Shuhui's father a pure-wool scarf, and Shuhui's mother a dress-length of woolen cloth. He'd given her a length of fabric before, but she'd never had it made into a dress, and he wondered if the color he'd picked was too "young" for a matron like her. Actually, Mrs. Hsu didn't look middle-aged at all. She must have been a real beauty when she was young, and Shuhui took after her, not his father. Mr. Hsu—his full name was Hsu Yufang—was a chubby man somewhere in his forties or fifties, the short, dark, podgy type. He worked in a bank, but having too much self-respect to fawn on his superiors, he was stuck in a back-office department, managing paperwork and bureaucratic minutiae—a situation which did not bother him in the least.

"Take that cloth to a dressmaker right away," Yufang said to his wife, as they were admiring the gifts Shijun had brought. "Don't put it in a trunk and let it sit there, the way you did last time!"

"I can't wear such beautiful stuff! If I go out dressed like that, and you're next to me looking like a dumpy old errand boy, everyone will think I'm a shrew, spending all our money on my wardrobe!" She turned to Shijun. "You can't imagine how stubborn he is. I've asked him to get some new clothes made, but he just won't do it."

"That's because I've already looked in the mirror," Yufang put in. "No matter what I wear, I still look the same. I'll never be good-looking, so I may as well get to the good-eating part!"

That gave him the opening he needed to ask his wife what new delicacies had come into season. "I'll go to the market with you tomorrow, and look for something tasty!"

"I'd rather you didn't. You never shop carefully, and I'm trying to save up so we can have a nice meal for the Mid-Autumn holiday."

"If we want to have a feast, waiting till the holiday might not be the best idea. Food's more expensive then—why wait till the big rush?"

But his wife held to the traditional view. "We have to celebrate properly."

In the end, someone else came in and made the decision for them. It was a friend, asking for a loan to cover an urgent need, and Yufang gave him the better part of his month's pay. The man was a long-standing colleague, and when he came over it looked like it was just for the usual weekend chat, but then he seemed to have something private to say, so Shijun excused himself and went upstairs.

A short while later, Mrs. Hsu came in to get the charcoal brazier she'd put in his room. "Shijun!" she said, on her way through. "Your uncle Hsu is going to make his famous yellow croaker noodle-stew. You have to come and try it!"

Shijun accepted the invitation with a smile, and went back downstairs. Yufang was rolling up his sleeves, preparing for a stint in the kitchen. "Don't you worry—this is no trouble at all," he was saying to his guest. "I'm just whipping up a simple dish from things we have in the larder. Nothing fancy, I assure you!"

There were two cold dishes, along with the fish noodle-stew. Cooking was Yufang's pride and joy, but the great chef needed an assistant, someone to chop and mince and grind, so Mrs. Hsu was as busy as ever. And Yufang was very particular about his ingredients, each one on its own plate, the plates spread all around the room. Long after the guest had gone, Mrs. Hsu would be busy washing up. She'd bought this fish early in the day because Shuhui had said he'd like some fish. The mid-section went into the noodle dish, but she'd fry the rest for dinner, as originally planned. She put the head and tail back together, which made the fish, lying on the chopping block, look whole again. When Shuhui saw it, he wondered at its odd appearance. "Why does this fish have such a big head?" he asked.

"It's a dwarf," his father said.

Mrs. Hsu laughed heartily.

Shuhui stood there with his hands in his pockets, the white flecks on his gray sleeveless jumper standing out like flakes of snow. "That's a new sweater," his mother said. "Is it machine-made, or hand-knitted?"

"Hand-knitted."

"Oh? Who made it for you?"

"Miss Gu. You wouldn't know her."

"But I do—isn't that the Miss Gu who works with you?"

Manzhen had said she'd make a jumper for Shijun, and, thorough as ever, she made one for Shuhui too. She always had a ball of yarn in the pocket of her sweater, and she'd sit and knit while they relaxed in their favorite lunch place. She'd finished Shuhui's jumper first, so he was already wearing his. When she saw it, Mrs. Hsu felt a bit concerned. Like many doting mothers, she paid attention to details, even though they might not mean a thing. She said nothing further then, but the incident preyed on her mind. Shuhui came and went unpredictably, so it was hard to find a time to sound him out privately. But she and Shijun got along well. She thought she could glean something about her son by talking to his friend. Once children get to a certain age, a yawning gap opens up between them and their parents; the children's friends can be easier to reach.

The next day was Sunday. Shuhui went out, and his father also went out to see a friend. The postman brought a letter, and when Mrs. Hsu saw that it was from Shijun's family, she took it to him in his room. Shijun opened it right then, and she leaned on the door frame and watched him read it. "Is it from Nanking? Is your mother well?"

Shijun nodded. "She says she's coming to Shanghai to see the sights."

"Your mother's certainly got a lot of energy!"

Shijun frowned and smiled. "I think it's because I haven't been home in a long time, and she's worried about me. She thinks she should come and see how I'm doing. In fact, I was thinking of going home for a visit. I'd better write and tell her she needn't come. Traveling would be a lot of trouble for her, and she's not used to staying in hotels."

"No wonder she misses you. You're the only child she's got now! You can't blame her for worrying about you, living here in Shanghai by yourself. Has she ever urged you to get married?"

Shijun was silent for a moment. Then he said, with a slight smile, "On that topic, my mother is very forward-thinking. She's suffered from the old marriage system, which might be why she doesn't try to run my life for me."

Mrs. Hsu nodded. "That's the best way. The way the world's going these days, parents can't manage their children's lives, even if they wanted to! And it's not just because you're here in Shanghai, and your mother is in Nanking. Here I am in the same house with my son, and it's still no use. If he has a girlfriend somewhere, is he likely to tell us?"

"Oh, if he really was thinking of marrying someone, he'd be sure to tell you."

Mrs. Hsu gave a slight smile but said nothing. Then, a few moments later, she took up the thread again. "This Miss Gu, the one at your factory—what's she like?"

Shijun was stunned. For some strange reason, his face went red. "Gu Manzhen? She's great, but . . . well, she and Shuhui are just friends."

"Oh." Mrs. Hsu's tone showed that she only half believed him. This Miss Gu had to be a close friend of Shuhui's, or why would she be knitting things for him? Well, maybe she was an ugly girl, and that had put Shuhui off. Mrs. Hsu smiled again, and put the question to Shijun: "So I suppose she's not very pretty?"

Shijun broke out laughing. "No, no, she's . . . she's not ugly at all. But I know for a fact that she and Shuhui are just ordinary friends." He himself felt this was a weak claim, and no guarantee at all that Shuhui and Manzhen would not in time become a couple, which meant that Mrs. Hsu would continue to doubt him. Well—nothing he could do about that.

Shijun wrote back to his mother and told her he'd soon be home for a visit. His mother was delighted. She wrote again and asked him to invite Shuhui. Shijun knew his mother wanted to meet his friend, so she could see what kind of people her son was living with. He invited Shuhui to go to Nanking with him. The National Day holiday fell on a Friday, giving them a three-day weekend. The two of them decided that three days in early October would be the perfect time for a pleasure trip.

The night before their departure, Shuhui put on his coat after dinner, ready to go out. Mrs. Hsu knew that a female friend had just phoned. "It's so late," she protested. "Why are you going out now? You have to get up early to catch the train!"

"I'll be right back. A friend has asked me to take a few things to Nanking, and I need to pick them up."

"What? How big are these things? Will they fit in your luggage? I've already packed your bag for you." She went on fussing, but Shuhui was gone already.

A minute later, he was back, calling up from the bottom of the stairs, "Hey, we've got a visitor!" It turned out to be Manzhen. He'd run into her at the entrance to the alley, then brought her back to the house.

"Aren't you going out?" she asked Shuhui. "Go ahead. Really, it's no problem. I'm just popping in for a moment—I brought some snacks for your trip tomorrow."

"Oh, you shouldn't be buying things for us!" Shuhui protested. He led her up the stairs, dodging the neighbor's clothes line, which was strung with half-dry nappies. At the top of the stairs there was a charcoal stove and an empty soap dish, along with a tub of lanolin. When several Shanghai families share one building, it often becomes a vertical version of those dirty, cluttered courtyards in the north. Shuhui dressed so neatly, in his Western-style business suit, that no one would have imagined his house looked like this. He himself was thinking, It's only Manzhen, so it's OK, but what if I had a girlfriend who was high-class and pernickety—I'd better not bring *her* home.

When they'd climbed two flights of stairs, Shuhui gave her a big grin. "This way, please." He made a fancy flourish, ushering her through the door. Straight ahead, hanging on the wall facing the doorway, were a couple of decorative paintings and a leg of ham. In the center of the lamplit room, Shuhui's father was doing the washing-up. He had put the washbasin on a table, and was vigorously swishing the dishes around. This after-dinner task had fallen to him because his wife was stuffing cotton-padded jackets. Their other two children were at schools in the north, and she was making winter clothes for them. She wanted to send the bundles as soon as she could; cold weather would arrive soon in that region.

When the guest came in and was introduced as Miss Gu, Mrs. Hsu got flustered: she realized at once that this was the girl who'd made the jumper for her son. She stood up and offered Manzhen a seat, apologizing all the while for her appearance. "Look at me! Covered in cotton fluff!" She patted her clothes, trying to brush off the clinging bits of cotton. Hsu Yufang wore an old brown tunic around the house—it was lined, but short and sleeveless—and even though he'd never been one to bother about his appearance, he got embarrassed when this young lady arrived. He quickly put on a shirt. At this point, Shijun also came in.

"Have you had your dinner, Miss Gu?" Mrs. Hsu was inquiring politely.

"Oh, yes."

Shuhui sat with them for a while, but Manzhen urged him to get on with his errand, so off he went.

Up to this point, Yufang had not said a word, but now he turned and asked his wife where Shuhui was going. Mrs. Hsu knew her son was going to see a female friend, but she tactfully avoided mentioning that. "Oh, I don't know. I heard him say he'd be back soon. Please do stay for a bit, Miss Gu. It's an awful mess in here—why don't you go upstairs and have a seat?" She took them up to Shuhui and Shijun's room, and left Shijun there to keep Manzhen company.

Mrs. Hsu reappeared with a cup and tea leaves, then left again. Shijun poured hot water from a thermos into the teacup, and turned on the lamp. Manzhen saw an alarm clock on the table. She picked it up, and asked when their train would leave the next morning.

"Seven," said Shijun.

"Well then, setting it for five is about right, don't you think?" She released the tension on the spring, and the rasping sound rang out in the quiet room.

"I wasn't expecting you to come over," Shijin said, then paused. "Bringing us food and—"

"Didn't you say you feel guilty when Mrs. Hsu gets up early to make rice porridge for you? So I figured you'd be up even earlier to get the train, and you'd go hungry rather than bother her at that hour, so I brought a little breakfast you can take with you."

She kept her voice low, not wanting Mrs. Hsu to overhear. In order to catch what she was saying, Shijun had to walk over and stand close to her chair. He felt, at that moment, that he was standing at the edge of a beautiful, deep pond; his heart pounded and his brain was a blur. She'd finished speaking but still he stood close beside her. It might have been a few moments only, but it felt much longer. She must have felt so too; the lamplight showed her face turning pink. She looked around for something to focus on. "Oh," she said. "You forgot to close the thermos." Shijun looked, and sure enough, the flask was steaming like a little chimney, the cap still off—why was he in such a daze? He grinned, went over and put the cap back on.

"Have you finished packing?" Manzhen asked him.

"Oh, I'm not taking much." His leather case was on the bed. Manzhen went over, lifted the lid, and saw the rumpled mess inside.

"Here, let me do it. If your family sees it like this, they'll think you can't even pack a suitcase, and they'll worry all the more about your living here on your own."

Shijun was wondering if she really ought to be packing his suitcase; if people saw her doing that, tongues would surely start wagging. But he couldn't think of a simple, easy way to stop her. Manzhen could be quite strange sometimes. She could be extremely and uncomfortably self-conscious, but then again, entirely unselfconscious—and yet she was by no means a simple-minded person, someone who had no social awareness, nor was she the bashful type. These various contradictions took a lot of effort to piece together.

He brooded for so long that Manzhen finally asked him what he was thinking about. He gave a startled grunt, but couldn't frame a real reply. She was folding up an undershirt, and that gave him something to say: "When I get back, will that jumper be ready? The one you're knitting for me?"

"Are you definitely coming back on Monday?"

"Definitely. There's no reason to stay longer, and I don't want to miss work."

"But you haven't been home in a long time. Your parents will want you to stay a few extra days."

"Oh, no. That won't happen."

The suitcase lid tipped over and closed on Manzhen's hand. She raised it but a moment later it came down again. Shijun held it up for her. He sat to one side, watching her fold his undershirts, his necktie, his socks, feeling strange about it.

Mrs. Hsu came in with a dish of sweets. "Miss Gu, please try some—oh? You're helping Shijun pack his bag?" Shijun noticed that she'd put on clean clothes and a bit of face powder, apparently intending to stay and chat with the guest. But she didn't sit down after all; a few polite phrases and she was gone again.

"You're not taking your raincoat?" Manzhen asked.

"No—what are the chances it will rain? I'll only be gone a few days."

"Are you coming back on Monday, definitely?" The minute she asked, she realized that she was repeating herself, and that made her laugh. Under cover of that laugh, she quickly closed the suitcase, picked up her handbag, and said she'd be going.

Shijun could see that she was embarrassed, and made only a token effort to hold her back. "It's early yet. You should stay a little longer."

"No, I'd better go, and you should get some rest."

"Aren't you going to wait till Shuhui gets back?"

"No."

Shijun saw her down to the ground floor, and when they passed the doorway to the lower room, Manzhen bid Mr. and Mrs. Hsu goodnight. Mrs. Hsu came out and saw her to the front entrance of the building, all the while inviting her to come again whenever she could.

After she'd closed the door, Mrs. Hsu turned to Shijun. "Miss Gu is a nice girl, and she's pretty too." Mrs. Hsu must have seen something special in his relationship with Manzhen, Shijun thought, or why would she be praising Manzhen to him? He got embarrassed, and mumbled a vague reply.

He'd intended, upon returning to his room, to go to bed right away, but before he could spread out the quilt he first had to take the suitcase off the bed. He ended up sitting on the edge of the bed, opening the suitcase to take a look, then closing it again, feeling listless and low-spirited. Finally he stood up, locked the suitcase and put it on the floor. When he put the key in his pocket, his hand touched a packet of cigarettes; he took one out and lit it. Since he'd lit it, he might as well have a smoke before going to bed.

A glance at the clock told him it was eleven already. Shuhui wasn't back yet. The silence was broken by the rattling of Mrs. Hsu's hand-cranked sewing machine. She usually was in bed by this time of night; she must be waiting up for her son.

Shijun was thirsty, after his cigarette. He reached for the thermos, and when his hand touched the cap, he found it piping hot. What was going on? He took it off and saw that he'd neglected to replace the wooden bottle-stopper, which meant the steam was in direct contact with the metal cap, heating it up. Meanwhile, the water itself was growing cold. Why was he such a dolt today? First he'd forgotten to put the cap on, and then he'd forgotten the stopper. Manzhen had probably noticed, but had refrained from reminding him a second time. While all this was sinking in, Shijun was drinking some water, even though it had cooled down. The water was cool but his cheeks were hot.

Someone was whistling outside the window—it had to be Shuhui. When the night air was cold, he liked to whistle instead of knocking, so he could keep his hands in his coat pockets. Mrs. Hsu might not hear him, Shijun thought, since her sewing machine made such a racket. As he was still up, he could go down and get the door for her.

Heading towards the entrance, he went past the Hsus' room and heard Mrs. Hsu talking to her husband. Her voice was low, but a person's ears prick up when his name is mentioned; he can hardly help it.

"Who'd have thought it?" Mrs. Hsu was saying. "Shijun seems so quiet and reliable, but he's gone and stolen Shuhui's girlfriend!"

Yufang never whispered; he had a booming voice, even for secrets. "Shuhui—that little pipsqueak! He's nowhere near good enough for that young lady."

After one brief meeting, this old gentleman had formed a very high opinion of Manzhen. That alone did not mean much, but his wife did not like to hear him disparaging their son. She said nothing, but the sewing machine rattled on loudly. Shijun took advantage of the noise, and ran back upstairs, three steps at a time.

Mrs. Hsu's words came back to him. She had completely misinterpreted the situation, had mixed up their relationships completely. And yet, nestling in the flood of protests that filled his mind, a sliver of joy shone through, making it impossible to say exactly what his feelings were.

Shuhui, down in the alley below, whistled up at the window and pounded on the door.

4

They took the early train to Nanking, then a bus from the south-end train station to Shijun's neighborhood, arriving about two o'clock in the afternoon.

Walking into his childhood home always felt odd to Shijun: it seemed smaller, more cramped than he remembered, probably because those memories had been formed when he was small and the house loomed large for him.

His family lived on the upper floor, over their leather-goods store. They were rich now, and the shop no longer was their main source of income, but they were used to economizing, and didn't want to move. The shop itself was cavernous and dimly lit, paved with stone-green square tiles. A rickshaw was parked in the back, next to a seating area where the business manager and two elderly clerks could chat with clients and guests. Two old leather caps lay on the table, alongside an earthenware tea set, giving the place a domestic, relaxed feeling. The ceiling was two storys high, with a central sky-light. An internal balcony ran in front of the living quarters, which were screened from view by dark blue windows.

Shijun's mother must have been watching for them from a window that opened onto the street; she saw them the moment they arrived. When they came through the door, she called out to Ah Gun, the rickshaw driver, "Ah Gun! Second Young Master is here! Go and help him with his luggage!" He came out at once, and took their bags. Shijun led Shuhui to the upper floor. Mrs. Shen greeted them, half giggling with delight. She asked a thousand questions, and got the maid to bring water so they could wash their faces. Steaming platters soon appeared on the table; the food had been prepared before they arrived. She addressed Shuhui as "Young Master Hsu." Shuhui was a good-looking, well-spoken lad, which always impressed older ladies.

Shijun's sister-in-law brought her son out to see them. A year had gone by since Shijun had last seen her, and she'd aged noticeably since then. He'd heard she was having trouble with her kidneys and asked if she was feeling better. She said she was getting by.

"Why, she's even been putting on some weight," his mother said. "It's Vim who's not been well. He's just recovered from the measles."

Shijun's nephew had always been a sickly child; they called him "Vim" in the hope of making up for that. The child was a bit shy around Shijun, and when his mother saw that he looked ready to burst into tears, she quickly warned him, "Don't cry! If you cry, Grandma will get angry!"

"And what does Grandma look like when she's angry?" Mrs. Shen teased.

The boy made a howling sound, like an angry dog.

"And what does Mama look like when she's angry?" Mrs. Shen asked.

He howled again, and everyone laughed.

These two women live here alone, Shijun thought, with this one child to fill their time. My brother's gone, my father hardly ever comes home—they're like a pair of lonely widows, one old, the other young, with only this little boy to give their lives meaning.

Vim had been with them only a few minutes when Mrs. Shen asked Shuhui if he'd had measles. Shuhui said he had. "So has Shijun," Mrs. Shen said, "but still it's best to be careful. The child is better now, but he could still give it to someone else." She told the nurse to take the boy away.

Mrs. Shen sat and watched her son eat. She asked him all about his daily routine, what time he went to work, what time he got off, what he ate, and so on. She wanted to know whether his room was heated in the winter, and insisted he get a long leather coat; she pulled out a stack of fur-lined leather pieces and made him choose one, right then and there. She told her daughter-in-law to pack the other pieces back into the trunks.

"This Russian squirrel would make a good cape for Vim," the child's mother said.

"Children shouldn't wear leather," Mrs. Shen said. "We've never allowed that in our family. We think it's not good for them—it's too hot. When my sons were young, we didn't even let them wear padded silk."

That didn't go down well with the younger woman, but she said nothing.

Mrs. Shen's behavior was slightly erratic—she was excited, no doubt, by her son's all-too-rare visit. She was grinning at the servants, calling out orders left and right, running them ragged; she got them all mixed up, as if she had no experience in managing staff. Her daughter-in-law wanted to help out, but couldn't get a word in edgeways. Shijun, not realizing that he was the cause of his mother's odd behavior, thought she was simply getting old, and that made him sad.

Shijun and Shuhui were deciding where they'd go that afternoon.

"Why don't you go and see Tsuizhi?" Mrs. Shen suggested. "She's on holiday at the moment." Shi Tsuizhi was her daughter-in-law's cousin.

"Can't do that," Shijun said. "Shuhui has some things to deliver, and I have to help him find the address."

Mrs. Shen did not respond to this rebuff. She merely asked them to come back early, in time for dinner.

Shuhui opened up his case and took out the things he was going to deliver; Mrs. Shen got some paper and string and made a little parcel for him. Shijun stood off to the side, near a window, and happened to see his nephew on the opposite balcony. The boy was leaning through a window, waving to him and calling out, "Hi, Uncle!"

Seeing the little boy reminded Shijun of his own childhood. And that made him think of Shi Tsuizhi. They'd known each other since they were children. They weren't childhood sweethearts, but even so, Shijun remembered her well. Happy memories quickly turn vague, while unpleasant incidents, especially those dating from childhood, stick in our minds, and rise up again for no reason we can find.

Now he was remembering everything about Tsuizhi. They had met at his brother's wedding. Shijun was the ring-bearer, who walked at the head of the wedding procession. There were two little girls who held the bride's train, and one of them was Tsuizhi. Tsuizhi's mother supervised the wedding rehearsals; she kept finding fault with Shijun, nagging at him for walking too fast. Shijun's mother, on the other hand, was quite taken with Tsuizhi. She kept talking about her, saying she wanted Tsuizhi to be her goddaughter. Shijun was too young to see that this was a way of making friends with another family, and he got jealous when he saw his mother chasing after the girl. She told him to play nicely with Tsuizhi. He was older, so it was his job to keep her happy; he wasn't allowed to be mean to her. He tried to teach her to play Chinese chess. Tsuizhi, six years old then, kept climbing on and off the chair, uninterested in the game. She went so far as to climb up on the table; then, with her elbows planted on the board and her head propped in her hands, she stared at him with her big black eyes and said, "My mother said your father is a johnny-come-lately. Hah!"

That knocked Shijun off balance, but he kept on with the game. "I'm taking your horse. Now, you move your cannon here . . ."

"My mother says your grandfather was a leather-beater."

"I'm taking your high official. Hmm. Now you can send your chariot out. Hey! I've got your general!"

Later that day, when they were back at home, he asked his mother what his grandfather's line of business was. "Your grandfather ran a leather-goods shop," she told him. "The same business we have now."

Shijun was silent for a while. "Mother, was Grandpa a leather-beater?"

She gave him a sharp look. "Before he opened the shop, your grandfather was a craftsman. There's nothing shameful in that, it's no reason to fear gossip."

Then she added, her tone now severe, "Who told you that?"

Shijun told her. Even though she'd said it was nothing to be ashamed of, her mood and tone made him feel it was. But even more shameful was the way she chased after Tsuizhi and her mother, kissing and cooing at them.

On the day of the wedding itself, when they lined up for formal photos, the ring-bearer and the little bridesmaids were scrutinized by their mothers, who warned them not to blink when the flash-bulb popped. But when the photo came out, Tsuizhi's eyes were screwed shut. That pleased Shijun no end.

Over the next few years, he didn't get much taller, almost as if he'd stopped growing altogether. Adults would tease him, asking if he'd opened an umbrella indoors—old people liked to say children would stop growing if they did that. Tsuizhi laughed at him too. "You're older than me, how come you're not taller? *And* you're a boy—I guess you'll be a shorty when you grow up."

At their next meeting, a few years later, he towered over her. "Why are you so thin? You're skinny as a grasshopper." She'd probably picked that up from her mother.

Back then, Mrs. Shi couldn't see much good in Shijun, but over the past few years, her perspective had changed. Tsuizhi was growing up fast and a suitable match was required. They moved in a close-knit social set, and potential sons-in-law were all too old, too young, or too wild. Shijun was the steadiest, the most conscientious of all the young masters in that circle. Ever since she'd come to this realization, Mrs. Shi had invented reasons for Tsuizhi to visit the cousin who had become Shijun's older brother's wife. Years earlier, Mrs. Hsu had been full of plans for making Tsuizhi her goddaughter, but it hadn't worked out. Now the idea had surfaced again, and Shijun couldn't tell which side was behind it. It probably was his sister-in-law's idea. A god-brother and god-sister were considered a good match. Shijun thought it likely that his mother and sister-in-law filled their long, lonely hours with matrimonial dreams of this very sort.

He and Shuhui were out all afternoon, returning home at dusk. "Goodness me!" his mother said, when she saw him. "You were gone so long—we were starting to worry!"

"We'd still be out," Shuhui said with a smile, "if it hadn't started raining."

"It's raining? Well, at least it's not raining hard. We're expecting Tsuizhi to come for dinner."

"*What?*"

Shijun started to fume. His nephew walked by just then, clapping his hands and singing, "Uncle's girlfriend is coming, hooray! Uncle's girlfriend is coming!"

Shijun frowned so hard his eyebrows made a single line. "What's all this about her being my girlfriend? What a joke! Who's been telling him this nonsense?"

Actually, he knew very well it was his sister-in-law's doing. He'd been out on his own for two years now, had matured quite a bit, but when he came home he suddenly grew childish again. Something about the place rubbed him the wrong way—it was as if he'd never learned to control his temper.

After this outburst, he turned and stomped off to his room. His mother stayed out of it. "Amah Chen," she said, "take two washbasins in, so the young master and his guest can wash their faces." Shuhui too went to their room.

"When Tsuizhi gets here," Mrs. Shen said to her daughter-in-law, speaking in a low voice, "we shouldn't say anything too obvious. Don't tease them—if we say too much, they'll get stiff and embarrassed. It's better to let things take their natural course."

She needn't have spoken; her daughter-in-law was incensed, not in the least inclined to joke about this. "Well, of course. Besides, Tsuizhi would never stand for it. She's a stubborn one, that girl of ours. The only reason she agreed to come while Shijun is here is that they used to be playmates, back when they were little. If she thought we wanted to pair them up, she'd never have accepted the invitation."

Mrs. Shen knew she was defending her cousin. "Oh, of course," she said amiably. "Young people today are all like that! We have to let them do what they like. It's all up to fate anyway!"

Off in their own room, Shuhui asked Shijun who Tsuizhi was. "She's my sister-in-law's cousin," Shijun told him.

"They're trying to match you up with her, is that it?" Shuhui grinned.

"That's my sister-in-law's fondest wish."

"Is she pretty?"

"You'll see her soon enough, so you can decide for yourself. Ugh! I finally get a few days at home, and they won't give me any peace!"

Shuhui looked at him and laughed. "My, oh my! What a temper you've got!"

Shijun had been annoyed, but now he had to laugh too. "This is nothing. You haven't seen *her* temper yet! These grand young ladies in their little towns sit behind closed gates and reign like empresses!"

"'Grand young ladies in their little towns'—since when is Nanking a little town?"

"I'm looking at it the way you Shanghainese would. Isn't the whole interior, from the Shanghainese perspective, nothing but countryside and little rural towns?"

The maid came in, and called them to dinner. She told them that Miss Shi had arrived. Shuhui went with Shijun to the front room, his curiosity aroused. Shijun's sister-in-law was calling everyone to the table, and Shijun's mother was on the sofa chatting with Shi Tsuizhi. Shuhui took a good look. Her hair was done up in a topknot, with a fringe that reached down to her eyebrows. She had a small, narrow face, very pretty except for the slightly puffy eyes. She was the curvaceous type, with a strong bust line that added a few years to her appearance, though she had to be in her early twenties, at the most. Her outer gown was made of stiff blue cotton, but a silver-threaded, apricot-yellow cheongsam shimmered under the lapels. That dark, plain wrapper was an odd choice for a dinner party, but she knew this was a matchmaking session and hadn't wanted to dress up too much, as that would only add to her embarrassment. She was sitting with her arms crossed over her chest when Shijun came in; they smiled and nodded at each other.

"It's been a long time," Shijun said. "How's your mother?" He introduced Shuhui.

"Come and eat!" Shijun's sister-in-law called.

Mrs. Shen insisted that the two guests take the seats of honor, and she took the place next to Tsuizhi. Tsuizhi had never been good at talking to old ladies. The only person at the table she knew well was her cousin, and she was in a foul mood today, would hardly say a word. That made it a quiet meal. Shuhui was a good talker, but this old-fashioned family's conservative ways kept him from chatting with the young lady beside him, especially since they'd never previously met. Amah Chen stood in the doorway in case they needed anything. Vim hid behind her, then peeked out and asked, "Where is Uncle's girlfriend?"

That made his mother even angrier, but Amah Chen didn't know the game; she leaned over to the child, a big smile on her face, and said, "Don't you see her, right there?"

"No, that's just Cousin. Where is Uncle's girlfriend?"

His mother couldn't take it any longer. She put her rice bowl down, swept her son up, and took him away. "Time for bed! Look how late it is!" She herself carried him to their room.

Tsuizhi spoke next: "Our dog just had some puppies. Vim can have one, if he likes."

"Oh, that's right," Mrs. Shen said. "You promised him one."

"I wouldn't give you a puppy," Tsuizhi said with a smile, "if Shijun were living here. He doesn't like dogs."

"I've never said that," Shijun protested.

"You've never said it outright, but that's because you're so polite. You never say what you're really thinking."

That stopped Shijun in his tracks. He turned to Shuhui and asked, "Tell me, am I really such a fraud?"

"Don't ask me. Miss Shi has known you longer—I'm sure she knows you better than I do."

Everyone laughed.

The rain had nearly stopped, and Tsuizhi stood up to take her leave. "Oh, stay a little longer, won't you?" Mrs. Shen said. "I'll get Shijun to see you home."

"No, no, thanks very much."

"I'll be happy to do it," Shijun said. "Shuhui, you can come with us, since you haven't seen Nanking by night."

"Is this Mr. Hsu's first visit to Nanking?" Tsuizhi asked, with polite restraint. She addressed the question to Shijun, not Shuhui.

"Yes," Shuhui answered. "Even though Nanking is so close to Shanghai, I've never been here before."

Tsuizhi had not once spoken to him directly, and when he replied to her question, she blushed and said no more.

A few minutes later, Tsuizhi repeated her intention of returning home. Mrs. Shen sent the servants off to hail a horse-drawn cart. Tsuizhi went to her cousin's room to say goodbye. She found a cooking stove in the room, with a pot at full boil.

"Aha!" Tsuizhi said. "I've caught you! So you're pinching food from the kitchen, are you?"

"What do you mean—'pinching food'? This is beef soup for Vim. He's only just recovered from his illness, and needs nourishing food. That's his grandma's orders. Every day she tells Amah Wang to make him soup, chicken or beef. But now the whole house has gone to pieces; she's been running the servants off their feet, getting things ready for Shijun's visit. No one has time to make soup for my little boy. So I had to go out, buy the meat myself, and make the soup. These servants really know what's up—it won't be long, will it, till Second Master Shijun is in charge around here. What about that widow and her little child? Oh, just leave them out in the cold!" She started to cry.

The outburst was surprising, given her many years of experience as a daughter-in-law in an old-style household like this one. It was Shijun's comments that had set her off. Her family pride had been injured, and from that point on, the tiniest incident became, for her, a deep insult.

"That's just how servants are," Tsuizhi said, trying to help her. "If you don't stay on top of things, nothing ever gets done. Anyway, Mrs. Shen dotes on your little boy."

"Oh, don't be fooled by appearances," her cousin said disparagingly. "None of that is real—she only uses him to fill the time. The minute her son appears, she forgets her grandson. Vim recovered from his bout of measles ages ago, and still she won't let him come out and be with other people—he might infect Shijun! *His* health is what matters! This afternoon, she sent me to the apothecary for a dozen herbs and jabs, all for Shijun to take back to Shanghai. I said it wasn't necessary, all those things are easy to find in Shanghai, and she got angry with me. 'Yes, he could get this in Shanghai,' she said, 'but what are the chances of his doing that? Even if I buy medicine for him here, there's no assurance that he'll take it—young people are so stubborn! They don't know how to look after their own health!'"

"Is Shijun not well?" Tsuizhi asked.

"He's fine, perfectly fine. But here am I suffering all the time, and no one gets a doctor for me, or buys me any medicine. My face is all puffed up because of my kidney trouble, and she says I'm putting on weight! How's that for maddening? It's a hard life, being a daughter-in-law in this house!"

The last sentence was a hint to Tsuizhi, telling her the match would not go through, but that was just as well. Tsuizhi could say nothing to that, of course. Instead she asked about her cousin's illness and the medicines she was taking.

The maid came to tell them the cart had arrived, so Tsuizhi put on her rain cape and said goodbye to Mrs. Shen. Shijun and Shuhui got into the cart with her. The horse clopped along the cobbled streets, the goose-egg stones shining like shoals of fish in the wet gleam of the rainy night. Shuhui kept lifting up the canvas flap to look out at the streets. "Can't see a thing," he said. "I'm going up front." He was as good as his word, calling out to the driver to get him to stop, then hopping out and climbing up to sit beside him, even though it was still raining. The driver found it strange, but Tsuizhi smiled.

That left Shijun and Tsuizhi alone in the back of the cart. A silence quickly fell, and the seats seemed hard, the ride bumpy. They sat in silence as the murmur of conversation between Shuhui and the driver drifted back to them.

"Are you staying at Mr. Hsu's place in Shanghai?" Tsuizhi asked.

"Yes."

Several minutes passed. "Are you going back on Monday?"

"Uh-huh."

This last question gave him a sense of déjà vu—it was the same question that Manzhen had asked him twice. Thinking of Manzhen made him feel lonely. Rattling through the rainy night in a damp cart, he suddenly felt how strange, how unfamiliar to him, his home town had become.

Then he realized that Tsuizhi had spoken to him. "Huh? What did you just say?"

"Nothing much. I was asking if Mr. Hsu is an engineer, like you."

It was a simple, ordinary question, and when he asked her to repeat it, she got flustered. No longer waiting for his reply, she lifted up the canvas flaps and looked out. "So, aren't we there yet?"

Shijun didn't know which question he should answer first; it took him a moment to figure it out. "Shuhui studied engineering, like me, and now he's an assistant engineer in our factory. I'm an apprentice engineer, still in training, really."

Tsuizhi, still embarrassed, kept looking through the flaps while he explained. It looked as if she'd lost interest in what he was saying. "Uh-oh," she muttered. "I hope we haven't gone past my house."

Meanwhile, Shijun was thinking to himself, Tsuizhi is so annoying. She's always been like this.

The rain was a fine mist. Shuhui sat next to the driver and looked at the lights of the old, old city. He thought of Shijun and Tsuizhi, two young people, growing up in this ancient capital. Perhaps because he was on the driver's seat, raised up high like an emperor's throne, he felt sad and sympathetic towards everyone. Girls like Tsuizhi had an especially difficult time of it. They lived in a tiny social circle, with only one option in life: find a suitable match, get married, and become a daughter-in-law. A dismal fate indeed. Tsuizhi seemed to have a strong personality; it was sad to think of her being buried alive like that.

Shijun poked his head out and called to them, "Hey! This is it!" The cart stopped. Shijun got out, followed by Tsuizhi, her rain cape thrown over her head. She went around to the front to say goodbye to Shuhui. "See you next time." The horse-cart light shone on her uplifted face, in the misty rain.

"Yes, see you next time," Shuhui said, doubting he'd ever see her again. His spirits sank. She had no future with Shijun, much less with him, due to the differences in their family backgrounds.

Shijun saw her to the front gate and waited while she rang the bell. Someone came out to open the gate. When Shijun returned to the cart, Shuhui had already jumped down from the driver's seat and climbed into the back. Under the canvas tarpaulin, there was a faint scent of hair oil. He sat alone in the dark. Then Shijun came back and, standing beside the cart, poked his head in.

"How about going in for a bit?" he urged his friend. "Yipeng is here too—he's one of Tsuizhi's mother's nephews."

Shuhui blinked. "Yipeng? You mean Fang Yipeng?"

Shijun's sister-in-law's maiden name was Fang, and she had two younger brothers, Yiming and Yipeng. Yipeng and Shijun had studied at the same college in Shanghai, so both of them were Shuhui's former classmates. But Yipeng and Shuhui had never been close; they were different types. When Yipeng heard that Shuhui came from a poor family, he thought he could pay Shuhui to write a dissertation for him. Shuhui refused and Yipeng was miffed. Shijun never told Shuhui what Yipeng said about him behind his back, but Shuhui had a pretty good idea, nonetheless. Of course, all of that was well behind them now, something from the remote past.

Shijun hadn't planned to visit Yiming and Yipeng on this trip to Nanking, but since he had run into them he couldn't very well leave the house without a brief chat. He didn't want to make Shuhui sit alone in the cart; hence the invitation to go in with him. Shuhui got out of the cart. A pair of servants came out with umbrellas and led them into the compound. Tsuizhi was waiting for them at the gatehouse and led them through the front garden. The night was so dark and wet they could hardly see a thing. It wasn't raining hard, but the rain that had collected in the trees plopped down in large drops. The air was filled with the scent of sweet osmanthus. The Shi family lived in an old Western-style house; as they approached it they could see, through a set of French doors, a living room lit by a splendid chandelier and a lively group of people sitting there. There wasn't time to take a closer look—Tsuizhi was leading them to the main door, then through the entrance hall to the living room.

Mrs. Shi, Tsuizhi's mother, honored them with a slow, slight bow from her chair at the mahjong table, and greeted Shijun by name. Mrs. Shi was half as wide as she was tall. Yipeng was also at the table. "Hey, when did you arrive in Nanking?" he called out to Shijun. "I had no idea you were here! And Shuhui too! How super to see you again!"

Shuhui returned the greeting.

Yipeng's older brother, Yiming, was there also, along with his wife, Amy. She was considered a modern, daring woman, because she wanted everyone, regardless of their age or seniority, to call her Amy. But they stuck to their old ways and, if they were senior to her, called her "Little Yiming's wife," or, if they were junior, "Elder Sister-in-law." Shijun greeted her as "Elder Sister-in-law."

"Ah," she said, narrowing her eyes at him, "you sneaked back home without letting us know—trying to avoid us, are you?"

"I got here just this afternoon," Shijun said pleasantly.

"Right, and then you looked up Little Sister Tsuizhi, without a thought for us!"

"Oh, you can't hold a candle to Tsuizhi!" Yiming laughed at his wife.

Shijun could hardly believe they were joking like this in front of Mrs. Shi. The lady of the house herself made no objection; she sat there smiling.

But Tsuizhi wasn't smiling in the slightest. "What's going on here?" she demanded. "Why are you all making fun of me?"

"Oh, all right," Amy said, "we'll stop now. But Shijun, you have to come over to ours for dinner tomorrow. Tsuizhi, you come too."

Before Shijun could say anything, Tsuizhi cut in. "Sorry—I'm not free tomorrow." She was standing behind Amy, watching the game.

Amy reached around and grabbed her arm. "A person gives you a nice invitation like this, and you pretend you're too busy to come!"

"I really do have something else on tomorrow," Tsuizhi said, her expression stony.

Ignoring her, Amy picked up a mahjong piece and arranged it among her other tiles. "I'd like to borrow this mahjong set tomorrow. We'll have several tables going, and not enough tiles, so please bring them with you when you come, Sister Tsui. And Shijun, be sure to come early too."

"Please don't go to so much trouble tomorrow," Shijun said pleasantly. "I'll come another day, when I have more time. Tomorrow I'm taking Shuhui out to see the city."

"Both of you should come," Yipeng said. "Shuhui also."

Shijun went on making excuses but just then Yiming made a big move. The mahjong players were so busy matching up tiles they let the subject drop.

Tsuizhi went up to her room, then came back and stood at the table, watching the game again. Yipeng dropped a tile on the floor, and when he bent to pick it up he saw that she was wearing shiny new shoes of silver satin with gold-thread embroidery. "Wow!" he exclaimed. "What pretty shoes!" He threw out the remark without much thought—he'd never viewed Tsuizhi as much more than a child. In Shanghai, he chased only the top-class types. Little misses from the interior, like Tsuizhi, did not interest him; he found them stiff and conservative—not enough pizzazz. But once Yipeng had admired Tsuizhi's shoes, Shuhui had to take a look too. She hadn't been wearing them earlier, he knew that much. She must have changed into them because her leather shoes had got wet in the rain.

Shijun had now made it through his half-hour's courtesy call. He took his leave of Mrs. Shi, who wasn't too happy with him and responded with a curt goodbye. She told her daughter to see the guests off. Tsuizhi came out with them, but stopped at the front door. The same two servants came out with umbrellas to take them through the garden. When they'd almost reached the front gate, a dog burst out barking, then came running at them through the darkness. It was a big, wolfish dog. The two servants yelled at it, but it barked wildly. Then they heard Tsuizhi calling the dog's name as she came running across the garden.

"Oh, but it's raining!" Shijun called to her. "Don't come out!"

But Tsuizhi was out of breath, and didn't answer him. She reached down and grabbed the dog by the collar.

"It's OK," Shijun said. "The dog knows who I am."

"So he might," she said coldly, "but he doesn't know Mr. Hsu!"

That was her goodbye to them, as she hauled the dog away by its collar. The rain was now falling hard. Shijun and Shuhui hurried onward, stumbling in the dark. Their shoes were soaked through, squeaking at every step. Shuhui suddenly thought of Tsuizhi's shiny slippers, covered with needlework—surely they'd be ruined now.

They left the garden, got into the cart, and headed back to Shijun's house.

"This Miss Shi," Shuhui said, after some moments had passed, "she doesn't quite fit into her own social scene, does she?"

"What you seem to be saying is that even though she's a rich young lady she wears a plain blue wrapper coat."

Shijun's choice of words made Shuhui laugh.

"And even if this young lady does wear a plain blue coat," Shijun went on, laughing along with him, "it has to be better than anyone else's. All the girls at her school wear uniforms of plain blue cotton, but hers is always the brightest, sharpest blue—she gets her maid to add new dye each time it's washed, and now the maid's hands are stained with indigo."

"Where did you hear all this?" Shuhui wondered, with a smile.

"My sister-in-law told me."

"Isn't she trying to get you two matched up? Why would she tell you such things about Tsuizhi?"

"Oh, she told me this before she'd thought up the matchmaking idea."

"These married ladies, old and young, are quite a handful, aren't they? The way they nitpick at other people, especially other women. Even their own relatives get taken apart."

Shijun's sister-in-law was the ostensible subject here, but Shijun took the hint: Shuhui was suggesting that he was being a gossipy old woman. It had, moreover, just occurred to him that the reason he kept finding fault with Tsuizhi was to keep people from thinking he liked her: in other words, he was protecting himself at her expense. Taking a step back, he saw that criticizing a young lady, as he'd just been doing, must seem to Shuhui a strange departure from his usual manner. Shijun grew very quiet when he thought of that.

Shuhui had some sense of what he was feeling, and tried to rouse him by talking about Yipeng. "So Yipeng hasn't gone out and found a job yet? I didn't feel I could ask."

"He's not likely to get a job," Shijun said. "His family won't let him out on his own."

"Why not? He's not a young woman."

"Oh, but he's the kind of person who, when he goes to Shanghai to look for a job, never has enough money. He'll spend everything in his account, then ask his family to pay his debts for him—he's done that more than once. So now they keep him locked up at home."

Shijun had learned all this from his mother, who told him about it behind her daughter-in-law's back—the latter of course would never have discussed her brothers' failings with anyone.

Their conversation made the trip home seem short. Because they planned to wake up early to go to Oxhead Mountain, they went straight to their room to get ready for bed, but Mrs. Shen sent a servant with two bowls of dumpling soup. "We've just had dinner," Shuhui protested with a smile. "I really can't eat any more."

Shijun asked a maid to take one bowl to his sister-in-law, and he took the other to his mother, to see if she would like some. This sign of filial attentiveness pleased her greatly. His being a good son meant that she could be motherly, and that was an opportunity she seized at once.

"Sit down for a minute," she said. "There's something I want to talk to you about."

Shijun frowned, sure that this would be about Tsuizhi. But no, that wasn't it.

Mrs. Shen had been planning carefully what to say, knowing that if she said the wrong thing she'd only upset him. "You come home so seldom," she started out, her words slow and somber. "It's not as if I'm constantly picking on you. But that wild outburst of yours today . . . it made your sister-in-law very angry. Surely that was obvious."

"But I wasn't speaking to her. Why did she take it personally?"

"You're just trying to defend yourself. Losing your temper with me doesn't matter, but you should show more self-control around others. You're an adult now—when your brother was your age, he was married already. He had a child by then!"

Shijun knew where this was headed now—sooner or later, Tsuizhi's name would be mentioned. "Oh, please, not that again!" he said with a smile. "I'm going to bed now. We're getting up early tomorrow."

"I know you hate hearing about this. And I'm not asking you to get married right away . . . still, you should be thinking about it. There's no harm in making friends with someone who might be suitable. Take Tsuizhi, for example. You two have played together since you were little, and—"

Shijun had to cut her off. "Ma, Shi Tsuizhi and I do not get along. I am not thinking of getting married, but even if I were, I would not want to marry her." He had decided to be very clear about this.

Despite the rebuff, his mother stayed calm. "It doesn't have to be Tsuizhi. But someone *like* her—that would be good!"

Shijun felt very pleased with that conversation. He had finally laid out his position regarding Tsuizhi, and his mother had accepted it. That would put an end to it.

They had wanted to go hiking early the next day, but it rained all night and into the morning, which put paid to that plan. They were considering what to do next when a messenger arrived from the Fang household. "Second Young Master and Young Master Hsu are invited to the house, whenever they are free to come," he told them.

"I'd rather not," Shijun said. "I've already been over to see them."

"You should go," his mother urged. "Yipeng is your old classmate, after all. Young Master Hsu knows him too, doesn't he?"

"He and Shuhui don't get along."

"You should go," his mother half whispered. "For your sister-in-law's sake." She gestured towards her daughter-in-law's room. "She hasn't come out this morning—she's still angry. She says she's not feeling well. Her family has sent an invitation, and if no one accepts, it won't look good."

"OK, OK," Shijun said. "I'll go and tell Shuhui."

His main objection to the invitation was that it had been made to both him and Tsuizhi; but since she had said she wouldn't go, he figured that changing his course would be safe enough. It hadn't occurred to him that Tsuizhi would follow the same line of reasoning. Amy had phoned the Shi household that morning, insisting that she come over, and since Shijun had been very firm in his refusal, she gave in. When Shijun arrived, Tsuizhi was already there; they both felt very odd about it, and could almost hear a trap snapping shut around them. Shuhui had come too. There were lots of people, and three mahjong tables were filled already. But none of the young people played mahjong.

"You'll all get bored, standing around watching others play," Amy said to Shijun. "Why don't you go to the pictures? I can't get away, so please play host for me, and take Tsuizhi to see something."

"No need to look after me!" Tsuizhi frowned at Amy. "I'm fine here. I don't want to see a film."

Paying no attention to Tsuizhi, Amy bustled about the room till she'd found out where the latest film was playing. "You'll just have time to see it, then come back here to eat."

"Shuhui has to come too!" This was the best Shijun could do, under the circumstances.

"Oh, that's right," Amy said with a smile. "Mr. Hsu is going too."

Shuhui felt the pressure. He knew he was the odd man out, at least in Amy's eyes. He turned to Shijun. "Why don't you take Miss Shi to see the double bill? I've already seen both of those films."

"Stop fibbing," Shijun retorted. "When was that? Let's all go together!"

Amy told a servant to hire pedicabs for them. In the end, Tsuizhi's protests were to no avail; she had to go with them.

Tsuizhi was all dressed up today, in a long, rippling cheongsam made of dusty green silk with dark embroidery. They bought tickets for the balcony, and as they headed up the stairs, Tsuizhi tripped on the hem of her gown and almost fell. Fortunately, Shijun caught her by the arm. "Careful there! Are you all right?"

"I'm fine. Oh—blast! My heel's broken!" It had snapped off, leaving her with one high-heeled shoe only.

"Can you still walk?" Shijun asked.

"Yes, yes." She didn't want Shijun to hold her arm, not with Shuhui there, so she limped into the cinema ahead of them, bumping up and down with each step. The theater was dark already; she was glad no one could see her.

The film had had rave reviews, but Shijun hadn't been able to see it in Shanghai. Finding it on here in Nanking was a nice surprise. They got to their seats just as the opening credits were running. "Great!" Shijun whispered to Shuhui. "We haven't missed anything." He was sitting between the other two.

The film started, but Tsuizhi was agitated. "What a mess!" she whispered to Shijun. "How can I get back like this? I'm afraid I'll have to ask you to run home and get me some other shoes."

Shijun thought it over. "Here's another idea. When the film's over, we'll go out in front of the cinema, and I'll get a cab for you. That will get you home easily."

"No, that won't work. I can't bump up and down like this in front of other people. They'll think I'm a cripple."

Shijun thought, So go barefoot, why don't you? But he didn't say it aloud. He sat in silence for several moments, then stood up. "I'll get them for you now." He squeezed past Shuhui, without explaining what was going on.

He rushed out of the theater, but since the film was still playing, the road in front of the cinema was deserted, with not a single cab in sight. He headed down the street—it was raining still—and after much effort got a pedicab. When he arrived at the Shi household, the servant who opened the gate knew at once that this was his second visit in two days. Servants always know what's going on—Young Master Shen might well become a master in their establishment. The gatekeeper was very respectful, greeted him politely, and said right away, with a knowing smile, that Miss Tsuizhi had gone to the Fangs' place. Shijun noticed the man's certainty that he'd come to see Tsuizhi, and also the readiness to give him information about her, before he'd even said a single thing. That's what they're all thinking, he realized. Still, there was nothing he could do but nod and smile.

"Yes, I know," he said. "I've already seen Miss Tsui. Her shoe is broken. Go and get another pair so I can take them to her."

When the gatekeeper heard that, he thought Shijun had come directly from the Fang household, which made him wonder why they hadn't sent a servant instead. "Oh!" he exclaimed, looking directly at him. "Young Master Shen is doing this himself!"

Seeing the man's broad grin, Shijun knew he had become an object of fun—the young lady's errand-boy. His irritation rose another notch.

The servant invited him in, but Shijun felt skittish, fearing that Mrs. Shi would come out to keep him company. He declined the offer and said he'd wait at the gate instead. He was there quite some time. The servant returned with the shoebox and offered to complete the delivery. Shijun declined again, saying that he'd take care of it himself. The servant got him a pedicab.

Back at the cinema, Shijun felt his way through the dark to his seat. "Here are your shoes," he said, handing the box to Tsuizhi. She thanked him.

The errand had taken more than an hour, and the film was almost over. They'd reached the climax of the tragic storyline and people were pulling out their handkerchiefs, wiping their eyes and rubbing their noses. Having missed the first part, Shijun could make only wild stabs at the plot. He thought the young girl was the man's daughter, but that turned out to be wrong. He couldn't figure it out; when the film ended, he'd really only half understood what was going on. The lights came on and everyone stood up. Tsuizhi's eyes were red; apparently she'd been quite caught up in the story. She'd changed her shoes already, and put the broken pair in the box. She was very animated now, discussing the plot with Shuhui as the three of them went down the stairs. Shijun said nothing. Then, when they reached the entrance, he suddenly laughed.

"Seeing the end but not the beginning is very confusing. You two go on. I'm going back in to watch it again."

Giving them no time to reply, he turned back and pushed his way into the crowd around the ticket booth. It was grumpiness that made him do this, but also his aversion to all this chasing around, with and for Tsuizhi. If they went back to the Fangs', Amy and the others would keep on teasing him. Why not let Shuhui take her home? Shuhui had no part in this; he barely knew Tsuizhi. He could take her home and be done with it.

Whatever Shijun's reasoning, his sudden abdication was close to peevishness, and embarrassing to Shuhui. Tsuizhi also said nothing. They came out of the cinema to find sunlight everywhere and the ground almost dry. Tsuizhi laughed in surprise. "So now the sun comes out!"

"What mixed-up weather we're having today," Shuhui said. "Our plan this morning was to hike up Oxhead Mountain, but the rain canceled that."

"How's that for unfair!" Tsuizhi sympathized.

"It certainly is! I've been stuck inside all day."

She thought a moment. "Well, there's still time. If you want to go somewhere else, we can go together."

"OK, but I'm a stranger here. Where would you suggest?"

"We could go to Hsuanwu Lake."

Shuhui was happy to do that. He called a pair of pedicabs and they went to the lake.

When they arrived, they first took a stroll through Wuzhou Park. There wasn't much to see—as a park it was no different from any other. But the sky above wasn't bright blue; it was a soft, clear color, as vague as lake water. There was a little zoo with monkeys and, inside a wire-mesh enclosure, an owl which sat on a tree branch in the slanting sun, his big eyes flashing gold like a pair of yellow sapphires. They stood and watched him for a while.

After they'd seen the park, they rented a rowing boat. Tsuizhi had suggested the outing on a whim, a sudden flash of courage, but now convention tugged at her and she lapsed into silence. Once they were in the boat, she took out her film program, spread it out on her knees and started reading. She came all this way with me, Shuhui thought, but maybe she regrets it now. Or maybe she's still angry at Shijun.

Evening on Hsuanwu Lake is lovely, and there were lots of boats out. Anyone who saw the two of them floating along would have thought they were a romantic couple. That's the effect of sitting in a boat together, and it made Shuhui wonder if any of the pleasure-seekers along the lake might be Tsuizhi's acquaintances. If they did run into anyone from her social circle, the resulting gossip could thwart any hopes of marriage for Tsuizhi and Shijun—and it would be all his fault.

Another boat came close to theirs; the two parties waved greetings to each other. The other boat was rowed by a girl in a checked trouser suit, with her hair bobbed short. A few wisps floated across her wide forehead, which tapered quickly to a narrow jaw. She had a purplish complexion and white, shiny teeth. The others in her boat called her "Big Girl," but in the Nanking accent "Big" turned into "Beeg." Shuhui tried to imitate the locals by calling her "Beeg Girl" too, but couldn't quite pull it off; Tsuizhi and Beeg Girl doubled up with laughter.

Shuhui wanted to try his hand at rowing, but when he dipped the oars he splashed water all over Tsuizhi. The water ran down her sleek cheongsam in little rivulets; she took out a handkerchief and cheerfully wiped them away. Shuhui was embarrassed, but Tsuizhi just laughed and dabbed at her face. Then, taking out a little mirror, she combed her hair with her fingers. Well, Shuhui thought, I'm not seeing any signs of a spoiled young miss. But if I told Shijun this, he'd say she was holding herself in check, treating me like a guest. He did feel that Shijun's negative view of Tsuizhi was biased, an inadequate assessment of her character. Still, the first opinion one hears does carry weight, and Shuhui couldn't shake it off entirely. One thing was clear: a rich girl like Tsuizhi would not make a good wife for him. Of course there could be no objection to a simple friendship—but these people in the interior were generally conservative, and a young lady like Tsuizhi wasn't free to arrange her own social life. If they became friends, the marriage question would immediately be raised, much to her family's displeasure, since he was poor compared to her. He himself would never think of social-climbing; he was too proud for that.

Shuhui rowed silently, thinking of all this. Tsuizhi too was silent. An assortment of snacks was provided with the boat, and she'd scooped up some roasted pumpkin seeds and was leaning back in her seat, cracking them with her teeth. She sat there nearly motionless, occasionally raising a hand to brush the shells off her dress. Looking across the water, they could see the old city walls, purple with age, sending back the glow of that soft, clear-colored sky. This was Shuhui's first encounter with the beauty of Nanking.

They stayed on the water till nightfall. When they were on the shore again, Shuhui asked Tsuizhi if she wanted to go back to the Fangs'.

"I'd rather not," she said. "It's too noisy and crowded there." But she didn't seem ready to go home either.

Shuhui thought for a bit, then offered to take her out to dinner. Tsuizhi said he should be her guest, since he was the visitor. "Well, let's decide that part later. But you should choose the place." Tsuizhi thought it over and remembered a Sichuan-style restaurant not far away. They hailed a cab and headed there.

What they didn't realize, while at dinner, was that the people gathered at the Fangs' were waiting for them. When it got to dinnertime, someone phoned Tsuizhi's house to see if she had arrived there. When Mrs. Shi heard that Tsuizhi was out with Shijun, she wasn't too worried, but still it was a bit unsettling. It was already eight or nine o'clock when a servant came to report that the young lady had returned. Mrs. Shi went to the front door to meet them.

"Where have you two been?" she called out. "The Fangs telephoned looking for you. They said you'd gone to a film and hadn't come back yet." She saw someone behind Tsuizhi, but instead of Shijun it was that friend of his, the one he'd brought the night before. Yipeng had told her, after the two young men had gone, that they'd all been at college together, and that Shuhui took jobs as a tutor while studying for his degree, since his family didn't have much money. Mrs. Shi hadn't paid much attention at the time, but now that Shuhui was here again, she was brusque with him. He bowed politely to her, and she pretended not to see it. "Oh, and where's Shijun?" she asked.

"Shijun missed half of the film, because he came here to get some shoes for me. He went back to see the second showing."

"Well, where did you go after the cinema? Why are you back so late? Have you had dinner?"

"Yes. Mr. Hsu and I went to a restaurant."

Mrs. Shi's face dropped. "What have you been up to, my girl? Running off like that, all by yourself, not telling anyone where you are!"

Accusing Tsuizhi of going off "all by herself" obviously meant that Shuhui didn't count for anything. It was such a slight that he wished he hadn't brought Tsuizhi to her door; but having come this far now, he couldn't easily turn around and leave.

"Oh, Ma, don't worry so much. I'm a big girl now, not a little child—did you think I'd got lost?" Tsuizhi steamed through the door. "Mr. Hsu, please do come in! Amah Chen, bring us some tea!"

She swept into the living room and threw the shoebox on the sofa. Shuhui, for whom retreating was now as hard as advancing, followed her in. Mrs. Shi would not let them be. She almost trod on their heels, then took the seat directly opposite, searching for hints about their relationship. The maid brought tea. Mrs. Shi took out a cigarette and asked Shuhui if he'd like one.

"No, thank you," he said, bowing from the waist. "Please don't trouble yourself."

Mrs. Shi sat there smoking, eyebrows raised high, and made small talk by asking when he was going back to Shanghai. After forcing himself to sit there a few minutes longer, Shuhui stood up and took his leave.

Tsuizhi saw him out, and even though Shuhui kept telling her to go back in, she insisted on seeing him to the front gate. They walked through the garden in the dim starlight. At first Tsuizhi was silent, but then she said, "Are you going back tomorrow? I won't be able to see you off."

She happened to look behind her as she spoke, and saw a maid quietly following them. Tsuizhi knew she had nothing to be ashamed of, but still she blushed. "What are you doing?" she said. "Sneaking around like that, scaring me to death!"

"The mistress asked me to call a cab for the guest," said the maid.

"Oh, please don't bother," Shuhui said. "I can get one myself."

The maid did not reply. She kept following them, barely stopping herself from smiling.

When they were almost at the front gate, Tsuizhi suddenly said, "Amah Wang, go and make sure the dog is tied up. Don't let him come rushing out like he did last night, scaring everyone."

The maid seemed a bit unsure. "Where is he tied up?"

Tsuizhi's anger flared. "Just go and have a look, will you!"

When the maid saw that Tsuizhi was cross, she didn't dare persist, and went back on her own.

Tsuizhi had driven the maid away, but then had nothing particular to say. She took another few steps, then suddenly stopped. "I'm going back."

"All right. Well, goodbye then!" Even before the words were out of his mouth, she had turned and was walking quickly away.

Shuhui stood there, frozen, for a moment. Then he glimpsed someone moving in the dark. The maid had not gone away after all, but was hiding behind a tree, peeping out at them. Shuhui found it irritating and funny. Then he remembered he'd told the maid he'd get his own cab—what address should he give the driver? He remembered Shijun's street, but not the house number. There weren't many people in Nanking he could ask, and if he went back to the Shi house in the dark, looking for Tsuizhi . . . well, the people there already took him for a complete good-for-nothing; if he returned in the middle of the night asking to see their young lady, they'd probably run him off. The whole thing seemed a joke to him, but at the same time he was a bit worried, and the harder he tried to recall the house number, the more elusive it became. Fortunately, Tsuizhi hadn't got very far. He ran after her.

"Miss Shi! Miss Shi!" he called out, surprising Tsuizhi, who suddenly turned and looked at him, her face tear-stained. Shuhui stopped and stared; his question flew right out of his head. Tsuizhi instinctively stepped into the shadows, wiping her eyes with a handkerchief. When he saw that she wanted to hide her tears, Shuhui pretended not to see them. "I'm so silly—I've forgotten Shijun's address!" he said with a smile.

"It's Wang Fu Street, No. 41."

"Oh, that's right. It's good I thought to ask or I'd never have found my way back—I'd be completely stuck, out on the streets!" He laughed, said goodbye again, then walked away without glancing back.

When he got to Shijun's house, they had just finished eating dinner and Shijun was playing with Vim. The day before, when they'd gone through Rain Flower Terrace District, he'd picked up some pebbles, and now he and Vim were playing the Stone Toss Game. He threw one stone in the air and grabbed another from the floor, then tossed one and grabbed two, gradually increasing the number, then reversing the sequence. There they were, a grown man and a little child, laughing away as they played together. Watching them made Shuhui's head spin, as if he'd stepped from dense shadow into a brightly lit room.

"Why are you back so late?" Shijun asked. "My mother was afraid you'd got lost, and blamed me for going back in to see the film, leaving you there. Where did you go?"

"Hsuanwu Lake."

"You went there with Tsuizhi?"

"Yes."

Shijun fell silent for a while. "I owe you an apology," he said finally.

After he'd heard that his friend had taken Tsuizhi to dinner, he felt even worse. But great though his remorse was, he still had no idea how much trouble had been stirred up by Shuhui's spending a day out on the town with Tsuizhi.

5

The next day, Sunday, was Shijun's last day in Nanking. His mother gently reminded him to visit his father.

Shijun didn't want to go to his father's "minor" residence. His mother didn't like it either, but failing to go would be, she thought, a major breach of decorum: he'd been away a whole year and everyone in the family knew he was in town. Shijun knew he'd have to go, but he'd always been one to put things off till the last minute.

He took himself there in the morning, hoping to catch his father before he went out. It was a fancy place, compared to his mother's. There were two manservants, and the one who answered the door, being new, didn't recognize him.

"Is the master up yet?" Shijun asked.

The man looked him up and down. "I'll go and see," he said. "What's your name, sir?"

"Just say that Second Young Master from the other house is here."

The servant took him into the parlor, then went off to announce his arrival. The parlor was filled with rosewood furniture. Shijun's father liked to put on a show, and the tables, high and low, were covered with ceramics and antiques. It filled a guest with mincing caution, afraid to stir hand or foot lest something valuable get broken. Shijun's eyes were drawn to a table that held a tray of visiting cards and invitations. Sifting through them, he found a pink wedding invitation addressed to "Mr. and Mrs. Shen Hsiao-tung," clear evidence that, in their social set, his father's concubine had the status of a first wife.

Hsiao-tung had apparently not risen yet. Shijun sat waiting in the parlor, and the morning sun shone on the sofa. The white sofa cover was old but very clean. The mistress here was a good housekeeper.

The mistress herself then appeared, her portable scales in hand, followed by a maid with a full shopping basket. When she passed the parlor, she looked in. "Oh, Second Young Master! When did you return to Nanking?"

Shijun never used any form of address when he spoke to her. He rose to his feet, stiff and straight, with a stern expression. "I came back recently."

The concubine had become an attractive middle-aged woman. She'd once been quite a siren, but now she wore conservative attire: her hair was swept up in a bun, her black poplin dress wasn't brand new, and only a dab of face powder showed. Shijun would have much preferred a boldly painted seductress. This housewifely appearance was too great a claim on his mother's position in the family; he found it disturbing.

She was always gracious towards him, her speech courteous without compromising her own dignity. "Li Sheng," she called to the servant, "why haven't you offered Second Young Master some tea?"

"I'm pouring it now!" came the answer.

She turned back to Shijun, and gave him a slight welcoming bow. "Please take a seat. Father will be down very soon. Little Three, come and greet your older brother. Come now!"

Her third child was descending the stairs, a book-bag on his back. She called him over and told him to address Shijun as "Second Older Brother." The child was about the same age as Shijun's nephew Vim.

"How old are you now?" Shijun asked, smiling at the boy.

"Second Older Brother asked you a question," the concubine prompted her son. "Answer him now!"

"He stutters, doesn't he?" Shijun said.

"That's his older brother. This one is Number Three. Last time you saw him, he was still a babe in arms!"

"Children grow so quickly," Shijun said.

"They certainly do."

She took the boy by the hand and led him out. Shijun heard her calling, from some other room of the house, "Where's the driver?

Tell him to take the young master to school, then come straight back so Father can go out."

She was sure that Shijun's conversation with his father would be short and superficial, but still she took strong defensive measures. She herself would not appear, but she sent her mother to sit in the next room. The old lady had always lived with her daughter. But while the daughter had achieved a full transformation, making herself a respectable woman, the mother still had the appearance and bearing of a procuress. The old one's even more disgusting than the young one, Shijun thought. She must have intuited this, because she refrained from coming over to greet him. He could hear her shuffling around, talking to a little girl. "Little Four, come here. Granny's going to show you how to make tinfoil ornaments. Here, first you fold it this way, then like this . . ." Shijun heard the little plop of an origami ornament landing in the basket as she finished each one—any conversation held in the parlor would certainly be audible to her. Her hearing must still be good, despite her age.

Just as the troops fell into position, a hoarse, harrumphing cough—which Shijun recognized immediately—issued from the upper floor. His father came down. The cough was familiar, but the man himself almost a stranger. Shen Hsiao-tung strode into the room, hands clasped behind his back. Shijun stood up and greeted him respectfully. Hsiao-tung nodded at him, told him to take a seat, and asked when he'd returned to Nanking. "The day before yesterday," Shijun replied.

"Lately there have been a lot of political rumors. Have you heard any particular news, there in Shanghai?" He started to pontificate about current affairs. Shijun had a low opinion of his father's views; he was an old-fashioned merchant who got his ideas from other businessmen, or went trawling through the papers, catching what he could.

After analyzing the entire national situation, Hsiao-tung fell silent. Then, even though he hadn't allowed his gaze to land directly on his son, he suddenly asked, "How did you get so dark? Been out in the sun a lot?"

"Oh, it's probably these few days in Nanking, going out to the parks."

"Are you on leave from your job?"

"No, no special leave. We had a day off for National Day, and since it fell on Friday we had three days off."

His father never asked about his work, because the two of them had fought so hard over it. When the talk veered in that direction, Hsiao-tung looked for something else to say. "Great-uncle died. Did you hear about that?"

Shijun started to say that his mother had told him, but rearranged his response and simply said the news had reached him.

There were several old, long-surviving elders in their family, and Hsiao-tung had always treated them with great respect. He went to their homes every New Year, to offer holiday greetings. He went with Shijun's mother, though they scarcely met otherwise, and never usually appeared in public together. But the old relatives had died off, one by one; Great-uncle was the last. There would be no more holiday visiting for Hsiao-tung and his wife.

Hsiao-tung told Shijun about Great-uncle's stroke. "It was such a sudden thing . . ." He himself had high blood pressure, and the mention of his uncle's case made him worry about his own health. He pondered a while, then said, "Dr. Liu once wrote me up a prescription, but I don't know where it's gone. I'll have to look for it tomorrow, buy the herbs and try it out."

"Why don't you ask Dr. Liu to examine you again?" Shijun asked.

Hsiao-tung had always tried to hide his symptoms and avoid treatment, so he parried the suggestion. "I'm not sure if he's still in Nanking."

"He is. He's the one who treated Vim's measles."

"What? Vim had measles?"

Here they all are in Nanking, Shijun thought, and he gets their news through me, the one who lives in Shanghai. His father had no knowledge of events taking place at home.

"That Vim," Hsiao-tung said, "he's always getting sick. I don't know if he'll make it to adulthood. He reminds me so much of your older brother. It's been five years since he passed away!" Suddenly, he started to weep.

Shijun was alarmed. He'd already seen his mother wobbling

around, seeming positively elderly, and now his father, for the first time ever, was crying in front of him—wasn't this another sign of advancing age?

His father had not cried like this when his brother died, five years earlier—what sorrow had beset him today? Maybe he was feeling his age, and the loss of the son who'd been his right-hand man, unlike this younger son who refused to help out. By yearning for the dead, he also could express his disappointment in the living.

Shijun sat very still. A thousand thoughts flashed through him: how badly his father had treated his mother, how his mother's pain had cast a shadow over his own youth. He summoned up all of this, in order to harden his heart.

"Amah Zhang," the concubine shouted from upstairs. "Please tell the master there's a phone call for him!" She called the maid, but really she was calling the master. The sound of her voice reminded Shijun there was no need to be sad on his father's account. His father had a nice, warm home. Hsiao-tung stood up and headed towards the stairs.

"I'm going now, Father," Shijun said. "I have some things to take care of."

Hsiao-tung paused. "All right, go ahead."

When Shijun followed his father out of the room, the concubine's mother smiled at him. "Are you leaving already, Second Young Master? Aren't you staying for lunch?"

"He's got something to do," Hsiao-tung said, much annoyed. When he reached the foot of the stairs, he turned and nodded at Shijun, then headed up the staircase. Shijun left.

When he got home, his mother asked him what his father had talked about.

"He talked about Great-uncle, and his own blood pressure. He seemed worried about it."

"Yes," his mother said. "It's very possible that your father will suffer a stroke. I don't mean to invite misfortune by talking about it—but I've been worried that you'd stay away too long, and never have a chance to see him again."

My father must fear the same thing, Shijun thought, and that's why he got emotional. Shuhui's being here makes it hard for my mother to cry in front of me—who'd have imagined that I'd see my father crying instead?

"Are you getting enough money for your household expenses?" he asked.

"There's never been a problem with that. He sends someone with money every month. But . . . please don't think I'm money-grubbing, but I do worry about what will happen if your father dies. She'll control his money then."

"But . . . surely Father has made arrangements to prevent that . . ."

Mrs. Shen laughed bitterly. "But when it comes to that point, he won't be there to manage things. She controls it all—even the man himself! She won't let him come and see me! And I'm not likely to go running over there like some opera heroine, braving all opposition to stay at his side!"

Shijun knew his mother had good reason to worry. There had been several cases like this among their relatives: the husband died at his concubine's house, and the wife was prevented from bringing the body home. There was a huge hullabaloo, and in the end the wife would set up the memorial hall and hold a funeral even though she had no coffin to display. And that was the least of it. The real headache came when the property was divided. Shijun could only hope that when the time came he'd be earning enough to support his mother, sister-in-law and nephew, so that there'd be no need to fight with *that* woman for the family property. This was his fervent hope, but he didn't want to fill his mother's ears with empty assurances; all he could do was urge her to stop thinking sad thoughts. His mother, wanting his last day at home to be cheerful, let the subject drop.

They were taking the night train to Shanghai, so he and Shuhui had time to see a few other places, then return to the house for an early supper. With Vim in her arms, his sister-in-law said, "He's just got used to you, and you're leaving already. Next time you're home, he'll think you're a stranger again!"

Yes, thought Mrs. Shen, because it will be another year till you come back—of course the child will forget who you are! The thought made her eyes redden, so she forced a smile and teased her grandson instead. "Vim, how would you like to go to Shanghai with Uncle? Wouldn't that be a good idea?"

"Oh, yes, Shanghai's great!" her daughter-in-law said. "You want to go with Uncle? Oh, yes, you should go!" The more she urged him, the closer Vim clung to her. "What a mama's boy!" she teased. "No hope for you at all!"

Shijun and Shuhui hadn't brought much luggage, but on the return trip they were loaded down. Besides the usual fruit and snacks, Mrs. Shen made them take two roast ducks flavored with sweet osmanthus, which had just come into season, and a big box of health-boosting medicines that she wanted him to take as injections. She had planned to see them to the station, but Shijun convinced her it wasn't necessary. The entire household gathered at the front door to see them off; Mrs. Shen laughed through her tears and told her son to write to her the minute he arrived in Shanghai.

Once they were on the train, Shijun felt a big release of tension. They bought two Shanghai newspapers and lay on their bunks reading. The train started moving, puffing mightily as it left Nanking. The lights of the old capital city receded into the distance. People say time flies like a train, an analogy that makes good sense: a train really does steam across time. Shijun's old family home, all those ancient ways and sad people, all that bottomless anger and remorse—all of it was left behind. The train steamed onward, into the darkness.

Shuhui took the upper bunk. Shijun looked up and saw his friend's foot hanging over the edge, a patch of yellow mud stuck to the sole of his leather shoe, along with a wad of fine grass. They were indeed "traveling shoes." Shijun thought what a poor traveling companion he had been for his friend. Out of sorts the whole time—constantly racing around, shrugging people off, like a man rushing to keep an appointment somewhere else.

They arrived in Shanghai early in the morning. "Let's go straight to the factory," Shijun suggested. His goal was to see Manzhen as soon as he could; he didn't want to wait till the lunch break.

"What about our luggage?" Shuhui asked.

"We can bring it along, and put it in your office for now." Taking the luggage to Shuhui's office would be a good opportunity to see Manzhen.

"That's fine for most of these things," Shuhui said, "but these ducks are greasy, and there's no place to keep them there. I'd better take them home. I'll do that—you go to the factory."

Shijun took the bus to the factory by himself. He checked his watch when he got off. It was well before eight o'clock. Manzhen would not have arrived yet. He paced around the bus stop. It was still early—too early for her to arrive, he knew—but waiting makes a person anxious. And then, working out the time it would take him, he realized that Shuhui could arrive at any moment. What if Shuhui stepped off the next bus and saw him still standing there, forty-five minutes after his early arrival . . . wouldn't that look strange?

His back got prickly when he thought of that. Off he went towards the factory. There was a fruit stand near the bus stop, and even though he'd eaten a handful of tangerines on the train, from the large supply his family had given them, he stopped and bought two more. He tore off the peel and ate them, slowly. Then he felt he couldn't hang around any longer, not with Shuhui due to arrive soon. Now that he thought about it, Manzhen must have appeared by now—might she have come early, and already be in the office? What a fool he'd been, waiting here all this while! This reasoning was a bit fuzzy, but it made him walk towards the factory, this time at a rapid clip.

Then he heard someone calling him from behind. "Hey!" He turned, and there she was, walking towards him in the early morning sun, holding her wind-tossed hair with one hand and smiling with delight. When he saw her, light flooded through him.

"You're back now?" she said.

"Yes, I'm back now."

There was nothing particularly funny about this, but they both started laughing.

"Did you just arrive?"

"Yes. Just got off the train." He didn't tell her he'd been waiting for her.

Manzhen took a close look at his face. He rubbed it, feeling a bit embarrassed. "Just splashed myself with water, there on the train. Not a real wash."

"No, it's not that . . ." Manzhen said. She looked carefully at him again. "You still look the same. I kept thinking you'd look different when you came back."

"I was only gone a few days. How could I change that fast?" But it did feel like a long trip, to a faraway place.

"How is your mother? And the rest of your family?"

"Everyone's fine."

"Did they say anything when they saw your suitcase?"

"No . . ."

"Didn't they say you'd packed it nicely?"

"No, they didn't!"

They were walking along and chatting when Shijun suddenly stopped. "Manzhen!" he said.

Manzhen thought he looked upset. "What is it?"

But Shijun didn't answer. He just started walking again.

Manzhen started having visions of disaster: something had happened in his family, he was going to quit his job, his family had arranged a marriage for him, he'd fallen in love with someone, or maybe he'd run into an old girlfriend. "What is it?" she asked again.

"Nothing."

She fell silent.

"I didn't take a raincoat, and it rained."

"Oh? It rained in Nanking? It didn't rain here."

"It wasn't that much, just one night, and during the day we could go out. But we went out at night too, when it rained." He realized he was talking nonsense and stopped abruptly.

Manzhen was getting rather worried. "Are you OK?" She looked at him with a smile.

"I'm fine." Another pause. "Manzhen, I have something to tell you."

"What is it?"

"I have a lot of things to tell you."

Actually, this was the same as saying it. And she had understood.

Her face was perfectly calm, but he could see that she was very, very happy. The world was suddenly bathed in light that made everything transparent, all of it real and precise. Never had he felt so clear-minded. It was like sitting down at an exam, and seeing right away that he knew every answer—he was that excited and, at the same time, strangely calm.

Manzhen's expression changed. "Hello, Mr. Chen." It was the manager at the factory, walking behind them. They had reached the front gates. "I'm late today," Manzhen said, speaking quickly now, "and so are you. I'll see you later." She rushed in and ran upstairs.

Shijun was happy, of course, but after a whole morning of turning it over in his mind, his confidence ebbed. He wished he had expressed himself more clearly, and received a clearer response. Manzhen was very good to him, that much was certain, but when he weighed up all the instances in which she'd expressed her liking for him, none of them could be viewed as incontrovertible proof: they could be signs of ordinary friendship, or maybe naiveté.

They were a threesome at lunch again, Manzhen chatting and smiling in her usual way, as if nothing were going on. Shijun felt that even if she didn't love him, there ought to be some kind of reaction, after his words to her that morning—a little embarrassment maybe, some awkwardness. He didn't know how a woman reacted to something like this, but whatever that response might be, surely it couldn't be pure nonchalance? And if she did love him, the serenity of her self-control was almost frightening. A woman can be so cool and calm that she's nearly inhuman. Such acting ability! All women are actresses, one might say.

After they'd left the restaurant, Shuhui went into a tobacconist's for cigarettes. Shijun and Manzhen stood on the street, a fair distance from the shop, waiting for him.

"Manzhen, when we talked this morning, I didn't express myself clearly," Shijun said. But words still eluded him. He looked down at their shadows, there in the autumn sun. The edge of the street was strewn with fallen leaves, and he stirred them with his toe, then picked out the largest one, burnt yellow, and stepped on it squarely, cracking it to pieces.

Manzhen too was looking away. She kept glancing around, waiting for Shuhui. "Let's talk about it later. You can come to my house."

He went to her home that evening. After she finished at the factory, she went to a teaching job from six to seven, and after supper she tutored another two children. Shijun knew her schedule by heart. The only time he could see her, and try to say something to her, was at exactly suppertime.

Watching the time carefully, he rang the Gu family's back-door bell at precisely ten minutes after seven. The family had rented out the rooms on the lower floor, and the door was opened by the elderly maid who worked for the tenant. She was in the middle of making supper, dashing about with wok and cleaver, the room filled with smoke and cooking smells. "Mrs. Gu," she shouted up the stairs, "you have a guest!" She sent Shijun up the stairs on his own.

Shijun had been to Manzhen's house once before, that day he'd brought the potential tenant. Her family had the habit of scurrying into corners when a guest appeared, which must be hard on the children—how could those rambunctious little ones suddenly become pin-drop quiet? He didn't like to impose, so he hadn't returned.

This time, however, he could hear loud conversation and laughter as he climbed the stairs. "It's too noisy!" one of the older children complained. "I'm trying to do my homework!" Loosely stacked on the table in front of him were his textbooks, a ruler and a set square. Manzhen's grandmother was pushing at his things with a pair of chopsticks. "Oi! Time to shut up shop! We're setting the table now." But the boy's head stayed bent over his geometry calculation.

Granny looked up and saw Shijun. "Oh, we've got a guest!" she called out with a smile.

Shijun greeted her politely, addressing her as "Elder Mrs. Gu."

He walked into the room and found Manzhen's mother in the midst of cutting her children's hair. He nodded, greeted her as "Auntie Gu," and asked when Manzhen would be back.

"She'll be here soon. Please come in and sit down. I'll get you some tea."

Shijun protested politely, but Mrs. Gu put down the scissors and poured him a cup of tea.

"Ma!" a child complained. "My neck is itchy!"

"It's just the bits of hair," she told him, pulling his collar up and out, holding him in the light, then carefully picking out the hairs.

Elder Mrs. Gu took out a broom and started sweeping. "Look at all this hair!" she exclaimed.

"Oh no, let me do it," her daughter-in-law said, taking the broom from her. "This is what they call 'tidying up right under a guest's nose'!"

"Careful, or you'll tidy that hair all over our guest's feet!" the older woman said. "Let him go—give him a nice place to sit in the other room."

Mrs. Gu turned on the light in the adjoining room, and motioned Shijun in. She herself stood in the doorway, leaning on the broom and chatting with him pleasantly. Then she invited him to stay for dinner—a simple meal, she said, nothing fancy. Shijun accepted, a bit embarrassed about having come right at suppertime. Mrs. Gu went downstairs to attend to the cooking and add a few dishes to the meal. She bustled about in the kitchen.

Shijun stood alone at the window, looking into the alley, but there was no sign of Manzhen. He knew this was her room, but everything he saw belonged to someone else: her mother's sewing basket and spectacles case, a child's gym shoes, et cetera. On the wall was a large photograph of her father. A sweater of hers lay on one bed—it must be her bed. This room felt almost like a dormitory, with no flavor of its own. The only things he could find that belonged to her were the books on the shelf. She had magazines, novels, foreign fiction and her old textbooks, including an English grammar with a worn-through spine. Shijun looked through all of them. There were several he had never read, but because they were hers, they felt like his too.

Manzhen returned. "Oh, have you been waiting long?" she asked, smiling as she came in.

"No, not long at all." He smiled back.

Manzhen put down her handbag and her books. There was tension in the air and it made her self-conscious, as if her every move were being scrutinized. She blushed and went to the dressing-table mirror to smooth her hair and adjust her collar. "The tram was packed today, everyone crammed in together. I've got dirt marks on my socks."

Shijun went over and stood at the mirror too. "What do you think? Did I catch the sun when I was in Nanking?" Standing close behind her, he couldn't see much change in his own complexion, but did see her cheeks turning red.

Manzhen gave him a quick glance. "It's always like that when you tan. It's red at first, and turns to brown a few days later." Only then did Shijun realize that he too was blushing.

Manzhen leaned over and studied her socks, then gave a little cry of dismay. "A hole—from riding on that crowded tram. Unbelievable!" She took another pair from a drawer, and went to the other room to change them. When she closed the door, Shijun was alone again. He was feeling rather perturbed, and thought she seemed displeased. He took another book from the shelf, but just then Manzhen opened the door and invited him to the supper table.

The table was crowded with people, and Manzhen sat diagonally across from him. To Shijun it seemed that he'd been trying all day long to sit down with her, but other people were always around, and she was slipping away from him. Hope dissolved, and he felt stranded.

Mrs. Gu had made an extra dish for the meal—stir-fried hard-boiled eggs—and had sent a child to buy smoked fish and stewed pork. She set these dishes close to Shijun, but her mother-in-law wanted her to pick through the delicacies and put the best bits right in his bowl. "I thought maybe these modern young folk wouldn't like us hovering over them," Mrs. Gu said with a smile.

The children gobbled their food in silence, then left the table. They bristled with hostility towards Shijun, and Manzhen was reminded of her own attitude towards her sister's erstwhile fiancé, Zhang Yujin, back when she was twelve or so, and he came to the house to see Manlu. Children that age have the instincts of tribal barbarians, loyal to family above all else. To them, a boyfriend is a home-wrecker—a raider come to carry off Big Sister.

When they had finished eating, Mrs. Gu got out a cloth to wipe the table. "Why don't you two go and sit in there?" she said to Manzhen.

"Yes," Manzhen said to Shijun, "let's go into the next room and let the children study in here, where they've got more light."

She poured him a cup of tea. They sat down, and she immediately pulled out the torn sock and started mending it.

"Aren't you tired?" Shijun asked. "Here you've finally got a moment to rest and you're working on this."

"If I don't do it, my mother will. She has enough to do, what with all the cooking and cleaning and laundry. She does all of that."

"You had a girl helping here before. Did you let her go?"

"You mean Ah Bao? We let her go a long time ago. When you saw her here, she was just helping out till she could get a new position."

Her head was bent over the mending, her hair falling forward to reveal a tender spot on the back of her neck. Shijun paced back and forth, wanting, when he passed, to lean over and kiss that spot. But of course he didn't. He just touched her hair with his hand. Manzhen seemed not to have felt it. She kept on mending the sock, head bent low, but the needle had a mind of its own—it rose up and pricked her finger. She made no sound, just looked at the tiny drop of blood welling up, and wiped it on her handkerchief.

Shijun kept looking at the clock. "You have to go to your next job soon, don't you? Maybe it's time for me to go?" He felt terribly disappointed. There was no chance to speak to her, because she was so busy. He'd have to wait till Saturday, and today was only Monday— the week stretched out, interminably.

"Don't go yet," Manzhen said. "Wait till I'm done with this, and we'll leave together."

A whole new world opened up before him. "I'll see you to your tutoring job. Do you take the tram, or a pedicab?"

"It's not far," Manzhen said. "I usually walk there."

Shijun felt a surge of boundless hope.

Manzhen stood up, glanced in the mirror, and put on her overcoat. They went out together, Shijun holding her books for her.

When they got into the alley, Manzhen remembered how her sister and Zhang Yujin used to go out for a stroll after supper. Manzhen and the other children in the alley would trail after them, clapping and shouting. Manlu and Yujin would hide their displeasure in small pretend smiles, trying to ignore the fuss. Thinking back on that, Manzhen felt ashamed of her behavior, especially since her sister and Yujin hadn't got married after all. All they'd had was a little piece of happiness, a moment that vanished all too quickly.

"I was very happy this morning," Shijun said.

"Oh? You looked quite unhappy."

"That was later on. When I thought I'd misunderstood what you meant."

Manzhen said nothing. He heard her laugh, a little peal of amusement coming to him through the darkness. Finally, Shijun stopped worrying. He took her hand.

"Your hand is cold," she said. "Are you warm enough?"

"I'm fine. Quite warm."

"When I came home earlier, it was starting to get cold, and now the temperature has really dropped."

All this talk was just a smoke screen. Behind that screen, he was holding her hand. That feeling could not be put into words.

The shops along the street had closed up. A big yellow moon hung low in the sky at the end of the road, exactly like a street light. It seemed a part of the human world tonight, as if it were rising from the blurred mass of humanity.

"I'm no good at talking," Shijun said. "I wish I had Shuhui's way with words."

"Shuhui is a perfectly fine person," Manzhen said, "but I almost hate him sometimes, because he makes you feel insecure."

"Yes, I have to admit, feeling insecure is one of my shortcomings. I've got way too many shortcomings, and no good points to make up for them."

"Really?"

"Really. But now I'm thinking there must be something good about me. Otherwise, why would you like me so much?"

Manzhen just laughed. After a few moments, she said, "You always say what you're supposed to say."

"Are you saying I'm a fake?"

"See? You have quite a way with words."

"That day you came to our place, before I went to Nanking, Shuhui's mother said that she never would have imagined that a nice boy like me would steal Shuhui's girlfriend."

"What? I'll never dare go to their house again!"

"Then I'll regret having told you this."

"Did she say that in front of Shuhui?"

"No, she was talking to Shuhui's father, and I happened to overhear them. Shuhui wouldn't fight with me."

"You mean—you wouldn't fight with him, right?"

Shijun thought it over. "I think some women like to have men fighting over them, fighting till there's blood everywhere. You're not like that."

"This isn't something one can fight over," Manzhen said. "But it's a good thing Shuhui doesn't like me, or you'd go off, far, far away, without saying a thing. I'd never know what it was all about."

Shijun had no answer to that.

He let her hand go when they passed a brightly lit fruit stall that stayed open late, then took it again and squeezed her fingers tightly.

But she shook free. "We're almost there. They might be looking from the window."

"Then let's move back a little bit."

They went back a few steps.

"If I thought you wanted me to fight for you," he said, "I'd fight to the finish."

Manzhen giggled. "Who's fighting with you?"

"Anyone who even tries will be sorry."

"I don't know what to make of you. I can never tell if you really are silly or just putting on an act."

"Eventually you'll realize that I am really silly, and then you will regret everything."

"I'll never regret this, unless you do."

Shijun wanted to kiss her, but she turned her face away and he kissed her hair instead. He could feel her trembling, and asked if she was cold. She shook her head.

She pulled his sleeve back a little and looked at his watch.

"What time is it?" he asked.

Manzhen paused for a long moment. "Eight thirty." It was time for her to go.

"Go," he said. "I'll wait for you here."

"No—you'd have to stand here a full hour."

"I'll find a place to sit. I think we passed a café just now."

"There is a café, but it's getting late. You should go home."

"Stop worrying about me! Get in there and teach your students!" He was so intent on pushing her away that he forgot to release her hand; she took two steps and was tugged back. They laughed.

Then she did go, rushing off to ring the doorbell. When she rang it, Shijun had to scurry out of sight.

A huge leaf drifted down from a London plane tree that stood by the roadside, a leaf the size of a bird. It slid past his head, crackling slightly, then crackled again as it settled on the ground. Shijun walked slowly down the street. A pedicab driver was calling for customers, calling from one end of the street to the other, but there were no takers. It was a lonely, almost deserted stretch of road.

It suddenly occurred to him that the child she tutored could have fallen ill, and if the session were canceled, she'd come out to the street to look for him. He went back and stood at the corner, waiting.

The moon had gradually risen higher, and now the ground was lit by its glow. Another pedicab passed in the distance, its hanging lamp creaking rustily, like the cold, empty sound a child's swing makes when the wind is blowing at night.

He had to kiss her, later that night.

Shijun strolled down the street, looking for the café they'd passed earlier. All her little inconsistencies rose up in his mind: here was a girl who knew herself and the world, and yet she could be utterly naïve, or deeply embarrassed. Is that because she likes me, Shijun wondered. Could she really like me that much? A shiver ran through him.

It was the first time that he'd ever told a girl that he loved her, and the first time the girl he loved loved him back. Reciprocated love might not be all that unusual, but when a person finds himself in this situation, it comes as a stunning surprise. Shijun had often heard of someone else having fallen "head over heels in love," but other people's lives bore no relation to his and Manzhen's. He knew they were entirely different from everyone else, just as this experience was entirely different from everything else in his life.

The street made a turn, and he heard music. Someone was playing an Eastern European tune, a dance tune, on the violin. Following the sound, he found the little café. It exuded light and color. A yellow-bearded foreigner pushed the door open and came out. The glass door swung on its hinges, letting out a stream of warmth and conviviality. Shijun stood outside and decided he couldn't mix with people, not in his current state. He was too happy. Great sorrow and great happiness are, in this regard, similar—they both require distance from others. He had to stay out in the cold, on the street, walking aimlessly about, listening to the music.

Early that morning he'd waited for her at the bus stop; later he'd gone to her house and waited for her in her room. Now he was again waiting for her.

He'd once told her that back when he was in school the happiest day was Saturday, because then he could look forward to Sunday. He had not the slightest premonition that the times spent looking forward to something would be his happiest times with her; that their Sunday would never dawn.

6

Shijun's mother had asked him to write as soon as he arrived, and he wrote her a short note that very night. He didn't have any stamps, so planned to get Shuhui to post it for him from the office. He went in early the next day, as a pretext for seeing Manzhen.

Manzhen had not yet arrived. Shijun took the letter from his pocket and put it on Shuhui's desk. "Here—I forgot to give you this earlier." He settled in for a little chat.

Manzhen came in and said good morning. She was wearing a light pink dress trimmed with black-and-white braid around the sleeves. Shijun couldn't remember seeing it before. She wasn't smiling openly, and avoided looking at him directly, almost as if he weren't in the room. But her happiness spilled out, undeniable. Every glance, every gesture was infused with irrepressible delight. Shuhui was taken aback. "My, my, isn't Manzhen pretty today?" He spoke without thinking, and for some reason Manzhen could not answer right away. She blushed. Shijun got nervous.

Fortunately, Manzhen recovered quickly. "What you mean, I guess, is that I'm usually very ugly."

"Oh, don't twist my words!"

"But that's obviously what you meant."

They didn't have to hide their relationship from others, certainly not from Shuhui, but Shijun had not told him anything. He had no desire to discuss Manzhen with anyone: talking about it would only miss the point, like scratching a shoe to get at an itchy spot underneath the leather. And yet he half wished, illogical though it was, that people did know about them. He and Shuhui lived together, saw each other from dawn to dusk, and still his friend had no idea what was going on. Love, they say, is blind, but apparently those who stand right next to it are completely blind.

There was a lot of politicking in their factory. Mr. Ye, whose birthday they had celebrated, had built up a faction within the company and was siphoning off funds for his own benefit; the evidence was there for all to see. He went from bold to brazen, counting on the support of the most senior manager—until matters came to a head, and he was toppled by all those who'd refused to connive. Shijun wasn't affected, since he worked on the factory floor, but Shuhui worked in the company office, with the upper management. He'd long been wanting to extricate himself from the mess. At this very juncture, a friend recommended him for a position at another factory, giving him an opportunity to leave. He resigned immediately. Shijun took him out for a goodbye lunch, and Manzhen came too. This marked the end of their daily lunch dates as a threesome.

When the three of them were together, there was a certain feeling that Shijun enjoyed a lot. He liked watching the other two and listening as they joked back and forth. It was nothing but light chatter, but it gave him deep pleasure. A childlike pleasure—that's how it felt. Shijun's own childhood had not been happy; when he heard people talking about the happiness of childhood, his mind turned to the times the three of them spent together.

They held the farewell party for Shuhui at a famous old restaurant. Afterwards, a colleague at the factory told them that they hadn't ordered the real specialities of the house, and Shuhui made Shijun agree to a second meal at the same place.

"And here we are again," Manzhen said. "This time, it's your treat."

"No," said Shuhui, "this is *your* chance to throw me a party!"

The banter went on, neither willing to yield. When the time to pay the bill came, Shuhui claimed he had no money on him.

"No problem," Manzhen said. "I'll lend you the money, and you can pay me back."

But she couldn't get him to agree that it was a loan. As they were leaving the restaurant, he made her a deep, formal bow. "Thank you so very much!"

She bowed in return. "No—thank *you* very much!"

Shijun laughed so hard he could hardly stand up.

Shuhui's new job was at a factory in the distant district of Yangshupu. He lodged in a dormitory, coming home only at the weekend. One week, a letter came for him, and his mother put it on his desk. Shijun glanced at it, saw a Nanking postmark, and felt curious, since Shuhui had said he didn't know anyone there. A female friend had asked him to deliver a package to a Mrs. Ling, but the Lings were not direct acquaintances of his. There was no return address on the envelope; it never occurred to Shijun that Tsuizhi could have sent it. He didn't recognize her handwriting, though they'd known each other since childhood. His mother had once urged him to start up a correspondence with her, but nothing had come of it.

By the time Saturday came around and Shuhui returned home, Shijun had forgotten the letter. Shuhui opened it and found a brief note. Tsuizhi wanted to take some entrance exams for Shanghai colleges, and hoped he could send her some exam schedules. Shuhui didn't consider this anything he ought to hide from Shijun if his friend were to ask, since Tsuizhi's reason for going outside the family was easy to imagine. She probably didn't have permission yet, and was keeping quiet about her plan. But Shijun never asked, so Shuhui didn't mention it. A few days later, he went to the two colleges she had listed, got the exam information, and sent it to her with a short note. She wrote back right away, but this time Shuhui waited a long while, then replied only briefly. She didn't write again. In fact, ever since he'd returned from Nanking, he'd thought about her a lot. But remembering the interest that she'd shown in him only made him feel sad and hopeless.

January came around, and Tsuizhi wrote again. The letter sat on Shuhui's desk a whole week, and Shijun wondered again about the Nanking postmark. Maybe Shuhui had a Shanghainese friend who'd moved there recently. He thought he'd ask Shuhui that weekend, but it slipped his mind; it wasn't really any of his business anyway.

That Saturday morning at the factory, a phone call came for Shijun. It was Yipeng—he was in Shanghai and wanted to have lunch.

Shijun already had plans with Manzhen. "I'm meeting a friend at a restaurant," he said, "but you're welcome to join us if you like."

"Is the friend male or female?"

"It's one of my female colleagues. Not a girlfriend. Don't say anything foolish when you see her, or she'll be offended."

"A female colleague, eh? One of those office girls? No wonder you're always staying in Shanghai. I've been wondering why you're so busy—now I know it's all rendezvous in little restaurants! Heh, heh! I'm going to tell everyone when I go back!"

Shijun wished, with all his heart, that he could unsay the invitation, but a firm retort was his only option now. "What utter nonsense! Miss Gu is not that kind of girl. You'll see that right away when you meet her."

"Listen, Shijun. Get this Miss Gu to bring along a friend for me. Don't leave me out in the cold."

"Why are you going on like this?" Shijun frowned. "What do you take her for?"

"OK, OK. I'll stop. Can't you take a joke?"

Yipeng might be full of loose talk with Shijun, but he straightened himself out for the meeting with Manzhen. Still, since he knew she worked for a living, he was more off-hand, slightly careless, than he would have been with a young lady from a wealthy family. Manzhen couldn't tell; she thought the flippant tone was his normal manner. But Shijun knew what was going on, and it made him angry.

Yipeng had a few drinks, and got tipsy. Suddenly he giggled and said, "I don't know what got into Amy, but she's been playing matchmaker for us!"

"Who is 'us'?" Shijun asked.

"Me and Tsuizhi."

"Goodness! That's great! That really is great!"

"But," Yipeng urged him, "don't you go around blabbing about it. It's not a done deal yet!" He smiled again, and gave a little sigh. "It's all her doing, and Yiming's too. I'm not ready to get married! Getting married means losing your freedom—you know that, don't you?"

"Oh, enough of that! You need someone to keep an eye on you!" He clapped his cousin on the shoulder.

Yipeng seemed pleased, and Shijun was happy too. It wasn't for selfish reasons; he wasn't thinking that if Tsuizhi got married, his mother and sister-in-law would have to abandon their plan. He wasn't thinking that way at all. He'd been so happy lately, the world looked different to him. Even Tsuizhi had turned into a lovely young woman. Yipeng was a lucky man, and they'd be a happy couple.

Manzhen sat smiling while they discussed family matters. Shijun's sister-in-law had asked him to buy her a dress-length of fabric, and now he asked Yipeng to take it to Nanking for him. The two of them went to Shijun's room to fetch it. Manzhen went home by herself. When they walked into the Hsus' apartment, Shuhui was already there. He'd just arrived home for the weekend, and certainly had not expected to see Yipeng coming in through the door. Shuhui had a poor opinion of Yipeng—who seemed a big windbag to him—and greeted him with a casualness that conveyed complete indifference. Fortunately, since Yipeng didn't know the meaning of self-doubt, the slight did not register.

Shijun got the fabric out and gave it to Yipeng. Yipeng opened the package to have a look. It was deep gray silk, brocaded with little sprigs of plum blossom. "I say!" he exclaimed. "It's the same fabric Miss Gu was wearing today! I sat there thinking her dress was very plain, almost like a widow's. I never realized it was a present from you!"

"Oh, you're just making things up!" Shijun said, a bit embarrassed.

"Whoever heard of such a coincidence?" Yipeng countered.

"There's nothing strange about it. My sister-in-law asked me to buy some fabric, which is quite out of my league, so I asked Miss Gu to help me pick it out. She bought herself a length of the same stuff."

"So I am right! I knew all along you two had a special friendship. When is the wedding?"

"Your head must be full of weddings, you talk about them so much. If you keep this up, I'll tell everyone!"

"No, no, don't do that!" Yipeng said hurriedly.

"What's this?" Shuhui asked. "Is Yipeng getting married?"

"Nothing but wild accusations," Yipeng cut in. "Pay no attention to him!"

After a few more rounds of banter, Yipeng said goodbye, and Shijun and Shuhui saw him to the door. At some point that afternoon it had started to snow, and flakes were drifting down from the sky.

They went upstairs together. Shijun felt guilty and embarrassed after all that talk about his relationship with Manzhen—Shuhui hadn't heard anything till Yipeng came and opened his big mouth. He and Manzhen were planning to see a film, but since Shuhui came home so infrequently, Shijun sat down for a chat instead of rushing off. Looking for something to say, he told Shuhui about the match that seemed to be developing between Yipeng and Tsuizhi. This was not a complete surprise to Shuhui. He'd read Tsuizhi's latest letter as soon as he got home, and learned of her unhappiness due to her hopes for studying in Shanghai being dashed—her family wanted her to get engaged. She didn't mention the name of the potential fiancé, and Shuhui assumed it was someone he didn't know. It had not occurred to him that it could be Yipeng.

Her letter seemed to suggest she hoped he would respond somehow, but what could he say? He had plenty of courage, if it came to that, but her family was not the only obstacle he had to consider. He had to think of Tsuizhi's own happiness. She was used to being pampered, had no experience of hardship; if she made a rash decision, based on a burst of emotion, she'd certainly regret it later on. Perhaps he let this consideration weigh too heavily on his mind, but he was an ambitious young man, afraid of tying himself down just as his career was starting.

And now she was going to marry Yipeng. If she were marrying someone halfway decent, Shuhui would have let it go. He would not have been so crestfallen. He lay across his bed, arms folded behind his head, staring out of the window. Big flakes of snow swirled in the air.

"Want to come to the pictures?" Shijun asked.

"All that snow out there, and you want to go out?" He pulled his feet onto the bed without removing his shoes, reached down to unfold the quilt, and covered himself with it.

Mrs. Hsu came in to retrieve their guest's teacup, and was surprised to see her son lying in bed in broad daylight. "What are you doing in bed? Are you unwell?"

"I'm fine," Shuhui said grumpily. He heard, in her question, the insinuation that he was wishing himself sick, and that irritated him.

Mrs. Hsu peered at his face and felt his forehead. "You are looking a bit off color. I hope it's not a cold. Have a little wine—it'll warm you up. I'll get it for you."

Shuhui made no reply. Mrs. Hsu fetched her special bottle of home-brewed cooking liqueur flavored with Guangzhou orange rind. "I'm telling you—there's nothing wrong with me!" Shuhui said impatiently. "Let me sleep and I'll be fine."

"All right, all right. I'll put the bottle here, and you can decide whether you want some or not." His mother was annoyed. "And take your shoes off," she said, as she headed for the door. "Have a good sleep."

Shuhui said nothing. He waited till she'd left, then sat up to remove his shoes. As he was unlacing them he saw the bottle on the table. He poured himself a cup and drank it down, hoping it would relieve his frustration. But "wine goes to the stomach, worries are in the heart," and there's quite a distance between the two. The heart cannot be drowned in wine. White-hot alcohol won't cauterize a heart—pour as much as you like over your troubles, and it still won't burn them away.

He drank cup after cup, ignoring what he was doing. Shijun went downstairs to phone Manzhen and ask if she still wanted to go out in the snow. They decided not to see a film; he'd go over to her place instead. Their phone conversations were never brief. By the time he'd hung up the phone and returned to the upper floor, the room, much to his surprise, reeked of alcohol. "Blimey! Didn't you say you weren't going to have any? You've finished the whole bottle!"

Mrs. Hsu was going past the door just then. "What's got into you today?" she said, raising her voice at her son. "I let you have one cup to warm you up—why did you drink so much?" She sighed in frustration. "Wine that's been aged for years, gone in a flash. I opened that bottle only a month ago, and now it's empty!"

Shuhui fell onto the bed, ignoring her, his face a flaming red. He saw Shijun putting on his coat, preparing to go out. "Are you still going?"

"I promised to go over to Manzhen's."

Shuhui saw the shy look on Shijun's face, and suddenly realized that Yipeng's teasing was based on something real. Shijun's eager high spirits, not in the least dampened by the snow, sent a blast of cold loneliness through Shuhui. He turned over, burying himself in the bed.

At Manzhen's home, the two of them sat close to a little stove and chatted. It was a tiny kerosene stove that had been used for cooking, but now served to heat her room. When Manzhen held a match to each of the little openings, it looked as if she were lighting a ring of candles on a birthday cake.

It was Saturday afternoon, so all her younger brothers and sisters were at home. Shijun was on good terms with them now. He'd never liked being around small children; spending time with his nephew, even that one child, could be a trial for him. But Manzhen's siblings, who made quite a throng, stirred his affections.

The children galloped around like ponies, up and down the stairs. They pounded across the adjoining room, peered through the doorway, and raced off again. Then they went into the alley to make a snowman, leaving the rooms filled with silence. The kerosene flame burned on and on, turning a gorgeous blue. Rippling blue, blue as water.

"Manzhen, when should we get married? Last time I was at home, my mother said she hoped I would marry soon."

"But I think it would be better not to depend on them financially."

That was Shijun's feeling too. He had struggled so hard for the freedom to make his own career, broken with his father and run off to Shanghai to work; if he turned around now, and asked his father to support him and his new wife, it would feel like a major defeat.

"Well, but how long should we wait?" he asked.

"I think we'd better see how things go. My family still needs me."

"You're carrying too much family responsibility—I hate seeing all that pressure on you. If we got married, the two of us could find a better way."

"That's what I'm afraid of!" Manzhen said, smiling at him. "I don't want to drag you into this."

"Why not?"

"You're just getting started in your profession. Supporting a household would be a big distraction. Supporting two households could mean the end of your career."

Shijun gazed at her, his mouth lifted in a little smile. "I know you're always thinking of what's good for me, but . . ." He paused. "But sometimes I hate you for that."

She said nothing then, but when he kissed her, she asked, in the lowest of tones, "Do you still hate me?"

The tea water on the stove had come to a boil, but they didn't notice. Over in the next room, Mrs. Gu heard the steam jiggling the kettle lid and called out, "Manzhen, is that the water boiling? Time to make the tea."

Manzhen called back in reply, then quickly stood up and adjusted her hair in the mirror. Then she rushed out to get the tea leaves and brewed a cup for her mother.

Holding her teacup in both hands, Mrs. Gu stood in the doorway and quoted the old phrase: "If the tea leaves stand up straight, a visitor will soon appear!"

Manzhen used her mouth to point towards Shijun. "Isn't he here already?"

"Mr. Shen doesn't count. He's not a visitor."

That was a big hint; it left Shijun quite abashed.

Mrs. Gu picked up the kettle to fill the thermos flasks.

"I'll do that," Manzhen said. "Sit down, Ma, and take it easy."

"No, if I stop now it'll be hard to get going again. It's almost time to start supper." After a few pleasant remarks, she left the room.

Dusk was falling. Every evening at this time, a street merchant came down the alley, calling out his wares. He came every day without fail, selling mushroom-flavored dried bean curd. It was an ancient, drawn-out cry: "Bean . . . curd! Five-flavor mushroom-tasty bean . . . curd!"

"Nothing stops that man," Shijun said with a smile. "Rain or wind, it's all the same."

"Yes. He's never missed a day. But his bean curd doesn't taste good. We tried it once."

They sat in the gloom listening to the old, wavering cry as it faded in the distance. The daylight faded also, along with the vanishing sound. That bean-curd seller—he must have been Old Father Time himself.

7

Arriving home from work one day, Manzhen learned from her grandmother that Manlu wasn't feeling well and their mother had gone to see her. Mrs. Gu might not be back till late, so they shouldn't wait for her to have supper. Manzhen helped Granny warm the rice and put the meal together.

"Your mother wants to know why your sister's been so unwell since she moved into that new house," Granny told her. "She thinks the house itself is the problem, since they didn't get a feng shui master's advice on the alignment. But I think she's got 'rich person's disease.' Your brother-in-law is rolling in money. Back when they first got married, they were lodgers in a single, upstairs room, but then—just like that, right before our very eyes—he got his own property and his own house, all custom-built. Your sister is lucky indeed. What a man she married! It's just as people say: no need to be a pious vegetarian if the gods already like you."

"Wasn't there a fortune-teller who said she'd be a good-luck charm for her husband?"

Granny clapped her hands together. "That's right! I'd nearly forgotten. And it's all come true. I'll have to ask your mother who that fortune-teller was—I'll go for another consultation."

"That was decades ago, back when Sister was born," Manzhen reminded her. "I don't think you could find him now."

After supper, Manzhen went to her tutoring job. Since she got back from that job rather late, it was usually her mother who came down to let her in, but this time her grandmother opened the door. "Ma still isn't back?" Manzhen asked. "Granny, you go to bed and I'll wait up for her. I'm not ready to sleep anyway."

She waited a full half-hour. "Your sister is not well," Mrs. Gu said, the moment she came in. "You should go and see her tomorrow."

"What are her symptoms?" Manzhen asked, throwing the bolt on the door.

"She says her stomach is bothering her again, and her joints ache." Mrs. Gu leaned in close to her daughter, in the dark of the kitchen, and whispered in her ear, "It's those abortions she had—that's what's wrong!"

Manlu had other symptoms as well, but Mrs. Gu, preferring to deceive herself, would rather not think about it.

They went upstairs. The right seam-pocket of her mother's dress bulged visibly—probably a wad of cash stuffed in there by Manlu. Manzhen held her tongue. She had told her mother, over and again, not to take money from Manlu. Now her mother was hiding the fact that she'd done just that. Parents, when they get older, can be a little afraid of their own children.

When they went to bed, Mrs. Gu carefully laid her dress on a chair. She still had not mentioned the money.

"Ma," Manzhen said, amusement seeping into her tone, "how much did she give you this time?"

Mrs. Gu pushed the bedding aside and jumped out of bed. She felt around in her dress pocket for the tied-up handkerchief. "I don't know," she said. "I'd better count it."

"Don't count it now," Manzhen said. "You should get back into bed so you don't catch cold."

But her mother untied the handkerchief, took out the wad of notes and counted them. "I told her to keep it, but she insisted. She said I should buy a few treats for myself."

"Since when would you buy treats for yourself?" Manzhen said with a smile. "You'll use it to buy groceries and pay bills! Ma, how many times have I told you not to take money from Big Sis? If that Zhu fellow finds out, he'll accuse her of sneaking money out to her family!"

"I know." Her mother sighed. "And on top of that, I have to listen to your grumbling, all for the sake of a few measly dollars!"

"Ma, I'm telling you: don't keep doing this. He'll start thinking we're all under *his* roof. You know he would—he's that kind of man!"

"He's rich now—why would he be so petty?"

"Don't you know why? Rich people are always the stingiest. They think their money's worth more than other people's!"

Mrs. Gu sighed again. "Child," she said, "you shouldn't assume your mother's got no sense of dignity. Of course I don't want to be his dependant—he's not in our family. But is it really better to depend on you? You're under so much pressure, working day and night, it hurts me to see the load you're carrying." She wiped her eyes, using the handkerchief in which the money had been wrapped.

"Ma, please stop worrying. We just have to scrape by for a little while—in a couple of years, we'll have turned the corner. It'll be much easier for me when Weimin is old enough to work."

"But you're a grown woman now—how can you sacrifice your whole life for your younger siblings? You should get married soon."

"Oh, there's plenty of time for that. I'll wait till Weimin is grown up, at least."

"And how long will that be? Is that young man of yours going to wait?"

Manzhen sputtered a laugh. "If he can't, that's his problem." A white hand rose from the covers; she turned off the lamp.

Mrs. Gu thought this might be a good time to find out if Manzhen and Shijun were secretly engaged. Then, depending on how her daughter responded, she could find out about his income and family situation. Mrs. Gu lay in the darkness, thinking. "Are you asleep?" she asked.

"Yes," Manzhen mumbled.

"If you're asleep, how can you answer?" Mrs. Gu asked with a smile. At first she thought her daughter was pretending to be asleep, then remembered she'd been out all day long, working hard, then stayed up late to unlatch the door for her. She must be tired. Mrs. Gu felt embarrassed, and said no more.

The next day was Saturday, and Manzhen went to her sister's to see how she was feeling. Her sister's new house was on Hongqiao Road, in a fairly isolated area whose inconvenience, in terms of location, was overcome only by the fact that its residents all had their own cars. Manzhen had not visited before, but her mother and grand-mother had taken the younger children several times. They said it was very fancy, the inside like a plush cinema, the outside like a public garden. Entering that garden for the first time, Manzhen passed a tall hedge of evergreen trees bordering a lawn. On the other side of the hedge, a gardener was cutting the grass. The silence of the sunny afternoon was broken only by the whirring click of the lawnmower—a drowsy sound swimming in soft quiet. A good place, Manzhen thought, for her sister to recuperate.

The interior was splendid, of course, but Manzhen didn't stop to look; she went straight up the stairs, following a maid to her sister's bedroom. The bed faced a set of tall windows framed with curtains, layers and layers of cascading purple gauze. Manlu sat on the bed, her hair uncombed.

"Feeling better today?" Manzhen asked. "Well enough to sit up?"

"A little better. Did Ma get back all right last night? It's such a long way, I worried about letting her go back so late. Next time I'll ask her to stay overnight."

"She'll just say she's needed at home," Manzhen said amiably.

"That's because the house runs on too tight a budget, with no maid to help out. Oh—that's right, I meant to ask Ma if she knows where Ah Bao is these days."

"I'll ask her when I get back. Do you want to hire Ah Bao again?"

"I didn't keep her after I got married, because she's so young. I thought I should have someone more reliable. But now I think it's better to keep the servants you already know."

The phone rang. "Could you get it?" Manlu asked.

Manzhen ran over and picked up the receiver. "Hello?"

The other party was surprised. "Oh—is that you, Second Sister?"

Manzhen recognized Hongtsai's voice. "Yes. Wait a moment, Brother-in-law. I'll get my sister for you."

"What a surprise! We hardly ever get to see you. What brought you to the house today?"

Hongtsai kept on talking as Manzhen carried the phone to Manlu's bedside; the receiver crackled on and on, unintelligibly.

Manlu picked up the receiver. "Hello?"

"I bought a refrigerator," Hongtsai said. "Has it been delivered yet?"

"No."

"What? How can it not be there yet?" He hung up.

"Hello, hello—where are you now? You said you'd be home for lunch and . . ." She broke off, then slammed the receiver down. "Cuts me off when I'm still talking," she fumed. "Your brother-in-law has turned into a different person, I tell you! This isn't a man who's got rich—he's got crazy!"

Manzhen started chatting about other things, hoping to distract her.

"I heard Ma say you're very busy these days," Manlu said.

"Yes, that's why I haven't been able to come to see you, even though I've been wanting to come."

They went on talking, till a car horn sounded outside and Manlu froze, listening intently. She recognized the sound of the car. A moment later, Hongtsai came striding into the room.

"What's this?" Manlu said, with a direct look at him. "Back so soon?"

"Yes. Aren't I allowed to come back? Isn't this my home?"

"Well, that's hard to say! The way you disappear, gone all night, then all day."

"I'm not going to fight with you! Aren't you embarrassed, carrying on like this in front of Second Sister?"

He plopped down and lit a cigarette. "It's no wonder your sister is unhappy," he said to Manzhen. "I'm so busy now. She's here all alone, bored silly—it's enough to make a person ill, even if she didn't have health problems already. And you don't come to see her."

"What's this all about?" Manlu demanded. "Now you want to blame *her*? Second Sister is very busy—how could she have time to sit with me? She works all day, then goes off on tutoring jobs."

"Since you're a tutor," Hongtsai said, "why don't you tutor your sister? I got her a tutor once, a foreigner who wanted thirty dollars an hour—that's a month's salary for some people! But she wouldn't stick with it, gave up after a few lessons."

"How can I study when I'm so sick?"

"You see! With that kind of attitude, how can a person learn anything? I like to study, but I have to spend so much time on business that I've never had a chance to dig in, the way I wish I could. That's always been my ambition. Hey—Second Sister! Why don't you tutor both of us?"

"That's a good joke, Brother-in-law! I'm no scholar—I only know enough to tutor little children."

They heard the sound of hard-soled shoes approaching the bedroom.

"Must be the nurse who gives me my injections," Manlu told her sister.

"What kind of injections?"

"It's glucose," Hongtsai answered for her. "Look at all the medicines we have here, enough to open a pharmacy! It's quite something, this illness of your sister's!"

"Her color looks good," Manzhen ventured.

Hongtsai burst out laughing. "After all the makeup she's slathered on, how can you possibly tell? You don't know how it works, do you? You haven't seen those women who, even when they're lying in their coffins, are covered in cosmetics!"

The nurse was already in the room, giving Manlu her injection. Manzhen thought Hongtsai had gone too far, ridiculing her sister in front of the nurse, but Manlu made no retort. She was pretending not to hear. When had Manlu become so saintly? And with Hongtsai getting wilder and ruder by the minute . . . Manzhen found it hard to bear. She stood up to take her leave.

"We can go together," Hongtsai said. "I'm leaving too. I'll take you home in my car."

Manzhen tried to refuse, saying she'd get a taxi.

"You've just come back and now you're going out again?" Manlu said to her husband, pulling a long face.

"With the sort of interrogation I get when I come back, why would I want to stay here?"

In days gone by, that would have sent Manlu into a spitting rage; she'd have latched on to him, and dug her claws in. But once people have money, they have to maintain some sense of hauteur. She wouldn't make a scene in front of the nurse.

Manzhen picked up her handbag and headed towards the door, but Hongtsai blocked her path. "Wait a moment, Second Sister. I'll be ready right away." He dashed off to the next room, mysteriously.

"I won't wait for Brother-in-law," Manzhen said to her sister. "I don't need a lift home."

Manlu scowled, thinking it through. "Let him take you. It'll be faster." Her own sister wouldn't make a pass at her husband—she felt safe on that front. And Hongtsai, even with his weakness for women, wouldn't take such a risk.

Hongtsai came back. "OK, we're off!"

Manzhen thought the nurse would think her silly if she kept protesting, so she gave in. She and Hongtsai went downstairs together.

"This is your first time here, isn't it?" Hongtsai said. "There are a few rooms you have to see. I put lots of effort into this, even hired a designer." He showed her the living and dining rooms. "Come and see the study—it's the best of the lot. I got a good deal on the murals. An art student did them for just three dollars a square foot. If I'd gone with the artist the designer recommended, it would have run into the thousands!"

The walls were full of angels, Mother Mary, Cupid holding a bow, and the Goddess of Peace accompanied by doves, all in oils. Colorful scenes and figures were packed in tightly together, filling every inch from floor to ceiling. The floor was covered with intricately designed Arabian tiles and the windows were of many-hued stained glass. It made the eyes glaze over, the head spin.

"When I come home all worn out," Hongtsai said, "I come in here for peace and quiet."

Manzhen had to stifle a laugh. Hadn't Manlu said her husband was going crazy? Even a man in a state of perfect sanity would quickly grow unhinged, if he came to this room seeking rest.

They went out of the front door and found the car waiting for them. "When I bought this car, I got taken for a ride!" He quoted the price, a staggering sum. Everything he said was a boast of some kind, but Manzhen was impervious. She had no idea what a car should cost.

Once they were in the car, it suddenly became clear why he'd run off when they were leaving Manlu's room. He'd tidied himself up, dousing himself in cologne. It was unmistakable, once they were in that confined space. The empty gestures of an effeminate youth— that's the impression created by a man who only dabs on a little cologne. How much odder, then, a middle-aged broker who reeks of scent.

"Where to?" the driver asked.

"Let's go for coffee," Hongtsai said to Manzhen. "I'm so busy, you're so busy—we hardly ever get a chance to chat."

"I've got something to do," Manzhen said pleasantly. "That's why I left so soon. I would have stayed longer if I could, since I rarely get to see my sister."

"Yes, we hardly ever see you." Hongtsai had to content himself with that. "I hope you'll come to the house more often now."

"I'll come whenever I can."

"We'll take Second Sister home first," Hongtsai said to the driver. "Do you know the way?"

The driver did, and the car rolled along noiselessly. The vehicle's speed was a point of pride for Hongtsai, but today he resented it. Manzhen had always seemed far above him, an unattainable woman, and even though people say, "Money fills a man with courage," and he certainly had grown more daring as his wealth increased, he still was a little afraid of her. He sat in one corner of the car, whistling tunelessly. Manzhen stayed silent, exuding coldness. Hongtsai exuded cologne.

When they had reached her neighborhood, Manzhen told the driver to let her out at the entrance to the alley, rather than going in.

"No, let's go in," Hongtsai urged. "I'd like to see good old Mother Gu. I haven't had a chance to chat with her in a long time."

"She took the children to the park today. Granny is the only one at home today, and I'm going out soon."

"Oh? You're going somewhere?"

"I'm going to the cinema with a colleague."

"If I'd known that, I would have taken you directly there."

"No," Manzhen said lightly. "I wanted to come home because Mr. Shen said he'd come here to pick me up."

Hongtsai nodded. Then, looking at his watch, he exclaimed, "Oh, five o'clock already! I can't stop now, I have to meet someone. I'll come again soon to see you and your family."

Hongtsai was out on the town all night long; when he got home, it was nearly daybreak. He came stumbling in, stinking of drink, and threw himself on the bed, shoes and all. He hadn't turned on a light, but Manlu flicked on the lamp next to the bed. Her eyes were bloodshot, her hair a mess—she hadn't slept a wink. She heaved herself up into a sitting position. "Where have you been?" she yelled. "You'd better tell me what's going on, or you'll pay for this!"

Even if he were sober, a blazing attack like that would have made Hongtsai pretend to be drunk. He lay stiff on his back, eyes shut, ignoring her. Manlu grabbed a pillow and whacked him on the face. "Playing dead!" she scowled. "Yes, you might as well play dead!"

Hongtsai lifted the pillow off his face and cried out, in a beseeching tone, "*Manlu!*"

That took her by surprise. It was ages since he'd shown any sign of tenderness towards her. It must be that he still loved her, and the alcoholic stupor had revealed his true feelings. She softened a good deal. "What is it?"

Hongtsai took her hand in his.

"What's going on?" she grumbled, but without real rancor. Twisting herself up and around, she sat on the edge of the bed, next to him.

Hongtsai put her hand on his chest, looked at her, and smiled. "I'll do everything you say. I won't go out anymore. But . . . there is something I want."

She was immediately suspicious. "What is it?"

"You won't go along with it."

"Tell me what it is. Why can't you spit it out? Oh—you want something terrible—that's it! How can you lie there like that, refusing to tell me what it is?" She threw herself at him, beat him with her fists, pummeled him so hard the wine churned in his stomach.

"Ugh! I'm about to be sick as it is—call Amah Wang and get her to pour me a cup of tea."

But Manlu returned to her haughty self-control. "I'll get it for you." She rose to her feet, made a solemn show of pouring and carrying the tea, then held it to his lips so he could take the hangover remedy in tiny, careful sips.

Hongtsai took a small swallow and smiled again. "Manlu, how did Second Sister get to be so pretty?"

Manlu's face went pale. "What are you saying? When did *you* get to be so crazy?" She put the cup on the table, and left it there.

Hongtsai stared into space. "Actually, there are girls who are prettier, but for some reason I keep thinking about her."

"What cheek! Wipe that crazy idea out of your head! Let's get this straight: even if she agreed, I wouldn't. I'm the one who raised the money, year after year, so that girl could go to school. I sacrificed everything so she could become who she is—do you think I'm going to turn around now and let her become somebody's concubine? You seem to think all the women in my family are fit only to be concubines—well, you'd better shake off that idea, right this minute!"

"Enough, enough. Here I am trying to make a joke and you won't play along. Should I just ignore you? Would that be better?"

But Manlu, thoroughly incensed, wouldn't let the matter drop. She went on grumbling and muttering. "I should have known you were up to no good! Eating from the bowl but staring at the pot! You get two dollars to your name, and think that makes you an emperor—they'll fall into your arms, they're all money-mad like you. Even I was not so low as that! When I married you, it wasn't for your money—surely that much is clear!"

Hongtsai sat up abruptly. "Can't you ever let that go? Everyone knows I used to be a penniless devil, but what were you? A filthy tramp! You shameless bitch!"

This verbal attack was more than Manlu had bargained for—it took her by surprise. "So now you're insulting me!" she cried.

Hongtsai gripped the side of the bed, his eyes red and inflamed.

"I'll do more than that—I'll give you a few smacks, how's that? I'll smack you, you filthy, shameless bitch!"

It looked to Manlu as though he might really hit her, using his drunkenness as an excuse. If it came to blows, she'd be the loser. So she burst out crying, her eyes filling with tears. "Hit me then! Go ahead, hit me, you thankless beast! That's what I deserve, for taking up with you in the first place—I should have known better! What else could I expect but to be beaten to death?" She fell back on the bed, burying her face and shaking with sobs.

This change of tune made Hongtsai back down, but still he sat on the edge of the bed and glared at her. After a few minutes he suddenly let out a big yawn, sprawled back across the bed and fell asleep, just as he normally did. In no time at all he was snoring, though she went on sobbing for a long time. In the beginning she wept to defuse the situation, but then real grief took hold of her. Her whole future looked murky; she couldn't bear to think of it. Outside, the sun was rising, and the lamp that had been left on in the room, fading in the daylight, grew pale and melancholy.

Hongtsai had slept for less than two hours when a maid came to wake him at the usual time. Early morning was the critical time for trading, so even though he had several phones at home and a direct line to his company, he always went into the office then. He could nap later in the day, in the hotel room he kept for that purpose.

That afternoon, Manlu's mother telephoned with Ah Bao's new address. Manlu had not brought her maid along when she moved in with Hongtsai, because he liked to chat with the girl, and Manlu found that worrying. But then the situation changed, and she'd decided it would be good, after all, to have the girl by her side, as a way of hanging on to Hongtsai. That was before she'd seen how fickle he was—and that his sights were set higher than Ah Bao.

She took down Ah Bao's address.

"When Second Sister got back," her mother said, "she said you were doing better."

"I'm much better now. I'll come and see you when I'm feeling up to it." Earlier she had said she would ask her mother to come for an overnight visit, but she made no mention of that plan now. She was keeping her distance, because of Manzhen. Her sister had done nothing wrong, and her mother, certainly, was not involved, but Manlu's tone was chilly, perhaps unconsciously so.

Mrs. Gu was not a worrier, but her daughter was a rich lady now, and there's always a gap between the rich and the poor. She could tell that something wasn't right. "That's fine," she replied. "Come as soon as you are well. Granny misses you too."

For the following two months, Mrs. Gu paid no visits to her daughter, nor did she receive any messages from Manlu, either by phone or post. Then one day while shopping in the city, Manlu popped into her old neighborhood. It had been such a long time since she'd been there, and now she was wafting through in her large, long, latest-model car, gazing out at the alley while the neighbors stood and stared—a triumphant, resplendent return to the old homestead. Her younger brothers were learning to ride a bicycle, helped by a young man who held the handlebars, and Manzhen was watching from the back door, leaning against the doorway with her arms crossed. Manlu stepped out of the car.

"Oh, my goodness!" Manzhen cried out. "Sister is here!"

The young man looked up at once, obviously curious, but Manlu's glittering gaze was already upon him, sizing him up. His glance was no match for hers—he quickly looked away. All he got was a fleeting impression of a middle-aged lady in a leather coat. Now that she'd risen so high, Manlu's appearance had to match her station in life. She no longer wore stage-style makeup—false eyelashes, black eyeliner, bright red rouge. The change was tantamount to dropping her weapons: she'd turned into a middle-aged wife. She hadn't realized the effect till earlier that day, while shopping in a fabric shop. She was looking at some purply-red cloth, thinking of buying it, when a clumsy clerk held up a length of dark blue stuff. "Is the dress for you, madam? This blue is nice and dignified." Manlu got angry. So you take me for an old lady? she thought to herself. Then I'll buy the red, for sure! She did buy it, but her displeasure did not abate.

Her mother too was unhappy that day, because Jiemin had fallen and hurt his leg. When Manlu went upstairs, she found her mother bandaging her little brother's knee.

"Oh, dear!" Manlu said. "How did *that* happen?"

"It's his own fault!" Mrs. Gu grumbled. "He was dead set on learning to ride a bicycle. I knew he'd have an accident! They all went crazy, when they got that bicycle, all of them mad about learning to ride it!"

"Where did it come from? Is it new?" Manlu asked.

"It all started with Weimin saying he wanted to go to school by bicycle, to save on the tram fare. He'd been wanting one for a long time, but I didn't get one for him. Mr. Shen bought a bicycle and gave it to him." Mrs. Gu drew her eyebrows together in a tight line. She'd been quite pleased when Shijun presented them with the bicycle, but after her darling got injured, her anger fell on the bestower of the gift.

"Who is this Mr. Shen?" Manlu asked. "I saw someone out there. Is that him?"

"Oh, so you've seen him already?"

"Is he a friend of Second Sister's?"

Mrs. Gu nodded. "A colleague of hers."

"Does he come here often?"

Mrs. Gu sent Jiemin away before she answered, her voice low. "He's here almost every day."

"Does that mean they're engaged?" Manlu asked with a smile.

Mrs. Gu knit her brow and smiled in turn. "What should I say? It has me worried, the way they go around together all day long, and still nothing's been said about marriage."

"Ma, you have to ask Second Sister what's going on."

"Asking her is no use! She talks nonsense, says she'll wait till the little ones are grown up, and then get married. *He* won't wait, I keep telling her! But from the look of things, Mr. Shen isn't the least bit impatient. I'm the one who suffers, getting more nervous by the minute."

"Oh, no!" Manlu suddenly exclaimed. "Do you suppose our little miss has fallen into this man's trap?"

"No, not Manzhen."

"It's not like that. The more innocent they look, the easier it is for them to be seduced. Appearances are no guide in a case like this."

"But Mr. Shen seems an honest man."

"Hah! An honest man! I can see the devil in his eyes, the way he looks at a woman!" She couldn't help raising a hand to her hair and smoothing it, with a self-satisfied air. It didn't occur to her that Shijun, having heard her story already, had looked at her with such interest due to simple curiosity.

"I still think he's an honest man. If you don't believe me, talk to him and see for yourself."

"That is exactly what I'm going to do. I've seen my share of men—I'll find out what kind he is."

Manlu had a husband now, so if she wanted to get acquainted with Manzhen's boyfriend, Mrs. Gu had no objection. "Good!" she said. "You can help me keep an eye on things."

Just then, Manlu heard Manzhen at the head of the stairs, talking to Granny. Manlu gave her mother a warning look, and Mrs. Gu fell silent. Manzhen came in and got her coat from the closet.

"Going out?" her mother asked.

"To the cinema," Manzhen said. "I'd change the plan, but the tickets have already been bought. Stay a while, Sister, and have dinner here."

She rushed off. Shijun never came upstairs, depriving Manlu of the chance to examine him.

Mrs. Gu and Manlu stood side by side at the window watching Manzhen and Shijun as they left together while the children in the alley rode back and forth, learning how to pedal.

"Ah Bao was here a few days ago," Mrs. Gu mentioned to her daughter. Ah Bao was now back in service with Manlu.

"Yes, she told me a letter had come here, from her home town, and she wanted to fetch it."

"Uh-huh . . . and how about the master? Is he still at it?"

Manlu knew that Ah Bao had been gossiping, telling Hongtsai's mother-in-law about his drinking and carousing. "That Ah Bao has a big mouth!" she said with a smirk.

"You'll say the same of me, I know, but I think you should stop quarreling with him. It's not good for your relationship."

Manlu was silent. She didn't feel like telling her mother her problems, even though she needed a shoulder to cry on. No one better than a mother for this role, but her mother never had the right balm—her advice always left her daughter unsure of whether to laugh or cry.

"How old is the master now?" Mrs. Gu went on, half whispering. "Almost forty, isn't he? Don't believe it when people say a man doesn't want children. Once they get to a certain age, they want them very much! I think you've done everything you should, except for this."

Manlu had had two abortions; the doctors said she couldn't have any children now.

"I remember you said the country wife had no sons, just one daughter, right?"

"What?" Manlu spoke languidly. "Didn't Ah Bao report on this too? Someone came from the countryside and brought the child to us."

Mrs. Gu was surprised. "Really? Doesn't the child live with her mother?"

"Her mother died, so they brought her to her father."

Mrs. Gu was stunned. *"Her mother died? . . . Really? . . .* Oh my goodness! Your granny's always said you'd have good fortune, child, and now you've got it made! How could you keep so quiet about this?"

She was grinning from ear to ear. But Manlu only smiled wanly.

Mrs. Gu went on. "Don't forget—a motherless child is to be pitied. You should be good to her."

There was a shoebox among the pile of shopping parcels that Manlu had acquired on her trip to town; she took it out and showed it to her mother. "Look at these," she said. "I buy her leather shoes, I teach her to read—what else do you want from me?"

"How old is she?"

"Eight."

"What's her name?"

"Beckon—as in 'Beckon little brother.'"

Mrs. Gu sighed. "Wouldn't it be good if she really could beckon a little brother!" She sighed again. "They say you've got good fortune, but how can you have good fortune without a son?"

Manlu's smile disappeared. "How you do go on about this great good luck of mine, knowing all the while I've got it rough!" She turned away, leaving her mother with a view of her back and to listen to the impatient tap of her fingernails on the windowsill. Her nails were long and sharp.

For one long minute, Mrs. Gu said nothing. Then she spoke her mind: "You should watch yourself, young lady!"

To her surprise, Manlu started sobbing. Mrs. Gu stood next to her, speechless.

Manlu wiped her face with a handkerchief. "Men are so fickle. Back then, he was willing to risk a charge of bigamy to bring me under his roof, but now that his first wife is dead, he won't go through a formal marriage procedure."

"Why bother about that?" her mother asked. "Didn't we all see you two get married?"

"That ceremony didn't count. His wife was still alive then."

Mrs. Gu frowned and screwed up her eyes, peering at her daughter's face. "I don't understand," she said. And yet she was beginning to grasp Manlu's situation, which was indeed precarious.

Mrs. Gu thought for a bit. "Well, in any case, you shouldn't quarrel with him. Even if he has someone else, you came first, before her."

"What good is that? So what if I came first, the other later? Beckon's mother came before me, and that's a frightening thought. The two of them were engaged by their families when they were little children, but when she died, off in the countryside, her family had to scrape together the money for a coffin."

Mrs. Gu let out a long sigh. "No matter which way you look at it, it all comes down to this: you need a son! Easy to manage, back in the old days. The wife picked out a concubine for her husband, then raised the child as her own. But you won't like that way of solving the problem." Even she felt it to be an old-fashioned, backward idea; a moment later, she was laughing at her own suggestion.

Manlu forced herself to laugh also. "Ma, that's quite enough!"

"Well then, how about adopting a child?"

"Enough, I say! We've already got one motherless child—if we go and get another, we might as well open an orphanage!"

Mother and daughter were so engrossed in their talk they didn't notice that dusk had fallen, turning the room cave-like. It was Granny who reached in from the adjoining room and turned the light on. "What are you doing, sitting here in the dark? I was just wondering if you two had gone off somewhere. Won't you stay for dinner, Young Mistress of the Gu House?"

"I'll cook you something light and tasty," Manlu's mother offered. "Something that won't upset your stomach."

"Well, let me phone home, and tell them not to wait for me for dinner."

She phoned, partly to find out where Hongtsai was.

Ah Bao answered. "The master has just come back. Should I call him to the phone?"

"Uh . . . no, don't bother. I'll be home too, right away." Manlu hung up, and said she had to leave. Her grandmother didn't know the details of the situation, and pressed her to stay.

"Let her go," Mrs. Gu said. "Her husband's waiting to eat dinner with her."

Manlu hurried home. She went upstairs, into the bedroom, just as Hongtsai was leaving the room; he'd come home only to change his clothes.

"Where are you going now?" Manlu asked.

"None of your business!" He slammed the door behind him.

Manlu ran after him, but Hongtsai was down the stairs in a flash, leaving a trail of cologne.

Beckon, the little girl, chose this moment to come running out, eager to see the shoes Manlu had promised to buy her. She'd been playing in the maid's room, but when she heard the click of high-heeled shoes she came running out.

"Ah Bao!" she cried. "Mother's here!"

It was the maids who'd told her to call Manlu "Mother," and Hongtsai had heard it before, but today he was spoiling for a fight with Manlu. "*What?* That damned piece of dirt? You're calling her 'Mother'? As if!"

Manlu grabbed a ceramic flower-pot, intending to hurl it at him, but Ah Bao wrestled her back.

Manlu was speechless with rage; by the time she got her voice back, Hongtsai was gone. "Who'd want *her* for a daughter—that wretched dirty kid, that snotty-nosed beggar-brat? I wouldn't have her, even if you gave her to me!" Her hatred fell on the child, who stood wide-eyed with amazement, following the show. The girl's dead mother, if she were watching from somewhere, must have been pleased; her victory-laugh was ringing in Manlu's ears.

When Beckon had first come to live with them, Manlu thought that pampering the girl would help her reach Hongtsai. Hongtsai wasn't a soft-hearted man, but surely he had some feeling for his own daughter. But instead of serving as a bridge, Beckon became a bone of contention, and a witness to Manlu's repeated humiliation—hence the viciousness of her attack on the girl.

The girl was thin and dark, with pieces of white yarn woven into her little braids. She stood staring dumbly at Manlu, who reached out and gave her a hard slap. Manlu ripped open the box of shiny new shoes, dumped them on the floor, and raised one of her heels. She stamped as hard as she could, in a flurry of wild kicks. But leather shoes are tough, not easy to tear. In the end, they were flung down the staircase, bouncing down to the lower floor.

Manlu's mood swings must have seemed to Beckon as wild as her father's.

Manlu went back to her room, skipped supper and went to bed early. Ah Bao brought a hot-water bottle and tucked it into the quilt. Seeing the maid reminded Manlu of another grievance.

"What did you say, last time you were over at the Missus's? I can't stand it when servants gossip."

Ah Bao still referred to Manlu as "Eldest Young Lady," and Mrs.

Gu as "Missus." "I didn't say anything," she hastily assured Manlu. "It was Missus who asked me—"

"Oh, so now it's the Missus's fault?" Manlu said icily.

Ah Bao knew that Manlu had a bellyful of anger, and no one to vent it on, so she didn't answer back. She slipped around the room, straightening things up, then got out.

Going to bed early makes the night even longer. Manlu, facing the long, slow night ahead, felt she was walking into a black tunnel. It made her very afraid, but she had no choice but to brace herself and enter.

There was a reading lamp at the head of the bed, and a clock, ticking loudly in the silence. Manlu reached over, picked up the clock and put it in a drawer.

When she opened the drawer, she saw a stack of flashcards, the ones she'd been using to help Beckon with her reading vocabulary. She grabbed them by the handful and hurled them towards the spittoon. In fact, her anger was almost spent, and what she felt now was sorrow and pain. Each card had a picture on the back: rice paddy, cat, dog, cow, goat. A few cards fell around the edges of the spittoon, and even into her slippers.

Manlu tossed and turned, sorting through the days to find the moment when Hongtsai's attitude towards her had changed. Ah! That day her sister came to see her, when she was sick in bed—the day he came home tipsy and told her, letting drink take the blame, that he lusted after her sister. She'd bawled him out soundly for that.

If she allowed him to fulfill that fantasy, maybe he'd settle down and stop running around. He was always looking for a new face, but her sister seemed to have inspired true infatuation in him.

She hated what she was thinking, hated it so much her teeth tingled. Come what may, she'd stick with him: she'd made that decision when she married him. She'd been ready to drink coarse tea and eat plain food the rest of her life, never imagining that he'd grow wealthy. When he got rich, it was like winning the lottery—how could she win all that, only to watch it fizzle away into nothing?

Something ice-cold was sticking to the top of her feet. The

hot-water bottle had lost its heat, which meant it was late, some-where in the middle of the night. In the depth of the night, a steam train on a nearby track let out a long, singing whistle.

That "mother's wisdom" she'd heard that day suddenly seemed not so unreasonable after all. It would be good to get a child. All she needed was someone to bear the child for her. Why not her own younger sister? She was the one Hongtsai wanted. And, as her own younger sister, she'd be easier to keep under her thumb.

When her mother first raised the idea, she couldn't have imag-ined that Manzhen would enter the picture. Manlu had to smile when she thought of that. There was ferocity in that smile, though she couldn't see it herself.

Then she came to her senses. "This is insane. I've been saying Hongtsai's gone crazy, and here I am on the same path!" It was an enormity, a huge and horrible idea: she took the idea and cast it from her mind, as hard and far as she could. But it would come back, and she knew it. Like the black shadow of a wild beast that, once it has been down a trail, knows how to trace its way there again, it would keep sniffing till it found her once more.

She was very afraid.

8

Early afternoon, two or three o'clock, is the quietest time in most households. The children are at school, the young people at work, leaving only decrepit old troops to guard the hearth. That's how it was at Manzhen's: her mother and grandmother were the only ones at home at that hour.

It was roughly then that Mrs. Gu heard a knife-grinder coming down the alley, calling out for customers. Taking two knives, she went downstairs, but returned a few minutes later, calling loudly from the staircase. "Mother! Guess who's here! It's Yujin!"

Granny, a bit befuddled, didn't recognize the name. "What? Who?"

By then, Mrs. Gu had brought the guest in. Granny saw at once that it was her niece's son, the man who'd once been betrothed to her eldest granddaughter.

Yujin smiled and greeted her politely, addressing her as "Grand-aunt."

The old lady was thrilled. "My, but you're thin!" she clucked at him.

"Oh, we country folk always seem thin and dark, I suppose," he said with a smile.

"How is your mother?"

Yujin paused, and before he could answer, Mrs. Gu cut in. "She passed away."

"What?"

"I was shocked too, when I saw his black armband!"

Granny stared at Yujin, all in a daze. "When?"

"It was in March. I didn't write to you about it because I wanted to come and tell you myself." He described his mother's illness, and tears streamed from Granny's eyes.

"It's unbelievable," she said. "How can it be that an old woman like me keeps on going, and a young thing like her passes away first!"

Yujin's mother had lived into her fifties, but no matter how many years rolled by, Granny saw everyone in the generation below hers as a child.

"But Cousin was still a lucky woman." Mrs. Gu sighed. "She had a good son in Yujin here."

"Oh, yes!" Granny agreed. "Yujin, I heard that you are the director of the health clinic. What an achievement for such a young man."

"It's not that impressive, really. You know the saying: top-rank in the countryside, seventh-rank in the city."

"You're too modest," said Mrs. Gu. "My husband used to say you had a lot going for you. He said you had a great future ahead of you. Don't you remember that, Mother?"

Back then, they'd betrothed Manlu to Yujin precisely because Mr. Gu had so much confidence in the young man.

"Did you come to Shanghai on business?" Mrs. Gu asked.

"The clinic needs some equipment, so I came here on a buying trip."

Mrs. Gu asked where he was staying. He told her he was in a hotel.

"You must come and stay with us," Granny said at once. "Hotels are always inconvenient."

Mrs. Gu echoed the sentiment, but Yujin hesitated. "Wouldn't that be too much trouble for you?"

"Oh, not in the least! We really mean it! Haven't you stayed with us before?"

"And," said Granny, "it just so happens we've got a spare room. One of the downstairs tenants has moved out."

"Last year, when Manlu got married, we started renting those rooms out," Mrs. Gu explained. There'd been no mention of Manlu up to that point.

"Did you know Manlu got married?" Granny followed up.

"Yes, I heard about it," Yujin said pleasantly. "How is she doing?"

"She's a lucky girl," Granny said. "This husband of hers is very good. He's a successful businessman, and they've built their own house on Hongqiao Road."

Manlu's having landed them a solid-gold son-in-law was, in Granny's eyes, a first-class miracle, the most gratifying event in all her years as a grandmother. Once she started talking about it, she couldn't stop.

Yujin took it all in, responding just enough to show he was listening. "Oh . . . uh-huh . . . well, that's wonderful."

Mrs. Gu thought he seemed a little uncomfortable; apparently he still had feelings for Manlu. If news of her marriage hadn't reached him already, he might not have come to their house, for fear of stirring up jealousy or suspicion.

The knife-grinder called from the back door, saying the knives were ready. Mrs. Gu jumped up, ready to go downstairs. Yujin stood up too, and tried to take his leave. But the two women insisted he stay, and at last he smiled and agreed. "OK then, I'll come back this evening with my luggage. Right now, I have to see to some business."

"Well, come back early," Mrs. Gu said. "Be sure to have supper with us."

That evening, Yujin came back with his luggage. Mrs. Gu had prepared the room for him. "Weimin! Jiemin!" she called to her sons. "Come and help!"

"Oh, I can do it," Yujin said, and carried his suitcase in. The boys followed him into the room, hanging back a little.

"This is Yujin," Mrs. Gu told her sons. "You can call him Brother Jin. Jiemin, you were too little when he was here last, you probably don't remember him. But Weimin, I'm sure you remember. You were crazy about him. When he left, you cried so hard—all day, and into the night—that Father couldn't sleep. He got angry, and smacked you for it."

Weimin was a teenager now, fourteen years old and as tall as his mother, and the story embarrassed him. He blushed.

Granny came in. "Don't worry about unpacking now," she said. "Come and have supper."

Mrs. Gu went into the kitchen to fetch the food, and Granny led Yujin upstairs. Their supper had been delayed because they were waiting for him, but Manzhen couldn't wait, because she had her tutoring job to go to. When Yujin came in, she was sitting at the table with her rice bowl. He froze. For a moment, he thought he was seeing Manlu—the Manlu of seven years ago.

Manzhen put down her bowl and chopsticks, stood up and greeted him with a smile. "Brother Jin, don't you know who I am?"

Yujin couldn't bring himself to say she'd seemed, for a moment, too familiar. "Second Sister, right? I don't think I'd have recognized you if we'd met somewhere else."

"Last time you saw her," Granny said, "she was younger than Weimin is now."

Manzhen picked up her chopsticks. "I'm sorry," she said. "I had to start eating because I'm going out soon." Her bowl held plain rice with a bit of pickled vegetable—such a simple meal that it made Yujin feel ill at ease. By the time Mrs. Gu had brought in the serving-bowls filled with different kinds of food, Manzhen had finished eating.

"Stay and have something with us," Yujin urged her.

"No, I've had enough," she said with a smile. "Mother, you sit here."

She got up, poured herself some tea, then stood leaning against her mother's chair, sipping from the cup. Her mother put some spicy meat into Yujin's bowl.

"Ma," she said, "don't you remember that Brother Jin doesn't like spicy food?"

"Goodness me! That's right, and I'd completely forgotten."

"What a memory the child has," Granny said. She didn't know that Manzhen remembered because she'd hated Yujin, back when she was little, for stealing her big sister away. She knew he didn't like spicy food, so she had poured pepper sauce in the bottom of his rice bowl. He'd known, at that time, that she was playing tricks on him, but the incident had faded from his memory. He was amazed that she remembered his tastes after so many years. And, at the same time, her voice, her smile, her every gesture was utterly familiar to him: these traces of her presence had danced in his dreams for years, and now he beheld them with waking eyes. Fate is cruel, but it's a cruelty that suffuses sweetness into the suffering.

Manzhen finished her tea and left. Yujin's head was spinning. In days past, he'd been a frequent guest, and they always gave their guests a special set of old-fashioned bone chopsticks, round at the tips and squared-off at the finger grip, extra-long and heavy. These were the chopsticks he'd used before, in their house, and now he was here again, sitting at the dinner table with young and old, just as before, except that Manlu wasn't there. The tides of time swept over him, as he sat in the dim amber glow of the lamp.

Like most country-dwellers, Yujin was an early riser, and went to bed at nine thirty. Mrs. Gu waited up, ready to open the door when Manzhen came home, and Granny wasn't sleepy so she stayed up too, talking with her daughter-in-law about her niece's life, recounting all the details and weeping as she spoke. Then they talked about Yujin, both women singing his praises.

"That's why Manlu's father thought so highly of him," Mrs. Gu said. She sighed. "Luck's not with us. Such a fine young man, and we didn't get him as a son-in-law."

"This kind of thing is always up to fate," Granny opined.

"How old is Yujin now? Isn't he the same age as Manlu? And yet he's not married yet—I can't help but feel we owe him something."

"Yes, indeed. His mother's only son, thirty years old and still not married. She'd be right to blame us for that. And no grandson to wear mourning when she died!"

"This child, Yujin." Mrs. Gu sighed. "He's a fool for love."

The two women felt silent, their thoughts turning in the same direction. Granny was the first to put it into words. "Actually, he and Manzhen would make a good match."

"Yes," Mrs. Gu said softly. "If we gave him Manzhen, as a reward for his faithfulness—wouldn't that be perfect! But Manzhen's already got this Mr. Shen. Rather unfortunate."

Granny shook her head. "This business with Mr. Shen—I'm not sure it's a done deal. They've known each other nearly two years now, and if things go on like this, we might find we've waited for nothing."

Mrs. Gu was a little displeased with Shijun's way of handling things, but she felt she should defend her daughter; and Shijun, after all, was her daughter's boyfriend. "Well," she said with a sigh, "Mr. Shen is a good man, even if he is a bit slow to act."

"To put it crudely," Granny said, "he should either shit, or get off the pot!" She cackled with laughter. Mrs. Gu had to laugh too.

On the third evening of Yujin's visit, Shijun came to the Gu house. It was after dinnertime, and Yujin was in his room. Manzhen told Shijun they had a house guest, a doctor who worked in a rural village. "How many doctors would be willing to work under such conditions?" she asked. "I really admire his dedication. Let's go and see him."

They went to Yujin's room and Manzhen asked him about life in the countryside, the situation in the village, and so on—she was interested in everything. Shijun was instinctively jealous. He sat to one side, listening silently, but since he generally was quiet around new people, Manzhen didn't see anything unusual in his behavior.

When Shijun was ready to go, Manzhen saw him to the door and told him about her sister and Yujin. "That was seven years ago, and he's still not married. It looks as though he hasn't forgotten her."

"Ah," Shijun said, "what a tender-hearted guy! He must be a true romantic."

"Oh, yes. It seems obsessive, but I think it's his great strength. You have to be a bit prone to obsession, if you run off to a poor, remote village to set up a health clinic. It's a hard, thankless task."

Shijun made no reply. He went out to the alley, gave her a brief nod and quick goodbye, then left.

After that, whenever Shijun came for a visit, Yujin was at Manzhen's house. If Yujin was in his room, Manzhen would drag Shijun along, and the three of them would sit and talk. She was doing this half on purpose, because lately she'd been feeling that spending time with Shijun, tête-à-tête, tended to heat things up; and if they continued in that vein, they'd end up brushing everything aside and getting married right away. Because she didn't want that to happen, she was happy to have a third person around. She was following, one might say, a deep design but, naturally enough, Shijun couldn't see that. He was just getting rather cross.

The factory had changed its policy and now provided lunch for its employees. The two of them had been used to going to little restaurants on a daily basis, but Manzhen urged him to save his money, so now they ate at work, and thus had fewer opportunities to talk together. Manzhen thought this was for the best, and her manner towards him grew slightly distant. She didn't know that matters of the heart are not that easy to arrange: you can't put feelings in a freezer and expect them to keep, without any change.

On Saturdays, Shijun usually went to her place, but one week he phoned instead, intending to invite her to the cinema. Mrs. Gu answered the phone. "It's Mr. Shen," she called out to Manzhen. They were in the middle of a meal; when Mrs. Gu went back to the table, she put a cover on Manzhen's rice bowl, to keep her food warm. She knew that when the two of them got on the phone, the conversation would not be short.

Manzhen ran off to the phone and indeed did not return for quite some time. Yujin had been wondering what sort of friendship she had with this colleague of hers, and suddenly it was clear to him. He felt disoriented—soft in the head—for allowing himself such wild daydreams after only a few days' acquaintance, when the girl had a sweetheart all along.

Jiemin liked to chatter about school life during a meal; he told his mother every little detail—who got put into detention, who got into a fight with whom—all in a voice pitched high with self-righteous animation. Today he was telling her about a play they'd be performing and his role in it, as an elderly doctor.

"All right, all right," his mother said. "Hurry up and finish your meal."

Jiemin stuffed two more bites into his mouth, and continued: "Ma, you have to come to it. The teacher said this play is really special. He picked the script for us, and it's great, it's a world-famous play!"

Mrs. Gu was not grasping anything he said. She looked him over carefully. "You've got rice on your face."

That took the wind out of his sails. Feeling deflated, he made a halfhearted effort to wipe his mouth.

"It's still there," his mother said.

"He's keeping it for a snack a bit later," quipped his older brother Weimin.

Everyone at the table laughed, except Yujin. He'd been staring into space, and the sudden burst of laughter caught him off guard; he wondered if he'd made a silly slip of some sort. He looked from one face to another, but it was no use—he couldn't figure out what was going on.

That afternoon, Yujin had some business to take care of, so he left right after lunch, and didn't come back for dinner. Shijun and Manzhen had dinner out too, and when they got back, Yujin had just arrived. When they went past his door, they heard laughter inside; Jiemin was getting Yujin to show him how to behave like a doctor. Yujin showed him how to use a stethoscope, and how to take a patient's blood pressure. When Manzhen and Shijun looked in from the doorway, Yujin couldn't go on. "OK, that's all I have to teach you, just these two things." But Jiemin wouldn't let him be. Children always like something new: when Shijun was teaching them to ride a bicycle, he was their favorite, but now that Yujin was here, their affections for Shijun had cooled. Under normal circumstances, this wouldn't have bothered Shijun, but he had grown extra-sensitive; even the children's fondness for Yujin was enough to make him jealous.

Yujin stifled a yawn.

"Jiemin, let's go upstairs," Manzhen urged. "Brother Jin wants to sleep."

"No, no," Yujin protested. "It's still early. I haven't been sleeping well these past few days. I guess I've turned into a country bumpkin, can't sleep when I hear the sound of a car horn."

"Or maybe it's the radio from next door," Manzhen said. "It's really awful, playing all the time."

"I'm just not used to sleeping here," Yujin said with a smile. "I wish I had some books so I could read myself to sleep."

"Oh, I have some. Jiemin, go upstairs and get some of my books."

Jiemin brought a big pile of books from her shelf; some were books that Shijun had given her. She went through them one by one, handing them on to Yujin. "Maybe you've read these already?"

"No, I haven't read any of these. I'm telling you, I'm thoroughly countrified, never get around to reading books." He stood in the lamplight, leafing through a volume.

"Goodness!" Manzhen cried. "This light isn't bright enough. We'll have to change the bulb."

Yujin tried to stop her, but Manzhen insisted on going upstairs for a light bulb. Shijun was at a loose end. He thought about leaving, but that didn't feel right either. He took a book in his palm and flipped through it, scanning a few pages. Jiemin was rattling on about his play; he told Yujin the whole plot.

Manzhen came back with a light bulb. "Shijun, help me move the table over."

Yujin quickly took the table's other edge; they put it under the light fitting, and Manzhen nimbly jumped on top.

"Oh, let me do it!" Yujin protested.

"That's OK, I've got it."

She reached up and unscrewed the light bulb, and the room briefly fell into darkness. In the moment before it grew dark, Yujin saw the heel of Manzhen's foot; he was standing next to the table, so there was no way of avoiding seeing it. That heel was slender and strong, like Manzhen herself. Over the past few days, she'd told him how things were, and he knew she was supporting all seven people in her family. Her constant cheerfulness, the absence of any complaint despite the great burden she carried, impressed him deeply. He'd found that her approach to life was different from other people's: she faced it head on, with a smile. His feelings had shifted; Manlu's loveliness paled by comparison.

The bulb sprang into life, lighting her hands, making her face glow. Manzhen crouched down and jumped off the table.

"Is it bright enough now? But you'll be lying in bed when you read—I don't think it's enough."

"Oh, no, it's absolutely fine. Don't go to any more trouble!"

"Got to do this properly," Manzhen declared. She ran upstairs and came back with a desk lamp. Shijun recognized it as the one from the head of her own bed.

Yujin sat on the edge of the bed, reading in the lamplight. Did he feel an extra warmth in that light? Shijun had been wanting to leave, but feared that would make his displeasure obvious: Manzhen would surely laugh at him for that. His own sense of logic told him his jealousy was groundless. After they were married, she'd be just as attentive to his friends, and he wouldn't object, now would he? He wasn't such an old fogey as that—he wasn't so petty. But much as he tried to reason with himself, it was hard to bear.

Hardest of all was the fact that when he left, he was on a dark street, while they stayed together in the lamplight, like a family.

Mrs. Gu kept a careful eye out, and when she saw Manzhen and Yujin getting along nicely, her hopes began to rise. Shijun seemed to be around less, which made her secretly happy; she thought Manzhen must be pushing him away.

It was Saturday afternoon once more, after lunch, and Mrs. Gu had spread two sheets of newspaper on the table so she could sort through several pecks of rice, picking out the wild seeds and bits of sand. Yujin sat across the table from her, chatting. He said he planned to leave on the Monday, which made her sad.

"We want to go back to our old home town too. We still have some land there, and two little houses. Granny is always saying how much she wants to go home. I've often talked to her about going back, and we were always thinking of your mother. I said we'd go back to the countryside and, in our spare time, put together something to eat and invite her to come and play cards with us; we'd be a bunch of old sisters getting together for fun. We never imagined we wouldn't see her again!" She sighed heavily. "It's a pity there aren't any good schools in the countryside, and it's so hard for the young ones to study there. When they get a bit bigger, they can stay in town in dormitories. Manzhen will be married by then, and Granny and I really will go back home!"

The way she spoke made Yujin feel Manzhen's wedding was quite some way off in the future, and maybe not certain after all. "Isn't Second Sister engaged?" he asked with a little smile.

"No," said Mrs. Gu, keeping her voice low. "She doesn't have anyone. That Mr. Shen comes around a lot, but it's not at all clear that Manzhen will take up with someone like that—someone about whom we know so little."

Yujin caught the hint, and knew that Mrs. Gu was on his side. But what about Manzhen? Was her relationship with Mr. Shen as platonic as that? Yujin had his doubts. But it's always easier to believe what one wants to believe, and Yujin was no exception. His heart was stirred.

The bitterness and frustration he'd been feeling were fully equal to Shijun's.

Shijun didn't come that afternoon, nor did he telephone. Manzhen wondered if he were ill, then thought he was probably busy and would come later in the day. She stayed in her room, leaning on the windowsill and looking out at the street. After a long while, she walked into the next room, quite dispirited.

"Aren't you going to the pictures?" her mother asked. "Brother Jin is leaving on Monday. You should take him out to see something."

"No, let me invite you!" Yujin said. "I've been here in Shanghai all this time, and haven't seen a single film!"

"I remember you used to love them. Why did you lose interest in them?"

"Films are addictive. Once you start watching them, you want to watch them all the time. But I haven't seen any these past few years, out there in the countryside, and that broke the habit."

"There's one you have to see. But I don't know if it's still playing." Manzhen looked through the newspaper, flipping the pages back and forth, but the one with film advertisements was missing. Leaning over the table, she folded up a corner of the spread on which her mother was sorting rice.

"This is an old newspaper," her mother said.

"Oh? Isn't this today's paper?" Manzhen smiled, and pulled out the sheet beneath.

"OK, OK," Mrs. Gu said. "Go ahead and take it. I'm due for a rest anyway. This rice is no good, it's full of sand. I can't see straight anymore." She cleared the table, and went out.

Manzhen studied the page till she found the listing she wanted. "Today's the last day," she said to Yujin. "You really have to see this."

"Come with me," he urged.

"I've already seen it."

"If it's as good as you say, it's worth seeing again."

"Now you're trying to trick me! No, I'm staying at home today— I'm too tired to go out. I'm not even going to my brother's play."

"He'll be disappointed."

Yujin was holding one of the books she had lent him, a volume he read every night before falling asleep. The paperback spine was curled up, and the cover had come off. "Look at this. What a mess I've made of your book!"

"Oh, it's just an old tattered book, nothing to worry about. Brother Jin, are you really leaving on Monday?"

"Yes. I've already stayed a week longer than I intended." He didn't say he'd stayed longer because of her; he'd been saving that to tell her on the day he left. That way, if she turned him down, he could leave straight away and that would be the end of it. If he instead had to stay on for several days after a refusal, it would be very painful. But now he was reconsidering this plan, due to this unexpected opportunity for private conversation.

He hesitated, then finally spoke. "I'd really like to invite Auntie and your granny to come out to the countryside. Maybe when Weimin and the others are on their spring holiday from school, you can all come and stay a couple of days. We could put you up at the clinic, it's cleaner there. Or do you not get a break then?"

Manzhen shook her head. "We get hardly any holidays."

"Can you not get a few days' leave?"

"I'm afraid not. We don't have a policy that allows it."

Yujin's face fell. "I'm really hoping you can come for a few days. The scenery is nice, and you could get to know me a bit better."

Manzhen suddenly realized that if he went on, he'd ask her to marry him. Overwhelmed by surprise, all she could think was that she had to stop him somehow. She couldn't let him propose: it would only cause needless pain. But try as she might, she couldn't think of anything to say; all she could do was listen to the pounding of her heart. Her head drooped as she slowly scraped the rice chaff together, forming a little mound on the table.

"I'm sure you'll think I'm being too forward—I've known you only a few days, and I'm speaking out of turn. But I just can't help myself. And I can't come to Shanghai very often, so I won't have another chance to see you any time soon."

This is all my fault, Manzhen said to herself. When he came, I felt bad because I had played tricks on him, back when he and Manlu were together—all those naughty pranks. I felt bad, so I was especially nice to him. I wanted to get rid of my guilt, and instead I've made things worse.

Yujin smiled and went on. "Time has flown for me, these past few years—I've been busy all day long, every day, buried in my work. I didn't realize how old I'd grown. I didn't feel my age till I saw you again. Maybe I've met you too late? Is that an issue?"

Manzhen was silent. At last she smiled and said, "It is too late, but not because of that."

Now Yujin fell silent for a moment, but then asked, "Is it because of Mr. Shen?"

Manzhen just kept smiling. She said nothing, but it was a tacit acknowledgment. She was putting it this way on purpose, telling him she had to turn him down because she'd fallen in love with someone else already; she thought it would be less painful for him. But even if she had met him first, and Shijun afterwards, she knew that she'd still prefer Shijun.

Suddenly she saw why Shijun had been so strange lately, why he'd stopped coming around. It was all because of Yujin . . . Shijun had completely misunderstood. Manzhen got angry—how could he be so distrustful? Did he really think she would change her mind so easily? And even if she had changed her mind, hadn't he once promised her, hadn't he once said that he'd fight to the finish to get her back? All those things he'd said that night, in the moonlight—was it all empty talk? He hadn't lifted a finger. The minute a third party appeared, he slipped away with nary a word. What a wretched man!

Manzhen was so busy getting angry with Shijun she almost forgot Yujin was there. Meanwhile, a welter of emotions was churning in Yujin. He sat across from her, utterly forlorn, then stood up and said, "I'm going out for a bit. See you later."

He left, and Manzhen was hit with a second wave of distress. She picked up the book she had lent him, her heart full of grief. The cover was falling off. She rolled the book into a tight cylinder and rapped the table with it.

It was almost time for sunset, and it looked as though Shijun would not come today. That man was too much—how could he be so awful! Now she wanted to go out. She didn't want to sit at home waiting, waiting for someone who wouldn't come.

She went into the next room, where her grandmother was resting on the bed, her joints aching in the clammy, overcast weather. Her mother had put on her spectacles and was doing needlework.

"Jiemin's play is tonight. Are you going, Ma?"

"No, Granny and I are both under the weather. My back is aching and my joints are swollen."

"Well, I'll go. He'll be disappointed if none of us shows up."

"How about Brother Jin?" Granny asked. "You should get him to take you."

"Brother Jin has gone out."

Granny searched Manzhen's face, and Mrs. Gu kept her expression neutral, saying nothing. Manzhen half guessed what the two older women were thinking, but she too said nothing. She simply got her things together, then went to her little brother's school to see the play.

A little while after she had gone out, the telephone rang. Mrs. Gu answered, and it was Yujin. "I won't be back for supper," he said, "so please don't wait for me, Auntie. I'm at a friend's house, and he wants me to stay here, so I won't be back tonight." He sounded cheerful enough, but it was a forced cheerfulness. It was obvious to Mrs. Gu that Manzhen had rebuffed him. He was embarrassed, and now was staying somewhere else.

As if Mrs. Gu's distress weren't great enough already, Granny started to nag, asking for all the details. "He's staying at a friend's place? What's this all about? And Manzhen went out by herself. Did those young people have a tiff? They were fine a moment ago—I heard them laughing and talking."

Mrs. Gu heaved a frosty sigh. "Who knows? Manzhen's temper—it wears one out, it does. Well, let's not bother about her anymore!"

Having decided not to fret over Manzhen, she cast about in her mind for something else to think about, and remembered her eldest daughter. The last time Manlu had come to see them, she'd wept and sobbed when she told her mother about her marital problems; it had been quite a while since then without any word from her, and that was rather worrying.

Mrs. Gu phoned Manlu and asked her how she was feeling. Manlu could tell, from her mother's tone, that she was thinking of paying her a visit. Ever since the time Manzhen had come to see her and all that trouble with Hongtsai had broken out, Manlu had decided not to let her family members come to her house: she would go to them instead. And so she said, "I'm going out tomorrow, I'll come and see you then."

Mrs. Gu gasped, thinking how awkward it would be if she came while Yujin was still there. "Tomorrow's not good. Come later, in a few days' time."

Manlu thought that strange. "Why?"

Mrs. Gu didn't want to go into things over the phone, so she spoke vaguely. "I'll tell you when I see you."

This stumbling reply only whetted Manlu's curiosity. She was bored anyway, staying at home by herself in her lonely boudoir; she went to her old home that very evening in the car, to find out what was going on.

All the younger children were at the school play, leaving their mother and grandmother to eat dinner by themselves, then sit in the lamplight sorting rice. Manlu suddenly appeared, frightening the life out of Mrs. Gu; she was afraid there had been a big row, and Manlu was running home to them. She searched her daughter's face, found no sign of tears, but couldn't put her fears to rest. "Is something wrong?"

"Oh, nothing's wrong. I've been wanting to come and see you, and you said tomorrow's no good, so I came today."

Before Manlu had even sat down, her grandmother was blurting it all out. "Yujin has come to Shanghai, didn't your mother tell you?

He's staying here with us. His mother has passed away, and he came especially to give us the news. Such a wonderful young man—haven't seen him for years, and he's more capable than ever. He came to Shanghai to buy equipment for their clinic. An X-ray machine, no less! He's barely thirty years old, and already the clinic director, but his mother had a hard life, only had a few years of retirement before she died. I was so sad when I heard the news. Of all my nieces and nephews, she was the kindest to me. I never thought she'd be gone before me!" The tears welled up in her eyes.

Manlu heard only the first few bits, about Yujin coming to Shanghai and staying with them. Her ears started ringing the moment she heard that, and nothing else went in. She was so shocked she couldn't quite believe her grandmother. She turned and asked her mother, "*Is Yujin staying here?*"

Mrs. Gu nodded. "He went out earlier. He's staying at a friend's place, and won't be back today."

Only then did Manlu let her breath out. "Is that why you told me not to come tomorrow?"

Mrs. Gu laughed wryly. "Yes! I didn't know what to do, thought it might be a problem if you saw him. It's awkward!"

"Oh, it's no problem."

"Well, good. It's been a long time. And we're relatives anyway, so there's no reason for anyone to gossip—"

Just then, the doorbell rang. Manlu leaned forward in her chair, checking her appearance in the long mirror that hung on the opposite wall. She fluffed up her hair, and regretted coming in such a rush that she hadn't changed her clothes.

"Has Yujin come back?" Granny asked.

"I don't think so," Mrs. Gu said. "He said he wouldn't be back tonight."

"It can't be Manzhen and the children," Granny said. "It's only eight o'clock, they wouldn't be back so soon."

Manlu felt the air in the apartment tightening, as in a theater when the curtain goes up, and she was the female lead, but she wasn't ready, didn't know her lines, and her mind was filled with fog.

Mrs. Gu opened the window and called down, "Who is it?"

A few cold drops splashed on her face. It was raining. The old woman who rented the other downstairs room was standing at the back gate and calling out, "Who's there? Ah! It's Mr. Shen!"

When Mrs. Gu heard it was Shijun, anger washed over her. She turned back to Manlu and said, "Let's go into the next room and sit in there. I don't want to see him. It's that Mr. Shen. It makes me so angry—if it weren't for him—"

Once she'd got that far, she stopped and heaved a big sigh, then told her daughter the whole story. Yujin had come to Shanghai, and since he still hadn't married, Granny thought that giving Manzhen to him would be a good way to make amends for the broken engagement nearly a decade ago. He seemed interested in Manzhen, and Manzhen was getting along fine with him, but there was this Mr. Shen, who happened to have met her first . . .

Shijun had not planned on coming today, but his Saturday visits to Manzhen were a regular part of his life. He fretted all day, stayed away, then arrived in the evening. The darkness was thick in the stairwell; usually, Manzhen would have turned on the upstairs light by the time he'd got this far, but tonight there was no one to do it for him. Apparently she wasn't at home. He felt his way through the gloom, and when he reached the half-landing, the floor was hot under his feet. Someone had set a coal brazier there, and a simmering pot of stew—kicking it over would be no fun at all. That gave him a fright. He crept forward even more cautiously. When he got to the upper floor, he found Granny sitting alone at the newspaper-strewn table, picking through the rice in the lamplight. Something about the scene made him uneasy. The old lady now saw him as her beloved great-nephew's rival, which made for an abrupt change of attitude on her part. Never in his life had Shijun been received so coldly. He forced himself to smile and offer a polite greeting. She looked up, pulled her face into a smile, grunted in reply, then went back to rice-sorting.

"Has Manzhen gone out?" he asked.

"Yes."

"Where did she go?"

"I don't know. Maybe to the cinema?"

Shijun now recalled that when he'd passed the lower room, the one used by Yujin, the light was off. Yujin too had gone out: they must have gone to the pictures together.

A woman's coat was draped across a chair and a handbag lay on the table, so apparently they had a female guest. Could it be Manzhen's older sister? He vaguely recalled seeing a car parked by the gate below.

Shijun had planned to take his leave right away, but the rain was falling harder now. He'd not brought a raincoat, and it would be hard to get a pedicab. He was trying to decide what to do when a gust of wind rattled the open window, making quite a racket. Granny hurried over to close the window, and the door to the next room blew open. Mrs. Gu was in there, and every word she said came through clearly: "If it weren't for that, she could marry Yujin. Just think! Then she wouldn't have to work so hard. And Granny's been longing to go back to her village, it would please her no end. We're different branches of the same family anyway, so it's not like we'd be depending on them more than we should."

The other woman said something inaudible to him—probably telling Mrs. Gu to keep her voice down—and the conversation faded to a murmur.

Granny closed the window clasp and turned around, her expression unchanged. It looked as though she hadn't heard anything, but it was hard to tell if it was deafness or mere pretense. Shijun gave her a quick nod and muttered his goodbye. Never mind the rain—hammers could be falling from the sky, and he'd still be racing out into the open air.

Impatience burned in him, but once he stepped into the black stairwell, he had to feel his way carefully; he longed to rush out in a fury, and the impossibility of doing that only increased his frustration. There in the darkness he thought to himself, Her mother's not to blame for judging people this way—after all, Yujin has an established career and real status in the world, whereas I've barely got started, and no one can tell how I will turn out. Manzhen does admire him, but she feels we've got a secret agreement and doesn't want to break it, even though we're not formally engaged. Are those two regretting they didn't meet earlier? Well, I'm not going to cause her pain on that account.

He steadied his heart, pulling himself in line with this new idea. When he reached the bottom of the stairs, he saw the old woman tenant from the ground floor scrubbing wash-rags in the kitchen.

"Oh, Mr. Shen," she said. "It's raining so hard out there—didn't you ask them for an umbrella? I've got one here. Why don't you take it?"

This old woman, someone he barely knew, was offering him the warmth of human kindness—which, at this moment, only made him feel the cold more acutely. Forcing a smile, he went through the back door and into the steady rain.

Back upstairs, Granny went into the next room. "He's gone." She paused briefly. "It's raining hard now. Manzhen and the others will get soaked."

When Granny came in, Mrs. Gu stopped talking. The three women, three generations together, sat in silence and listened to the dripping rain.

Mrs. Gu had just finished telling Manlu her woes. She told her daughter every last detail of the story about Manzhen and Yujin, holding nothing back, because Manlu had her own husband and she'd married well, rising high above the treetops, whereas Yujin had stayed unmarried, all on her account. Dispatching her younger sister to comfort him was a splendid solution, wasn't it? Mrs. Gu was certain her eldest daughter would approve.

But in fact Manlu was shocked and angry. What made her angriest was hearing her mother assume that she, Manlu, had joined the family's elder generation, and could be included in discussions regarding the children's marriages. It was as if none of it could touch on her directly. She'd lost her right to be jealous. Her mother was such a busybody—what made her think she could match her sister with Yujin, when Manzhen already had someone? It would only put Yujin through the wringer again. She knew that if Yujin had fallen for Manzhen, she herself was the prime object of his affection, given the sisterly resemblance. That poor man—still chasing an illusion!

Her heart was touched to the core. She had to see him and warn him, tell him not to be a fool for love. She told herself she had no other motive, wanted only to see him for a moment and set him on the right path. But who could say whether she still embraced some wild hope, especially since Hongtsai was being so cruel, making her life miserable.

She couldn't very well say anything in front of her grandmother, so she stood up and took her leave. Her mother went downstairs with her, and when they passed Yujin's room, Manlu reached in and turned on the light. "I want to take a look," she said. It was her old bedroom, but the furniture had been replaced with a temporary set—just a simple bed, table and pair of chairs. It made the room look empty. Yujin's towel hung on the chair, his hat was on the table, along with his fountain pen and a comb. Her mother had washed and folded his underclothes, and set them on his bed. Next to the pillow was a book. Manlu stood in the lamplight staring at it all. A few years along life's road and he'd become a stranger to her. This had been her room for all those years, and now it was an unfamiliar place. She felt herself floating away, as if she were dreaming.

"He's leaving the day after tomorrow," Mrs. Gu said. "Granny said we should make some extra dishes and throw him a little party, but we don't know if he'll be back tomorrow."

"All his things are here. If he doesn't come tomorrow, he'll come the next day to collect them. Call me when he comes. I want to see him—there's something I want to tell him."

That gave Mrs. Gu a good scare. "Is that a good idea? What if your husband finds out? That would only cause trouble!"

"I'm not doing anything underhand. What's there to be afraid of?"

"Well, of course that's so. But if *he* finds out, he'll pick away at it, looking for a reason to find fault with you!"

"Stop worrying, will you?" Manlu snapped impatiently. "Anyway, no one's going to drag you into it!" It was hard to explain, but every time she talked with her mother, even though they both meant well, the conversation ended with Manlu losing her temper.

Yujin did not come the next day. He came the following afternoon, just before his train's departure, and only to collect his things.

Manlu had not waited for her mother to telephone; she came early in the day and had lunch. Mrs. Gu was full of foreboding, fearing that if the two of them met, the flame would reignite and the crack in her daughter's marriage would split wide open. But her daughter had never been one to listen to warnings; there was no way to hold her back. Nor could one simply stick close to her, in order to prevent a tête-à-tête; trying to keep tabs on her would be only too obvious.

Yujin arrived and was in his room packing, when he looked up and saw a slender wisp of a woman in a purple stretch-silk cheong-sam. He didn't know when she had come in, but here she was, leaning on the rail at the head of his bed and gazing at him with a slight smile. Yujin flinched with surprise, then realized it was Manlu—and flinched again. He couldn't think of anything to say, but as he looked at her, his heart sank.

At last he mustered a smile, and gave her a slight nod. But he still didn't know what to say, and his head felt as empty as a clean bowl, devoid of words. The two of them stood there silently, letting time wash by; it rippled through them like water.

It was Manlu who spoke first. "Are you leaving soon?"

"The two o'clock train."

"Do you have to go?"

"I've been here almost a month already."

Manlu rested her elbows on the bed rail. She lowered her eyelids and ran one hand over the other. "You shouldn't have come here, you know." Her voice was very soft. "You hardly ever have a chance to visit Shanghai—you should have gone off and enjoyed the city while you were here." She paused. "I hope you will forget all about me."

The tack she had taken made it hard for Yujin to come up with a good reply. She thought he was still in love with her. He couldn't refute that, directly.

After a moment's thought, he said, "There's no point in bringing up the past. I've heard you have a good home now, and that is a great comfort to me."

Manlu laughed lightly. "Yes, you've heard them say that. They see the surface only, and don't know how I feel."

Yujin didn't dare reply to this. He was afraid that if she kept talking, she'd lay out all her troubles, and the conversation would grow even more intense. Another long silence fell. It took all his efforts to keep from looking at his watch. He noticed her dress, and wondered if she'd chosen the color by chance. She used to have a deep-purple silk cheongsam that he liked very much. There's an "elder sister in a purple dress" in a story written by Bing Hsin, and Yujin had once written Manlu a letter in which he addressed her thus. She was older than him, by two months.

Manlu smiled as she looked him over. "You haven't changed. Have I?"

"People are always changing," he said pleasantly. "And I've changed too, especially my temperament. Maybe it's because I'm older, but when I think of the past, I laugh at myself for being so childish."

He was rejecting their whole past. Those few memories that she cherished—he was almost ready to deny them. The purple dress started to itch ferociously, till her whole body was on fire. She wanted to rip the dress off, tear it to shreds.

Fortunately, her mother came in just then, carrying a food basket. "Yujin, you didn't come back yesterday—Granny made a few special dishes, to give you a good send-off, but since you didn't come yesterday we've packed it all up so you can eat it on the train."

Yujin thanked her politely.

"I'll ask Mrs. Liu, from downstairs, to hail a taxi for you."

"Oh, I'll take care of that myself," Yujin said hurriedly.

Mrs. Gu helped him carry his luggage. He gave Manlu a rushed goodbye, and Mrs. Gu walked him out, all the way to the mouth of the alley.

Manlu was alone in the room, tears falling like streams of sand. The room itself had not changed since she was last here, two days earlier: his towel still hung on the chair, though his hat was gone from the table. But when she tried to recall how she'd felt under that lamplight—all those warm, tender feelings—it gave her a jolt, as if she'd stepped into some other world.

The book near his pillow was still there, turned to some particular page. She hadn't noticed it yesterday, but there were quite a few novels on the table too, all of them her sister's books. And the desk lamp—that was her sister's too. Second Sis had been very sweet to Yujin, lending him her books, lending him her lamp, so he could lie comfortably in bed and read. All that sweetness of hers was easy to imagine. And their mother had encouraged her, looked for ways to send her in with tea, or even just plain water—all day long, the typical landlord's daughter, finding reasons to run to his room, waltzing back and forth in front of him. And because she was young, people thought her a guileless innocent, all her motives perfectly pure, no matter how much she pranced around. Manlu hated her, hated her to the bone. She was so young, with a bright future stretching out in front of her, not like her older sister, whose life was already over. The only thing Manlu had were memories of her time with Yujin; stark and lonely though they might be, those memories were worth keeping. But now her sister had stepped on them, smashed them to pieces, till they lodged like slivers in her heart. She couldn't touch those memories again—if she did, her heart would break.

Her sister would not let her hold on to them, those dream-like memories, in peace. Why was she so cruel? She had her own sweetheart. Her mother had said the man was feeling jealous. Maybe that was Manzhen's plan—to make him jealous. No real reason—she just wanted to make her sweetheart jealous.

"I've been good to her," Manlu thought to herself. "And this is how she repays my kindness. Never a thought for what I've done for her. For whom did I sell my youth, if not her? If it hadn't been for them, I'd have married Yujin long ago. I am a fool. Such a fool."

She sobbed uncontrollably.

When Mrs. Gu came back, she found her daughter leaning over the bed, crying so hard her shoulders heaved. Mrs. Gu stood by her side in shock, then after a long while said, "Didn't I warn you? But you wouldn't listen. No good could come of seeing him. Look how upset you are!"

The sun shone on the floor, thick and yellow. A room from which someone has gone to catch a train always feels a bit messy. Two old sheets of newspaper wrapping were scattered on the floor. Mrs. Gu picked them up, one by one. "Don't be sad," she said. "Things are better this way! And here I was afraid that if you saw Yujin just when you're so unhappy at home, getting into all these fights with your husband, you'd feel something for him again—it's good that you do understand how things are!"

Manlu made no reply. The sobs came in bursts, wrenching her whole body.

9

Walking back to his room that windy, rainy night, Shijun decided never to go to Manzhen's place again. But it was a decision that couldn't last. After all, it was her mother whose talk had needled him; Manzhen herself had had nothing to do with it. He couldn't simply walk away, not after they'd come so far together. Even if she had changed her mind, they'd have to meet and talk it out.

He got this clear in his mind, but did nothing about it the next day—which meant another sleepless night. On Monday, he went to the factory office to look for her. Talking with her in the office was harder to manage now that Shuhui had gone and his replacement had taken over. Shijun had stopped frequenting the office, to avoid attracting attention. When he went this time, he simply said, "Let's go out for dinner tonight, at that coffee shop near the Yangs'. Then you can go straight there for your tutoring job."

"I'm not tutoring tonight," she said. "They told me yesterday that the children are going to a wedding."

"That's great—we'll have more time to chat. We could go somewhere else if you'd rather."

"Let's go to my house. You haven't come by in a long time."

Shijun thought for a moment. "What do you mean? I was there two days ago."

Manzhen was surprised. "Really? Why didn't they tell me?"

Shijun said nothing. Manzhen guessed, from his reaction, that he'd been treated unfairly. This wasn't the time to ask, so she smiled and said, "I happened to be out that evening. Jiemin's class was putting on a play, and it was his first time on stage. I had to go and cheer him on. We got soaked by that big rainstorm on our way home.

Someone got the sniffles, and now we're passing the cold around between us. Let's not go to a restaurant tonight. I should stay away from oily food. My throat is raspy as it is!"

Indeed, her voice had a wispy softness that only tugged harder at him. He agreed to go to her house for dinner.

He arrived at dusk. As he started up the stairs, the light on the upper floor went on. Her mother had flicked the switch. A coal brazier and cooking pot sat on the landing, just as they had two days ago; the simmering soup filled the air with the thick, warm scent of ham. Shijun often had ham soup at their house; Mrs. Gu, knowing he liked it, had prepared it especially for him. This sudden change of attitude must mean Manzhen had said something to her—Shijun was a bit embarrassed.

Mrs. Gu seemed embarrassed too. She gave him a big grin as he came in. "Manzhen's in there," she said, and went off to tend to the soup. Shijun went in and saw Granny shelling peas. Granny gave him a knowing smile, and gestured towards Manzhen's room. "Manzhen's in there," she said. All this clearing of the way made Shijun a little uneasy.

He went into the next-door room and found Manzhen leaning over the windowsill, looking out at the alley. He stole up behind her and placed a hand over hers. "What are you looking for, gazing out of the window like this?"

Manzhen gasped. "You scared me! I've been standing here for ages—how did I miss you coming in?"

"Maybe you blinked." He kept his hand over hers.

"Why haven't you been in such a long time?"

"I've been busy."

She made a face at him.

"It's true!" he said. "You remember Shuhui's little sister, the one who's been at school in the interior? She's come to Shanghai to take some entrance exams, and she's working on her maths. You know Shuhui's not living at home now, so the job fell to me. Every evening, after dinner, I tutor her for two hours." He paused. "Where is Yujin?"

"Gone already. He left earlier today."

"Oh."

He sat down on Manzhen's bed and fiddled with her desk lamp, switching it on and off. Manzhen slapped his hand. "Don't do that! You'll break it. Tell me—when you were here the other day, what did my mother say to you?"

"Nothing."

"You're not being frank with me. I wasn't being frank with her, and that's why you got treated badly."

"I was? When?"

"Say no more! Anyway, I've explained things to her, and now she knows she was rude to someone who deserves better."

"Well," he said with a smile. "She probably thinks my intentions towards you are not sincere."

"What? Is that what you heard her say?"

"No, no. I didn't even see her. Your sister came that day, didn't she?"

Manzhen nodded.

"They were in here talking, and I heard your mother say—" He broke off, unwilling to reveal how calculating her mother had been. "I don't remember clearly. Anyway, the point was that Yujin would make an ideal son-in-law."

"Well, maybe he's an old lady's idea of a perfect son-in-law."

Shijun looked at her. "I thought he was an all-round favorite here."

Manzhen stared at him. "I wasn't going to say this, but since you've raised the subject—you owe me an explanation!"

"Huh?"

"You thought I liked Yujin—right? You have no faith in me."

"What? No! I was just teasing you. I know it's just that you think he's a wonderful man. And a man of strong feelings. After all these years of loyalty to Manlu, how could he, in the space of a few days, turn around and fall in love with her younger sister? It's simply not possible."

There was still a sour tinge to his words when he spoke of Yujin. Manzhen had been planning to tell him that Yujin had proposed to her, to banish any suspicions he might have. But now she didn't want to. She too thought it odd that Yujin had fallen in love with her, after all those years of "faithfulness" to her sister, but Shijun's tone made it sound ridiculous. She didn't want anyone laughing at Yujin. She'd shield him from that, at least.

Shijun saw her biting her tongue, and gave her a searching glance. He too fell silent. Then, after a long pause, he laughed. "Your mother's right, you know."

"About what?"

"Getting married right away. If we go on like this, misunderstandings are bound to crop up."

"Maybe from your side. But I don't get suspicious. I could mention, for instance, this sister of Shuhui's—"

"Shuhui's sister? She's barely fourteen years old!"

"Well, I haven't been poking my head around corners, trying to find out. Hey—don't you go thinking I'm serious!"

"But maybe you are," he teased.

Manzhen was starting to lose her temper. "I'm not talking to you anymore!" she said, whirling away.

Shijun caught her by the hand. "Let's be serious then."

"Haven't we already decided to wait a few years?"

"Why, really? You can still work after we're married, can't you?"

"But what if—we have a baby? Once we have children, I can't go out and work, and you'll be stuck supporting two households. I've seen plenty of cases like that, a man supporting his family, and his in-laws too. He's so desperate for money, he'll take any job he can find. What happens to his career then?" She paused. "Now what on earth are you smirking about?"

"How many children should we have, do you think?"

"Ugh! I've got nothing more to say to you!"

"No, really. Look—I can work hard too. That's how people get by. You should try to see things from my point of view. Don't you think I feel bad, watching you wear yourself out like this?"

"I'm fine—don't worry about me."

On this point, she was adamant. He'd tried, so many times, to talk her out of it. His spirits fell, and he was silent. Manzhen looked into his face. "You must think I'm terribly cold-hearted," she said, smiling gently at him.

Shijun wrapped her in a sudden embrace. "If I say it's for your sake, you won't do it," he murmured. "But if I say it's all for me, that I'm selfish and I need this, what will you say then?"

She would not answer this question; she pulled away so he couldn't kiss her. "I'm coming down with something," she said. "I don't want you to catch it."

"I'm coming down with something too."

Manzhen laughed. "What a silly you are!"

She slipped her hand out of his and ran into the next room. Her grandmother had got through only half the peas. "Here, let me help you shell them," Manzhen said.

Shijun came out too. There was a desk against the wall, behind Granny's seat, and he leaned against it, pretending to read the newspaper but in fact watching Manzhen, smiling at her all the while.

Manzhen couldn't concentrate on the peas. Her heart stirred, and she thought, We could get married now, and sort things out afterwards. Lots of people have to cope with big households, and they get by, don't they?

She was sunk in thought when her grandmother suddenly cried out, "Whatever are you doing?"

Startled, Manzhen looked up and realized she'd been throwing pea shells on the table, peas on the floor. She blushed and laughed, bending down quickly to pick up the peas. "I'm just like Guo the Idiot, the one who made things worse, the more he tried to help!"

"I've never seen you like this before," Granny said. "Not even looking at what you're doing!"

"I'll just do a few more. My nails are so short for typing, there's almost nothing left. Even shelling these peas makes my fingers sore."

"Aw—I knew you'd be no use!" Granny said, pulling the peas away from her.

Manzhen had started to change her mind, but Shijun didn't know that and he was still downcast. After dinner, Granny took out a pack of cigarettes and offered them to him. She'd found them in a drawer when she was cleaning out the lower room; the children had wanted to play at smoking, but their mother wouldn't let them. Shijun casually took one and started smoking it. After Granny had gone, he asked Manzhen if the cigarettes were Yujin's. He remembered hearing Yujin say that in the countryside, these Fairy brand cigarettes were considered top-notch; even when he was in Shanghai, he went on buying them, out of habit. Which is to say, he was in the habit of economizing.

Shijun was smoking Yujin's cigarettes and asking Manzhen about him—but Manzhen didn't want to talk about Yujin. When she'd arrived home that afternoon and found that he'd already gone, taking his luggage and heading straight to the train, she knew he was avoiding her. Chances were, she'd never see him again. She'd refused him, and in so doing had lost him as a friend. There was nothing she could do about it, but still it made her sad.

Shijun saw her sitting there with a long face. He remembered all the times she'd talked to him about Yujin, and talked too long; now she wouldn't speak of him at all. Something must have happened between them. She wasn't telling. And he wouldn't ask.

His spirits remained low, and he went home early, crying off by saying he had to tutor Shuhui's sister.

Not long after he'd gone, the doorbell rang again. Granny and Mrs. Gu, thinking it was someone coming to see their tenant, didn't respond, but then they heard footsteps on the stairs. "Who's there?" they called out.

"It's me," Shijun called. "I'm back again!"

That gave them all a shock, Manzhen included. His feelings must be running high, to make him come twice in one day. She felt he was going too far, acting like this in front of her family. It was very embarrassing—but at the same time, it made her strangely happy.

Shijun came to a stop before he'd reached the doorway. "Have you gone to bed already?" he asked.

"No, no," Mrs. Gu said. "It's early yet."

He walked into the room, and everyone looked at him with half-teasing smiles. But when she saw that he was carrying a suitcase, Manzhen was surprised; she looked at his face again, and knew that something was wrong, despite his seeming good cheer.

"I'm going back to Nanking, on the night train," he said. "I thought I'd come here first and let you know."

"Why are you going so suddenly?" Manzhen asked.

"There was a telegram just now, saying that my father's ill and I'm needed at home."

He stood there with the suitcase still in his hand, as if he didn't plan to sit down. Manzhen too was numb with confusion and stood there with a shocked expression on her face. It was Mrs. Gu who asked what time the train was leaving.

"Eleven o'clock," Shijun said.

"Well then, there's still time. Come in and have a seat!"

Shijun sat down at last, slowly unwound his scarf and set it on the table.

Mrs. Gu said something about brewing tea and went out; she gathered up the children and told them to come with her. Granny went out also, leaving the two of them alone.

"Did the telegram say what's wrong with him?" Manzhen asked.

"My mother sent it. It must be fairly serious, or she wouldn't know anything about it. My father lives at his other place, you know."

Manzhen nodded.

Shijun saw her sitting in silence, and thought she must be worrying that he'd be gone a long while. "I'll come back as soon as I can," he said. "I can't miss too many days at the factory."

Manzhen nodded again.

The last time he'd been to Nanking, they didn't yet know each other well, so this would be their first real parting. After a long moment, Manzhen finally said, "I don't know your address there." She looked for pen and paper.

"You don't need it now," Shijun said. "I'll write as soon as I get there, and put the return address on the envelope."

"You should give it to me anyway."

Shijun leaned over the desk; she leaned from the side, watching him write. They felt the chill of loneliness.

When Shijun had finished writing, he picked up the paper and looked at it. "I'll be back in a few days. There won't be any need for letter-writing."

Manzhen said nothing. She'd taken his scarf from the table and was running it through her hands.

Shijun looked at his watch, and pulled himself up. "I'd better go. Don't see me out—you're coming down with something."

"I'm fine."

She put on her coat, and went out with him. The iron gate at the end of the alley wasn't latched yet, but the street was almost deserted, and there weren't any cabs. Most of the houses were dark, but yellow lamplight pooled all around one shop that was still going strong, a purveyor of hot water, with its milky-white steam billowing out from beneath a thick black pot-lid. It was a warm spot, a place that gave people a tender feeling when they walked past late in the evening. The weather had turned cold and the nights were getting sharp.

"I don't have much of a connection to my father, but last time I went back and saw him, I felt sad for some reason."

Manzhen nodded. "I remember you said that."

"My biggest worry is the family's financial future. None of this is unexpected, and yet my thinking is completely scrambled."

Manzhen reached out and took his hand. "I wish I could go with you. I could hide away somewhere, and you could come and see me when something happens and you need someone to talk to. That would keep your spirits up."

Shijun looked at her and smiled. "You see? Even you have to admit it would be easier if we did get married. Then we could go together, and you wouldn't have to stay here all alone, missing me."

Manzhen gave him a look. "If you can talk like that, you can't be very worried after all."

A cab approached from down the street. Shijun hailed it, and the driver crossed over to meet him. Shijun suddenly thought of something. "They won't read my mail," he said, his voice low and urgent, "so you can write . . . long letters."

Manzhen giggled. "Didn't you just say I won't need to write, since you'll be back so soon? Now I know you're tricking me!"

Shijun laughed too.

She stood under the street light and watched him go.

The train arrived in Nanking early the next morning. Shijun rushed to his mother's house, but the shop front wasn't open yet. He went in the back door and found the rickshaw driver brushing dust off his vehicle. "Is my mother up yet?" he asked the man.

"Yes, she'll be headed over there very soon." The words "over there" came with a tilt of the head that meant the concubine's house.

That gave Shijun a shock. If she's going there, he thought to himself, Father's condition must be serious. A leaden feeling seeped into his legs.

The rickshaw driver scrambled up the stairs to announce Shijun's arrival, and Mrs. Shen came out smiling. "You got here so fast! I was just saying to your sister-in-law that you'd probably arrive on the noon train, and she should send the driver to meet you then."

Shijun's sister-in-law was eating breakfast porridge with Vim; she got up and told the maid to bring another place setting and some sausage.

"Have some breakfast first, then come with me," his mother said.

"How is Father doing?" Shijun asked.

"He's better now, but he gave us quite a scare two days ago! I had to go and see him, even under these conditions. He looked awful—his tongue was stiff, he couldn't speak properly. He's getting injections every day, and the doctor's orders are for complete rest. He's not out of danger yet. I'm going every day now."

Shijun could not imagine his mother going there on a daily basis, facing the concubine and that witch-like mother of hers. His mother was the sort of woman who could face any hardship, as long as her dignity was not threatened. And her dignity was rooted in the traditional hierarchy: she'd never let a concubine take precedence over her. Nursing a sick husband was her clear duty now, but since someone "over there" was doing that already, her presence must be greatly resented, her path strewn with difficulties. Shijun thought of the detachment with which his mother usually spoke of his father, the coolness in her manner when contemplating the possibility of his falling ill and dying. "I'm past worrying about all the rest," she used to say, half laughing, "but if nothing is set aside for us, what are we going to live on, after he passes away? If it weren't for that, I wouldn't care if he died right now. He might as well be dead, since he never comes here anyway!" Her words still rang in his ears.

After breakfast, the two of them went to his father's. Mrs. Shen rode in her rickshaw and hired another for Shijun. Shijun arrived first, jumped out and rang the bell. A male servant came out, very surprised to see him, and greeted him as "Second Young Master." Shijun went in and saw the concubine's mother in the living room, braiding her granddaughter's hair. A maid knelt on the floor, tying the little girl's shoelaces.

"The one from the Drum Tower is here, is that it?" the old lady said, tugging on the girl's hair. "Stop fidgeting! Your father's sick, you have to behave! Amah Zhou, take her out to play. Don't let her eat anything she shouldn't, you hear?"

"The one from the Drum Tower" must be my mother, Shijun thought. Our house is in Drum Tower District, isn't it? They're using place-names instead of personal titles.

At that moment, "the one from the Drum Tower" herself came in. Shijun let his mother precede him up the staircase. It was the first time he'd seen her through other people's eyes, noticing how heavy and pale she was. Going up those stairs took great effort: she was striving to seem serenely absorbed in her natural, wifely duty.

Shijun had never been upstairs before. The bedroom decor bore traces of the concubine's former occupation—it was full of heavy rosewood furniture—along with a few touches of respectable domesticity, like the curtains in "Scholar's Garden" green over white gauze, and the walls painted light green to match. It had the messiness of a sickroom. Hsiao-tung lay alone on the double bed, with an iron-frame single bed set up as a nurse's cot beside it. The concubine was bending over him so that his head was almost buried in her bosom as she fed him kumquat juice with a little silver spoon—a sensuous display, though it was hard to say whether Hsiao-tung appreciated it. His wife came in, and the concubine raised her eyelids a fraction, offered a brief greeting and went on spooning kumquat juice into him. Hsiao-tung did not open his eyes.

But Mrs. Shen smiled at him and said, "Look who's here!"

"Oh! It's Second Young Master!" the concubine said.

"Father," Shijun said.

Hsiao-tung labored to reply. "Oh, you're here. How long is your leave from work?"

"Don't talk," Mrs. Shen said. "Didn't the doctor tell you not to talk?"

Hsiao-tung made no response. The concubine pressed the spoon against his lips, but he shook his head impatiently and set his jaw.

"You don't want any more?" she asked with a smile. His refusal only led to a further display of tender care: she pulled out the snowy-white handkerchief tucked into her dress and wiped his mouth, then plumped the pillows and smoothed the quilt.

"When are you headed back?" Hsiao-tung asked Shijun again.

"Don't you worry," Mrs. Shen said. "He's not leaving. Please don't try to talk."

Hsiao-tung fell silent again.

Shijun could scarcely recognize his father. Of course it was because he'd lost weight, but also because his father was lying in bed, without his glasses—Shijun wasn't used to that.

When she heard that he'd come on the night train, the concubine quickly offered him a seat on the sofa near the window. "Second Young Master, do come and sit down. You haven't had any rest at all."

Shijun pulled out a newspaper and started reading, Mrs. Shen sat in a chair near Hsiao-tung's bed, and the room became very quiet.

Downstairs, a child burst out crying, and the concubine's mother called up to her daughter, "Come and take him, will you, please?"

The concubine was just then using a little glass rod to press out kumquat juice. "One above, another below," she grumbled lightly. "Two masters but there's only one of me! The older one gets unhappy if anyone else makes the juice for him—he says their fingers aren't clean enough."

She bustled about, busy with this and that, and a short while later a maid came in with a big platter of fried noodles, two bowls and two sets of chopsticks. The concubine came in behind the maid, and invited Mrs. Shen and her son to eat.

"I'm not hungry," Shijun said. "I had something at home just now."

"Try just a little," the concubine urged him.

Shijun saw that his mother wasn't budging. Eating nothing at all would be too rude—he picked up the chopsticks and ate a little. His father lay on the bed, his eyes taking in the simple pleasure of watching his son eat. His lips curved in a smile. Shijun sat next to his father's sickbed eating noodles that slipped down easily—despite the cold, hard lump in his chest.

At lunchtime a table was set up for them in the sickroom. Shijun sat in that room the whole day long, and his mother wanted him to go back so he could rest, but Hsiao-tung said, "Shijun's staying here tonight."

That did not please the concubine. "Oh, my!" she said. "But we haven't got a proper bed for him. I don't think he'll be comfortable here!"

Hsiao-tung pointed to the little iron-frame bed she had been using.

"You mean he should sleep here? But you'll need someone to tend to you at night, and he's not used to hopping out of bed at all hours—you'll wear him out!"

Hsiao-tung said nothing.

The concubine looked at him carefully, and had to relent. "Well then—Second Young Master, if something comes up, just call for me. I'll sleep lightly, in case you need me."

She supervised the rearrangement of the bedding: her things went to the bed that she'd share with two of her children, and Shijun was given a fresh quilt. "So sorry to put you through this," she said to Shijun, "but at least we've got a nice, new quilt for you."

The bedroom walls glowed apple-green in the lamplight. The whole room was thick with the sense of marital intimacy, leaving Shijun to wonder how in the world he'd landed here. The concubine ran in and out all night long, full of loving concern, bringing her husband water and medicine, helping him relieve himself. Shijun was embarrassed; putting him in the sickroom's spare bed was only making things more difficult for her. He'd force his eyes open, only to hear her say, "Don't get up, Second Young Master. Let me take care of things. I'm used to it." She was startled out of sleep by the slightest sound and ran in with her hair half-undone and her sleeping gown half-unbuttoned, with the red silk chemise showing through. Shijun was afraid to look at her—he'd suddenly recalled the story of the Phoenix Pavilion and the beauty who cast alluring glances at the son while nursing the ailing father, in order to sow division between them. Was she trying to make him go after her? This concubine had always seemed to him a crafty, scheming woman. But then he realized she probably was worried about that iron box, the one in the corner of the room; she feared there would be some midnight transfer of property from father to son, and kept running in to check on things.

When Mrs. Shen returned home that day, she worried about Shijun's lack of appetite due, no doubt, to the unfamiliar food at that place over there. The next day she brought two dishes from her own kitchen: steeped lettuce hearts and vegetarian goose—a kind of thin, chewy tofu cut into strips. The lettuce was a gourmet dish. The lettuce hearts were marinated till they turned translucent green, then stuffed, one by one, with a bright red dried rose.

"I noticed you had several of these at breakfast yesterday," she said to Shijun with a smile. "I thought you might like some more."

Hsiao-tung saw them and wanted some too. He was eating rice porridge, a perfect complement to steeped vegetables—it would make a tasty meal indeed. "It's been so long since I've had this!"

That made the concubine angry.

Hsiao-tung's spirits rose greatly over the next few days. His accountant came to consult with him—even though Hsiao-tung was sick, the staff needed to get instructions from him because he kept the books in his head. The man sat at his boss's bedside, bowed over to hear the confidential information relayed to him in whispers.

"Father," Shijun said when the accountant had left, "I think you shouldn't tire yourself out with work. If the doctor finds out, he'll scold you for sure."

"But what can I do?" Hsiao-tung sighed. "I have to keep at it. This illness has shown me how false my hopes have been—I can't rely on any of them!"

Shijun knew his father's temperament: further chiding would only provoke further complaint. He'd say he had no choice but to bury himself in work—each day's earnings depended on the effort made that very day. He couldn't stop, he had to feed his family. But in fact, he didn't have to operate from such a stressful position, as if he were still living hand-to-mouth. He was making a mistake common to those in business: he treated money as an all-consuming end and devoted all his energy to it. The result was that he lived besieged by constant, nagging worry.

In this house, the telephone was set up in the bedroom, and Shijun took a few calls for his father. Once when someone was needed to conduct a transaction, Hsiao-tung told his son to handle it for him.

"Do you really think he can he manage it?" Mrs. Shen asked.

"He's been out and about in the world," his father said, smiling. "Surely he can handle a small matter like this!"

Shijun took care of several transactions for his father, who said nothing to him directly, but praised him to his mother: "He does a good job. Thinks it through carefully." Mrs. Shen then found an opportunity to pass the compliment on to her son. She could hardly contain her glee. Shijun had always been awkward around people, a stranger to the world of business; he hadn't developed a good rapport with his Shanghai colleagues, and his career had suffered as a result—which was frustrating for him. But here in Nanking, he was the son of Mr. Shen, which meant doors were already open to him and people were accommodating. It was all very gratifying.

Gradually, the decision-making shifted over to him. The accountant would come to ask the old boss about something, and Hsiao-tung would say, with evident delight, "Go and ask Second Young Master! He's the one managing things now, not me. Go and ask him about it!"

Shijun suddenly had become an important person. As soon as she saw him, the concubine's mother would say, "Second Young Master, you're getting too thin! All that work you're doing—my, what a good son you are!"

And the concubine herself would say, "Now that he's here, things are much better for the old master. It takes so much strain off him!"

Then her mother would say, "Second Young Master, please make yourself at home, and if you want anything, you just need to ask. The lady of the house has been through such a scare that she hasn't been able to look after you properly."

The two of them, working in unison, plied him with polite phrases, but behind his back they were aghast with fear. "If the old man dies now," the daughter said to her mother, "we're lost! The whole business has been taken over by someone else. No wonder people say a businessman is heartless; all he cares about is his money and his son. That is so true! Here am I, a wife to him for all these years—ten years and counting—and he hasn't made any provision for me."

"Control your temper, I say. Try a little gentleness. He's taken good care of you so far, and he's even a bit afraid of you. Remember that time he ran off to Shanghai to see some dancing girl? You threw a fit, and that ended it."

But the situation this time was harder to handle. The concubine considered her options and decided to make her appeal through the children. That same day, she fetched her youngest son and brought him to see his father. "He's been going on and on at me," she told Hsiao-tung with a smile. "He keeps saying he wants his father. So, you see—Father's right here! Didn't you say you wanted to see him?"

The child didn't know what to do; he turned dumb and shy, stood at the bedside with his head hanging, staring at the quilt. Hsiao-tung reached out and patted the boy's face, but his heart was sad. A man who's past middle age often feels lonely: everywhere he looks, all he sees are dependants—no one who can support him, no one in whom he can confide. That's why he leaned on Shijun so much.

Shijun had been wanting to go back to Shanghai. He said as much, very softly, to his mother, but she begged him to stay a few more days. Given the precariousness of his father's health, Shijun did not want to upset him. He said no more about leaving, but did say he wanted to stay at his mother's house. Staying at the concubine's was awkward, and the worst of it was the impossibility of carrying on a proper correspondence. Manzhen's letters went to his mother's house, and his mother brought them over to him, but he'd had no opportunity to sit down and write a good long letter in return.

When Shijun told his father he wanted to go back to the other house, the older man nodded. "I want to go too. It's in a quiet neighborhood, a good place to recuperate."

The concubine had a cough from staying up at night, and her day-and-night vigilance, due to her constant fretting lest the old man transfer the strongbox to Shijun, had worn her out completely—her nerves were at breaking-point. Hearing now that Hsiao-tung wanted to leave her house, she turned deathly pale and silent.

Mrs. Shen was dumbstruck too. It took her some moments to recover enough to smile and say, "You're just now starting to get better, won't a move be too tiring?"

"It'll be fine. We'll hire a car, and Shijun and I will ride in it together."

"You mean today?"

Hsiao-tung had been thinking about this a long time but wanted to avoid a fight with the concubine. His plan was to keep quiet right up to the moment of departure and then, once he'd announced his intentions, leave at once. "Can't we do it today?" he said now. "Why don't you head back first and tell them to get the room ready. We'll come along a bit later."

Mrs. Shen agreed, but she and Shijun exchanged glances, each thinking the same thing: his getting out of there was not a done deal.

After Mrs. Shen left, there was a short, sharp laugh from the concubine. "Right then—I'm the one who needs to rest—what a nice way to put it!" The rims of her eyes turned red.

Hsiao-tung closed his own eyes; his face looked very tired.

When he saw the quarrel brewing, Shijun wanted to avoid getting caught in the middle. He jumped up and made his escape by saying he wanted an evening paper and would ask Li Sheng to fetch one. All the servants were upset, whispering urgently to each other.

They must have heard the news already. Shijun paced up and down in the living room.

The maids were calling for the manservant: "The master wants to see Li Sheng."

"He went out to get a paper for Second Young Master," someone replied.

Li Sheng reappeared soon thereafter and brought the paper to Shijun. Then a maid came in. "Li Sheng, the master wants you to call a cab." Shijun got nervous when he heard that. The cab seemed to take a long time; he flipped through the paper, glancing at the same pages several times, till finally he heard the sound of a car horn.

Li Sheng was out in front of the house, telling a maid to go upstairs and report the arrival of the cab. "Why aren't you going?" the woman said. "You're the one who called the cab."

"Go, I tell you!" the man said, his face long and stern. "What are you afraid of?"

The two of them argued back and forth, neither willing to do it. In the end, Li Sheng came into the living room, arms hanging stiffly at his sides, and reported, "Second Young Master, the car is here."

By this time, Shijun had remembered he still had to get his clothes and other things from his father's room, so he went back upstairs. He could hear the concubine's loud voice even before he'd entered the room. "What are you doing? You're taking *that* with you? You're taking it all? How can you do such a thing? Are you going to abandon us, leave us forever? Your own children, the ones you're raising?"

Hsiao-tung's voice was equally tight and angry. "I'm not dead yet, you know. Of course this goes where I go—for convenience's sake!"

"Convenience! This is *not* about convenience!"

There was the sound of a struggle, then a huge crash. Shijun ran into the room and found—to his relief—his father sitting on the sofa, panting hard, accusing the concubine of trying to give him a heart attack. The strongbox was open, and the room was strewn with stock certificates, bank books and signed promissory notes. Apparently he'd tottered over to get something out of the box, and the concubine had got upset and tussled with him, trying to wrest it away. He'd lost his balance but fortunately had not fallen down, though a chair had been knocked over.

The concubine's face was white with fear, her mouth an iron-hard line. "How can you do this to me? I've waited on you hand and foot all through your illness, and now you just take off like this—how fair is that, I ask you?" She collapsed into a chair, head and shoulders pressed into the seat back, and burst out crying.

At this point her mother came in. "Don't take it so hard," she urged, patting her daughter on the shoulder. "Just because he's going now doesn't mean he's not coming back! What a silly goose you are!"

This was said for the master's benefit: she wanted him to see her daughter as a heartbroken girl, desperately in love with him. But Hsiao-tung's heart had been chilled by the sight of his concubine reaching for the stocks and certificates, trying to pull them out of his hands. The general chaos gave him the opportunity he needed. "Amah Zhou, Amah Wang!" he called. "Is the car here yet? Why haven't you told me? Useless creatures! Come and help me down the stairs, this instant!"

Shijun grabbed the most essential of his belongings, then followed his father down the stairs and into the waiting car.

Things were not yet in order back at the main house: not in her wildest dreams had Shijun's mother imagined they'd get out of the other place so quickly. The rickshaw driver and the maids carried the master up the stairs and helped him into bed. Mrs. Shen gave him her bed, and set up a pallet for her own use. They hadn't brought all the medicines with them, so she called a doctor, who wrote up a new prescription. Then she rushed around finding something for Shijun to eat, and started making plans for an elaborate dinner. The house had been quiet for so long that the servants had never been through anything like this, and they stumbled as they scurried about. Mrs. Shen's daughter-in-law ran around behind her, consumed with haste; her hair flew, her voice cracked. There might have been something touching in this opera scene called "The Return of Father," but if so, it got lost in the frenzy.

That night, after Shijun had got into bed, Mrs. Shen came in and, for the first time in days, had a good talk with her son. She wanted to know all the details of her husband's departure from the other house, but Shijun, wanting to spare her the worry, didn't tell her his father had almost fallen over.

"I didn't want to tell you how worried I was," she told him, smiling now. "When you said you wanted to move back here, all I could think was, your father's been so kind towards you, and that woman is ablaze with anger. Who's to say she wouldn't murder the old man, if you weren't there with him?"

Shijun chuckled. "Oh, it's not that bad, is it?"

For Mrs. Shen, Hsiao-tung's return was an unexpected blessing, and this great boon was all her son's doing. It brought her untold pleasure. It's not that she and her husband had achieved any deep reconciliation—he still behaved towards her as he always had—but since he was sick he could not refuse her ministrations, and that alone brought her great satisfaction.

Oddly enough, the addition of a sick man to the household stirred things up right away. Paintings that had been stored in trunks for years were brought out and hung up, a big carpet was retrieved from somewhere or other and spread out on the floor, new curtains were made up. Mrs. Shen said that since the master had returned, lots of people were bound to come and see how he was doing, and the house had to be presentable. Hsiao-tung had some antique knick-knacks of which he was fond, but which had been left at the other place. They were much on his mind, so he sent a servant to fetch them, but the concubine was angry with him, and wouldn't give them up. Hsiao-tung flew into a rage, smashing a teacup on the floor, pounding on the bed and yelling, "You people are so useless! Can't even do a little thing like this! I'll go there myself—we'll see then if she tries to keep my things from me!"

It was Mrs. Shen who calmed him down. "Don't get so upset about such a little thing. It's not worth it! Didn't the doctor tell you not to get worked up?"

The smashed teacup was from a set she'd brought with her when she got married. For years, she wouldn't let anyone use them, and now that she had, Vim had broken one, and Hsiao-tung another. Mrs. Shen joked about it. "I'm going to take the rest of the set to the fortune-teller's, and see what their fate might be!"

Hsiao-tung had praised her steeped lettuce hearts, so now she was steeping and curing and pickling and fermenting everything in sight: bamboo hearts, sausages, vegetables, noodles. It was a long time till the New Year holiday, but already she was making big plans for the celebration. She even spent money on the servants, giving them a new set of blue cotton clothes each.

Shijun had never seen her so happy. For most of his life, his mother's face had been glum. He was used to seeing her crying; it had no effect on him. But this happiness of hers—it made him feel depressed.

There was no certainty that his father would not go back to the concubine's house. They would of course have to see each other again. Once they did, the women there would find a way to lure him back, and his interest in his first wife would cool again. If Shijun stayed in Nanking, things would be a bit better, since his father depended on him so much. If he left, his father would be deeply disappointed. His mother had been pressing him to stay, asking him to quit his job in Shanghai. Resigning his position had never occurred to him before, but now the thought haunted him. It would be a big blow to Manzhen, if he did that. She valued his career so highly, she'd endure any hardship to help him succeed. If he went back and, of his own accord, left his job—what could he say to her then? Wouldn't she be hurt and disappointed?

At first he had longed to get letters from Manzhen. Now, when a letter from her arrived, he almost shrank from it.

10

Shijun told his family that he had to make a trip to Shanghai, in order to resign from his job and wrap things up. He stayed with Shuhui's parents, the night that he arrived. The next morning, he went to see the head of the factory so he could submit his resignation. It took him till noon to complete that process, so it was only then that he went to the office to look for Manzhen. He hadn't told her anything about his plan to quit, because he knew that if he told her, she would object. He'd thought it over and decided to "act first, get permission later."

Entering the office, he saw Manzhen's old gray sheepskin coat hanging on the back of a chair. She was leaning over her desk, copying a document of some sort. Sitting at Shuhui's old desk was the new clerk, a man who'd adopted the Americanized manners of their boss; his feet were propped up on the desktop, putting on full display a pair of striped socks and leather shoes—the soles of which had not been wiped clean. He and Shijun exchanged brief greetings, and then the man crossed his legs again and went back to his newspaper.

Manzhen turned and smiled. "Oh! When did you get back?"

Shijun went up to her desk and casually leaned over, trying to see what she was writing. She was being very mysterious about it, using a pair of blank sheets to hide her work as she wrote, leaving only two lines visible. She covered up the whole thing to keep him from seeing it, but he'd seen enough to know it was a letter to him. He grinned, but couldn't insist that she let him see it then and there, since they were not alone.

"Let's get some lunch," he said, still leaning on the edge of her desk.

Manzhen looked at her watch. "Sure, let's do that." She got up and put on her coat.

"Aren't you going to post that letter?" Shijun asked when they were ready to go. He reached back and took the sheet of paper from her desk, folded it up, and put it in his own coat pocket.

Manzhen smiled but didn't say anything till they were out of the office. Then she said, "Give it back to me. You're here now, so what's the point of writing?"

Shijun paid her no attention; instead he pulled the letter out and read it as they walked along. A little smile grew on his face as he scanned the page. That made Manzhen peek over his arm to see which part he was reading. When she saw, she blushed and pulled the letter out of his hand. "Read it later. When you're back at your place."

"OK, OK. I won't read it now. Give it here, and I'll put it away."

Manzhen asked him about his father's illness and he gave her a brief report, then slowly worked around to his decision to resign, starting from the ground up. He told her he'd spent a sleepless night on the train back from Nanking, realizing that if his father did not recover, the burden of supporting his mother, sister-in-law and nephew would suddenly fall on him. That would be a heavy load. The good part was that his father now relied on him to handle the business, which meant that he, not the concubine, was gaining control of the family's finances, thereby assuring a secure future for his mother and widowed sister-in-law. That was why he'd had to give up his position at the factory. It was of course only a temporary measure; he'd resume his career later on.

His explanation was well prepared, the phrasing tactfully smooth, but it hid from view the anguish in his heart. His mother's joy, for instance: it was so much like a beggar child finding a broken bauble and treating it as some great treasure. That heart-wringing happiness was something he had given her—and now that he'd made it happen for her, he could not bring himself to deprive her of it. There was another reason too, but he couldn't tell it to Manzhen, nor could he quite admit it to himself: all the obstacles to their plan to marry. The truth was that if he inherited his father's business, everything would be easier to arrange. Then, after they were married, support-ing a few in-laws would be no trouble at all. But if he did not seize this opportunity, he'd end up having to support his mother, sister-in-law and nephew on his meager factory salary, and there they'd be—he with his dependants, Manzhen with hers, and she unwilling to add to his burden. Their prospects of marriage would recede, almost to the point of vanishing. It felt as though he'd already waited an eternity; he could not make her understand how hard this waiting was, for him.

And there was something else as well. Back in the beginning, he'd never worried about the strength of their relationship, but ever since that incident with Yujin, he'd not been entirely free of worry. People say the mind dreams more when nights are long, and he was feeling the truth of this saying.

None of these were things that he could share with Manzhen, so of course she didn't understand his decisions. How could he have suddenly patched things up with his family, and left his job, without consulting her? She was hurt and upset. His work had meant a great deal to her. She was fully prepared for the sacrifices needed so that he could progress in his career; but he had tossed it aside. She was on the point of saying all this, but when she saw how crushed he was, she couldn't add to his burden. Keeping a smile on her face, she let a single question rise to her lips: "Did you tell Shuhui?"

"Yes."

"What did he say?"

"He said it was a pity."

"So he feels that way too."

Shijun looked at her. "I know you're not happy about this."

"Well, but you're happy now, I think. Off in Nanking, meaning that we'll never see each other. But I guess that doesn't bother you."

When Shijun heard her sticking to one tune only, the sweet petu-lance of a girl in love, he felt much relieved. There hadn't been a single word of accusation to charge him with giving up on himself.

"I'll come to Shanghai every week, how's that? This is all a tem-porary arrangement, the best we can do for the time being. You don't really think I won't miss you, do you?"

He stayed in Shanghai another few days, and they saw each other every day. On the surface, everything seemed the same, but after they'd parted he could feel that something was not right. When he returned to Nanking, he wrote to her straight away. "I miss you so much," the letter said. "But since I've just come back, I don't have a good excuse for going to Shanghai right now. Why don't you and Shuhui come to Nanking for the weekend? You've never been to Nanking before. I've told you all about my mother and my sister-in-law, so it's almost as if you know them already. I think you'll feel comfortable with them. Please come. I'll write to Shuhui too."

When Shuhui got his letter, he debated with himself for quite some time. He didn't want to go to Nanking. He phoned Manzhen. "I think it's best to wait till the spring," he told her. "It's too cold now, and anyway I've just come back from there a little while ago. But you should go and see what it's like, since you've never been there before."

"If you're not going, I'm not going either," said Manzhen. "If I go by myself, it will seem too . . . too sudden."

Shuhui had already half guessed that Shijun was inviting them because he wanted his parents to meet Manzhen. If that's what it was all about, he couldn't refuse his friend; he'd better go to Nanking with Manzhen.

The two of them went to Nanking that very weekend. Shijun met them at the train station. He saw Shuhui first; Manzhen had a soft green wool scarf wrapped around her head, and he almost didn't recognize her. The headgear accentuated her jawline, which might have made her even prettier—he really couldn't tell. He liked the way she usually looked and disliked any change.

Shijun got a horse-cart for them.

"What? Putting us in a cart so we can freeze to death?" Shuhui accused his friend. "Brrr!"

"Nanking *is* cold," Manzhen said, smiling.

"Colder than Shanghai," Shijun agreed. "I forgot to tell you to wear warmer clothes."

"I don't know how that would have helped," Manzhen said. "We wouldn't go off and get padded clothes just because we're visiting Nanking."

"When we get home, I'll ask my sister-in-law to lend you some padded trousers."

"What makes you think she'll wear such a thing?" Shuhui teased.

"How's your father feeling?" Manzhen asked. "Is he any better?"

"Much better."

Manzhen studied his face. "Then why do you look so worried?" A slight smile played across her face.

"He's at it again, the same as when I came last year." Shuhui grinned. "He's worrying that we'll spit on the floor or grab food from the table, and then he'll be embarrassed in front of his family."

"What are you talking about?" Shijun protested.

Manzhen laughed, and tightened the scarf around her head. "The wind is really strong. Good thing I've got this head-wrap. Otherwise my hair would be a mess!"

But a moment later, she had unwound the green scarf from her head. "No one here seems to be doing this. I guess it's not the fashion here. It looks too strange, if I'm the only one. Makes me look like a Sikh in a turban."

"A Sikh wears a red turban." Shuhui laughed. "How about a green-headed fly?"

Shijun chuckled. "Keep your head wrapped up, so your ears stay warm."

"I don't care if my ears are warm or not," Manzhen said. "The problem is the tangles in my hair!"

She took out a comb and mirror, but as soon as she'd combed her hair, the wind gusted and she had to tie the scarf around her head again. She decided to keep her head wrapped up till the moment just before they arrived.

In all the time that Shijun had known her, and all the times they'd gone out together, he'd never seen her acting so skittishly. He could not but be amused by these signs of stage fright.

Shijun had told his family that he'd invited Shuhui and a young lady friend of his, Miss Gu, to come and stay for a few days. Miss Gu was another of their colleagues at the factory. When he put it this way, he was not intentionally deceiving his family. He simply felt they were too ready to pass scathing verdicts, too ready to assume that other women could not meet their standards. He didn't want all that tense scrutiny; he wanted them to meet her in a normal, relaxed way. Once they'd got to know Manzhen, they'd approve of her—he was sure of that.

The cart stopped in front of the leather-goods shop and the three of them got out, Shijun with Manzhen's suitcase in his hand. Some customers were in the shop, picking out fur pieces with which to line their jackets. The rolled-up pelts were tied to the end of a rope, then dropped from the upper floor. The rope slithered through the air, bringing down a little curl of leather, skin-side out, with only a few bits of fur poking out. The red bundles looked like swaddling cloths wrapped around a snugly sleeping, furry little creature. Upstairs, behind the colored windows, the goods were managed by his mother, or else his sister-in-law.

Today it was his mother—and she must have seen them, because suddenly she started shrieking, "Amah Chen! Someone's here!" Her voice was so shrill, it sounded as if they kept a giant parrot upstairs. Shijun frowned.

A leather-goods shop always has a special scent, the odor of leather and camphor, and once the pelts are lifted out of the trunks, they're lovingly wrapped in silver paper. As a child, Shijun had felt that the downstairs shop was a darkly forested palace, magnificent and luxurious. Since then, it had become an ordinary scene in his eyes, with only a trace of special sentiment. He'd often imagined Manzhen coming here, seeing his home for the first time. And now here she was, right beside him.

As they went up the stairs, Shuhui, who already knew his way around, pointed out the pair of monkey pelts hanging on the wall. "Those are called Golden Monkeys," he said to Manzhen. "They're from Mount Emei in Sichuan Province."

"Are they called that because there's a golden tinge to the yellow fur?" she asked.

"There are supposed to be three golden stripes on the head," Shijun said. "That's how they got that name."

Manzhen peered at the skins but it was dark in the stairwell and she couldn't see any stripes.

"When I was little, this corner of the staircase always seemed mysterious," Shijun said. "And a little scary."

The younger mistress of the house stood at the head of the stairs and welcomed them into the living quarters. She and Shuhui exchanged greetings, and he introduced Manzhen to her. "Please come in and have a seat!" she urged them. No matter how hard Shijun tried to dodge the issue by saying that Manzhen was a friend of Shuhui's, she still was a female guest from Shanghai whom he'd invited to visit, and thus the object of close attention. *Shijun never thinks our local girls are good enough for him,* his sister-in-law thought to herself, *but this Shanghai girl doesn't look all that special. Not much of a trend-setter, I'd say.*

"Where is Vim?" Shuhui asked.

"In bed. He got sick again."

The boy's mother blamed his grandpa for this. Hsiao-tung had been showing his grandson how to read basic characters, and giving him treats for performing well. The treats had made the boy sick. Every time Vim got sick, his mother found someone to blame, and this time the blame fell on the boy's grandmother as well. Mrs. Shen had poured all her energies into making tasty snacks, trying to tempt Hsiao-tung's appetite, and Shijun's appetite too—how could a child resist all those goodies? Mrs. Shen was in such high spirits these days: the sight of all that happiness was too much for her doleful daughter-in-law to bear. Vim was sick again, and of course there was his grandpa's illness—yet Shijun had to pick this very moment for a visit from his Shanghai friends. His lack of consideration was nothing new, but did his mother really have to join this mad chorus of unruly voices?

Mrs. Shen came out and Shijun introduced Manzhen to her. Mrs. Shen was very polite to Manzhen, and warm towards Shuhui. Shijun's sister-in-law took a few turns around the room, then left. The table was laden with food, but Shuhui said they'd already eaten on the train.

"Well then, I'm the odd one out," Shijun said. "I've been waiting till you got here to eat."

"You should all have a bite," Mrs. Shen urged them. "Miss Gu, and Young Master Hsu, please sit down and eat with Shijun."

They sat down, and Mrs. Shen told the servants to take the guests' luggage to their separate rooms. Sitting with the others, Manzhen felt a dog's tail brushing up against her. She looked for it under the table.

"He comes around whenever we're eating," Shijun said. "Vim has spoiled him, feeding him scraps from the table."

"Is this the dog that Miss Shi gave you?" Shuhui asked.

"Yes. But how did you know about that?"

"Last time I was here I heard Miss Shi say her family's dog had had a litter, and she wanted to give Vim a puppy." He patted the dog, then fell silent. A moment later, a slight smile played across his face and he asked, "Did she get married?"

"Not yet," Shijun answered. "But I guess it will be soon. I haven't seen Yipeng lately."

"Oh, I know," Manzhen joined in, "that must be the Mr. Fang who came to Shanghai for a visit."

"That's right," Shuhui said. "You still remember him? When we went out to lunch with him, he said he'd got engaged—Miss Shi is his fiancée. The two of them are cousins by marriage."

After they'd eaten, Manzhen said they should pay their respects to Mr. Shen, and Shijun led them into his father's room. They'd just finished their lunch, and Hsiao-tung too had just finished his; he stood against the bed, inviting them in, but his words of welcome were followed by an enormous, rumbling burp. He never burps, Shijun thought to himself, and now today he makes such an awful noise . . . well, maybe he does burp occasionally, but I haven't noticed. Everyone in his family seemed crude to him today. Even his mother and sister-in-law were not up to snuff.

Shuhui asked Hsiao-tung about his illness. As the saying goes, an invalid soon becomes a physician, and Hsiao-tung knew more about his condition than any doctor could. Since he'd given the management of his business over to Shijun, he had lots of time to ease into the role of the old man, the elderly master of the household, so he bought a guide to herbal medicine and proceeded to treat any and every ailment with which the maids were afflicted. His confidence in the tonics he prescribed was increased by the fact that no one, as of this moment, had yet died from them. He himself was under the care of a Western-medicine doctor, but he still thought Chinese medicine more effective for some illnesses. There was no one in the house who he could really talk to—Shijun was practically a deaf-mute. Even on this first meeting, Shuhui struck him as very personable. Shuhui could start up a conversation with anyone.

Chatting with Shuhui put Hsiao-tung in high spirits. When Mrs. Shen came in, he asked if Vim was feeling any better, and she told him the boy still had a slight fever. "That medicine that Dr. Wang prescribed isn't the right thing," Hsiao-tung said. "Bring the boy to me and I'll take a look. I'll write him a prescription."

"Goodness!" said Mrs. Shen. "Please take it easy, Grandpa—don't get involved in this! You'll scare the boy's mother. Besides, don't they say that even a famous doctor shouldn't treat the members of his own family?"

Hsiao-tung had to let it go.

He'd nodded at Manzhen when they were introduced but, because she was a young woman, refrained from looking at her directly. Suddenly he turned to her and asked, "Miss Gu, have you been to Nanking before?"

"No," she replied.

"I think I've seen you somewhere before, but I don't remember where."

Manzhen looked at him carefully. "I don't know. Could we have met in Shanghai? Do you often go to Shanghai, sir?"

Hsiao-tung gulped silently. "It's been a long time since I was in Shanghai."

There'd been quite a fuss, the last time he'd been there. The concubine had rushed into the city after him and fetched him back. In Shanghai, he usually stayed with Mrs. Shen's younger brother. The two men got on famously, despite the problems in the marriage through which they were related. Mr. Shen's brother-in-law always took him out on the town, to "see the sights." Hsiao-tung was just going along with the crowd, having a good time, but the concubine saw it as a dark plot hatched by Mrs. Shen: that devious old first wife of his must have told her brother to take the master out and get him all smitten with some taxi-dancer so that she, as second wife, would be supplanted by a new favorite. No amount of discussion could ever clear this up. Mrs. Shen herself had been deeply wounded by her husband's trips to Shanghai, and even quarreled about it with her brother.

"Oh! I know!" Hsiao-tung suddenly let slip. Who did this Miss Gu look like? A well-known taxi-dancer, Li Lu. That's why he thought he'd seen her before!

The unguarded exclamation had burst from his lips, and now everyone in the room was looking at him, waiting to hear what he'd say next. How could he tell them that this nice young woman reminded him of a taxi-dancer he once knew? He paused for a long minute, then finally said to Shijun, "I know—let's ask these two to take a birthday gift to your uncle when they go back to Shanghai. His birthday's coming up soon."

"I was thinking of taking it myself," Shijun said. "That way I could give him my birthday greetings in person."

"But you just got back from Shanghai—are you really planning to go again?"

"It would be good for him to go," Mrs. Shen put in. "My brother's got a big birthday this year."

Shuhui winked and gave Manzhen a knowing look. "You see? Shijun is quite a big-shot now, shuttling backwards and forwards between Shanghai and Nanking."

In the midst of all this chatter, a maid came in and said, "The Fang family's Second Young Master is here, along with Miss Shi. They're downstairs looking at leather coats."

Mrs. Shen smiled. "They must be arranging her trousseau. Why don't you go down and see them, Shijun? Ask them to come up for a visit."

Shijun glanced at his friends and invited them to join him in greeting the visitors. As they were heading down the stairs, he muttered to Shuhui, "Speak of the devil . . ."

Shuhui frowned. "Aren't we going out today?"

"Yes, we'll go in just a little bit. We can go off on our own, and my sister-in-law can look after them."

"Then I'll go now and get my camera, to save myself another trip upstairs."

Shuhui went back to get his camera out of his suitcase; Shijun and Manzhen went down to meet the as-yet-unmarried couple, Yipeng and Tsuizhi. The little dog that Tsuizhi had given them came out too, wagging its tail and weaving through the room, happy to see its former mistress. Yipeng beamed at Manzhen. "Miss Gu! When did you get to Nanking?"

Tsuizhi had to give Manzhen a sharp glance when she heard that. "Oh, so you've met each other before?"

"Of course!" said Yipeng. "Miss Gu and I are old friends!" He gave Shijun a broad wink.

Shijun did not like hearing this kind of joke, especially since Tsuizhi, who had no sense of humor at all, was apt to take it all too seriously. He looked to see how she was reacting.

"Has Miss Gu been here several days already?" she asked.

"No, we've just arrived," Manzhen answered.

"The weather these past few days has turned suddenly cold."

"Oh, yes."

The polite stilted talk of women making their first acquaintance always sent cold fear running through Shijun. He could not understand why. He did not feel himself to be such a timorous man.

"Oh, we've got someone else here," Yipeng said. "Let me introduce you." One of Tsuizhi's classmates had come with them, and was off in the back trying on coats in the mirror. The girl students of those days clung to old ways; even after they were engaged, they dragged along a school chum when they went out. Tsuizhi was still prone to this kind of childishness. This school friend was Miss Dou—Miss Dou Wenhsien. She was a few years older than Tsuizhi, and a shorter, smaller person. She took off the coat she'd been trying on, and Yipeng, who was very good at playing the gentleman, helped her on with her own mink overcoat. Tsuizhi had a leopard-skin coat. Leopard skin is a common enough thing, but it falls into distinct grades, the lower end being no different from ordinary housecat. Tsuizhi's was top-notch: a brilliant, gleaming yellow, the black spots so black they seemed to have come from a plump ink-brush. It was a coat that looked best on a girl in her late teens; it had an energetic, almost feral gleam.

"I don't think we have anything here that could match your two coats," Shijun said.

"That's no way for a salesman to talk!" Shuhui called out, as he came down the staircase.

"Oh, Shuhui's here!" Yipeng said. "I didn't know you'd come too."

"Congratulations!" Shuhui said in greeting. "So when can we toast you at the wedding banquet?"

"It'll be soon," Yipeng said. "We're here putting together the trousseau."

Yipeng was all smiles. Tsuizhi smiled too, though her expression was more subdued. She leaned down to pat the dog, scratching him gently under the chin. The dog stretched out its neck, begging for more.

"What are your plans for today?" Yipeng asked. "Let me take you to dinner at Six Splendor Spring."

"What's all this?" Shijun said. "You don't need to play host for us."

"But I do. I'm going to Shanghai at the end of the month, so it'll be your turn to take us out."

"You're going to Shanghai?"

Yipeng tilted his head towards Tsuizhi and laughed. "Have to take her shopping."

"Shanghai's the place to go for shopping," Dou Wenhsien put in. "If you want to shop, or see a film, that's the place to go!" A fashion-conscious girl like her, if not fortunate enough to live in Shanghai, was always one step behind. Her pride took a hit when she spoke of it, her voice going squeaky with the strain.

Shijun's sister-in-law now came down the stairs, smiling and welcoming Wenhsien, whom she had met before. "Oh, it's good to see you again, Miss Dou."

"Hello, Cousin," Tsuizhi said, but she got teased for that.

"You should call me 'Sister' now, since we'll soon be even closer relatives!"

Tsuizhi blushed, and her face went solemn. "It's not nice to make fun of me."

"Well, come along everyone, let's go upstairs and relax a bit," their hostess urged them.

"Shouldn't we be going?" Tsuizhi said to Yipeng. "Didn't you say you'd invite Wenhsien to go to the cinema with us?"

Yipeng turned to Shijun and his friends. "Why don't you come with us?"

"They've just arrived from Shanghai—why would they want to see a movie in Nanking?" protested Shijun.

"Where are you three planning to go?" his sister-in-law asked him.

Shijun thought for a moment, then conferred with Shuhui. "How about Pure Coolness Temple? I don't think you went there, last time you were here."

"Then you all should go and see the temple," their hostess declared. "It's good that Yipeng has a car—otherwise you'd spend all day going back and forth. You'll have to get back here in time to eat. Shijun's mother is putting together a nice welcome dinner for his guests."

"OK, sounds good to me." Yipeng was happy to go along with her plan.

So they all went to Pure Coolness Temple, six of them squeezed into the one car. Shuhui was quiet at first, then rallied and started cracking jokes, none of which seemed funny to Shijun; somehow his friend seemed silly today. Tsuizhi and her friend were being typical girl students, huddling together to trade little in-jokes and remarks. The two were inseparable even after they got out of the car at Pure Coolness Mountain. Wenhsien walked half a step behind

Tsuizhi, snuggling her hands under the collar of her friend's coat, to keep warm. The two of them kept up their own private conversation, ignoring Manzhen. Yipeng felt it was awkward, but it wasn't a gap he could fill; if he chatted with Manzhen, Tsuizhi would get suspicious. It thus fell to Shijun to keep Manzhen company, and the two of them walked up the hill together.

The broken, eroded stone steps seemed to go on forever. Somewhere in the distance, there was an army base; the faint crackle of a loudspeaker announcement came drifting on the wind. The sound of shouted slogans, filtering through bland afternoon light, gave the place a desolate feel.

The temples in the lower Yangzi River region have outer walls that are painted a dull red. Inside those walls, there's a courtyard with rooms on all four sides, where families live. An old woman, dressed in rags, was sitting on a shabby old kneeling cushion made of bound grass and trimming garlic bulbs. She had a little brazier and a rolled-up sleeping mat; a gaggle of children were playing on the high threshold of the room behind her. They looked like war refugees, but they were just the local poor, who lived like refugees year after year.

"I've heard that the monk in this temple has a family," Tsuizhi said, "and that they all wear monk's robes."

That piqued Shuhui's curiosity. "Really? Let's go and see."

"Yes, it's true—let's go and have a look," Tsuizhi said.

Yipeng smiled. "Even if it is true, they're not going to let you see them."

A cauldron-sized incense burner stood in the center of the courtyard, on a raised platform of green-tinged stone. Manzhen sat down on the stone dais.

"Are you tired?" Shijun asked.

"Not really."

She paused, then suddenly looked him in the face and smiled. "What should I do? I've got a blister on my foot, and it's just burst."

She was wearing a pair of gray doe-skin pumps, low-heeled but still thin and wobbly. Boots had not yet come into fashion for women in those days, and cotton-soled shoes were too flimsy for climbing up to temples. Thicker soles could be made of felt, of course, but a girl who wore them out of the house risked looking like an old charwoman. That's why most young women, even in the depths of winter, went around in stockings and leather pumps.

"What should we do?" Shijun exclaimed. "Let's go back."

"But that would ruin it for the others."

"They'll be fine. We two can go back on our own."

"Then let's take pedicabs, instead of getting a ride in their car."

"All right. I'll go and tell Shuhui, and ask him not to say anything to Yipeng yet."

Shijun took Manzhen back to his home, each in a pedicab. Even though Nanking winters can be bitterly cold, heating stoves are not a standard feature of the houses there; it's quite different from Peking. Shijun's family was being especially high-minded and austere this year. Except for the stove in Shijun's father's room, the only heat in the house was provided by a shallow brazier in the living room, and even it had an additional function: an earthenware bowl of water chestnuts was gently steaming away on the brazier's iron grating.

Manzhen huddled close to the fire but could not stop shivering. "I guess the cold really got to me this time."

"Let me find something you can wear," Shijun offered. His first thought was to ask his sister-in-law for some knitwear, but then he remembered how difficult she could be. Besides, both she and his mother wore their hair combed up and slicked back in a married woman's bun, and their clothes were sure to carry the heavy scent of hair oil. In the end he went and got one of his own sweaters, something he'd worn in middle school—an old, brown jumper with that kind of round, ribbed neck that his mother called a "dog-collar neck." It was too big for Manzhen; the cuffs fell past her wrists, leaving only her fingers exposed. But he liked the way that old sweater looked on her. He sat facing her in the dim firelight, his heart content. It felt as though she'd become part of his family.

The water chestnuts cooked through, and they peeled and ate them. "Your fingernails are too short," Shijun said. "I'll get a knife."

"No, don't go," she said.

The truth was, he didn't want to move, it was so cozy here.

Then he dug around in his pocket shyly, pulled something out and thrust it at her. "Here, have a look. I got it in Shanghai."

Manzhen opened the little box and found a ruby ring.

"You got this back then? How come you never mentioned it?" She smiled at him.

"Because you were angry with me then." He smiled back at her.

"That's just you overreacting. When was I angry with you?"

Shijun toyed with the ring, his head bent over it. "When I left my job, they gave me half a month's salary. That's when I bought the ring."

So he'd bought the ring with his own earnings—Manzhen felt much better about it now. "Did it cost a lot?" she asked.

"Hardly anything. Want to guess how much? Just sixty dollars. Strictly speaking, it's not real. But it's not fake either. It's made of gem dust."

"It's a beautiful color."

"Go ahead—try it on. I'm afraid it'll be too big."

The ring went on her finger, and he took her hand in his. She gazed silently at the ring.

Suddenly he smiled again. "When you were little, did you ever take one of those red-paper rings that come wrapped around a cigar and wear it on your finger?"

"Yes! Did you do that too?"

The ruby ring did remind one of those circlets of bright red paper, edged with shiny gold.

"Did you see the ring that Tsuizhi's wearing?" Shijun asked her. "It must be her engagement ring. It's got a diamond the size of a wristwatch."

Manzhen giggled. "Oh, what an exaggeration!"

"Maybe my mind's playing tricks on me—this stone I bought looks so small."

"I've never liked diamonds much. They say diamond is the hardest substance in the world, and even the gleam of diamonds seems hard to me, like a steel needle poking my eye."

"Well then, how about pearls?"

"There's not enough color in a pearl. I like rubies, especially if they're made of gem dust."

That made Shijun laugh out loud.

But the ring was indeed too big for her. "I was afraid of that," Shijun said. "We'll have to take it back and have it adjusted."

"I'd better not wear it for now."

"I could get some string, and wrap it around the back of the ring—then it would fit, at least for the next few days. How about some silk thread?"

But Manzhen held him back. "Don't go and ask them, please!"

"All right, all right."

He noticed a strand of yarn hanging from her sleeve; the old sweater he'd lent her was unraveling.

"We can rip off a bit of this wool and use it to wrap the ring."

He pulled on the yarn, snapped a piece off and wound it around the back of the ring. Then he gave it to her to try on.

Just then, he heard his mother talking to a maid in the other room. "Take this food to the old master's room," she was saying. "The young people aren't in a hurry to eat. We'll keep dinner till Miss Shi and the others have returned."

They were talking just outside the door; Shijun jumped up and scurried back to the seat opposite Manzhen's.

Amah Chen went past the open door, heading towards his father's room with a tray of steaming hot food. It probably had been intended for them, but then his mother had redirected it and kept the maid from coming in. She must have figured out that something was going on between them. He was planning to tell her anyway, in another day or two—no harm if she cottoned on a bit early.

Shijun was thinking this through when Manzhen pointed out that the others had returned. There was the sound of footsteps on the stairs, then Mrs. Shen's voice greeting them. "Oh—but where are the others?" she asked. "Where's Tsuizhi?"

"You mean she's not here?" Yipeng was clearly surprised. "We thought they'd come back already!"

Shijun hurried out to see them, but Yipeng and Dou Wenhsien were the only ones there. "What about Shuhui?" he asked.

"Shuhui's missing, and so is Tsuizhi," Yipeng said. "We don't know where they've gone."

"Weren't you all together?" Shijun asked.

"It's all Tsuizhi's fault," Yipeng replied. "She was dead set on seeing a monk's wife, said she had to see what kind of person that would be. But Wenhsien said she couldn't walk another step, so I suggested she and I have a cup of tea in Sweeping Leaves Tower, and wait for Tsuizhi and Shuhui there. We waited for ages, and they never came."

"I got worried," Wenhsien chipped in. "I thought they must have returned already, so I said we should come back here to look for them. Until this happened, I wasn't even planning to come back here. I was headed home."

"Well, come in and stay for a bit," Shijun urged her. "They're sure to come back soon. The two of them are acting like little kids—running off like that!"

Shijun had already filled up on water chestnuts, but he picked at the snacks with them. They sat and chatted till the sun went down, still with no sign of Shuhui and Tsuizhi.

Yipeng started to get worried. "What if something awful's happened to them . . ."

"Unlikely," Shijun assured him. "Tsuizhi knows her way around Nanking, and she's got Shuhui with her. Shuhui's very smart—he knows how to steer clear of trouble." Shijun waved these words around, but inside he shuddered.

But all was well—it wasn't too much later that the missing ones returned, and were roundly berated by the others. "If you'd been gone much longer," Shijun said, "we'd have formed a search party and gone up the mountain with lanterns and torches!"

"You frightened Yipeng to death!" Wenhsien chimed in. "Where on earth have you two been?"

"Remember we said we were going to look for Mrs. Monk?" Shuhui explained. "Well, we couldn't find her, but Mr. Monk made us stay and eat steamed buns with him—the vegetarian kind. Then we went back to Sweeping Leaves Tower to look for you, but you'd already gone. It took us forever to find a rickshaw, and then we had to send it off to find a second one. That's why we're so late."

"That area is so deserted," Yipeng said. "I was afraid you'd run into trouble of some kind."

Shuhui laughed. "I bet you all were thinking of that old martial arts movie, *The Burning of Red Lotus Temple*—you probably thought we'd been caught by a gang of outlaws. And all that talk about a monk who has a family—he might have kept Miss Shi there, and set her up as his second wife."

"That's just what I was thinking!" Shijun said. "I didn't dare bring it up, for fear of alarming Yipeng."

They all had a good laugh at that.

Tsuizhi was silent throughout all this, but her face gleamed with excitement. Shuhui also seemed unusually excited. He looked over at Manzhen, sitting near the stove. "Hey there," he teased, "and what happened to you? Losing face for all us Shanghainese—wimping out like that and coming back early!"

"Wenhsien was no better," Tsuizhi said. "Had to stop and rest, even though we'd gone only a few steps."

"Well, if you're still full of energy," Yipeng put in, "let's go out again."

"Where?" asked Shuhui. "I don't know Nanking, but I've heard there's a Confucius temple, with singing girls."

The girls all tittered.

"Must be in some novel you read," Shijun suggested.

"Well then," said Yipeng, "let's all go to the Confucius temple to hear some chanting. Could be quite worthwhile."

"But are the singing girls pretty?" Shuhui wanted to know.

Yipeng gave it a moment's thought. "I really don't know, haven't been there much. I'm not much of an expert on actresses and all that."

"Didn't you know?" Shijun said, speaking to Shuhui but throwing a wink at Tsuizhi. "Yipeng's on the straight and narrow now."

But Tsuizhi sat there stony-faced, pretending she hadn't heard this. The joke fell flat, and Shijun cursed himself for forgetting what he knew all too well: the girl had no sense of humor.

They got themselves all worked up over a plan to go out after dinner, but in the end it fizzled out. Manzhen had a blistered foot, so she didn't want to go, and Wenhsien said she'd better go home. After they'd eaten, Yipeng took Wenhsien and Tsuizhi home in his car. Shijun and his guests sat around the stove and chatted a little longer, then retired for the night.

Manzhen had a big bedroom all to herself. In the morning a maid brought a basin of water, a jar of Snow Flower face cream, and a battered old tin of Three Flowers scented face powder. Manzhen had already noticed that Mrs. Shen, a woman well past her youth, still wore a shiny layer of cream and face powder; her daughter-in-law, though a widow, did the same. Women in old-fashioned households seemed to feel that even if they weren't going out, they had to wear a lot of makeup—whitened skin and reddened cheeks—to keep the place festive and upbeat. If the older ones felt this way, the assumption must be even stronger for the younger ones. So Manzhen washed her face and patted on a little powder. Coming out of her room, she ran into Shijun. "How do you like my makeup?"

"It's makeup, all right. Looks a bit too white to me."

Manzhen pulled out a handkerchief and rubbed at her face. "There. How's that?"

"You've still got some on your nose."

"I'll bet I look like a white-nosed clown!" She laughed and rubbed her face again. Then they made their way to the dining room.

Mrs. Shen and Shuhui were already sitting at the breakfast table, waiting for them. Manzhen greeted her hostess as "Auntie Shen," and was met in turn with solicitous inquiries as to how she had slept, whether the quilts were thick enough, and if she had stayed warm.

"Very warm," she replied. Then she turned to Shuhui. "I'm so dizzy, you know. When I got up this morning, I was all turned around, and almost couldn't find my way to the dining room."

"That's where they got that old saying from," he told her. "'New to the place, she fumbles for the door, knocks her knuckles on the wok, trips over the bed.'"

It could be that Manzhen overreacted, but it sounded like something one would say of a new bride, and she blushed. "Where *do* you get these sayings of yours?"

"Young Master Hsu has such a way with words!" Mrs. Shen said. She turned and spoke to Shijun. "I was just telling Young Master Hsu how much your father enjoyed talking with him yesterday. Afterwards, he kept saying how happy he was that you have a friend like him—such a capable, lively person, someone who puts his best foot forward, not like other young men these days. He went on and on, till it occurred to me that if Young Master Hsu were a girl, your father would be trying to get him into the family, as your bride!"

Shijun and Manzhen found Mrs. Shen's casual witticism a tad startling. What could have made her start raising the subject of Shijun's marriage? Of course she was only joking, but it made them nervous.

Shijun focused on his rice porridge. "Ask the driver to buy some train tickets," he said to his mother. "They're leaving this afternoon."

"Leaving already?" she said. "But you've only just arrived. Why don't you stay a few more days? Shijun's going to Shanghai to wish his uncle a happy birthday, and you three could go back together."

Her ploy was unsuccessful, and she had to settle for the standard formula: "Well, come again in the spring, and stay for a few days at least."

By that time, Shijun was thinking, Manzhen and I might be married already. It was hard to tell whether his mother knew they were a couple.

"Where are you going this morning?" Mrs. Shen asked. "Maybe you should try Hsuanwu Lake. You could ride around in a boat, and that way Miss Gu wouldn't have to walk on her hurt foot." She directed a long stream of talk at Manzhen, starting with tips for treating blisters and moving on to inquiries about the latter's family. It could have been ordinary hostess-talk, but to Shijun it sounded like extra-special attention.

They spent the morning boating on the lake. Shijun went with them to the station, and when he saw Manzhen waving at him from the train carriage, her ruby ring glinting in the sun, he felt happy and safe.

He went home. His mother came out to meet him as he was going up the stairs. "Yipeng's here to see you," she said. "He's been waiting for you for hours."

That struck Shijun as odd: he'd seen his cousin the day before, and generally speaking, months could go by without their paths crossing. He walked in, and Yipeng rose at once. "Are you busy right now? If not, let's go out and find a place to chat. There's something I want to tell you."

"Why not talk right here?" Shijun asked.

Yipeng said nothing, but walked firmly to the door and took a good look around, then to the window, where he stood staring into the distance. Suddenly he turned and said, "Tsuizhi broke up with me."

Shijun stood still, rooted in shock. "When did this happen?"

"Yesterday evening. Remember how I saw the two girls home? I took Wenhsien home first, then Tsuizhi. When we got to her house, she asked me in. Her mother had gone to play mahjong, so we were alone. She told me she wanted to break off the engagement, and handed the ring back to me."

"That's all she said?"

"That was it."

After a long silence, Yipeng went on: "It would be easier to take if she'd given me some kind of hint, or some kind of reason—she really took me by complete surprise!"

"It seems to me that this sort of thing doesn't happen overnight," Shijun said. "You must have felt that something was wrong."

Yipeng's face showed his pain. "Didn't she seem happy to you, when we were here last night? No sign at all that anything was wrong."

Shijun thought back over the evening's events. "You're right about that!" he admitted.

Yipeng's frustration rose up again. "To tell you the truth, the match was mostly my family's idea, not mine. But it's been formally announced, everyone's heard, and now she's broken it off, for no apparent cause—everyone will think it's my fault, that I've been running around on her. They'll look down on me, I know it."

Shijun saw the distress on Yipeng's face, and couldn't think of anything comforting to say. "Well, if this is what she's like, better to find that out before you marry her," he said lamely.

Yipeng stared into space a good long while. "I haven't told anyone else," he said. "I came here and saw my cousin, but I didn't say anything to her. Now I'm thinking I should ask Wenhsien what she thinks—isn't she Tsuizhi's best friend? Maybe she'll have some idea of what's going on."

"Good idea!" Shijun finally felt the pressure lifting. "Miss Dou was with us all day yesterday. You should go and find out what she thinks."

With Shijun's encouragement, Yipeng went straight to Wenhsien's place. He returned the following day, and reported: "I went to see Wenhsien, and she's really smart. You might not guess it, just looking at her, but that girl has quite a head on her shoulders. I felt so much better after we talked. You know what she said? She said that if Tsuizhi is that kind of person, we wouldn't have had a happy marriage. She said it's better to find that out now, not later."

Yes—that's just what I said, Shijun thought to himself. He hears exactly the same thing from someone else, and comes back to tell me what I've already told him. Humph!

The whole thing made him smile. "That's right!" he said. "That's just what I said."

But once again, Yipeng seemed not to have heard him. "I think she's got it right," he said, bobbing his head in approval. "Don't you think so?"

"Does she have any idea as to why Tsuizhi . . ."

"She said she'd try to find out, and asked me to come back today for another chat."

Yipeng left, and didn't reappear till several days later. Shijun had been getting ready to go to Shanghai for his uncle's birthday, but that very day a letter came from his uncle, who said he didn't want a birthday party and was coming to Nanking instead; it had been many years since he'd seen his sister and her husband, and he was looking forward to a nice family gathering. Shijun had been planning to use this excuse to go to Shanghai, and the collapse of his plan left him very disappointed. A visit from Yipeng only made things worse.

But Yipeng was on good form, no longer moping about. He came in and sat quietly, smoking a cigarette. "Shijun," he said, after a long moment of reflection, "you've been my friend for many years, so tell me honestly: I'm a strange person, don't you think so?"

Shijun had no idea what this was about, but fortunately there was no need to reply, because Yipeng kept going.

"Wenhsien analyzed my personality, and I think she's got it right. She says that when I'm clever, I'm cleverer than anyone, but when I'm muddled, I'm the most muddled fellow there ever was."

Shijun couldn't keep his eyebrows from shooting up. He'd never thought of Yipeng as someone who "when he was clever, was cleverer than anyone else."

Yipeng got a little embarrassed. "It's true. You'd never guess it, but when I'm muddled, I'm the most muddled fellow there ever was. The truth is, I'm not in love with Tsuizhi. I'm in love with Wenhsien, and didn't even know it myself!"

Not long after, he and Wenhsien were married.

11

Shijun's maternal uncle, Feng Jyu-sun, had come to Nanking to avoid any birthday fuss, but Shijun's family held a party for him anyway. They didn't let their whole social circle know; it was to be just a small family gathering. Even so, it kept Mrs. Shen very busy. She couldn't have asked for better timing: these were the happiest days of her married life, and she wanted her brother to see how much she was thriving, basking in this late-in-life good fortune after years of undeserved suffering.

Jyu-sun brought with him a couple of tins of imported sweets and biscuits. "My daughter-in-law sent these for her godson," he said. Vim had always been such a weakling that his parents had feared he wouldn't make it to adulthood, so they set him up with multiple godmothers, among them Jyu-sun's own daughter-in-law. The boy's mother was happy to see signs of affection for her son, and promised to have a photograph taken and sent to the godmother, as soon as the boy's health permitted.

When Jyu-sun saw Hsiao-tung, his private thoughts ran thus: It's really an awful thing when a man our age gets sick. One bad spell, and he looks positively geriatric!

Meanwhile, Hsiao-tung was thinking, Those false teeth make Jyu-sun look like a buck-toothed granny. What a decline since I last saw him!

But these thoughts could not dampen the pleasure they felt, as brothers-in-law, upon seeing each other after so many years. Jyu-sun asked after Hsiao-tung's health, and heard that the latter was greatly recovered, except for some numbness in one finger of his left hand. Jyu-sun said he'd wanted to come and see his brother-in-law during his illness, but feared it would upset his concubine-wife. "I didn't think she'd want to see me at her door—she's really got the wrong impression about me, you know. I think you must have put all the blame on me, that time you went down on your knees and begged her forgiveness."

Hsiao-tung laughed. Just thinking of that adventure made his mind reel: he'd gone off to Shanghai for a good time and she'd chased him down, and thrown a huge fit. Going over it again with Jyu-sun—all that tricky ground they'd covered on that pleasure trip—was almost too much to process. Then suddenly he thought to ask: "Do you still remember a girl called Li Lu?"

Before the question was even out of his friend's mouth, Jyu-sun was slapping his thigh and exclaiming, "I almost forgot to tell you! There's news about her, not recent news, it's been a couple of years already. People say she had a wedding of some sort, but never really left the business. She's not a taxi-dancer anymore, she's a privately owned, ah . . . *entertainer*. So I said, well, let's pay her a visit—I'd like to see what sort of front she puts up now!"

"Did you really go?" Hsiao-tung asked.

"No, no. I'm an old man now, not as frisky as I used to be. Back in the day, I'd have been on her doorstep in a flash, just to get my revenge!"

When the two of them had first met Li Lu, she was at the top of her form. Jyu-sun had taken pride in his "frequent customer" status, and promised his guests full value for money. But Hsiao-tung, after spending a fortune on her without getting anywhere, walked out in disgust. Whenever Jyu-sun remembered that defeat—his first ever—his anger boiled over again.

Hearing about Li Lu's new situation, Hsiao-tung's view of her was confirmed. "Who would have imagined that she'd sink so fast!" he sighed.

Jyu-sun crossed his legs and smiled. "Sounds as though you're still hooked on her!"

"No, no. I'll tell you why I suddenly remembered her. A few days ago I saw a girl who looks just like her."

"Really?" Jyu-sun chuckled. "Where was that? Have you been hanging around there lately?"

"Don't be silly," Hsiao-tung said with a grin. "This was a proper young lady, but she looked just like Li Lu, and she came from Shanghai."

"It could be her younger sister. Li Lu had a lot of little sisters, as I recall, though they were snotty-nosed brats back then."

"What was her real family name? She wasn't really a Li, was she?"

"Her real family name is Gu."

Hsiao-tung stared. "That's it! This other girl's name is also Gu."

"Is she pretty?"

"Hard to say," Hsiao-tung answered in some confusion. "Not bad-looking, anyway."

"Unless she's really ugly, a girl from that sort of family is bound to take up that line of work."

Jyu-sun seemed very interested; he kept trying to find out where Hsiao-tung had met the girl, apparently bent on exposing her, to get his long-delayed revenge. Hsiao-tung made vague replies about seeing the girl at a friend's house; he didn't want to admit that his own son had brought her home.

That evening, when no one else was around, he had a talk with his wife. "Here's something strange," he began. "The minute I saw that Miss Gu, I thought she looked familiar. She looks just like a taxi-dancer Jyu-sun used to know. Jyu-sun says the taxi-dancer's family name was also Gu. He told me she's no longer a taxi-dancer, she's something even worse. This Miss Gu must be from the same family. The two of them look so alike—she must be the younger sister of that other one."

None of this sank in at first. Mrs. Shen simply muttered along, "Oh . . . OK . . . that's fine, dear." Then it hit home and shock rippled through her. "How could that be?" she gasped.

"Why ever not?"

"That Miss Gu seems a very nice girl to me, she doesn't look anything like that!"

"And what do you know about it? Women like that are good at

changing their manner. They go from nice to naughty, depending on who they're with. A secluded old lady like you, someone who's stayed inside all her life, never seen even a bit of the world—you're the easiest kind to fool!"

Mrs. Shen's throat tightened.

"I wonder if Shijun knows about her background," Hsiao-tung went on.

"How could he know anything about other people's families? He and that Miss Gu are office colleagues, that's all."

"*Colleagues!*" Hsiao-tung harrumphed. His suspicions about his son were raging. But the love of one's children overcomes all. He restrained himself, and tried a different tack. "Well, so she's a secretary now, but what was she before? Unless she's really ugly, a girl from that kind of family has to be in that line of work, once she's old enough."

Mrs. Shen was again at a loss for words. All she could do was put the blame on Shuhui's shoulders. "Well, if any of this is true, we'd better get hold of Young Master Hsu and tip him off. Shijun said she's *his* friend."

"I had a very good opinion of that young man," Hsiao-tung said. "Now I feel sorry for him. Still wet behind the ears, and already mixed up with a girl of that sort."

"I don't think he could have known about it. And, in fact, we can't be sure that any of this is true."

Hsiao-tung fell silent. Then, after a long pause, he said softly, "It wouldn't be hard to find out, now would it? But there's no need, really. It's not our problem."

Mrs. Shen spent the evening thinking it over. She wanted to have a good talk with her son. As it happened, Shijun was also looking for a chance to talk, to tell her that he and Manzhen wanted to get married. The next morning, Mrs. Shen went to the living room to polish the pewter candlesticks. The New Year was coming, and she took out all the incense-burners, candlesticks and such like, to get them ready for the holiday. Shijun came in and sat down across from her.

"I wish Uncle weren't going back so soon," he said pleasantly. "Seems like he just got here."

"New Year's coming," his mother said. "He's got things to take care of at home."

"I could go with him, take him back to Shanghai."

Mrs. Shen paused a long moment, then finally gave him a smile. "You're always pining for Shanghai, wanting to go there."

Shijun smiled back but stayed silent, so his mother filled in the gap for him. "I know, I know . . . now that you're used to life in Shanghai, everywhere else bores you to tears. Go and spend a few days there, but be sure to come back soon. The New Year's coming, the shop will be busy settling the accounts, and we've got our family celebrations too."

Shijun nodded and murmured his assent.

He didn't get up and leave straight away; he made small talk to keep the conversation going. After they'd chatted a while longer, Mrs. Shen suddenly asked, "Do you know Miss Gu very well?"

Shijun's heart leaped into his throat. To him it seemed that she'd purposely raised the subject so he could speak his mind—she was helping him out of a tight corner. His mother was so good to him. Now he could tell her all about Manzhen. But she wouldn't let him speak—she was pursuing her own train of thought: "I'm asking you because your father talked to me about her last night. He says Miss Gu looks like a taxi-dancer he used to know." She told him the whole thing: the taxi-dancer whose surname was also Gu, then this Miss Gu looking as if she could be the dancer's younger sister, and Hsiao-tung claiming that Jyu-sun knew the older woman, though he probably was using his brother-in-law to cover up his own dalliance with her.

Shijun sat silent for a long while after she'd finished talking. Then he pulled himself together. "I think it's just random guesswork on Father's part. How can we be sure any of it is true? There are lots of people who look like each other—"

"True," interrupted his mother, "and there are lots of people with the same family name. But put these two coincidences together, and you can't blame your father for getting suspicious."

"I have been to Miss Gu's home," Shijun said. "She has a lot of younger brothers and sisters, and her father has passed away, leaving just her mother and grandmother. It's a completely respectable family. Nothing at all like what you're describing."

Mrs. Shen frowned. "I said it didn't seem like her—she seems a very nice young lady to me! But your father's got a one-track mind. Once he's got an idea stuck in there, you could spend a lifetime trying to explain things to him and he still wouldn't listen. Isn't that what happened, back when it all fell apart? Didn't he blow his top over some teeny-weeny, minor things, and then that concubine got in there, and twisted everything around so that no one could get a word in edgeways?"

Shijun could tell, from her tone, that she knew all about Manzhen and him: she was not in the least deceived. The whole time that Manzhen had been staying with them, she hadn't dropped the slightest hint: clearly, he'd underestimated his mother. He'd never imagined her capable of so much cunning. The truth is that women raised in the old way couldn't do much else, so when it came to "pretending" they were top-notch. They were so used to keeping a tight rein on their own feelings that self-suppression was nothing to them. Pretending to be deaf and dumb was second nature, it took no effort at all.

"Your father wondered if you knew about Miss Gu's background," Mrs. Shen continued. "I told him there was no way that you could know, that she was Shuhui's friend, and you'd met her through him. Your father is a funny man—he liked Shuhui so much at first, but now he's turned against him. He says he's wet behind the ears, and will have trouble getting ahead."

Shijun stayed mute. His mother paused, then went on softly: "When you see Shuhui tomorrow, tell him to be careful, tell him he should steer clear of this."

"It's a personal matter," Shijun said coldly. "Anything a friend could say would be totally beside the point. The same goes, for that matter, if it's a family member who's trying to interfere."

That shut his mother up completely.

But Shijun himself felt he'd been too harsh: this was no way to speak to his mother. He calmed himself down and smiled at her.

"Ma," he said, "haven't you said you support freedom of choice in marriage?"

"Well, yes, I do. But . . . the girl has to be a decent sort."

Shijun lost his temper again. "Didn't I just tell you there's nothing the matter with her family?"

Mrs. Shen kept quiet after this. The two of them sat there in silence. Eventually a maid came in and said Uncle wanted to play chess with the young master. Shijun went off, and the subject was not broached again.

Mrs. Shen's confidence was undermined, as if she had done something wrong; she became entirely cautious in her approach to both husband and son, always smiling and never saying anything. Jyu-sun was planning to leave the next day, and Shijun had arranged to go with him. Mrs. Shen sent someone to get four of Nanking's speciality treats—pressed duck, duck gizzard, roasted sweetmeats and pine-nut pudding—then packaged them up and took them to Shijun's room so she could ask him to deliver the parcel to his uncle's family. "They sent treats for Vim, so I want to send something to their little ones. Will you be staying at Uncle's place?" she continued.

"No, I'll go over to Shuhui's."

"Then you should take them a gift also, since you're so often their guest."

"I know."

"Maybe you should take a little extra spending money?"

Then she repeated her entreaties to come back soon. In all the times he'd gone off to Shanghai, she'd never seemed so reluctant to let him go. She sat in his room a long while, clearly with something on her mind, but could not find the words she needed.

Shijun too was unhappy. His unhappiness made his mother seem very annoying.

They set out the next day, taking the afternoon train and eating dinner on board. Shijun saw his uncle home, went into the house with him, and stayed for a bit.

"It's getting late," his uncle said. "Why don't you stay here tonight? On cold nights like this, people get mugged for their padded clothes. It's a desperate time of the year."

Shijun laughed it off and said he wasn't afraid. He made his farewells, picked up his suitcase and took a pedicab to Shuhui's house. The Hsus had already gone to bed, but Shuhui's mother got up, threw on some clothes and made up a bed for him. She wanted to know if he'd had dinner. "Oh, yes, and then at my uncle's I had an after-supper snack of noodles."

It was Saturday, so Shuhui was at home as well. The two of them lay in their beds chatting, just like in the old days back in the student dormitory. "I've got something funny to tell you," Shijun said. "That day I saw the two of you off at the train station, Yipeng came by in the evening and told me Tsuizhi had broken off the engagement."

"What?" Shuhui was shocked. "Why did she do that?"

"I have no idea. But that's not even the funny part. Wait till you hear this . . ." He told his friend the whole story, how Yipeng had taken Tsuizhi home after dinner at Shijun's house, and she'd given his ring back to him, with no explanation whatsoever. Then Yipeng had gone to ask Wenhsien about it, since Wenhsien was Tsuizhi's good friend. Shuhui's mind was in shock as he heard this story; he kept drifting back to scenes from earlier that day, on Pure Coolness Mountain. He and Tsuizhi had plunged recklessly into the temple grounds, eager to uncover the monk's secret, but after winding around on one twisty path after another, they'd abandoned the quest and looked instead at the mountain peak. "Let's climb to the top!" they'd decided, in a burst of childlike glee. The sky was wide and high, the breezes sweet and caressing, and after they'd reached the top they sat and talked a good long while. What they said was of no particular importance, but inside they both were thinking that they'd never meet like this again—and couldn't bear to let it end. They lingered on the mountaintop till nightfall. The path back down was treacherous, much harder than the trek up, and he took her hand to guide her down. It would have been easy to kiss her, which he very much wanted to do, but he wouldn't let himself. He felt he'd already gone too far; and yet his conscience, that night, was clear. It never occurred to him that she might—suddenly, as if she couldn't take it anymore—break up with Yipeng.

He sat there stupefied, then was roused by a chuckle from Shijun. "'When he's clever he's cleverer than anyone'—"

"Who are you talking about?"

"Who else? Yipeng, of course."

"*Yipeng?* Cleverer than anyone?"

"I'm not the one saying that. It was Wenhsien. Eh? Didn't you hear what I was saying just now? Did you fall asleep?"

"No. I was just thinking about how strangely Tsuizhi is behaving. Why do you think she did it?"

"Who knows? Anyway, those spoiled-young-lady types are very hard to please."

Shuhui said nothing. He struck a match, there in the dark, and lit a cigarette.

"Let me have one too," Shijun said. Shuhui tossed him the packet and the box of matches. "I must be overtired," Shijun said. "Too tired to sleep."

The moon rose very late. Well after midnight, moonlight flooded the frost on the roof-tiles, a cold sheet of white that lit up the sky. Cocks started to crow, fooled into thinking that day had come. It was the season when lots of city folk kept a chicken, getting ready for the New Year feast. The sound of poultry everywhere made the city seem like a rural hamlet, and filled sleepers' heads with the echoing chill of empty spaces.

Shijun's mind was so stirred up, it seemed like hours until he fell asleep. When he awoke, Shuhui was fast asleep, his quilt sprinkled with bits of cigarette ash. Shijun felt sorry for coming in so late and keeping his friend from getting a good night's rest, so he was careful not to wake him. He got up and had breakfast with Shuhui's parents and younger sister. Shijun asked if she'd passed the entrance exam for the school she wanted. "Yes," said her mother, happily. "Thanks to your help, Teacher." After breakfast, Shijun checked on Shuhui, but he still was not stirring. He took his leave of Mrs. Hsu and set off for Manzhen's house.

When he got there, the downstairs tenant opened the door for him. The upstairs rooms were very quiet, and Old Mrs. Gu was sat alone eating rice porridge. "My!" she exclaimed, when she saw Shijun. "You're here early today! When did you arrive in Shanghai?" Ever since Manzhen's trip to Nanking, her mother and grandmother had assumed that the wedding plans were confirmed—there was even a ring to prove it. Old Mrs. Gu was therefore especially warm in her welcome to him. She called over to the adjoining room, "Manzhen! Get up! Guess who's here!"

"She's not up yet?" Shijun asked, smiling.

Manzhen answered for herself. "Some of us get up early all week long. On Sundays we're allowed to sleep in a bit."

"Shuhui's just as lazy as you are. When I left the house, he still hadn't raised the bed-curtain."

"That's right," Manzhen retorted. "He and I are both hard-working office staff, not like you big bosses."

"You're just hiding in there so you can hurl insults at me!"

There was a burst of giggles from inside the room.

"Come out here," Manzhen's grandmother called. "Stop yelling through the wall—what a racket you're making!"

There were several empty bowls on the table, and now that Old Mrs. Gu had finished her breakfast, she cleared the table by stacking them up. "You're early," she said to Shijun, "but the children are even earlier. They've gone off already, to watch a game."

"How about Mrs. Gu?" he asked.

"She went to see Manzhen's older sister. Big Sis has been in poor health recently, and wanted her mother to come and see her. Spent the night there too—she hasn't returned yet."

The mere mention of Manzhen's older sister stirred up unease in Shijun's mind. His face became a dark mask.

Old Mrs. Gu took the bowls and chopsticks to the downstairs kitchen. Manzhen was still in the inner room, putting on her clothes while asking Shijun how his family was doing, whether his nephew was feeling better, and so on. Shijun made his replies with forced good cheer, then told her about Yipeng and Tsuizhi's breakup.

"That comes as a surprise!" Manzhen said. "We all sat there hap-

pily over dinner that day. Who would have imagined this next install-
ment in the story?"

"Indeed. Such drama!"

"I think some people have seen too many films," Manzhen said.
"Sometimes they do things just for the sake of dramatic effect."

"All too true," Shijun agreed.

Manzhen had finished washing her face and came into the outer
room to comb her hair. Shijun looked at her in the mirror, and suddenly said, "You don't look anything like your sister."

"I don't think so either. But sometimes, even though we think
there's no family resemblance, other people see it right away."

Shijun said nothing. Manzhen turned to look at him. "What's
going on? Who says I look like my sister?"

Shijun still said nothing. Then, after a long pause, he let it out.
"My father once met your sister."

That gave her a shock. "Oh! No wonder he said he thought he'd
met me before!"

Shijun told her his mother's view of the situation. Manzhen was
a bit put out when she heard that his father, for all his overbearing,
pompous ways, was nonetheless a reprobate who slipped off to the
demi-monde in search of a good time. "So what did you say?" she
asked, when Shijun had finished.

"I said you didn't have an older sister."

Manzhen's face registered her disapproval.

"Of course there's no connection between your sister's situation
and yours. You've been working in an office ever since you finished
school. But we could spend a lifetime explaining this to them, and
they still won't see it clearly. It's better just to ignore the whole thing,
and let it fizzle out."

Manzhen was silent for several moments. Then she laughed
lightly and said, "In fact my sister's already married, and maybe if
you told your father that, he wouldn't be so stubborn—especially
since my sister is rich now."

"But . . . my father isn't the kind of man who thinks only of
money."

"I didn't mean to say that. Still, I don't see how we can keep this from him. It'll get out, one way or another. Our neighbors will tell the whole story to anyone who asks."

"Yes, I've thought of that. I think your family should move. I brought you some money. Moving is expensive, isn't it?" He took two wads of notes out of his pocket. "I saved this up when I was working here in Shanghai."

Manzhen stared at the money, her face expressionless.

"Take it," Shijun urged her. "Don't let Granny see it—she'll wonder what it's all about." He pulled a newspaper across the table, and hid the money under it.

"How is this going to work? Won't your father have to meet my sister at some point?"

Shijun paused, then eventually said, "We can figure that out when the time comes. As things stand now, we'd better . . . just not see her."

"How am I going to explain that to her?"

Shijun made no reply. He leaned over the table, pretending to read the paper.

"I can't do this to her—she's already sacrificed so much for our family's sake."

"I have nothing but sympathy for your sister and what she's been through," Shijun said, "but other people don't see it the way we do. To get along in society, sometimes you have to—"

Manzhen did not wait for him to finish. "Sometimes you have to show a little courage," she put in.

Shijun again fell silent for a long moment. "I see. I'm sure I've seemed weak to you, ever since I gave up my job." In fact, he'd quit that job mainly because of her. It was so unfair—words could not begin to express the unfairness of it all.

Manzhen had not said anything more. Shijun went on, his voice low: "I suppose you feel disappointed in me." In his heart he was thinking, *You probably regret your decision now. Especially when you think of Yujin.* All he could think of was Yujin, but Manzhen had no idea of that.

"I am not disappointed, I tell you. But there is one thing I want to know. Do you plan to go out and get a job? I can't believe you'd be willing to stay at home your whole life, like your father."

"My father may be behind the times, he may have an old-fashioned way of thinking, but that's no reason for you to disrespect him!"

"When have I ever disrespected him? It's you who don't respect people! I don't think there's anything wrong with my sister, no reason why she should be hidden away, kept from meeting people. She hasn't done anything wrong. It's all society's fault—this unfair society of ours! If you want to talk about immorality, I don't know who's more immoral: prostitutes, or the men who are their clients!"

Shijun thought she really ought not to have let loose with this hurtful tirade. His only reply was silence. Bitter pain coursed through his body as he sat there.

Manzhen suddenly pulled the ring off her finger and set it down in front of him. "No need to let this worry you so," she said with a sharp laugh. The words themselves were light and casual, but her throat betrayed her and her voice revealed the strain.

Shijun stared for a long moment, then finally smiled. "What's going on here? Weren't you just saying that a certain someone we know is a drama queen? Looks like it's got into you too!"

Manzhen stayed silent. Her face had gone white with nervousness, and when Shijun looked at her, his color changed too. He picked up the ring and threw it into the wastebasket.

He got to his feet, and struggled to collect up his hat and overcoat. To steady his nerves, he raised his tea glass from the table and emptied it in one swallow. Still his body was cold, and none of his muscles would do his bidding. He yanked the door to behind him as he went out, and the slam when it shut gave them both a great jolt: shock waves rippled through their nervous systems.

The room was chilly, so when the glass of hot tea was emptied, it misted the air with steam, like a human breath. In that wintery cold room, the vapor floated up from the glass in curly white wisps. Manzhen stared at it. The glass from which he'd drunk was still hot, but he was gone, and would not be back again.

She burst into tears. Hard as she tried to hold them in, the wailing sobs rose in her throat. She fell onto the bed, burying her face in the pillow, nearly suffocating herself. She may as well die of suffocation—anything to stifle these sobs, to keep Granny from hearing her crying. If anyone heard her, there'd be question after question, then warnings and advice—none of which she could bear.

Luckily, her grandmother stayed downstairs. Eventually she heard the old woman coming up the stairs; Manzhen grabbed a newspaper so she could lie in bed with her face covered, pretending to read. When she picked up the paper, she saw the two stacks of notes on the table; if her grandmother saw them, there'd be questions to answer, so she stuffed them under her pillow.

"Has Shijun left already?" her grandmother asked when she came in.

"He had something to do."

"He's not staying for a meal? I bought some meat for him. The woman downstairs went to the market and I asked her to get a bit of pork for us. So nice of her to do that! And I sorted a little more rice, even though your mother's not back yet, and I don't know whether she'll be back in time for lunch."

She prattled on, and Manzhen made no reply, just kept reading her newspaper. Suddenly there was a loud crack, the sound of an old woman's joints. Her grandmother bent down stiffly and fished around in the wastebasket for something to start the charcoal fire with.

The ring—it's still in that basket! flashed urgently through Manzhen's mind, followed by the hope that it would not be found.

But then she heard her grandmother's cry: "What? Isn't this your ring? How could it have fallen in the bin? What a careless girl you are!"

Then there came a flood of recriminations, as her grandmother used the corner of her apron to wipe the dust off the ring, then handed it to her. She had to put it back on.

"This bit of yarn here is dirty. You should pull it off. Don't wear the ring now—take it to a jeweler's and get it sized so it fits properly."

Manzhen thought of the coffee-colored old sweater from which he'd taken the wool, and how he'd wrapped the ring so that it would fit her finger. The memory of that moment was like a flight of arrows piercing her heart.

Her grandmother went back downstairs to light the stove. Manzhen threw the ring into a seldom-used drawer. But then, when she heard her mother returning, she got the ring out and put it back on her finger. Her mother kept a close watch on such things, and would be sure to ask why she wasn't wearing the ring. And it was a lot harder to pull the wool over her mother's eyes—not like Granny, who after all was getting old.

"Something is wrong with our doorbell," Mrs. Gu said as soon as she came in. "I rang and rang, but no one came."

"It worked fine when Shijun was here, just a little while ago!" Granny said.

Mrs. Gu's face widened into a big smile. "Oh! Shijun was here, was he?"

"He was here, then left," Granny said. "Don't you think he'll come back in a bit, and eat with us?" She was still thinking about that bit of pork.

"Hard to say," Manzhen said. "Ma, how is Big Sis feeling? Is she any better?"

Mrs. Gu shook her head and sighed. "It looks pretty bad to me. She used to say it was a stomach problem, but now she says it's something more serious—the disease has gone deeper, it's in her intestines now."

Granny gasped in dismay. Manzhen too was shocked. "Is it intestinal tuberculosis?"

Mrs. Gu was whispering now. "Her husband stays out night after night, even though she's so sick. He doesn't seem to care at all!"

Granny whispered back. "She's heartbroken and outraged—that's why she's ill!"

"When I think of all she's been through, I feel so sorry for her," Mrs. Gu said. "She's never had any happiness. People say money brings happiness, but that child's never had any!" Her eyes were brimming with tears.

Granny started down the stairs to finish the cooking, but her daughter-in-law tried to stop her. "Ma, I'll go and do the cooking."

"You should rest a bit," the older woman said. "You've only just come back."

Mrs. Gu sat down. "Your sister really misses you," she said to Manzhen. "She keeps talking about you. When you have time, you should go and see her. Oh—but Shijun's in town, so you can't go now."

"I can go," Manzhen said. "I want to see her too."

Mrs. Gu smiled at her. "Not a good idea. He came all the way to Shanghai to see you, so you should stick around for him. You can go to your sister's in a few days. Sick people can be temperamental, you know. They think of a certain food, or someone they want to see, and start pining for that. But once they've got it, they're not interested anymore."

After she'd sat and chatted for a bit, Mrs. Gu got up and put an apron on, then went downstairs to help Granny with the cooking. When they'd eaten, she got out some sheets and other things she couldn't leave dirty, intent on getting the laundry done before the holiday. Granny could handle only small items, so the two women worked on the washing together. Manzhen sat alone, staring into space. Her mother thought she was waiting for Shijun and, in fact, Manzhen was hoping, subconsciously, that he'd return. She couldn't bring herself to believe that he'd never come again. Even if he did come, surely he'd be plagued by misgivings. Then he'd ring the bell and no one would answer, and he'd think they were ignoring it on purpose. He'd leave again. The doorbell hadn't been broken earlier that morning—why did it have to break now? Today of all days. Yet one more thing to worry about.

Usually she liked to stand at the window watching for him, but today she didn't want to. She mooched around inside, glancing at the paper, glancing at her fingernails. The sun slanted its rays, and still he did not come. He was sulking, so she'd sulk too—even if he did come, she wouldn't open the door to him. But apparently fate was toying with her, for just when she'd made this decision, she heard a knock. Her mother and grandmother were in the washroom doing the laundry; they were sloshing about and couldn't hear anything over the noise of water and wet clothes. The woman downstairs must have gone out—she wouldn't have let someone stand there, knocking and knocking like that. Manzhen knew she had to go down and open the door, but still she hesitated. As she sat there wondering what to do, she kept listening, and realized that the pounding was coming from the kitchen—someone was chopping meat with a cleaver, and she'd heard it as a knock at the door. Her mind was in such a daze.

Suddenly her grandmother called out, "Hurry! Hurry! Your mother has hurt her back!" Manzhen leaped up, and saw her mother holding on to the door frame for support, breathing heavily. "I don't know how it happened," Granny said, "but she's thrown her back out."

"Ma, how many times have I told you—you should send the sheets out to be washed."

"And then," said Granny, "you tried to do too much. You wanted to get the whole load done in one day."

"It's because the holiday is coming," Mrs. Gu panted. "I had to get it done before the New Year comes."

"OK, OK," Manzhen said. "Ma, you should lie down and have a rest." She led her mother over to the bed.

"I think you'd better go and see an acupressure doctor," Granny said. "He can sort you out."

But Mrs. Gu did not want to spend the money. "No, it's all right. I just have to take it easy for a few days, and then I'll be fine."

Manzhen frowned but said nothing. She helped her mother take off her shoes, covered her with a quilt, then dried her wet hands with a handkerchief. Mrs. Gu turned her head on the pillow, so as to hear better. "Is that someone knocking at the front door?" she asked. "Why didn't you, with your sharp ears, hear it, when even I can hear it?"

In fact, Manzhen had heard it already, but she didn't want to make the same mistake twice, so she hadn't said anything.

"Go and see who it is," her mother urged her.

But the guest had already arrived at their door. Old Mrs. Gu led him in, exclaiming all the while, "Oh, it's you! How are you?"

The guest greeted her politely, calling her "Great-aunt."

"You've come at just the right time," Granny said. "Your cousin's mother has put her back out. Maybe you could take a look." She led him into the room.

Mrs. Gu sat halfway up, clasping the bedclothes in her arms.

"Now don't get up," Granny said. "Yujin is one of us, after all."

Yujin heard how she'd tried to wash too many things at once and thrown her back out. "Cover the area with cloths soaked in hot water," he advised. "Do you have any pine-resin oil? Rub some of that on her back—it will help a lot."

"I'll go out in just a bit and buy some," Manzhen said. She poured tea for Yujin. Seeing him reminded her of how happy she'd been last time he'd been there. That was only two months ago—how quickly our fortunes change! she thought to herself. Again she felt herself slipping into a stupor.

Old Mrs. Gu asked Yujin when he'd arrived in Shanghai. "I've been here a week already," he said. "But I haven't had a single free moment to come by . . ." He pulled out a wedding invitation and handed it to her, slightly bashful.

"Oh!" cried Mrs. Gu. "You're inviting us to your wedding!"

"Good!" said Granny. "It's good for you to get married!"

"Who's the bride?" Mrs. Gu asked.

Manzhen opened the invitation with a smile, and saw that the banquet would be held the next day. The bride's family name was Chen.

"Did you meet her in the countryside?" Old Mrs. Gu asked.

"No, it was last time I came to Shanghai. You remember I stayed with a friend for a couple of nights? They introduced me to her. We've been writing back and forth ever since."

Meet someone, write a few letters, and get married, Manzhen was thinking, despite herself. It's all happened so fast, in less than two months . . . She knew that Yujin had suffered a shock last time he'd been in Shanghai, though she didn't know about his meeting with her older sister. But, in any case, this was happy news for him, and she should help him celebrate. It was just that this had come right at the point when she had so much on her mind. Smiling took so much effort, and yet she had to smile. He didn't know the reasons for her heartache; if she didn't smile, he might think his wedding was causing her distress.

"After the wedding, will you two stay in Shanghai for a few days?" she asked.

"No, we're going straight back."

Seeing her the day before his wedding made him feel rather mixed up. He sat with them for a little while, then said he had to go. "Sorry, but there are still lots of things I have to take care of."

"We'd be happy to help if we could—it's a pity we didn't know earlier." She was smiling so hard her cheeks were sore. Yujin knew there was something strange going on; the moment he saw her, he'd noticed her swollen, red eyelids and guessed she'd been crying. No sign of Shijun either, so maybe they'd had a falling-out? But he made himself stop right there. Here he was, a man getting married the very next day—it was not the time to be thinking about other people's problems. Going on like this was pure foolishness.

He stood up and picked up his hat. "Please come early tomorrow."

"We'll certainly be there," Mrs. Gu said.

Manzhen was about to see him to the door when suddenly she heard a flurry of impatient knocking, and the woman downstairs calling out, "Mrs. Gu, your daughter has sent someone to see you!"

Manzhen had already given up hope, convinced that Shijun wouldn't come back, but her heart sank again when the person at the door wasn't him.

When Mrs. Gu heard that Manlu had sent someone, she was very surprised, and wondered if her daughter had taken a turn for the worse. She pushed the quilt back and felt around on the floor for her shoes. "Who is it?" she called out. "Tell him to come in."

Manzhen went down the stairs. It was the Zhu family's driver. He came up the steps and stood outside the entrance to their apartment. "Mrs. Gu, my mistress has asked me to come and fetch you."

"What's going on?" Mrs. Gu asked, her voice trembling.

"I'm not sure," the driver replied. "I heard that she's very ill."

"I'm coming," said Mrs. Gu.

"But can you walk?" asked Granny.

"I'll manage."

"All right, please go back to the car," Manzhen told the driver.

"You go with me," Mrs. Gu told her daughter.

Manzhen agreed, and slowly helped her mother to her feet. But when Mrs. Gu tried to stand up, the pain radiated from her spine throughout her abdomen, a pain so intense it made her want to vomit. And yet she would not let herself cry out, for fear that the others would prevent her from going.

Mrs. Gu had not wanted to tell Yujin about Manlu's illness: a man filled with wedding joy shouldn't be burdened with tales of woe. But Old Mrs. Gu could not be silenced, and she soon told him all about it. Yujin asked what sort of illness it was. Mrs. Gu told him the whole story from the beginning, omitting the part about Manlu's husband's callous disregard, his apparent lack of interest in whether his wife lived or died. Such a contrast between Manlu's forlorn, lonely state and Yujin's bright prospects as a bridegroom on the verge of a happy union: the thought of her daughter's unhappy fate could not but drive a mother to tears.

There was nothing Yujin could say to comfort her. All he could do was wonder aloud, "How could she have fallen so ill, so quickly?" Seeing Mrs. Gu's tears, he suddenly realized that the same instinctive outpouring of strong feeling had to be the cause of Manzhen's swollen eyes. That made his wild guesses of a moment ago seem more foolish than ever. And here he was, in people's way, just when they were getting ready to go off to a sick woman's bedside. He gave them a quick goodbye and was off. On his way out, he saw a brand-new car parked by the back door—it must be Manlu's car. He studied it a moment.

A few minutes later, Mrs. Gu and Manzhen were riding in that car along Hongqiao Road. "I didn't want to let Yujin know about this," Mrs. Gu said, wiping her tears away.

"Well, it doesn't matter," Manzhen replied. "But I don't think we should tell Manlu about his marriage, at least not now. It's not good to tell sick people anything that might upset them." Mrs. Gu nodded and agreed.

When they got to the Zhu household, the maid Ah Bao greeted them like family: she went on and on about the master's misbehavior, how he hadn't come back for days, and they'd sent someone to find him, but he couldn't be found—it was all so aggravating. The story came with stamping and crying, and wild hand gestures, and took forever to tell. She led them into Manlu's room, walked up to the bed and called out in hushed tones, "Mistress, your mother and sister are here."

"She's asleep," Mrs. Gu whispered. "Don't wake her."

But Manlu had already raised her eyelids slightly. When Mrs. Gu saw how pale and weak her daughter had become, much worse than she'd seemed that same morning, it gave her quite a start. She leaned over and stroked her daughter's forehead. "How are you feeling now?"

Manlu closed her eyes.

Mrs. Gu stared at her in silence, her mind wandering.

"Has the doctor been?" Manzhen asked Ah Bao in an undertone.

Manlu answered, in a voice so faint they could barely hear her. "He was here. He said that . . . that tonight we need to be especially careful . . ."

So the doctor is saying that tonight will be critical, Mrs. Gu thought. But why is he saying this to the patient herself? Then she realized the doctor was not to blame, since no one in the house was taking responsibility—the only one he could speak to was the sick woman herself. Manzhen had grasped the same point, and she and her mother exchanged silent, meaningful glances.

"Ma, you should sit down," Manzhen urged her mother, drawing her over to the sofa.

Manlu's ears were alert. "What's the matter, Ma?" she asked.

"She's thrown her back out," Manzhen replied.

Manlu raised her head towards her mother. "If I'd known that . . . you don't really need to be here, since Manzhen's come too. That's good enough."

"It's nothing serious," Mrs. Gu said. "I sprained it a bit, but if I just take it easy it'll be fine."

Manlu said nothing for a long moment. "But in a little while you should go home," she finally said. "If you get too tired, I'll feel . . . I'll feel bad."

Sick as she is, Mrs. Gu thought to herself, she's still thinking of me. That's when you really can see a person's true character. People with hearts like that are supposed to live a long, long time.

These reflections made her sinuses tingle, and a moment later two big tears rolled down her face, but fortunately Manlu had already closed her eyes again.

The lights had been turned on in the room, making it suddenly seem very late. The doctor had said this would be the critical time; uncertainty hung in the air. Mrs. Gu and Manzhen sat in the lamp-light, both of them preoccupied.

Manzhen was thinking about the argument she'd had with Shi-jun. It seemed to her that even though it had begun as a disagreement over her sister, he had the wrong attitude about it; she could see that the two of them had been seeing things differently, over the past little while. Even if her sister were to die, the problem would still be there. She told herself, over and over, that even if her sister died, it wouldn't make things better—till suddenly she wondered if she were in fact wishing for her sister's death. That thought left her flooded with guilt, utterly ashamed of herself.

Ah Bao came in and invited them to eat dinner. The meal was laid out in an informal dining room on the upper floor, for just the two of them. "What about Beckon?" Mrs. Gu asked.

"She never eats at the table," Ah Bao said.

Mrs. Gu insisted that the girl be brought out. Ah Bao had to fetch the child.

"Goodness! Why doesn't she ever seem to grow any taller?" Mrs. Gu asked, in a friendly tone.

"Yes," said Ah Bao. "She looked just the same when she first came here. OK then, greet your grandmother! And this is your Second Aunt. Quick! Greet them politely or you won't get anything to eat."

"She's just scared," Mrs. Gu said. Seeing the child struggling to get away, she could imagine what a hard time her daughter had, try-ing to cope with this girl. She couldn't help but sigh to herself, Ah! Here's where Manlu missed a chance for good luck! And because she wanted to improve her daughter's fortunes, she made a great effort to please the child, picking out all the best bits of food and putting them in her bowl—the chicken liver from the soup, and then the chicken's tail, which she called the "needle-and-thread purse." "Here! Eat the 'needle-and-thread purse,' it'll help you with your sewing!" And then, a little later: "As soon as your mother's well, I'll ask her to bring you over to our house to play. You've got so many little aunts and uncles there, and they'd be happy to play with you."

At the end of the meal, Ah Bao brought them hot damp cloths to wipe their hands. "The mistress says that when you've finished eating, Mrs. Gu, you should let the driver take you home in the car."

"That daughter of mine!" Mrs. Gu exclaimed. "She's always been like that. Once she makes up her mind, there's no arguing with her. She simply won't listen."

"Ma, you really should go back," Manzhen said. "If you stay here all night, it'll only make her feel bad."

"There's nothing to worry about," Ah Bao put in. "Your other daughter is here, so everything will be all right."

"But didn't the doctor say we should be especially careful tonight? I'm afraid that if I go back, and something happens, well, Manzhen's still young after all, and she's never had to deal with something like this."

"That's just the doctor's way of putting things," Ah Bao said. "There's really no need to worry. If anything happens, we'll send the car for you at once."

Mrs. Gu really did want to go home and rest. She was used to doing everything for herself, and when she came here, the tea was brought, the food was served—it was too much for her. She'd already spent the previous night in this house and found it uncomfortable.

Mrs. Gu went back to Manlu's room to say goodbye, and while she was there Manzhen reminded her, "Ma, on your way back, go to a pharmacy and get the driver to buy you some pine-resin oil. Rub some of that on your back, and you'll feel better tomorrow."

"That's right," her mother said. "I'd already forgotten. And I have to cover my back with cloths soaked in hot water."

All of that was Yujin's advice for her backache. Thinking of him suddenly reminded her of something else. "Are you going to the wedding tomorrow?" she whispered to Manzhen. "I think you'd better go." It seemed to her important that Manzhen, in particular, attend the wedding banquet; if she didn't go, it might look as though she were displeased. Manzhen knew what she meant, and nodded.

Manlu had heard all this, and asked, "Who's getting married?"

"It's an old classmate of mine," Manzhen said. "Ma, if I run out of time, I'll go there directly, so don't wait for me."

"Don't you want to come home first and change your clothes?" Mrs. Gu asked. "That outfit is too plain. Why don't you borrow something from your sister? I remember she's got a purple stretch-silk dress that would be just right."

"Yes, yes," Manzhen agreed impatiently.

After she'd issued a few more instructions, her mother finally left.

Manlu seemed to have fallen asleep. Manzhen turned off the lights, except for the one at the head of the bed. The room smelled of medicine. Manzhen sat alone, thinking back over the day's events. That morning, even before she'd got out of bed, Shijun had arrived, and the two of them had bantered back and forth through the wall; he'd laughed at her for sleeping in so late. But that was in the morning. It seemed far away now, like a dream.

Ah Bao came in. "Second Young Lady," she said in a whisper, "go and get some sleep. I'll stay here with her, and if she wakes up, I'll call you."

Manzhen had been planning to rest on the sofa and get some sleep there, but then she realized that even though Hongtsai had not been home in several days, he could come home at any time. Sleeping in her sister's room could be awkward. So she nodded and stood up.

Ah Bao leaned over to take a close look at Manlu. "She's fast asleep," she whispered.

"Good," said Manzhen. "I'd like to make a phone call to my mother, to reassure her."

"But," said Ah Bao, laughing a bit, "if you call at this hour, won't that scare her half to death?"

Manzhen realized she was right. Her mother would surely imagine that her sister had taken a turn for the worse. It would shake her up no end, after all the work they'd done to get her to go home. Her real reason for calling was the slim chance that Shijun might have come back; if he had, her mother would certainly report that fact to her. But now she saw that she'd better let it go and forget about calling. He wouldn't come anyway, and she knew it.

They'd arranged a room for her. Ah Bao took her through another room filled with furniture, all the things that Manlu had brought with her when she got married. They'd bought full, new sets of better furniture since then, so all the old things were piled up here, the tables and chairs covered with dust, the sofa wrapped in newspaper. This pair of rooms was usually left locked and unused, but the inner one had been equipped with a few basic furnishings as a temporary bedroom. Manzhen wondered if her mother had slept here the previous night. She didn't want to detain Ah Bao with small talk. "You should go back," she urged. "Somebody should be with my sister."

"Don't worry," the maid replied. "Amah Zhang is with her. Is there anything else you need, Second Young Lady?"

"No, I'm fine. I'm going straight to bed."

Ah Bao stayed in the room until she'd got into bed, then turned the light off and left.

Manzhen was used to living in a big family, with people all around, and the feeling of being alone in a cold, still room was strange to her. The house was in an especially quiet, remote area, so it was almost perfectly silent at night—even the sound of dogs barking was rare. Too much quiet feels strange. Manzhen suddenly remembered Yujin's trouble when he first came to Shanghai, how the city noises kept him awake at night. Here she was, facing the same problem, but from the opposite direction. Thinking of Yujin brought back, in a great rush, all the things that had happened that day. They loomed in front of her again, filling her mind with tumult. Then from her bed in that deathly still, empty room, she heard a train going by, with long bursts of its whistle. Hard to tell if it was coming from the northern station, or the western one, much less where it was going. In any case, when she heard it she knew, for a fact, that Shijun was returning to Nanking. He was headed further and further away from her.

She heard a car out on the road. Might it be Hongtsai, coming home? The car went past without stopping and she relaxed. Why was she so nervous? There was no cause for such anxiety. Even if Hongtsai did come home drunk, there was no way he'd blunder into this room by mistake—it was at the other end of the house from his. But for some reason, she kept listening for the sound of car tires.

Hongtsai had once taken her home in his car, after splashing on a bucketful of cologne; sitting next to her in the backseat, he'd reeked of it. Why was she suddenly reminded of that? Because she was again smelling that cologne. And the scent was growing strong, then even stronger, in that dark room. All the hairs on her body stood on end.

She sat up suddenly.

Someone else was in the room.

12

Yujin's wedding was held in a community hall, hired through people they knew. The place was full of guests, most of them on the bride's side since Yujin didn't have many acquaintances in Shanghai. Mrs. Gu went, expecting to meet Manzhen there, but didn't see her even though she scanned the crowd throughout the ceremony. *What is the matter with her?* Mrs. Gu thought to herself. *I made it quite clear to her yesterday. She should know that even if she doesn't want to come, she has to put in an appearance. Why isn't she here? Could it be that Manlu's condition has got worse, and she can't get away?*

She got so agitated she couldn't sit still; her head was full of fears that Manlu was fading away, barely clinging on to life. Meanwhile, the wedding march was playing, the bride and groom had just left the hall, and the guests were sitting down to the feast. Everywhere she looked, smiling faces and happy laughter filled the place; she sat still amid all those cheerful folk, dumb with worry and confusion. She had planned to wait until the wedding pair reappeared, so she could offer her congratulations, but she simply could not wait any longer. She slipped out and hired a cab, heading straight for the Zhu household.

The situation there, at that moment, was entirely different from Mrs. Gu's imaginings. Manlu was fine, showing no signs of illness whatsoever; she was sitting on her sofa in a silk dressing gown, smoking a cigarette and talking to her husband. He was the one who seemed unwell: he had a pair of bandages plastered across his face and a hand wrapped in gauze. Still in a state of shock, he kept saying the same thing, over and over, "Never seen a woman like that. *She actually bit me!*"

He'd been pushed off the bed, crashing to the floor so hard he almost lost his grip on her. He'd felt a burst of heat in his nose, and then a stream of blood was let loose. The ferocity of her screaming rattled his brain, and then she bit him so hard he screamed too; in the end he'd had to grab her by the hair and knock her out, by hitting her head on the floor. He couldn't tell, in the dark, if she was dead, and would drag him too into the grave. He turned on the light, and saw that she was still breathing. He carried her unconscious body to the bed and stripped off her clothes: she looked like a luscious corpse. This was his chance to romp to his heart's content; he wanted to die on her, this first night being, he had a strong hunch, their last also.

"You can hardly blame her," Manlu said mildly. "Did you think she'd treat you like a rich playboy with money to spare, and fall into your lap?"

"That's not it at all. You've never seen her like that—she went completely crazy! If I'd known she had a temper like that—"

Manlu cut him off. "I know that temper of hers, and that's why I told you it wouldn't work. She'd never go along with it. But you were so sure I was being jealous—you got all spiteful, as if I were your worst enemy. You pushed me so hard I had to give in and find a way to get you what you wanted. Now you come to me all scared and jittery—what *are* you after? Seems to me you'll do anything, just to make me angry!" She threw her cigarette at his face, almost burning him.

Hongtsai frowned. "Don't go on blaming me like that. Tell me what to do."

"What do you think?"

"We can't keep her locked up forever. Sooner or later your mother will come here asking about her."

"Don't worry about her. She'll be easy to manage, unless that Mister Fiancé has an opinion on all this."

Hongtsai was on his feet at once, pacing the room. "What a mess that would be!" he groaned.

Manlu's rage rose up again when she saw him whimpering like that. "Well, what do you want to do?" Her voice dripped with sarcasm. "Just let her go? You think they'll let you get away with this without making a fuss? Doesn't matter what you offer—this is not a business deal, they're not going to be bought off with money."

"That's why I'm so worried."

Manlu snorted. "Why are *you* worried? *She's* the one who should be worrying. She's been to bed with you—she can't change that fact, no matter how angry it makes her. Give her a couple of days to cool off, and I'll speak to her. If she's at all reasonable, she'll come down off her high horse and face the facts."

Hongtsai's doubts were not entirely assuaged; his self-confidence always wavered when he was dealing with Manzhen. "What if she won't listen to you?"

"Then we'll have to keep her in there a few days longer, till her temper wears off."

"Can't lock her up for the rest of her life."

"Can't, you say? Wait till she's got a baby. I promise you—once that happens, you won't be able to get rid of her. Leave her then, and she'll accuse you of abandoning her!"

When Hongtsai heard that, his gloom finally dissipated and his spirits rose. But then he shook his head, bothered by something else. "With a temper like that, is she going to accept secondary status?"

"Well, if she doesn't"—Manlu's voice was icy cold—"I'll step aside for her. How's that?"

Hongtsai knew this was said in anger, not a real offer. "What are you talking about?" he protested. "I'd never go along with that! I'm going to make this up to you, fine good wife of mine. A wife like you is rare indeed! It's time to show you how much I admire and respect you."

"OK, OK, that's enough. No need to pour it on so thick—just stop winding me up, that would be enough."

"You're still angry with me!" He took her hand in his, and pouted shamelessly. "Look how she's beaten me up—doesn't that move your heart, just a little?"

Manlu gave him a big shove. "That's what you deserve! Pity the poor woman who throws herself at your feet—you treat *her* like dirt! Look in the mirror and ask yourself: isn't that the truth?"

"All right, all right. No need to put on such an act for me. I can't handle all this carrying on from you two sisters—what a pair you are!" He was feeling good again, and Manlu could see that his superior, cocky air was returning.

She was itching to clip him round the ear, give him a good drubbing, but she held herself in check. She had promised herself to get a firm grip on him this time, by dangling her sister in front of his eyes, the way old ladies used opium to keep their sons from running off to brothels. Once a man had sunk into that sweet swamp, his ties to home were assured.

Husband and wife were deep in their private talk when Ah Bao appeared, a little flustered, and announced the arrival of Mrs. Gu. Manlu crushed her cigarette. "I'll handle this," she told her husband. "You should get out of here."

Hongtsai jumped to his feet.

"Go and hide in that room you were in yesterday, and wait for my signal," she continued. "Don't go running out of the house."

"Look at me! With a face like this, how can I go out? My friends would all laugh at me."

"Since when did you care about things like that? They'd just think you'd been fighting with your wife, and she was the one who beat you up and gave you a black eye."

"Who'd believe that? They all know I have a good, fine wife."

"Go on, get out of here." Manlu couldn't help giggling. "You think I'm fooled by your fine talk?"

Hongtsai quickly went out through a side door, passed through the next room and went down the back stairs to the ground floor. Manlu got busy: she undid her hair and messed it up, then grabbed a cold, wet cloth and rubbed the makeup off her face, threw her dressing gown off and buried herself in the quilt. Her mother came in. Manlu put on her sick face, but her mother could tell, the minute she saw her, that Manlu's health had improved. "Oh! You're looking so much better! Not at all the same person I saw yesterday!"

"Really?" Manlu sighed. "Well, if so, it's because I've just had two injections of adrenalin to keep me going."

Mrs. Gu didn't quite grasp all of that. She kept up her own happy line of commentary: "And your voice is so much stronger too! You really gave me a scare, yesterday." And just now, while waiting for Manzhen, she'd filled herself with fears that her elder daughter had slipped into a critical state, till she had to rush back to check on her. But of course she didn't mention this part.

She sat down next to the bed, and squeezed her daughter's hand. "Where's your sister?" she asked.

"Ma, something terrible has happened. That girl—she almost put me under, I tell you. If the doctor hadn't given me those two shots, the strain would have done me in."

"What?" Mrs. Gu was overwhelmed.

Manlu looked down at the covers, her expression pained. "Ma, I don't know how to tell you this."

"What's she done? Where is she?" Mrs. Gu stood up quickly and looked all around.

Manlu held on hard, and pulled her mother back. "Ma, sit down. I'll tell you, but please don't raise your voice. Hongtsai, that good-for-nothing, hasn't been home for days, but last night he came home drunk as a dog, and blundered into the room where Second Sis was staying. I was lying here sick, didn't know what was going on. By the time I found out, the terrible thing had already happened."

Mrs. Gu sat there frozen. "No, no, no!" she finally responded. "Your sister has someone already. How could he? How could he be so reckless? Daughter of mine—I am shattered. This is a disaster!"

"Ma, don't shout! The more you shout, the harder it is for me to think."

Mrs. Gu glared at her. "Where is that Hongtsai? I'll have it out with him!"

"He's hiding his face, of course. He knows he's made a huge mistake. 'Don't you know you've ruined her life?' I said to him. 'How can she get married now? Answer me that!'"

"That's right," Mrs. Gu said. "What did he say?"

"He agreed to marry her officially."

That proposition, so unexpected, stopped Mrs. Gu in her tracks. "Marry her officially? But what about you?"

"He and I are not officially married."

"This will not do," Mrs. Gu said bluntly. "It makes no sense."

"Oh, Ma—" Manlu sighed. "I'm not going to live long anyway. I can't be bothered about all that."

Mrs. Gu's heart ached. "Don't talk that way."

"Even if I don't die straight away, I'm so weak and unsteady—how can I manage a social life? I'd rather hand all that over to her. She'd be the official Mrs. Zhu, the one who goes out and meets people. I could stay at home, and take it easy. She's my sister after all—she'd never use her position to harm me!"

Manlu talked her mother into a state of stupefied sorrow. "Even so," Mrs. Gu began, "it still will not do. It's too unfair on you."

"I'm the one who married this good-for-nothing! And if I hadn't been so sick, this never would have happened. I'm so ashamed—I hardly know what to do." She wiped her tears away.

Mrs. Gu was also crying. Her tears this time were for Manzhen too. She would not want to live with Zhu Hongtsai, that much was sure. And yet, they had to find a solution of some sort, now that things stood as they did. Manlu's idea was not a perfect solution, but to Mrs. Gu it seemed a way forward, while all other avenues were blocked.

Mrs. Gu mulled the situation over, then stood up and said, "I'll go and see her."

Manlu sat bolt upright. "Don't do that—" She lowered her voice, and continued in a conspiratorial whisper, "She's kicking up a fuss, you know. She says she's going to the police."

"What?" Mrs. Gu was shocked. "That child doesn't understand how things work! If she goes out and broadcasts this, the shame will fall on her!"

"That's right," Manlu agreed softly. "We'd all lose face. Hongtsai has a good position in society now. If this got out, it would be embarrassing."

Mrs. Gu nodded. "I'll go and speak to her, set her straight."

"Ma, I don't think this would be a good time to see her. You know what a temper she has—when has she ever listened to you? And right now she is throwing a fit."

That gave her mother pause. "She shouldn't carry on like that."

"Indeed. I'm in a corner here—the only thing I could think of was to tell people that she's ill and needs to rest. No one can go into that room to see her, and she can't come out."

This last phrase sent a chill through Mrs. Gu—something wasn't right, but she couldn't tell what.

Manlu saw her mother sitting in a daze, not responding. "Ma," she said, "don't worry. In a few days, when she's calmed down, we can have a little talk with her. Once she agrees, we can arrange the wedding right away. Hongtsai has agreed. Now it's up to her. But what about that Mr. Shen? Are they engaged?"

"Yes, they are. What can we say to him?"

"Is he in Shanghai now?"

"He came yesterday, early in the morning."

"Does he know that she came here?"

"No. He came early in the morning, but left and didn't return."

"That's strange," Manlu muttered softly. "Did the two of them quarrel?"

"Now that you mention it, Granny told me that Manzhen dropped her engagement ring into the bin. Could she have thrown it there on purpose?"

"They must have quarreled. But why? Was it because of Yujin, do you think?" Manlu's heart always ached when she thought of the close relationship between Yujin and Manzhen.

Mrs. Gu thought it over. "It couldn't have been Yujin. When he dropped in yesterday, Shijun was long gone. Their paths never crossed."

"Oh? Yujin came by yesterday? Why?" A wave of jealousy swept through her, erasing all else.

"To deliver his wedding invitation—oh dear! I wasn't going to tell you, and now I've let it out! All this stress is making me all confused."

Manlu couldn't believe her ears. "*What!* He's getting married?"

"Yes. Today."

"Yesterday you said you were going to a wedding. It was *his* wedding, wasn't it? Why didn't you want to tell me?"

"It was your sister's idea not to tell you right now. She said it's not good for a sick person to hear news that might be upsetting."

But this in itself was disturbing. When Manlu saw how considerate Manzhen had been, she realized that she alone, in all their family, cared about her older sister's feelings—the same sister who had now done this awful thing to her. Manlu was overcome with shame. She'd made a terrible mistake in heaping so much blame on her sister over Yujin. But it was too late now for regrets. She had to steel herself, face the situation as it stood. Once you mount the tiger, you can't get off—she'd have to stay evil till the bitter end.

Manlu lay there thinking these dark thoughts, fingering the telephone cord and twisting it around her hand till it coiled up on her wrist like a little serpent.

"But I can't just go off and leave her here!" Mrs. Gu suddenly burst out. "What will I say to the others?"

"Granny's not a problem. You can tell her what happened, though it's possible she'll let it slip. Do what you think is right. The younger ones are too little to understand anyway."

Mrs. Gu gave her a big frown. "You call them little, but Weimin will be fifteen in the spring."

"If they ask, tell them Manzhen is ill, and she's resting at my house. Tell them it's lung disease and she won't be able to work anymore. You'll have to cut down on expenses, and since living costs in Shanghai are so high, you'll have to move inland."

"Why?" Mrs. Gu asked, bewildered.

Manlu spoke in a conspiratorial tone. "To get away from Mr. Shen, in case he comes looking for her."

Mrs. Gu fell silent. She'd been in Shanghai for many years, and the thought of moving away, uprooting her whole family, was hard indeed.

But Manlu did not give her time to think about it. She phoned Hongtsai's office and asked for Little Tao, a quick, sharp-witted assistant who was, moreover, fully literate. Manlu often got him to run errands for her, since none of the household staff were half as satisfactory when it came to managing things. She told him to come over right away. "I'm going to send him to Suzhou to find a house for you," she told her mother.

"Suzhou? Going back to our old place in the country would be better. Granny's always saying how much she wants to go back."

But Manlu didn't like the thought of all those old acquaintances everywhere, and besides Shijun knew it was their home town and could easily track them down. "Suzhou's better," she said. "It's closer. Anyway, it won't be for long. Once we know the date of the wedding, we'll send for you so you can come and do the honors. After that, of course you'll live in Shanghai and the children can go to school here. When Weimin graduates, he won't have to rush out and look for work. He can have a few more years of schooling, and even study abroad after that. I'll get Hongtsai to foot the bill. You've been through so many years of hardship, Ma. Now you should sit back and enjoy the good times, here with me. But I won't let you do the laundry anymore. You're getting older, Ma—you shouldn't be doing heavy work. Yesterday you got overtired and hurt your back. I don't think you know how much my heart ached when I heard that!" She dazzled her mother with fine talk, laying special emphasis on the gloriousness of Weimin's future career.

Little Tao arrived while they were talking. Manlu ordered him to go to Suzhou right away, rent a house that was ready for immediate occupancy, and wait for her family to arrive. She'd send a telegram telling him which train they'd be on, so he could meet them at the station and take them there. All of these arrangements were made in her mother's presence. Manlu then told her mother to rush home and start packing. She put her in the car with Little Tao, who was headed to the station. Mrs. Gu had wanted to ask again to see Manzhen, but she couldn't very well make her request in front of Little Tao, so she had to go along with the arrangements, which included a wad of notes given to her by Manlu.

Riding back in the car, Mrs. Gu was rather fearful; she didn't know what she'd say if Granny and the other children asked her about Manzhen. Apparently they were still at Yujin's wedding, because when she rang the bell, the old maidservant who worked for their tenants, the Liu family, opened the door. "Mr. Shen is here," the old woman said. "All of you had gone out, so he's been waiting a long time."

Mrs. Gu's heart leaped into her throat. She was so startled that everything Manlu had told her to do almost flew clean out of her head. All she could manage was to pull herself together sufficiently to see Shijun.

Shijun, after the big quarrel with Manzhen, had spent the whole of Sunday wandering around on his own. He'd got back to Shuhui's late that night and hadn't slept a wink. He telephoned Manzhen's office the next afternoon, and when he heard she hadn't come to work, he thought she must be ill, so he rushed over to her house. But none of the Gus were at home, and the Lius' servant told him that Manzhen had gone to her sister's the day before, in a car sent by her sister, and hadn't come back yet. Shijun remembered hearing that Manlu was sick. He assumed that Manzhen and her mother were taking turns sitting with her—which meant that her return home was by no means certain. The Lius' maid had been very kind to him. She let him in, and found him a place to sit while he waited. Since no one was at home upstairs and the door was locked, she got a chair from her employers' place and took him into the only unoccupied, unlocked room. It was the room formerly occupied by Yujin.

"That Dr. Zhang who used to stay in this room came by yesterday," the old woman told Shijun.

That startled him. "Oh? Did he stay here again?"

"I don't know. I wasn't here last night."

Just then, someone called out, "Amah Gao! You're needed here!" Off the woman went.

The room had been empty for a long time and the dust had piled up, making it a bit hard to breathe. Shijun sat alone and listless. Then he stood at the window, writing with his finger in the dust. He wrote, then rubbed it out, his mind a whirl: he'd been planning and rehearsing what he'd say to Manzhen to try to patch things up, but now that Yujin was on the scene, and apparently had seen her, he wondered if the doctor knew about their breakup. She wouldn't tell Yujin about it, would she? What an opportunity this was for Yujin—

seeing her just when she was hurt and angry. Thinking of that nearly made Shijun's heart explode. All he could think of was finding Manzhen and putting everything back the way it was before—that's what he wanted, more than anything.

Finally the doorbell rang. Amah Gao, with Shijun standing right behind her, opened the door for Mrs. Gu. He greeted her politely, this being the first time he'd seen her on this trip to Shanghai. But Mrs. Gu did not respond, which struck him as odd; she even seemed alarmed. He thought this meant that she knew about the breakup, and was angry. That made him feel ashamed, which strangled the words in his throat. Mrs. Gu had been fretting about seeing him, and when he suddenly appeared, it threw her off balance: she wanted to pour out everything to him. She had so much anguish, and no one to help her talk it through—at that moment, Shijun looked so familiar, she almost broke down in tears.

But the staircase was no place to talk, so she invited him upstairs. She led the way, reaching into her pocket for the key, since the upper-floor door was locked. Feeling for the key, her hand brushed against the big bundle of cash Manlu had given her. Those worn, warm notes in a big, thick wad. Money has a strange power of its own: touching those notes made her feel contrite towards Manlu. She'd made a promise to her oldest daughter, and if she spilled the secret now and told Shijun—well, young men are headstrong and impulsive. He'd be outraged, he'd call in the authorities, it would be a complete mess. On the other hand, young men are not to be counted on. That engagement ring was thrown away when he and Manzhen quarreled over some trifle—what were the chances that, after hearing what had befallen her, he wouldn't react badly? Likely as not, the marriage would not go through. Hongtsai's offer would be canceled, of course, and the Gus would be left with nothing. Once she'd given it some thought, it seemed to her that there were many reasons not to tell Shijun.

Mrs. Gu pulled the key from her pocket and tried the lock. So many thoughts had gone through her mind, leading to a complete change of direction, that now she was nearly faint with confusion. Her hands were sweaty and shaking, and no matter how she tried, she could not turn the key in the lock. In the end, Shijun did it for her. They went into the room and Shijun made small talk. "Has Granny gone out too?"

Mrs. Gu, her head still in a whirl, barely managed a grunt in reply. "My back hurts," she finally managed to say. "I came home before the others." She moved away to pour tea for him.

"Oh, please don't bother," Shijun insisted. "You should take it easy. Where did Manzhen go? Do you know when she'll be back?"

Mrs. Gu had her back to him as she poured the tea. She poured two cups, brought them over, then finally replied, "Manzhen is sick. She's at her sister's place, and wants to rest there for a few days."

"Sick? What kind of sickness?"

"Nothing serious. I'll ask her to phone you in a few days, when she's better. How much longer will you be in Shanghai?"

She was eager to find out how many days he'd be in Shanghai, but Shijun did not answer her question. "I'd like to go and see her," he said. "What's the house number, on Hongqiao Road?"

Mrs. Gu hesitated. "The number . . . well, I don't know. I'm so fuzzy about these things, I only know what the house looks like." She gave a forced laugh.

Shijun could tell that she was trying to deceive him, which struck him as bizarre. Could it be that this was Manzhen's idea? Had she told her mother not to give him the address, because she didn't want to see him? But even if that were the case, the older generation always urges peace and reconciliation. Even if Mrs. Gu were upset with him and thought him in the wrong, she would, at the most, treat him coldly; she wouldn't try to prevent them from seeing each other. Suddenly he remembered that Yujin had been there, according to Amah Gao. Could this all be because of him?

Mrs. Gu's attitude, whatever its cause, made their conversation pointless. He stood up, took his leave and was gone. He went to a nearby shop, borrowed a telephone book and looked up the Zhu household on Hongqiao Road. Only one listing. It had to be Manzhen's sister's place. He copied down the house number and got a cab. It was a big house, surrounded by a decorative brick wall. Shijun rang the bell and a little square window in the metal gate opened up. The guard's face appeared.

"Is this the Zhu household?" Shijun asked. "I'm looking for Miss Gu, the second sister in the Gu family."

"What's your name?" the man asked.

"My family name is Shen."

The man closed the window with a clang. Then came the scraping sound of footsteps on a cinder drive, receding into the distance. He must have gone inside to report his presence. But Shijun waited for a very long time, and no one came to open the gate. He wanted to ring again, then thought he'd better not. This house stood alone on the street, no neighbors on either side, just empty land and vegetable plots stretching out all around; it was a cold, deserted, lifeless part of town. No birdsong even. The afternoon sky was dark and heavy. Suddenly, in the midst of all that stillness, came a sound carried by the wind: a woman crying. The wind blew past, and the sound disappeared. Where did that sound come from? Shijun asked himself. Could it have come from the house? The Hongqiao cemetery must be close by. Maybe it came from there, someone crying over a recent death. He listened carefully, but the sound did not come again. Only a sad, wrung-out feeling.

Just then, the gate-window opened and the guard reappeared. "Miss Gu is not here."

Shijun was taken aback. "How can that be? I've just come from the Gu household, and Mrs. Gu told me her second daughter is here."

"I already asked," the man said. "She's not here." He clanged the window closed again.

She's finished with me, Shijun thought to himself. She doesn't want to see me. Fear took hold of him, then he raised his hand and knocked on the gate. The man opened the window again.

"Excuse me, but is the lady of the house here?" He had met Manlu once before, and now he thought he might be able to get her to help him talk her sister round.

"She's not feeling well," the guard said. "She's resting."

Shijun had no further recourse. The pedicab driver who had brought him, unable to find customers in this remote district, circled around and asked if he'd like a ride back to the center of town. The guard watched Shijun get in and move off, then closed the gate-window.

Ah Bao had been standing behind the gate throughout all of this, hidden from view. She'd been sent by Manlu, who wasn't sure the guard would handle it properly. "Is he gone now?" she whispered to the man.

"Yes, he's gone."

"The mistress said all of you should go into the house. She has something to say." Ah Bao went around to all the servants, calling them together.

"In the future, if anyone comes looking for Second Sister, tell them she's not here," Manlu instructed them. "Second Sister is resting, recovering from an illness. Do exactly as I say, and I'll make sure you are rewarded. This illness makes her sometimes crazy, sometimes not, but in either case she's not allowed to go out. She's been placed in my care by our mother, and if she gets out I'll hold you responsible. *She absolutely cannot go out.* Is that clear?"

The servants chorused their assent. Manlu distributed their annual bonus pay, which she had doubled. All the servants left, except Ah Bao, who had already grasped the situation.

"Mistress," she said in a low voice, "perhaps you should ask Amah Zhang to take Second Sister's meals to her. Amah Zhang is very strong. Just now, when I went in, she almost knocked me over. I can't hold on to her." She lowered her voice even further. "It looks as if she really is sick," she whispered. "She can barely stand up."

"What kind of sick?" Manlu frowned.

"A bad chill. The wind comes streaming into her room, through the window she broke. All that cold air blowing on her, day and night. It's no wonder she got sick."

Manlu mulled this over. "We'd better do something about the room. I'll have a look."

"Be careful when you go into her room, Mistress."

Manlu got a bottle of cold medicine and went to see Manzhen.

The pair of rooms at the back of the house, the outer and the inner one, were both locked. She unlocked the outer room and stationed Ah Bao and Amah Zhang there as guards. As she approached the inner room, she heard, through the door, a sudden long moaning sound. It gave her quite a shock. In fact it was the casement of the broken window creaking back and forth in the wintry wind. Every time it crashed shut, pieces of broken glass fell down the side of the house, with a sharp tinkling sound. Manzhen had broken the windowpane the night before, when she'd screamed and screamed and no one could hear her. She'd cut her hand, then wrapped it with a handkerchief. She was lying on the bed, motionless. When Manlu opened the door and came in, Manzhen gave her a long, hard look. Her older sister, the one who'd been deathly ill only the day before, was now up and walking around, which meant she'd been faking. From the look of things, that sister was part of the plot against her. Manzhen was already shaken by feverish chills, and when she realized what her sister had done, a wave of fiery heat surged through her body, making her head swim. Her face turned bright red, and her vision went black.

Manlu too was shaken. "What's this?" she asked, with a forced smile. "Why is your face so red? Have you got a fever?"

Manzhen did not reply.

Manlu strode across the room to a chair that had been knocked over, reached down and righted it. The wind came through the broken window, swinging the casement back and forth; metal hit metal with an ear-splitting, heart-piercing crack.

Suddenly Manzhen sat up. "I want to go home. Let me go this minute, and we can forget it ever happened. A mad dog bit me, that's all."

"Second Sis, let's not fight about this. I'm angry too—of course I am. I gave him an earful, I did, but what's the use? What can we do about it, really? What he did is terrible, hateful, horrible. But he really is crazy about you—I know this for a fact. It's been going on for years, since before we married. He idolizes you. But he's always kept his distance, out of respect for you. If he hadn't been so drunk last night, he never would have dared. If you can bring yourself to forgive him, he'll make it all up to you, treat you perfectly from now on. His feelings for you will never change."

Manzhen grabbed a ceramic bowl from the table and hurled it at the floor. It was a bowl of food that Ah Bao had just brought her: the sauce spilled across the floor and the bowl shattered into several pieces. She picked up a big, sharp shard and held it up in front of her. "You go and tell Hongtsai that if he comes in again, he'd better be careful. I've got a knife."

Manlu said nothing. She leaned down and wiped the oily splashes off her feet with a handkerchief. "Let's not get so excited," she finally said. "We won't discuss this any further now. Wait till you're feeling better, and then we'll talk again."

"Are you letting me go or not?" Leaning on the table for support, Manzhen struggled to her feet and made for the door. Manlu pulled her back, and for a moment the two were locked in a struggle.

Manlu was a bit wary, since Manzhen was still wielding the broken piece of the bowl, sharp as a blade. "What's the matter with you?" she complained. "Have you gone crazy?"

The chunk of ceramic slipped from Manzhen's hand and smashed to pieces. "You're the one who's crazy!" she panted. "You're the one who set everything up—you colluded with him, you plotted all of this to hurt me. Are you even human?"

"I plotted to hurt you? I've had to put up with so much, I've suffered till I bled, all because of you and—"

"You won't even admit what you've done?" Manzhen's rage boiled over. Her hand swung out and landed a ringing blow on the side of her sister's head. She struck with such force that even she went dizzy. Both of them stood rooted in shock. Manlu instinctively raised her hand, intending to rub her head, but the hand paused in mid-air, and stayed there. Manzhen saw her sister standing in a stupor, half her face bright red from the blow, and all her sister's goodness came to mind. For years and years, she'd depended on her older sister's support, without ever so much as thanking her. Of course, families don't think in terms of generosity and recompense, and there exists a deep bashfulness between people whose bodies and lives are closely related. Many things, it seems, are better left unsaid.

For Manlu, all this had led to the belief that her younger sister looked down on her. That ringing slap made both sisters think of the thick account-book in which their relationship was recorded. And that made Manlu remember all the wrongs she'd suffered. Pain and anger surged through her, and her hatred fell on the virtuous victim's face—the very face that Manzhen was wearing.

She gave a cold, hard laugh. "Well, I never realized we had such a brave martyr in our family! If I'd taken that approach, our whole family would have starved! When you're a dance-hall girl, when you're a prostitute, people treat you like dirt and you just have to take it—you can't put on airs and graces. I'm no different from you. We're sisters, the same flesh and blood. So why am I beneath contempt, while you get to ride high in everyone's eyes?" Her voice kept rising in pitch till by the end she'd broken down, and tears coursed down her cheeks.

Ah Bao and Amah Zhang, still standing guard in the next room, were startled by the sounds of the struggle; they pushed the door open, ready to intervene, but when they heard Manlu saying something about being a dance-hall girl and a prostitute, they knew she wouldn't want anyone to overhear. Ah Bao gave Amah Zhang a sharp look and they both retreated. But just as they were about to latch the door, Manzhen rushed forward and lunged through. Manlu couldn't block her entirely, but she did grab her arm, and once again the two of them were fighting.

"What? You still won't let me go?" Manzhen shouted. "This is against the law, you know! Are you going to keep me locked up for the rest of my life? Or maybe you'll just kill me?"

Manlu did not reply; she wrenched herself free, throwing her sister back with a sweeping shove. Manzhen, still weak with fever, was thrown off balance. She staggered back, then fell to the floor in a sitting position, her outstretched hand landing on a shard of the broken rice bowl. She cried out in pain. Manlu had already run across the crackling broken bits to the door and closed it behind her. A key turned, and Manzhen was locked in again.

There was a gaping wound in her palm, oozing blood. She raised her hand to look at it and noticed the red-jewel ring on her finger.

Her ideas about sexual purity were different from those of women in earlier times—when she thought of Shijun, she had no sense of guilt or failure. Nevertheless, when she looked at the ring, she felt a stab of pain.

Shijun . . . Was he still in Shanghai, or not? Would he come here looking for her? Had her mother been? She knew better than to think she might rescue her. Even if her mother did know what had happened, she'd never call the police; she would not want any public airing of the family's dirty secrets. Besides, Mrs. Gu was convinced that a woman is supposed to stick with one man, for life. In her eyes, the goose was already cooked: the only solution was for Manzhen to marry Hongtsai and settle into some sort of wifely role. The tiniest bit of pressure from Manlu, and her mother would have no opinion of her own. If—and this was the only hope—her mother were willing to tell Shijun the whole story, then he'd be brought into the discussion. But was Shijun still in Shanghai, or not?

She pulled herself to her feet, gripping the windowsill. The broken pane was a jagged blade, like the peaks of a sawtooth mountain. The garden lay below, the lawn cropped and bare in the winter air, stretching out for what seemed a very long way. The wall stood tall on all sides—she'd never before noticed how high it was. The once-purple blooms of a bauhinia bush had shrivelled up, and the dry, cane-like branches shivered in the wintry wind. She suddenly remembered hearing, as a child, that bauhinia bushes are haunted by ghosts. She didn't know why people said that but, because they did, bauhinia always seemed gloomy to her. If she died here, wouldn't her ghost haunt that bauhinia? But she had no business falling into such dark, death-seeking thoughts: death would not relieve her rage. If only she had some matches—she'd set the whole house on fire and maybe manage, in the confusion, to escape.

Suddenly she heard someone in the next room. A carpenter was hammering away at something. A hatch was being installed in the door of the outer room, so that in the future her meals could be delivered more safely, but Manzhen didn't know what the plan was. She thought the door was being boarded up, to keep the crazy person locked up inside. The hammer blows rang out again and again, pressing on her heart; if felt like they were nailing up her coffin.

Then she heard Ah Bao talking to the carpenter, who responded in a local Shanghainese dialect, his voice soft with age. To Manzhen, it sounded like the voice of the outside world, and her heart turned over, full of hope. She pressed herself against the door and started shouting, asked him to take a letter to her family, told him her family's address, then Shijun's address. She said she'd been cruelly mistreated, had fallen into a trap, then been locked up. She went on and on, she no longer knew what she was saying, till even she did not recognize her own raspy, cracked voice. Screaming and crying like this, pounding on the door with her fists—wasn't that exactly what mad people did?

Suddenly she stopped. The next-door room was eerily quiet. Ah Bao had certainly already explained to the workman that the girl inside had a severe mental illness. And she herself was beginning to suspect that she was indeed near the edge of real madness.

The carpenter resumed his work. Ah Bao stayed with him, chatting and keeping watch. In that gentle, calm voice of his, the man told her they'd caught him just as he was getting ready to go back to his home in the countryside, for the New Year celebration. Ah Bao asked him how many children he had. Listening to them talk was like standing outside a house on a windy, snow-filled night, looking through a window at the family gathered in the bright lamplight. She felt so lost, so terrified. She leaned against the door, all her strength gone, tears flowing from her eyes.

She suddenly realized that her legs could no longer support her, and stumbled across the floor to the bed. Collapsing there felt soft and sweet, but a moment later all her joints were aching. She tossed and turned, unable to get comfortable, her breath so hot it felt like fire in her nostrils. These were the symptoms of a bad cold, she knew, but she'd never known they could be so severe. Each and every pore of her body seemed to be leaking sticky sweat; it was painful beyond words. Night was approaching, and the room grew steadily darker. She did not turn on the light, and soon lost track of time. At long last she drifted off, though the fierce burning of her wounded hand kept her from sleeping soundly.

She awoke in the middle of the night and saw a line of light under the door. That startled her. Then the sound of a key in the lock, followed by deep, unbroken silence. She was constantly on her guard now—sleeping fully clothed, not even taking her shoes off. She pushed off the quilt and sat up, but as soon as she did so the world started spinning and she almost fainted. By the time her head had cleared, the line of light under the door was gone. She waited a long time, but heard nothing, except the thumping of her own heart. It had to be Zhu Hongtsai. A rush of strength came to her, from some unknown source. She got up, turned on the light, then stood by the window, bracing herself. She must have had some confused notion of jumping out of the window, if it came to that. She'd leap, and take him with her. But long minutes passed in perfect silence. Nothing stirred. The tension slowly seeped out of her overwrought nerves and she realized that she was standing in a cold draft. The buffeting of the northwestern wind on her feverish body made for a bizarre sensation indeed. Blustering cold, burning heat, churning back and forth—it was dreadful.

She walked over to the door, tried the knob and it opened. Her heart was pounding again. Could someone be helping her, secretly letting her escape? The outer room, full of piled-up furniture, was dark and cave-like. She turned on the light. No one there. She saw the newly installed opening in the door, with a little shelf extending from it, on which was placed a lacquered tray that held a teapot, a teacup and a little plate of food. Then she understood: no one was helping her escape. They were only sealing off the connection between this room and the outside world. This was the little portal they'd use to deliver her meals. From the look of things, this was a long-term plan. When she saw that, she felt as though she'd fallen into a deep icehouse. She tried the outer door, but of course it was locked. The little hatch was locked too. The teapot was still hot to the touch. She poured a cup of tea, her hand shaking, and drank. She was very thirsty. But the taste was peculiar. She told herself her taste buds were wrong, but her mind danced with suspicion—maybe they had put something in it. She took another mouthful and it really was awful. Now her suspicions were fully raised, and she had to put the cup down. The thought of returning to that bed in that room filled her with loathing, so she lay down on a sofa in the outer room, on top of the old newspaper wrapping. There she slept all night, with the light still on.

The next morning, at breakfast time, Ah Bao must have looked through the hatch and seen her moaning in a delirium. Her temperature was too high, she could not focus her senses, but she had the impression of someone opening the door and carrying her into the next room. She was put to bed, and the maids kept up a steady supply of food and drink. Her head was so foggy she didn't know how much time passed, but one day her mind cleared a bit. There was Ah Bao sitting by her bed, knitting something and singing a little ditty under her breath, a song about the names of flowers, one for each of the twelve months. Manzhen thought she was back in the past, when Ah Bao worked for her family. I must be very sick, she thought, since Ah Bao's up here, nursing me, instead of working in the downstairs rooms. But why isn't my mother here? Then she remembered the desk-drawer key for her office. Shuhui would need the documents she'd locked in that drawer—she had to get the key to him. She started worrying about this, and murmured out loud, "Where is Jiemin? Tell him to take the key over to the Hsus' house."

Ah Bao thought at first that she was simply raving, and couldn't catch her meaning. But when she heard the word "key," she thought Manzhen meant the key to this room, and was still trying to get out. "Don't worry about that, miss," she said. "You just get yourself better. When you're well again everything will be easier to sort out."

The mismatch between question and reply bothered Manzhen. There wasn't much light in this room, the broken window having been boarded up. She looked around and, bit by bit, all of it came back to her. All those deranged, frenzied events, the ones she'd thought were caused by her feverish delirium, were not just dreams. Not dreams, after all.

"Second Young Miss, wouldn't you like something to eat?" Ah Bao asked.

Manzhen lay flat on the bed, unresponsive. After a long while, she shook her head slightly. "Ah Bao," she said, "I think you'll recall that I've been quite good to you."

There was a short pause. "Oh, yes. Always generous, it's true."

"If you help me now, I'll certainly remember it."

Ah Bao pulled out a bamboo knitting needle and scratched her head with it, her face arranged so as to express uncertainty. "Second Young Miss," she began. "We servants are dependent on our masters, so we have to do as they say. I'm sure you understand."

"I do understand. I don't want to cause you any trouble. I just want you to deliver a letter for me. I may not be as wealthy as my sister, but I will find a way—it wouldn't go unrewarded."

"It's not that, Second Young Miss. They're taking such precautions, you know. If I went out on an errand, it would only raise suspicion."

The maid's persistent refusal filled Manzhen with chagrin: if only she had some cash on her. Promises of future reward, no matter how large, were just empty talk, utterly unpersuasive. She was so exasperated that she unconsciously wrapped her hands together, making one big fist. In order to hide her ring from view, she always wore it the wrong way around with the stone turned towards her palm. When she made a big fist, that hard, full surface pressed into her skin. That gave her an idea. Women like jewelery, she thought to herself. If I give her this ring, she might change her mind and help me. If she doesn't like the ring, it still can act as a surety—I'll buy it back from her, at a good price, once I get out of here.

She pulled off the ring. Even though the sight of it bothered her, parting with it was hard. She handed it to Ah Bao. "I know you're in a difficult spot," she said in a low voice. "Take this for now. It's not worth much, but it means a lot to me. I'll be sure to come back later and redeem it from you."

At first, Ah Bao would not accept the ring.

"Take it, take it," Manzhen insisted. "If you don't take it, that'll mean you don't want to help me."

After a further show of resistance, Ah Bao accepted the ring.

"Find a way to get me a pen and paper," Manzhen said. "Bring it with you next time you come." Her plan was to get Ah Bao to take the letter to Shuhui's house. That way, if Shijun had already gone back to Nanking, Shuhui could still forward it to him.

"Are you going to write to your family?" Ah Bao asked.

Manzhen shook her head on the pillow, but said nothing. Then, after a pause, she said, "I'll write to Mr. Shen. You've met him before." Mentioning Shijun's name brought tears to her eyes; she turned her head away.

Ah Bao told her not to worry, that everything would be fine. Then she got up and left, locking the door behind her as usual. She went straight to Manlu's room.

Manlu was on the phone. Judging from the impatient rasp of her voice, she must be talking to her mother, whom she was calling every day, urging her to hurry up and get the family moved to Suzhou. Ah Bao picked up the cigarette butts and newspapers from the floor, and tidied up the dressing-table. She put the lid back on the jar of Snow Flower face cream, and picked out, one by one, the loose hairs from the hairbrush. When Manlu had finished talking on the phone, Ah Bao went over and closed the door. Then, with a mysterious smile, she pulled the ring from her pocket and showed it to Manlu. "Just now, Second Young Miss insisted that I take this as a deposit. She promised she'd pay me well, if I delivered a letter for her."

"Really? Who does she want to write to?"

"To that Mr. Shen."

Manlu picked up the ring and studied it. She'd heard about this ring from her mother. It was a gift from Mr. Shen, so it must be serving as an engagement ring. "Well, it's not worth anything," she said to the maid. "But give it to me anyway. Of course I'll give you something for it." She unlocked a drawer and took out several bundles of notes.

Ah Bao stole a glimpse—five or six stacks, each one a pile of ten-dollar notes. Back when Manlu was often close to broke, she'd send Ah Bao out to sell or pawn her jewelery; by this means the girl had acquired some knowledge of the market for valuables. She'd been fairly sure the ring was not worth much and she'd get more by turning it over to her mistress. And now she had reaped a small fortune. Of course she had to pretend to refuse it.

"Take it!" Manlu said, pouting at her and tossing the cash onto the table. "For staying true to your duty."

Ah Bao thanked her then and tucked the money away. "Second Young Lady is expecting me to get her a pen and paper," she reminded her mistress.

Manlu thought it over. "Then don't go in to see her," she decided. "Let Amah Zhang do that." A further refinement then occurred to her, and she sent Ah Bao over to her mother's place, ostensibly because they needed more people to help them pack up, but also to hurry them along; she wanted to make sure they got out of Shanghai straight away.

Mrs. Gu still could not believe that she'd be ringing in the New Year in Suzhou. But Manlu was exerting tremendous pressure on her, and since Mrs. Gu held to the custom that prohibits moving house in the first month of the New Year, her only choice was to move before the holiday. All those sheets that she'd been rushing to get washed before the end of the year were used to wrap their possessions into bundles; there were lots and lots of bundles. When Mrs. Gu went through her things, she kept finding items she could not bear to part with. But transporting them on the train, as baggage, seemed frightfully expensive. On the other hand, they were all old, half-broken things, years and years of accumulated stuff. Putting them out on the street, exposing them to the bright light of day, piled up on a truck for all the world to see—that was not a pretty thought, either! Ah Bao saw that she was stuck, and agreed to take all those things back to the big Zhu house, which after all had plenty of spare room. (In fact, once Mrs. Gu had gone, Ah Bao called in a secondhand-goods dealer and sold the whole lot to him.)

As she prepared to depart, Mrs. Gu felt she was being punished, sent into exile. She grew afraid, and wondered if she ought to trust Manlu so completely. But all her hopes, and their whole future, depended on her eldest daughter, and that made her reluctant to think ill of Manlu. Shijun had sent a letter to Manzhen, which Mrs. Gu hid and didn't show to anyone, so she had no idea what it said. For a long while now she'd kept it tucked in a fold of her clothing, but just before she left Shanghai she took it out and gave it to Ah Bao, asking her to give it to Manzhen.

Shijun's letter came from his home in Nanking. After he had gone to the Zhu house that day, trying in vain to see Manzhen, he was devastated, believing that she was deliberately avoiding him. When he got back to Shuhui's house, Mrs. Hsu told him his uncle had sent someone to look for him. He went to his uncle's house right away, worried in case something untoward had happened. In fact, nothing major had occurred. There was a young nephew, the son of his uncle's concubine, who attended school in Shanghai, though his mother still lived in Nanking. The winter holidays had begun, and the boy was going to his mother's for New Year's, but his father didn't want him traveling alone. He wanted Shijun to go with him. Shijun was happy to oblige, though he had hoped to stay in Shanghai a few days longer. Now his uncle was pressing him to leave right away. He reminded Shijun that his mother wanted him to return quickly; there would be a flurry of business when accounts became due at the year's end, and if he weren't there, his father would step in and try to manage things, since he didn't trust anyone else. That would not be good for his health.

Judging from the tone of his uncle's remarks, Shijun guessed that his mother had told her brother, before they left Nanking, to push her son to come home quickly. And it was a good bet that she had told him more than that; she probably had told him all her worries, or he wouldn't have become so insistent. He hammered away at Shijun from all directions, urging him to go back the next day. When Shijun saw his uncle up in arms, perturbed and persistent, it seemed to him that if he argued over such a little thing, there might be a major quarrel. So he agreed. In any case, he was feeling distraught and confused. Maybe he and Manzhen needed time to calm down. He'd go to Nanking and write to her from there. His thinking would make more sense in letter form.

He went back to Nanking and wrote to her—twice in fact—but never got a response.

That year, the New Year celebrations at their house were especially festive, with lots of people coming and going. All that merry-making wore his father out, and his illness suddenly returned in a more severe form. The situation was quite serious, and a problem for his father's doctor, who wanted to withdraw from the case. In the end, Shijun took his father to Shanghai to seek treatment there.

The first two days that he was in the Shanghai hospital, Shijun's father's condition was acute, and Shijun had to stay with him every minute. He was there day and night, keeping his father company. When Shuhui heard about this, he came to see them. Shijun's father had by then made a slight recovery. After they had talked a while, Shijun asked Shuhui if he had seen Manzhen recently.

"I haven't seen her in a long time," Shuhui answered. "Does she know you're here?"

"I've been so busy these last two days," Shijun said awkwardly, "I haven't had a spare moment to telephone her." He felt his father's gaze upon him, paying close attention, so he quickly changed the subject.

Stationed in the room was the nurse they had hired, a lively young woman named Miss Zhu. She wore her white nurse's cap at a jaunty angle, and had already formed quite a bond with them in the short time they'd been there. Shijun's father told him to get out the tea leaves they had brought and brew a cup for Shuhui. "Do you like Liu An tea?" asked Miss Zhu, having already noticed that they were particular about their tea. "A nurse who used to work here, Miss Yang, now has a job in a hospital in Liu An. She sent me ten pounds of tea leaves to sell for her. The price is quite reasonable too."

The mention of Liu An gave Shijun a strange feeling: that was Manzhen's old home town. "Liu An . . ." he said amiably. "Is that the hospital that's run by a Dr. Zhang?"

"Yes!" said Miss Zhu. "Do you know Dr. Zhang? He's a very nice man. He's the one who brought me this tea, when he came to Shanghai to get married."

This news struck Shijun like a thunderbolt. At first he didn't even hear the question that Shuhui had put to him, but then it suddenly resurfaced in his mind. "Who is this Dr. Zhang?" Shuhui had asked.

"Zhang Yujin," Shijun hurriedly replied, with a smile. "You haven't met him." Then, turning back to Miss Zhu, he asked, "Oh? So he got married? Do you know the bride's name?"

"I'm afraid I don't. I only know that the bride's family is in Shanghai, but after the wedding, they went back to Liu An."

Shijun did not pursue the matter further, realizing that his queries would not make the situation any clearer, and afraid that if he showed too much interest in the wedding of this Dr. Zhang, his father and Shuhui would think something strange was going on. When Miss Zhu saw that he'd lapsed into silence, she took this to mean he didn't want to buy the tea, but didn't want to refuse her directly. She was a tactful person, so she quickly looked at her wristwatch, then busied herself with a thermometer, checking Hsiaotung's temperature.

Shijun could hardly wait till Shuhui left. Fortunately, it wasn't too much later that Shuhui stood up and took his leave. "I'll go out with you," Shijun said. "There's something I want to buy."

The two of them walked out of the hospital together. "Where are you headed now?" Shijun asked.

Shuhui looked at his watch. "I have to get back to the factory. I slipped away before clocking-off time, so as not to miss the visiting hours at the hospital."

He hurried back to work. Shijun went into a nearby store to use the telephone. Expecting that Manzhen would still be at work, he dialed the number of the factory office. The male clerk who worked there answered the phone. Shijun greeted him, then asked for Miss Gu. "She's no longer working here," the man replied. "Oh—didn't you know that?"

Shijun was shocked. "Not working there? Did she quit her job?"

"I don't know if she ever submitted a formal letter of resignation, but I do know it's been days and days since she was last here. We sent someone to her house to look for her, but apparently the whole family has moved." Then, to fill the silence on Shijun's side, the man continued: "I don't know where they moved to. Do you?"

Shijun forced himself to reply in a lighthearted way. "I have no idea. I've just come from Nanking, and haven't seen her in a long time." He rounded off the conversation with a few courteous remarks, then hung up the phone. He went back to the counter, bought another phone token, and dialed Manzhen's home number. He had no reason to think the clerk was lying to him, but still he couldn't quite believe it. The phone rang and rang; obviously, the rooms there were all empty. They had indeed moved out. Shijun felt as if he'd that very day happily visited a friends' house only to ring up a mere two hours later to hear that they'd all moved out. It was a terrifying, dizzying experience. Like seeing a ghost.

He hung up the receiver, then stood by the phone a long while. He walked out of the shop and down the street, all in a daze. The slanting rays of the sun fell lightly on him, and the immensity of the world was unfurled; he had no place to go.

But of course he went back to her old neighborhood to ask around. Maybe the alley guard would know where the family had gone. And the downstairs tenants—they probably had moved out also, but if they'd left an address, maybe he could learn something from them. Her house was quite far from the hospital, and as he rode down the street in a cab, he suddenly remembered that he had told her, the last time they'd met, to move elsewhere. Could it be that she had moved because he'd asked her to? So off she'd gone, and because she was angry with him, she hadn't even written to tell him—could that be it? Maybe a letter from her had already arrived in Nanking, during the two days he'd been in Shanghai. Or, there was yet another possibility: maybe she had written to him, but his mother had intercepted it and kept it from him. But none of that explained why she'd suddenly left her job. That fact undid all of his guesswork.

The cab stopped at the entrance to the Gus' alley. He could no longer count the number of times he'd been here, but this time it all seemed very unfamiliar, from the moment he stepped into the alley-way. Maybe it was because he knew the people had gone and the house was empty, but the place looked dusty, dark, broken-down and cramped. Even the sky looked as if it had slipped downwards.

He remembered the first time he came here: the mystery that clung to Manzhen's family somehow gave the entire alley a trembling, self-protective air, but also a trace of something sweetly joyous. It was in that state of mind that he had seen the group of maids washing rice and doing laundry at the communal tap—what a fresh, cheerful scene that was. But on this keen, cold winter's day, the alley was empty. Just one maid was standing at the window of the little wooden shack at the entrance, where the guard lived, caught up in an intense conversation. She wore cotton trousers and a jacket, hugely swollen at the waist, her belly rising so high that her white apron stuck out in front of her. She leaned on the window, pressing her face close to the man inside. Seeing this, Shijun did not stop to talk to the alley guard. He'd go in first, have a look around.

But there was nothing to see. An empty house with doors and windows tightly shut, and a black, foggy layer of ashes and dust covering the windowpanes. Shijun stood outside the door, then slowly walked over to the alley entrance. This time the guard saw him. The man came out with a nod and a smile. In the past, Shijun had often given him a tip when he left the alley late at night, having sat and talked in the Gu house well into the evening. By then the metal gate at the entrance to the alley would be closed, and he'd have to get the guard to open it for him. Now that the guard had greeted him, Shijun could ask about the Gu family.

"They moved at the end of the year," the man told him. "I have two letters for them here. If I knew the address I could forward them. Mr. Shen, do you have any way of finding it out?" He reached back into the shack, feeling around on the table till he'd found the two letters. The maidservant who'd been chatting with him was still standing there, leaning sideways against the window, but she quickly shifted her stance and got out of the way. In the past, servants could be counted on to transmit news about a family, but since the Gu family had no servants, even the alley guard, who usually acted like a local gazette, and knew everything about local events, had no clue as to developments in that household. Plus, of course, due to Manlu's situation, the family was more mysterious and close-mouthed than others. They didn't volunteer any information, so people didn't feel they could ask.

"There was a family by the name of Liu that lived on the lower floor. Do you know where they went?"

"Liu, Liu . . ." the guard muttered. "I think they moved to Hong-kou District. The Gu family left Shanghai altogether. I heard the cart-pullers say they caught the train at the northern station."

Shijun's heart thumped. "North Station?" Manzhen must have married Yujin, and gone back with him, along with her whole family. They'll depend on him now. Manzhen's mother's dream, and her granny's too, has finally come true, he pondered to himself.

He'd known all along that Manzhen's mother and grandmother wanted her to marry Yujin—and they weren't the only ones, he thought. Yujin had always liked Manzhen a lot, and even though Manzhen hadn't mentioned any further signs of affection from him, Shijun instinctively knew that she'd kept something from him. This wasn't a case of pure mistrust on his part. Once people grow really close to each other, they can feel any little gap that subsequently opens up between them. She'd never made any bones about the admiration she felt for Yujin; her feeling towards him amounted to hero-worship, even though he just went on silently with his work, expecting to spend the rest of his life as a small-town, country doctor.

Yes, of course, Shijun thought to himself. How can I compete with someone like that? My career had barely begun, and then it got cut off. She thinks I surrendered to family pressure, so she's very disappointed in me. She still has some feeling for me, since we've been together for almost three years. All the same, in all these years, we'd never quarreled—and then, right after Yujin was here, we had a big fight. That is not mere coincidence. Of course she wasn't looking for an excuse to row with me, but there was an unresolved place in her feelings for me, and when that spot got prodded, a quarrel broke out.

The alley guard gave him the letters. One was from Manzhen's brother's school, probably a report card. The other one was from Shijun himself, to Manzhen—the sight of his own writing on the envelope gave him a shock. Besides the postmark, there was also a circular stain of soy sauce: the bottom rim of a food bowl, set down on the letter by the guard. Shijun glanced at the two envelopes, then nodded to the man. "OK, I can try . . . try to get these delivered." He took them and left.

By the time he emerged from the alley, the street lamps were lit. He took out the letter he'd sent to Manzhen and checked to see which one it was. It was the second of his two letters to her. The first one must have already reached her. Most of what he had to say was in the first one; the second one wasn't really necessary. He ripped it to shreds.

A snack-seller's cry rose in the distance: "Mushroom-flavored, chewy bean curd!" He'd heard that vendor before. The man came every day, about this time, circling through the streets and alleys, calling out his wares. An old man with a long, thin body, carrying a basket. Every day, without fail, he stopped by Manzhen's alley. The sound of his cry brought to mind all the evenings that he'd whiled away at her house. "Bean . . . curd! Five-scented, mushroom-flavored, chewy bean . . . curd!" A long, lonely, sinking cry, slowly drawing nearer, till Shijun was mesmerized.

Then it occurred to him that he could go to Manzhen's sister's house and ask for news there. He'd been there before, and knew the house number. But it was a long way away; it might be too late by the time he got there. He walked a little further, then went to a nearby taxi rank. He arrived at Hongqiao Road before the sky had darkened completely, got out of the cab and rang the bell. The gate-window opened as before, and the guard's face was revealed. It looked like the same man he'd seen before.

"I'd like to see the lady of the house. My name is Shen Shijun."

After a moment's pause, the man replied, "I think she's gone out. I'll go and see." He closed the window.

Shijun knew this was the way servants in rich families responded to visitors' inquiries, since they didn't know whether their masters wished to see this particular person. And yet he couldn't keep himself from fearing that Manzhen's sister might indeed have gone out. Actually, if the brother-in-law was at home, that would do just as well. But he'd forgotten to mention that.

As he'd expected, he had to wait a long time. Finally he heard a bolt being drawn, and a little side-door opened. The guard stepped away and invited him in. Once Shijun had walked through, the guard threw the bolt again, then led him towards the house, along a cinder driveway lined on either side with a thick wall of evergreen bushes. It was already dark in the garden, even though the sky was still lit, almost as bright as day. The pale light of the sun was reflected in the pale gold of the moon, arched and thin, like an eyebrow.

Shijun passed beneath a window, and Manzhen heard, from her upstairs room, the sound of footsteps below. Hard-soled leather shoes on the driveway. Nothing unusual, except that no one here, neither servants nor masters, wore that kind of shoe. The servants wore cloth shoes, Manlu usually had embroidered slippers, and Hongtsai's shoes were made of vicuna hide. They had very few visitors here. So who was this? With great difficulty, Manzhen raised herself to a half-sitting position, listening carefully and straining to see out of the window, even though it was mostly boarded up. All she saw was that blank, bright sky and the sickle moon. Maybe Shijun has come, she thought. No, I'm being crazy now. I lie here wishing and wishing he'll rescue me, and the minute I hear footsteps I think it must be him. The distinct footsteps came closer, then receded. Something about this bothered her. Doesn't matter who it is, she thought, I'll call out for help. But after all her fever her voice was nearly gone, though she did not at first realize that, since it had been days since she'd spoken to anyone. She opened her mouth to shout, but to her surprise, the only sound her throat would emit was a weak, dry rasp.

She was alone in that dark, dark room. Ah Bao hadn't been back since the time she'd taken the ring from her. Amah Zhang had just left, heading to the kitchen for some New Year's sticky pudding. It was the first month of the new year, and there was still a lot of it in the house, so the servants could go off and have a snack whenever they liked. Amah Zhang had just heated up a big bowl of sticky-pudding soup, and was just about to have her first mouthful, when Ah Bao came slinking in and said the mistress wanted her. Amah Zhang put her bowl down. "She's asking for me?"

Ah Bao nodded briefly, then whispered in her ear, "She wants you to keep watch on the back room. Keep a sharp eye out!"

Thinking that some new mishap had occurred in Manzhen's quarters, Amah Zhang raced towards the stairs as fast as her feet would carry her. Ah Bao was right behind, but when she got to the foot of the stairs, there was the gate guard leading Shijun through. Shijun had seen Ah Bao at Manzhen's house before; even though he'd seen her only once, he must have remembered her, because he was looking straight at her. Ah Bao recoiled sheepishly, afraid that if he struck up a conversation and asked where the Gu family was now, she'd end up giving him a garbled, inconsistent story. So she hung her head and pretended not to recognize him, heading straight up the stairs.

The guard led Shijun into the living room and turned on the light. It was a huge space, luxuriously furnished, but so empty of human presence that voices echoed. The radiators were turned on full blast, and as soon as Shijun was seated he had to take out his handkerchief to wipe the sweat off his face. The guard left for a few minutes, then came back with tea, which he set down on a low table in front of Shijun. There were two teacups. Shijun looked up and saw Manlu walking towards him from the far end of the room, a long way off. She was wearing a calf-length black cheongsam over a pair of black silk trousers; the diamond-sparkle of sequin piping shone through the long slit in the upper garment. She moved silently across the thick, lotus-gray silk carpet. She seemed much thinner than he remembered from that first meeting; so much flesh had melted from her eye-sockets that her eyes, in the lamp's uneven light, looked like two dark holes. Her makeup was, as usual, bright red and stark white. The term "painted skull" suddenly rose in his mind: he could only go by the words themselves, but that's what her face looked like.

He'd never in his life been in the company of a woman like this one. Feeling a bit alarmed, he got to his feet and gave her a half-bow. Before she'd even reached him, he was racing into his reason for coming. "I'm so sorry to bother you, Mrs. Zhu. I've just been to look for Manzhen, but the family has moved out. Are they living somewhere else now?"

Manlu merely smiled and followed his remarks attentively. "Mr. Shen, please have a seat. And have some tea." She sat down first.

Shijun noticed that she was holding a small paper packet in her hand. He couldn't help stealing glances at it, but couldn't guess what it contained. It didn't look like a letter. He sat down across from her. Manlu opened up the packet. Inside was another wrapping of silver paper. She opened up that wrapping and took out a ring with a red stone. Shijun's heart turned over when he saw that ring; he had no words to describe his feelings.

Manlu handed the ring to him. "Manzhen expected this. She said a Mr. Shen might come looking for her, and asked me to give this to him."

Shijun thought, Is this her way of answering my letter? He took the ring, moving woodenly, but then another idea came to him. Hadn't she already returned the ring to me? She gave it back to me, and I threw it into the wastebasket. Now why would she get it out, only to give it back again? It's not like it's worth a lot of money. If she was determined to give it back, why didn't she just post it to me? Why make such a big deal of it, getting her sister to hand it to me in person? Is this all out of spite? But she's not that kind of person. I know she's changed, but can a person change all her ways so completely? Is that possible?

He sat thinking a long while, then asked, "Well, is she still in Shanghai? I'd like to talk to her."

Manlu looked at him, her face broadening into a smile. Then, very slowly and gravely, she said, "I would say that's not really necessary."

Shijun paused, and his face turned red. "She hasn't got married, has she?"

Manlu's expression changed, but she did not answer immediately.

"Did she marry Zhang Yujin?" he continued.

Manlu raised the teacup to her lips and took a sip. She was simply improvising, and though she knew that Shijun was jealous of Yujin, she didn't want to state outright that Manzhen had married him, since that kind of falsehood would be easy to disprove. But it looked as though Shijun wouldn't give up unless she confirmed this story. Holding the teacup up, she peered at him across the rim. "Since you already know, there's nothing more for me to say."

Shijun had carried almost no hope with him when he entered this house, but her words still fell on his ears like thunder. He sat there stunned, unable to say a word. After a long moment, he forced himself to his feet, nodded, and said, "I'm so sorry for disturbing you." He turned and left.

But as he walked away, he felt something crunching underfoot. He looked down. That ring of his. He'd had it firmly in his hand— somehow his grip must have slipped, and it had fallen onto the floor. He didn't know when it had happened; there'd been no sound, of course, when it hit that thick carpet. He bent down and picked it up, then thrust it quickly into his pocket. How ridiculous it would be to lose that ring in this house, after making a big scene.

At this point, Manlu also stood up, but Shijun did not look at her. She might be smirking, or smiling in sympathy, but in either case he couldn't bear it. He rushed out of the room towards the front door, which the guard had already opened for him. Manlu saw him to the door, then went back in, letting the guard escort him to the gate. Shijun walked so fast the man behind couldn't keep up. A moment later, he had gone through the front gate and was out on the road. A car swept past, two bright beams of light preceding it. There was no pavement on Hongqiao Road, and his feet sank into the soft gray dirt along the road's edge, noiselessly. In that darkness, the light of the street lamps was ineffectual and blurry, as was he.

The ring was still in his pocket. If he'd taken a good look at it when he got home, he'd have seen bloodstains on the yarn that was still wrapped around it. The wool itself was coffee-colored, and dried blood is reddish-brown, so there the stain wasn't particularly noticeable, but the sticky dried blob had stiffened the yarn, and could be spotted by someone who looked carefully. If he'd seen that he'd surely have thought it odd, and grown suspicious. But that's the sort of thing one hears about in detective stories—in real life, it doesn't happen often. Shijun walked along the road, feeling the pressure of the ring in his trouser pocket. That red gemstone seared his leg like the lit end of a cigarette. He reached into his pocket, pulled the ring out, and without another glance at it, threw it into an empty field.

When he got back to the hospital that evening, his father asked where he had been, since he'd been gone so long. Shijun said something about running into old friends, and getting dragged off with them, till all hours. His father could tell that he was shaken and unhappy, and guessed that he'd gone off to see his girlfriend. The next day, Shijun's uncle came to the hospital to visit and stayed quite some time. Hsiao-tung talked a long time, and that night his condition deteriorated. From that point on, he declined steadily. He was in hospital for two whole months, and Mrs. Shen came to Shanghai to see him. The concubine came too, with her children. They all knew the end was near. Hsiao-tung died that spring, in the hospital.

When spring came, the purple flowers of Hongqiao Road's bauhinia bush reappeared. The whole plant was covered with little blossoms of dark, deep violet. A bird hopped around on Manzhen's window-sill, and since the room was so quiet, the bird thought no one was in there, and flew in. It flapped about wildly, but Manzhen, who was sitting in an easy-chair, seemed not to notice. She had recovered from her illness, only to find she was pregnant. These days she could only stare woodenly into space; her whole body felt numb. A sun-beam shone onto her foot, warm and soft as a purring cat pressing up against her. She was so far removed from the world that this little spot of sunlight felt sweet to her.

She never cried now, except when she imagined seeing Shijun some day, and telling him all that she'd been through. Thoughts of that far-off meeting made it seem he was there already, right in front of her, and she could talk to him. Then the tears streamed down her face.

13

Hsiao-tung's coffin was taken to Nanking by boat, with Shijun in attendance; Mrs. Shen and the concubine each traveled by rail, on separate trains. The death of her husband lifted a great weight from Mrs. Shen's heart. She was already used to living like a widow, and now that she no longer had to bear the affront of having her husband stolen by someone else, she could embrace a dignified widowhood in fact as well as in name. She was especially gratified by her husband's having died while in her care—in her arms, so to speak. Now that he was about to be safely buried, the case was closed: no one, but no one, could steal him away. All this left her feeling settled and serene.

There wasn't enough room in the house, so the coffin was set up in a temple and they took turns keeping watch, performing all the mourning rites there. After they'd got through that, the property had to be divided, at the concubine's insistence. She had lots of children, and wanted an exorbitant sum for their education; she also claimed that Hsiao-tung had promised to support her mother through her old age. It was common knowledge that the concubine had, for years, been squirreling funds away, not to mention all the valuables that were left behind when the ailing Hsiao-tung moved out of her house. But there was no way to prove any of this. Shijun was willing to placate her, in order to minimize strife; he urged his mother to accept the losses and be done with it.

But women can be so pernickety—and his sister-in-law too was part of the negotiations. Strictly speaking, the division of property did not extend to her, because she still lived with her mother-in-law, but somewhere down the road, her branch would have its own portion of the estate. It was of course her son's future, not her own, that concerned her. As soon as Shijun's back was turned, she complained about his weakling ways; or she called him a callous young lord, too high and mighty to spare a thought for his own hard-pressed relatives. She even suspected that his stay at the other household had turned his head; the concubine had heaped flattery upon him, and young men, of course, have no sense at all—hence his partiality towards that woman ever since. In fact, Shijun felt caught in a quagmire. It took all his powers of forbearance, but finally the matter was laid to rest.

When the hundred-day mourning period was complete, Shijun made the rounds to all their relatives, thanking them for their loyalty and support. One of the homes he visited was Shi Tsuizhi's. Her family's house was an old villa in the Western style, five rooms to a floor, with Chinese features throughout. The garden also mixed the two styles: in the middle of the grass lawn was a Chinese-style rockery and a little pond filled with golden carp. Shijun visited the house on a summer evening, just as the sun was setting. The trees were buzzing with cicadas and Tsuizhi was in the garden walking her dog. She had the dog on a lead, but in fact the dog was leading her, the leather strap a straight, taut line that pulled her along. Shijun greeted her, and she called out to the dog, "Lai-li! Lai-li!" Finally, she got it to stop.

"That's an old dog, isn't it?" Shijun asked. "I remember seeing you with a black dog a long time ago."

"That dog is the grandmother of this one," Tsuizhi told him. "This one is a litter-mate of the puppy I gave to your nephew."

"And he's called Lai-li?"

"It's also his English name—Riley. My mother wanted to call him 'Lai-fu,' like 'Ralph,' but everyone calls their dog that, so I changed it to 'Lai-li.'"

Shijun laughed—Tsuizhi had turned the old name-phrase "Come Hither, Wealth" into "Come Hither, Greedy Gain."

"Is your mother at home?" he asked.

"She's out playing mahjong."

Tsuizhi had come to pay her respects during the mourning ceremonies, but there'd been no chance for them to talk; Shijun, in his filial role as chief mourner of the deceased, could not leave his station in the mourning pavilion. This was Tsuizhi's first chance to ask him about his father's last few days, which she did, and Shijun told her how he'd stayed with his father in the hospital.

"Oh, so you didn't stay at Shuhui's house then? Did you see him at all?" she asked.

"He came to the hospital a few times."

Tsuizhi did not pursue the subject. She'd been wondering if Shuhui had left Shanghai; she'd written him a letter telling him that she'd broken off her engagement to Yipeng, but he had not replied. He'd never made an explicit advance—a consequence of her family's wealth, she thought, making him think she was beyond his reach. The initiative had to come from her, she felt. But when she got no reply, she regretted writing that letter. It wasn't that she felt she'd stooped too low—she never thought about him like that. She feared instead that her boldness had made him recoil, even if he had liked her. She'd felt depressed ever since.

Turning to Shijun with a smile, she asked, "Did you see Miss Gu when you were in Shanghai? How is she getting on?"

"I didn't see her on that trip."

"She and Shuhui are quite close, aren't they?"

This seemed strange to Shijun, until he realized she must have heard this from his sister-in-law. He was the one who'd told his family that Manzhen and Shuhui were friends, back when the two of them had come to Nanking, because he'd wanted to defuse any scrutiny of Manzhen. Thinking back to that visit was like remembering some distant, bygone era. It made his head swim. He forced a smile, and told Tsuizhi, "The two of them are just friends."

"I do envy people like her. Having a job like that—it's wonderful."

A quick, ironic laugh burst from Shijun. He couldn't imagine anyone envying the way Manzhen lived, always rushing from one place to the next, working so many jobs at once. But that was in the past— her life now, as the wife of a hospital director, had to be much easier.

"I do wish I could go to Shanghai and get a job of some kind," Tsuizhi persisted.

"Whatever for?"

"What? You think I couldn't do it?"

"No, no, it's not that. Aren't you studying at some college?"

"It makes no difference. Even if I wait till I've graduated, my family still won't let me go out and get a job." She heaved a long sigh. Apparently she had a heart full of woe, and no one to talk to. Shijun looked carefully into her face. She'd grown quite thin. He felt she had changed somehow, after the broken engagement. She was a quieter person now.

The two of them followed the dog around the lawn, walking slowly. "He's always got so much energy," Tsuizhi suddenly said.

"You mean Riley?"

Tsuizhui paused. "No, I meant Shuhui."

"Yes, he really does have a lot of energy. Going off for a chat with him always raises my spirits, if I'm feeling down." I really have nothing to say to Tsuizhi, Shijun thought to himself. That's why we keep coming back to Shuhui, the only thing we have in common.

Tsuizhi asked him to come in, but Shijun said he still had some other families to visit; he said goodbye and left.

He hadn't been to anyone's house over the past three months due to the mourning protocol, but now that the prohibition was lifted, social obligations gradually piled up again. Ever since his sister-in-law had tried to fix him up with Tsuizhi and been rebuffed, she'd felt a bit shamefaced towards her younger cousin: it was like "losing the pattern while the shoe is still being made." She never raised the subject again, and of course Tsuizhi's mother was even more silent about it. As a result, none of their other relatives knew the full story. When Yiming's ultra-modern wife, Amy, discussed it, she said Shijun was too bashful and Tsuizhi too stroppy: otherwise, they'd have been a perfect match. Now that Tsuizhi had a broken engagement behind her, she again became a problem for her family. Maybe Shijun was too suspicious, but it seemed to him that whenever he was invited somewhere, Tsuizhi was invited too. Tsuizhi had the same impression. She often went to Amy's to play tennis, and Amy would get Shijun to come over as well. At one of these gatherings, he met a

Miss Ding—a good tennis player, studying at the same Shanghai college he had attended. When Shijun got home, he mentioned her name a few times, and his mother immediately found an excuse to go to Amy's and get a good look at this Miss Ding. Shijun's father had said, before he died, that his only regret was not seeing Shijun married. At that time, Shijun's mother hadn't dared press the point, because she knew that if Shijun got married then and there, his bride would be Manzhen. But now that the coast was clear, she kept repeating, for Shijun's benefit, the dying wish of his father.

All around them, young people were getting hitched—somehow there seemed to be a sharp increase in weddings that year, and the invitations kept coming in, one after another, all through the autumn months. The person most affected was Tsuizhi's mother. Tsuizhi's age wasn't an issue yet, so she might not have worried so much if it weren't that Tsuizhi had tried to run away. She left a letter saying she was going to Shanghai to get a job, but fortunately the family found it in time and got her back from the station before she'd boarded the train. They didn't see anyone with her at the station, but Tsuizhi's mother was sure that someone had seduced her. From that point on, Mrs. Shi redoubled her efforts to get her daughter married. Otherwise, it was only a matter of time till some new horror erupted.

A match was proposed by someone: the potential groom was a young master from a big landowning family, surnamed Qin and rumored to be an addict of some kind. A meal was arranged so that the pair could meet, but Tsuizhi was determined not to go. She slipped out of the house early in the day, without a clear plan in mind. Her elder cousin, Young Mistress Shen, struck her as the only person who'd lend a sympathetic ear, so she decided to have a good cry on her shoulder. Cousin Shen was indeed supportive: she hadn't taken sides when Tsuizhi and Yipeng had broken up, even though the former was her cousin and the latter her younger brother. For a simple soul like her, anyone on her side of the family had to be a good person. Her brother was of course the best of men. And her cousin Tsuizhi? She too could do no wrong. The fault had to lie elsewhere. Right after the breakup, Yipeng married Dou Wenhsien—so it was all Wenhsien's fault. She'd plotted to split them up and then had stolen Yipeng for herself. Young Mistress Shen was thus very sympathetic to Tsuizhi.

But when Tsuizhi arrived at the Shen household seeking sympathy, her cousin, who almost never went out, wasn't at home. The elder Mrs. Shen had suddenly realized how long it had been since she'd visited her husband's spirit-marker at the temple, so she'd bought scented candles and spirit money, then gone off to kowtow and make an offering, taking Little Vim and his mother with her. Shijun was the only one in.

"Hey there!" he said the minute he saw Tsuizhi. "Does your family know you're here? They just telephoned, and I told them you weren't here."

Tsuizhi knew her mother must be getting worried, and phoning everyone they knew to find her. She took a seat, ignoring the whole issue, and asked if her cousin had gone out.

"She went to the temple with my mother," Shijun told her.

"Oh, so your mother isn't at home either?"

There was a book on the table, and she leafed through the pages. Shijun saw her settling in, evidently planning to stay some time. "Do you want to phone your family?" he asked. "Let them know you're here?"

Tsuizhi looked up abruptly. "Whatever for?"

Shijun was taken aback. "No harm intended. I just thought your mother might need you for something."

Tsuizhi bent over again and looked at the book. "She doesn't need me for anything."

Shijun was starting to understand that she'd run out of the house after a fight with her mother. He knew she'd been miserable for quite a while: he'd seen the signs. But he'd been staying out of intimate conversations, refraining from inquiring into other people's sorrows, because he too was depressed and didn't want anyone asking him why he was sad. Maybe because they were fellow sufferers, being with her now felt easier than being with others—at least he didn't have to keep up that fake smile, that pretend laugh. The dog that Tsuizhi had given them came forward timidly, wagging its tail. Tsuizhi put the book down and rubbed its itchy spots.

"That poor dog," Shijun said, making conversation. "He's stuck here with us, without any garden or anyone to take him for walks."

Tsuizhi appeared not to hear him. Shijun suddenly saw that her eyes were gleaming with tears, and fell silent. But then she broke the silence. "Have you played any tennis lately?" she asked.

"No. Do you want to play? We could have a game together."

"I hit the ball back, but I never get anywhere." Her voice was measured and quiet, perfectly normal, but when she spoke, tears spilled out from her eyes. She turned aside, brushing them away with an impatient swipe, but the tears wouldn't stop coming.

"Tsuizhi." Shijun, with a gentle smile, spoke her name. "What's the matter?"

She didn't answer, and he fell silent again. After a moment, he got up, went over, and sat down beside her, putting his arm around her shoulders.

The early autumn breeze came through the window and lifted the pages of the book one by one, making a patting sound. It was a clean, crisp, sweet sound.

Several moments passed before Tsuizhi shook his arm off. "Someone might see," she said softly, as if that were an explanation. In other words, it could be done, so long as no one saw. Shijun couldn't help grinning as he looked into her face. Tsuizhi blushed immediately, then stood up to go. "I'm leaving now."

"Heading home?"

"No!" she said in a big loud voice. "I'm not going back there!"

"Then where are you going?" He smiled again.

"None of your business," she said, pleasantly enough.

"Then let's play some tennis, how's that?"

At first she refused, but eventually she agreed.

The next day he went to her house to fetch her so they could play tennis again, but they ended up not going; they sat around talking instead, and he had dinner there. Her mother was being very nice to him, and nicer to Tsuizhi too. From that point on, Shijun was at their house every few days or so. Both Mrs. Shen and Young Mistress Shen knew what was going on, and were very happy about it, but they kept their opinions to themselves, afraid that if they cheered him on, he'd turn around and march away again. Nothing was ever said openly, but the air around him grew warm and light; wherever he went, off to Tsuizhi's house or relaxing in his own home, that warm light stayed wrapped around him.

On her birthday, he gave her a diamond brooch. The stones had been in his family for many years: they were taken from a pair of his mother's earrings. Four diamonds reset in a single line, on a little cylinder of white gold. It was a simple, tasteful design. Tsuizhi fastened it onto her collar at once, Shijun standing behind her as she looked in the mirror to find the right spot. "How did you know it was my birthday?" she asked.

"Sister-in-law told me."

"Did you ask her, or did she just tell you?"

"I asked her," he lied.

He looked at her in the mirror. She'd put on a little makeup today, but done her hair the usual way, with a long fringe hanging over her forehead and the rest gathered up in a topknot held in place with a strip of dark felt. She was wearing a short-sleeved dress made of dark red corduroy. Shijun ran his hands over her wrists. "Have you lost weight again? Your arms are so thin!"

Tsuizhi kept her chin raised as she worked at the clasp of the brooch. "I guess I'm sensitive to heat. I'm always thin at the end of summer."

Running his hands over her wrists might have been an experimental ploy. Now he moved close behind her, and kissed her on the cheek. Her face powder had a sweet scent. "Stop that! What are you doing?" she reprimanded him. "What if someone sees?"

"Who cares if they see?" he said. "It's OK now." He didn't say why being seen was no longer an issue, and she didn't press him for an explanation. She merely looked back towards him, holding her face at an angle, and they smiled at each other. Their pledge was formed in that moment.

In all the novels Shijun had read, the pairing up and marrying off of boys and girls seemed a terrific bother, but now he discovered that getting married is the easiest thing in the world.

The family kept the arrangements quiet because his father had died so recently; they skipped the formal engagement period and chose a wedding date in October. Whenever they had a moment to themselves, they eagerly discussed details of their future life together. Tsuizhi was still hoping that they eventually could have their own place in Shanghai, and she was full of ideas about the kind of house it would be, the furniture they'd buy, the color of the paint, or whether they'd have wallpaper instead—plans that were marvelously clear and specific. It was so different from his earlier experience. When he and Manzhen had considered their future together, it was always tenuous and vague, hard to imagine.

They had to buy several things for the wedding, and Shijun planned to do the shopping in Shanghai. "I'll go and see Shuhui while I'm there," he told Tsuizhi. "I want him to be my best man, and help us put this whole thing together. Don't be fooled by his slap-happy manner—he's very good at getting things done. I only wish I were as sharp and efficient as he is."

Tsuizhi said nothing at first, but a moment later she spoke out irritably in defense of her fiancé's character: "Why are you always singing Shuhui's praises? It's as if you think you'll never measure up to him. But you're better than he is. Much, much better." She threw her arms around him, burying her face in his shoulder. Shijun was taken aback, never having seen such ardor in her before. At the same time, he felt guiltily aware of his own doubts and anxieties, so unlike her unmarried affection for him. What he needed to do was find Shuhui, and talk it all through with him.

Shijun's first move, when he arrived in Shanghai, was to visit his friend's workplace dormitory in Yangshupu, since he knew Shuhui wouldn't be back at his parents' home till Sunday. Shuhui had finished work for the day, and Shijun noticed that his friend was wearing the gray sleeveless jumper Manzhen had knitted for him, back when she'd made one for each of them. Shijun had stopped wearing his sweater, but he couldn't very well ask Shuhui to do the same.

They went out for a stroll. "You've come at just the right time," Shuhui told him. "I was about to write and tell you I got a scholarship for a graduate program in America. Looks like I'm going back to my old life as a penniless student. But it's the only way I can get ahead—I'm not making any progress now. If I come back with a doctorate, my chances should be better."

"You're going to America? Where?"

"It's a little place in the Northwest, you've probably never heard of it. It doesn't matter—anyone with a PhD can quickly become a big boss here. If you're interested, I'll ask around once I get there and find a way for you to come over too."

"Well," said Shijun with a laugh. "I used to dream of going, but things aren't so simple anymore."

"Sounds like you're finally getting married," Shuhui said, smiling. "Is that it?"

Shijun could tell that his friend had misunderstood, and thought he was marrying Manzhen. It made him feel awkward. "That's why I wanted to come and talk things through with you," he said. "Tsuizhi and I are engaged."

"Shi Tsuizhi?" Shuhui was horrified. He broke out in a strange, cackling laugh. "What is there to talk over with me?" His tone bore traces of hostility, something more than simply indignation on Manzhen's behalf, as if he too had been insulted.

Shijun found it very irritating, since he couldn't lay out any of his doubts, not under these conditions. "I want you to be my best man," he said.

Shuhui was silent for a long while. "If you marry Tsuizhi," he said at last, "you'll be buried alive. Any man who marries her is condemning himself to the meek, cautious life of a wealthy woman's husband."

Shijun's reply came with a smile, but gave away nothing. "That depends on the man, I think."

His displeasure was evident to Shuhui, who blamed himself for being so censorious. What was he doing, opposing their marriage like this? Wasn't he being selfish? After deciding, for good reasons, not to pursue a relationship with Tsuizhi, now he wouldn't let anyone else have her? That was despicable. Once he realized this, he put aside all the warnings he'd thought of giving to Shijun.

"What's got into me?" he said, smiling. "Here am I picking a fight instead of offering my congratulations!"

Shijun smiled back.

"When did you two get engaged?" Shuhui asked.

"Very recently." He felt the need to explain, since he had once been so uninterested in her, as Shuhui knew very well. "Remember how my sister-in-law tried to pair us up? Well, she was still a child then, and I guess I was childish too. They were pushing us together, and I was simply resisting the pressure."

The way he said this made it seem that something like youthful willfulness had passed; that he was more adult now, ready to follow the path laid out for him, fully accepting the habits and manners of his class. Shuhui was aghast when he heard that. They were walking through the broad, vacant lots of Yangshupu as the factories shut down for the day, whistle after whistle hooting thinly through the air, the chimney stacks sending straight, taut lines of smoke into the red expanse of the sunset sky. A flock of returning ducks flew overhead, honking.

Shijun again asked Shuhui to be his best man, but Shuhui said he was afraid he couldn't, since he would be leaving so soon to take up his studies. But Shijun offered to bring the wedding date forward, and was sure that Tsuizhi would support that idea. In the face of such persistence, Shuhui could not refuse.

Shuhui asked his friend to stay to supper at the dormitory, and Shijun left afterwards. He was due at his uncle's house. He stayed there a few days, bought most of what he needed, and returned to Nanking.

Shuhui came to Nanking the day before the wedding festivities started. Holding a wedding always throws a house into commotion, but even in the midst of this upheaval, Mrs. Shen set up a guest room for Shuhui. Their house felt crammed and crowded, but the wedding events took place in a big venue. The ceremony was held at the Center Hotel, with dinner afterwards in a large banqueting hall.

When Tsuizhi appeared at the banquet, she'd already changed into a bright red cheongsam with narrow sleeves, made of silk velvet, over which she'd thrown a little wrap also made of bright red silk velvet. It was the latest fashion. Shuhui looked out across the hall to where she stood in the lights. It had been so long since he'd seen her, almost a full year. That last time, he'd congratulated her on her engagement to Yipeng, and now he was congratulating her again. Here he was, always the outsider—something stuck in his throat. As best man, he ought to be seated at the same table as the bride and groom, but since he was so good at entertaining others, they'd asked him to look after their other guests, and put him at another table. The party was in full swing there, perhaps because of him. The alcohol flowed freely, and they pushed each other hard. Shuhui wasn't good at drinking games, but neither would he give up, so in the end he drank more than anyone else.

The guests started taking turns to go up to the top table to toast the happy couple, and Shuhui joined in the fun; the crowd wanted the bride and groom to tell the story of how they'd fallen in love. There was a long stretch of awkwardness, till someone helped them out by changing the requirement to holding hands in public, right then and there. That gesture might have been a real challenge for couples in arranged marriages, but modern-style couples in love matches of their own making won't feel that it is embarrassing. But Tsuizhi could be very stubborn, and she was sitting with her head bowed. Shijun was wilting, so Shuhui had to get them out of this. Firmly grasping Tsuizhi's hand, he held it in the air. "Come on now! Shijun, hurry up and put your hand out."

At that moment, Tsuizhi suddenly looked up and stared into Shuhui's face. Shuhui must have been very drunk, because he kept holding her hand, without realizing it. Shijun thought Tsuizhi must be very angry: her face was drained of color, drawn and white, as if she were about to burst into tears.

After the banquet, as per usual, some of the guests followed the couple home, happy to continue harassing the newlyweds, but Shuhui did not join in. He'd already told Shijun he had to return to

Shanghai that same night; he was leaving the country soon, and still had a lot to get ready. As soon as he got back to the house, he said goodbye to Mrs. Shen, then quietly picked up his luggage, hired a cab and was gone.

The carousers did not leave till late that night. When a room is emptied of a boisterous crowd, it usually grows open and spacious, but here it was just the reverse: for some reason the room now felt cramped and small. The ceiling was too low, the air was stuffy. Shijun adopted a casual manner, and stretched out.

"Who was that little fat man, the one who was making all that noise?" Tsuizhi asked.

They went through all the guests, one by one, picking out in turn the most attractive girl, the craziest lady, the most ridiculous stunt they'd seen at the party. They became quite caught up in their discussion, and it kept them busy for some time. There were some long-stemmed dishes on the table, filled with sweets, and Shijun offered them to Tsuizhi, in the manner of a good host. She tried each of the various flavors. This wedding-night room had been converted from a living room, and when she refurbished it, Mrs. Shen had tried to suit the younger generation's tastes. Instead of red decorations everywhere—that dripping, blood-red look of an old-fashioned bridal suite—she'd chosen light, simple furnishings that made the place look almost like a Western-style hotel room. But on the table she'd put a pair of red candles, in silver candlesticks. Those dripping red candles were the only sign that this was a room for newlyweds.

"Shuhui was really drunk," Tsuizhi said.

"Wasn't he just! I'm a bit worried about his going off on his own to catch the train."

After a moment's silence, Tsuizhi said, "No telling where that train will be, by the time he wakes up." She was at the dressing-table, combing from her hair the red and green confetti the wedding guests had thrown at her.

Shijun told her about his uncle's concubine, an elderly woman who'd spent the last ten years at home, reading Buddhist scriptures and eating no meat; she'd nonetheless come out to see their wedding. Tsuizhi, still combing her hair, thought of something else: "Did you see that hairstyle of Amy's?" she asked. "It was really something."

"Oh? I didn't notice."

"They say it's the latest thing in Shanghai. Did you see any women with their hair like that, last time you were there?"

Shijun thought for a moment. "Couldn't really say. I suppose I wasn't paying attention."

Gradually they ran out of things to say. "I guess you must be tired?" Shijun asked her.

"I'm fine."

"I don't feel like sleeping—talking so late like this must have woken me up. I'd like to sit up for a bit and read. Why don't you go on to bed?"

"All right."

Shijun picked up a book and started to read. Tsuizhi kept combing her hair. She removed her jewelery, putting it away in the dressing-table drawers. When he saw her moving with such steady, slow care, Shijun thought she might be feeling shy about undressing and getting into bed, with him sitting there. "Does the light keep you awake?" he asked.

"Uh-huh."

"I can't sleep with a light on either." He got up and turned off the main light, then switched on a little table lamp so he could read. The room was now mostly in darkness.

Some minutes later, he looked over and saw that she hadn't gone to bed yet. She was clipping her fingernails, in the candlelight. It was now very late, and one of the candles had already burnt right down. Bad luck, according to the old folk superstition. Shijun noticed it, and though he guessed that Tsuizhi didn't place any stock in that, he still said, "Oh—the candle's out. Aren't you going to bed soon?"

After a moment's silence, Tsuizhi responded, "I am going soon."

Shijun heard a catch in her voice, and guessed she had been crying. Was it because of his aloofness? Surely it wasn't because a candle had gone out, was it?

He turned to get a good look at her, but just then she was using the fingernail clipper to trim the wick of the remaining candle. The red candle's bright flame sank down, the room went dark—then the trimmed wick flared and the light shone on her face, now very peaceful-looking. But Shijun knew that she'd been crying, just a moment earlier.

He crossed the room and stood next to her. "What's the matter?" he asked kindly. "Why so sad again?"

She gave him an impatient shove. Then suddenly, grabbing his clothes tight, she burst into tears. "Shijun—" The words came tumbling out between sobs. "You don't care for me. I've known it for a long time, but after all that trouble in my past, I couldn't say anything. What would people think, if I had another broken engagement? And now it's too late . . . it *is* too late, isn't it?"

It really was too late. The same thing was on his mind too, but she'd said it aloud. He admired her for having the courage to say it—but what good could come of that?

All he could do was try to comfort her. "That's not the way to look at it," he murmured. "Come what may, I'll always be . . . Oh, please don't worry, Tsuizhi. Don't do that. Please stop crying . . . Oh, Tsuizhi." He tried to fill her ears with consoling talk, but in his heart he was just as lost. They were, he felt, like two children who have made a terrible mistake.

14

The birth was going to be a difficult one, and Manzhen ought to have gone to hospital much sooner. The family had arranged for an obstetrician—a regular at Manlu's mahjong table—to oversee the birth at home. This doctor was highly complaisant: she'd seen her share of strange things on her rounds among the rich, and never once blinked. Manlu could rely on her discretion. But her medical skills were not the best, and there were complications. The doctor eventually recommended hospitalization, but the family kept putting it off, unwilling to let Manzhen leave the house. Not until the last possible moment, when things had grown truly desperate, did they get out the car and take her away. Manlu went along and tried, of course, to keep her in isolation, but the private and semi-private rooms were all taken. There was no time to look for another hospital, so Manzhen was put on the ordinary, third-class ward.

By the time she was wheeled out of the house, Manzhen was slipping out of consciousness. But when the car door closed and the vehicle crept down the drive, followed by the creaking of the metal gate as it swung wide, her senses cleared. Finally, finally, she was out. She made a vow never to return to that place. She hated that house. But it would come back to her . . . in nightmares. That hellish room, that vile garden, never to be erased from her mind: nocturnal visions of horror would take her there, again and again. It was a memory she could not outlive.

She gave birth, in the hospital, to a little boy. He weighed barely five pounds, and she didn't think he would survive. The night nurse brought the child so she could suckle him; she looked at his ruddy face in the dark yellow light of the lamps. She'd hated him before he was born, even though she knew he was blameless. Even now, as she cradled him in her arms, overwhelmed by the newness of it all, she still felt a tremor of detestation. Who did he look like? The newborn didn't take after anyone: he looked more like a skinned cat, bare red flesh where the fur had been. Still, Manzhen found something to make herself think he took after Zhu Hongtsai. He absolutely could not look like her. Some people say a child will take after the person who was on his mother's mind during the pregnancy. Did the baby look like Shijun? No, she saw nothing to make her think that.

The thought of Shijun threw her mind into a whirl. How she had yearned, through those long, wretched months of captivity, to see him again, face to face; to pour out her woes to him, the only one who could really comfort her. Somehow it hadn't fully dawned on her that she was having a child with another man—wouldn't that have some effect on him? How could she expect otherwise? But the Shijun in her mind had turned into an idealized figure: he loved her all the more, for having been through such a trauma. It was good that she'd had such infallible support in that time of intense pain. Holding his image close in her heart, keeping him always in mind— that had been her only source of comfort. But now that she stood on the verge of freedom, with the real possibility of seeing him soon, doubts awoke in her. What if he was in Shanghai right now, came to this very hospital to see someone, walked by this room, and saw her there—what luck! He'd have her out in a flash . . . wouldn't he? If in fact he saw her with this infant, what would his reaction be? Thinking about it from his point of view made the quandary clear.

She looked at the child greedily sucking her milk, as if he wanted to drink her up.

She had to find a way out of the hospital, maybe that very day, but she couldn't take the baby with her. Her own future was so uncertain, she had no idea where she'd end up. It wouldn't be a problem to leave him with Manlu. Her sister wouldn't mistreat the child—hadn't she always wanted a son? But this infant was too thin and weak. It didn't look as though he could live.

Suddenly she leaned over and kissed him lovingly. She and her child had met, she felt, at the boundary of life and death: one brief encounter, and they'd be parted. And yet, in this momentary meeting, the bond between them was closer than any on earth.

When the nurse came to take the baby back to the nursery, Manzhen asked for a glass of water. She'd made the request repeatedly, the first time when her temperature was taken, but still no one came. She was so thirsty she had to call out loudly, "Miss Zheng! Miss Zheng!" The patient in the next bed woke up, and coughed.

The beds were separated by a white partition, through which the two of them had already spoken briefly; the other woman asked if this was her first child and whether she'd had a boy or a girl. She too had been delivered of a boy, on the same day and almost at the same hour as Manzhen. From the sound of her voice, she must be quite young, but she had four children already. Her husband's family name was Tsai, and her given name was Jinfang. They were pedlars, selling eggs in a local market. When Manzhen heard Jinfang coughing, she apologized for waking her up.

"Oh, that's all right," Jinfang said. "These nurses are terrible. If you want them to do anything, you have to act like a street beggar and keep calling, 'Miss, Miss, Miss!' so they can't get away from you. It's really annoying, I tell you. I don't put up with rudeness even from my parents and parents-in-law, but here in the hospital they expect me to put up with this!"

Jinfang turned over in her bed. "Mama Zhu," she asked, "is your sister-in-law coming to see you today?"

The question made no sense to Manzhen. Who was "Mama Zhu"? Who was this "sister-in-law"? Then she realized that Manlu must have registered her as "Mrs. Zhu". Manlu had been making daily visits, and the hospital staff knew her as Mrs. Zhu too. That made them seem like sisters-in-law.

"That is your sister-in-law, isn't it?"

Manzhen muttered something vaguely affirmative.

"Is your husband away from Shanghai?"

"Uh-huh." Manzhen's heart sank.

It was now late at night, and all the other patients on the ward were asleep. The white frames around the windowpanes made a cross against the black sky. In the yellow light of the lamp, Manzhen told Tsai Jinfang her whole story. She'd never seen Jinfang's face, but the woman clearly had a good heart, and Manzhen was in desperate need of help. Her first idea had been to tell the doctor, before her family came to fetch her, that she was ready to leave. Or, if she couldn't get the doctor's attention, she'd tell a nurse what she needed, and get her to take the message. The problem was that the public ward was mostly left to its own devices, and the hospital staff wouldn't want to get involved in the third-class patients' family problems.

Her case, moreover, was bizarre. Would anyone believe her? All Manlu had to do was tell people that this patient was a mental case. She'd be bundled up and taken back to the house—no chance of effective resistance, in her weakened condition—because even though the hospital was full of people, they'd all steer clear of this sticky situation. And she did look like some kind of mental case, even to herself: long hair, tangled and wild, falling over her shoulders; she had no mirror, so couldn't see her face, but her arms were sickly white, wrists thin as sticks, bones sticking out like the points of a spiral-mollusk shell.

If she had had enough strength to stand, she could have slipped out quietly, all on her own. But her head spun if she so much as tried to sit up—oh, this detestable weakness of her own body! Well, she could ask Jinfang's husband to take a letter to her family, and then her mother could come and get her out of hospital. But was that really a good idea? She didn't know where her mother stood in all this, but it did look as though she'd been drawn into Manlu's camp—how else could they have kept her locked up for the better part of a year? That was the most painful aspect of the whole thing. She'd never imagined her own mother capable of this sort of treatment. Even this stranger met by chance, Tsai Jinfang, was showing more empathy.

Jinfang was outraged. "Your sister and brother-in-law—they're not even human!" she cried out. "They should be hauled off to the police!"

"Please, not so loud!" Manzhen warned her.

Jinfang desisted, and listened: the other patients in the ward stayed fast asleep, the huge room silent except for the little clicking sound of knitting needles, from the nurse who sat by the door.

"I don't want to take this to the authorities," Manzhen said, in a low voice. "Legal cases are always won by the side that has more money."

"You are so right," Jinfang said. "I lost my head just now. Little folk like us know very well that calling in the police only brings grief. Of course I know it's no use—once you're down at the station, it's money that does the talking! You'll never win a case against them. The best you could hope for is a settlement of some kind."

"I don't want their money."

It seemed that this sentiment only deepened Jinfang's respect. "Then you need to get out of here," she said. "My husband, Lin-sheng, will come tomorrow to take me home. We'll put you in my place, and you can leave with him. He'll help you walk, if you're too shaky."

Manzhen hesitated. "That's very kind of you, but what if some-one sees us? I wouldn't want you two to get dragged into this."

Jinfang laughed. "I'd be happy to see them try! If they come look-ing for me, they'll get an earful, they will, and a smack on the head!"

Manzhen was so grateful she couldn't say a word.

"But you've just given birth," Jinfang went on, "it's not good for you to be out and about."

"It doesn't matter," Manzhen murmured. "Anyway, I can't worry about that now."

Their whispered talk continued. To keep their voices low, they craned their necks towards the partition, which wore them out. They talked in fits and starts, till gradually the morning light dawned.

That afternoon, when visiting hours began, Manzhen waited anxiously for the arrival of Jinfang's husband. But Manlu and Hong-tsai arrived first—Hongtsai's first appearance in the hospital. He held a bunch of flowers and looked embarrassed. Manlu was carry-ing a basket of food; she was bringing Manzhen chicken soup every day. Manzhen shut her eyes the moment she saw them.

"Second Sister . . ." Manlu spoke softly, trying to rouse her gently. But Manzhen made no reply.

Hongtsai was feeling awkward, and he gaped around the room. "This room is no good at all," he said. "How could anyone stand it in here?"

"I know," said Manlu. "It's a terrible nuisance. All the good rooms were taken. I told them to inform me as soon as they've got a private, or even a semi-private room, so she can move out of here." She went off at once, to find the nurse.

After a bit of fuss, she came back with the baby. Hongtsai was all over the boy—here he was, a middle-aged man, finally holding his first son. He and Manlu teased the baby, who burst out crying, at which point Manlu made all sorts of strange cooing noises to calm him down. Manzhen lay there with her eyes shut, ignoring them. She heard Hongtsai ask Manlu whether she'd hired the wet-nurse who'd applied recently. Manlu said she'd turned the woman down because she had an eye infection.

The two of them chatted away cheerfully till Manzhen opened her eyes impatiently and scowled at them. "I'm trying to get some sleep," she said in a weak, angry voice. "I wish you'd go home."

Manlu stopped and stared, then quietly said to Hongtsai, "She's getting upset. Maybe you should go."

Hongtsai turned away guiltily and headed off, but Manlu followed and stopped him in his tracks. "Where are you going?" She kept her voice low.

Hongtsai muttered something. Apparently her suspicions were not allayed, but there wasn't much she could do. "All right then," she said. "But be sure to send the car back so I can get home."

Hongtsai left, and Manlu said no more about it. She sat next to Manzhen's bed, gently rocking the baby in her arms. After a long silence, she said, "He wanted to come earlier and see you, but he was afraid you'd get angry. A few days ago, when he saw you in such trouble, and the doctors said your life was in danger, he was so upset he couldn't eat anything."

Manzhen said nothing. Manlu pulled a big red carnation from the bouquet and dangled it in front of the child. His face swayed back and forth, following the flower. "You see!" Manlu said with a smile. "Such a little boy, and already he likes red!" The child grabbed the flower, then let it slip; it fell onto Manzhen's pillow. Manlu looked at Manzhen and didn't see any resentment in her expression. "Second Sis," she said softly. "So a man slips up after he's had too much to drink—you're not going to hold it against him forever, are you?" She put the baby into her sister's arms. "Second Sis, if only for the child's sake—please forgive him."

Manzhen was full of heartache, knowing that she'd soon leave her child. She hadn't expected to see him again, after that first meeting and parting. She wouldn't look at him, or say anything, but she held him tight and rubbed her cheeks on the top of his head. Manlu misread her sister's thoughts, and grew hopeful. She believed Manzhen was relenting, but didn't want to signal a change of heart. Extreme caution was needed; if she said the wrong thing, it could spark a reaction. Manlu kept quiet.

Jinfang's husband had arrived a good while earlier. Manzhen could hear them through the partition, talking softly to each other. Jinfang must have told her husband all the details of Manzhen's situation. They'd been eavesdropping on the conversations on her side, and when a long silence fell, they started chatting about ordinary things. Jinfang asked how many red eggs he'd dyed, and who was minding their market stall while he was away. They didn't have much to say to each other, and Linsheng would have left by now, if he hadn't been planning to take Manzhen with him. He was only biding his time. But he couldn't sit there in silence; they had to find something to say. It was hard for them—it may have been the longest conversation they'd ever had. Linsheng told his wife that his elder sister, who was also pregnant, was helping out with the egg stall. Jinfang told her husband how terrible the nurses were.

Manlu kept sitting there, and visiting hours would soon be over. The floor was covered with nutshells, from all the snacks and treats brought by the families of women who'd had babies. After they left, the housekeeper started sweeping up, swishing the broom around. She slowly made her way to their side of the room, hinting that it was time to go. Manzhen grew anxious. The sight of those nutshells made her think of sugared chestnuts. It was mid-autumn already, so chestnuts must be on the market. She'd been lost in a daze for almost a whole year, locked up in that house. "Is chestnut cake in season now?" she wondered aloud.

Manlu was happy to hear Manzhen expressing a desire for food. "Do you want some? I'd be happy to get it."

"Maybe there's not enough time."

Manlu looked at her watch. "I'll go right now."

Manzhen let the eagerness slip from her face. "Oh, it's hardly worth a special trip."

"You haven't had any appetite—if there's something you think you want, you should have it. The reason you're recovering so slowly is that you don't eat enough." She put on her coat, sent the child back to the nursery and rushed out.

Manlu waited till she was sure her sister had left, then raised her hand to tap on the partition. Linsheng was already on his way around the screen with a bundle of clothing. It was a plaid dress of Jinfang's, along with a woolen scarf and a pair of light green cloth slippers. He handed her the clothing without saying anything, then slipped out of sight. Manzhen saw the red dye on his hands and knew he'd been coloring eggs to celebrate the arrival of his child. A smile crossed her face, and her heart sank. She and Jinfang had each been delivered of a child, but in her case the birth was a bleak, lonely event.

She threw Jinfang's dress over her own clothes and wrapped the scarf around her head, covering half of her face. New mothers are always on their guard against the wind, so no one would find her head-covering odd. Getting dressed nearly wore her out, and when she stood up, her feet seemed to float, as if she were walking on cotton wool. Leaning against the wall for support, she made her way around the partition. Linsheng gave her his hand, and out they went. She caught a glimpse of Jinfang—a long, dark face and sparkling, mischief-filled eyes. Linsheng kept his expression neutral as he helped her towards the door. The nurse on duty was taking Manzhen's baby back to the nursery, so the way was clear: the whole place seemed empty. Once they got downstairs, there was little danger of anyone recognizing her. They went out through the front door to where the rickshaws waited, and Manzhen got into one. Linsheng told the driver to put up the hood so the wind wouldn't blow on her, and a screen went up in front, in case of rain. They went on a long ride, across Suzhou Creek. The sky was growing dark, and the street lights danced all around. Linsheng lived in a scruffy little alley in Hongkou District; he and his wife and their children had a one-room garret. Linsheng got Manzhen settled in, then rushed off to deliver a letter to her family. She also asked him to telephone the Hsus' building and find out if a Mr. Shijun Shen was in Shanghai; if so, he should leave word that a Miss Gu wanted Mr. Shen to come and see her at this new address.

Linsheng went out, and Manzhen rested on the family's wide bed, on the other side of which a little child, about a year old, was fast asleep. The dust-caked, peeling walls were decorated with newspaper pictures: pretty women from the fashion pages, droughts and floods from the news reports, fancy graphics and wedding photos from the society section. Some in color, others in sepia or black and white; sensuous, like petticoat ruffles fluttering overhead on a stage. Pushed up next to the bed was a long, low table covered with household items—a thermos flask, face-oil bottle, mirror, saucer, bowl cover—all crammed together so tightly one could scarcely have plucked one item out from the rest. A light bulb dangled from the ceiling, casting a crooked glare. Finding herself in such a cramped, jumbled room was like falling into a dream. There was even a child lying at her side, though it wasn't hers.

The oldest of the four Tsai children was a six-year-old girl, to whom her father had given, before he left, a bit of cash to buy some flat bread for their supper. When the woman neighbor with whom they shared a kitchen saw what was going on, she asked him who the lady guest was, and he told her it was his wife's younger sister. But it didn't look good, he knew. People were going to think he'd brought a girlfriend over while his wife was in hospital.

The little girl bought the flat bread and shared it out with her young siblings, saving one big hunk for Manzhen. When the girl set the bread on the table, Manzhen asked her to hand her the mirror.

She could scarcely recognize her own reflection. Her cheekbones jutted out, her skin was drained of color—even her lips were white—and her eyes were huge and lifeless. Staring into the mirror, she tried to comb her hair with her fingers, but it was useless. She flew into a panic, convinced that Shijun would appear at any moment. Providing, of course, that he was in the city.

And, as it happened, Shijun was in Shanghai. He'd arrived a few days earlier, but was staying at his uncle's house, getting ready for his wedding to Tsuizhi. At the top of his list was asking Shuhui to be his best man; after that, he had some shopping to do. He went to Shuhui's company dormitory in Yangshupu, instead of his parents' home, so Mr. and Mrs. Hsu didn't know that their son's friend was in town. Linsheng did telephone them, but Mr. Hsu told him that Mr. Shen was not in Shanghai.

Following Manzhen's instructions, Linsheng went next to her mother's home, but a new family had moved in, and had hung up a sign advertising dancing lessons. Linsheng asked the alley guard, who told him that the Gu family had moved quite some time ago, at the end of last year. When Linsheng got back and told Manzhen all this, she could hardly believe it. Now she could see the full extent of Manlu's scorched-earth policy. It was clear that their mother was in her sister's power; even if she could find her, there'd only be further trouble. The upshot was that she had no family to turn to, and no money either. Staying at Linsheng's place meant that he went to his sister's house to sleep: Manzhen felt guilty for inconveniencing him so much. She didn't, at that point, understand that the poor are more than willing to help each other in times of need; living at the mercy of the elements, they can sympathize right away when they see someone in distress. Theirs is not the sympathy of the rich, all shriveled up with reservations and inhibitions. It wasn't till much later that Manzhen grasped this; at the time, she marveled inwardly at having landed in the hands of this uncommonly good couple, Linsheng and Jinfang.

That night, she asked their oldest daughter for pencil and paper so she could write a note to Shijun, asking him to come immediately. Now that seeing him again was such a near thing, her mind clouded over. She couldn't, after all, have full confidence in him. The conservativism of his ways came back to her. Even if he forgave her completely, how could his feelings for her remain the same? Besides, if he really loved her, with a love that would prevail against all odds, they'd never have got into that terrible fight, the last time they were together. The root cause of that quarrel was his inability to stand up to his family. His family had opposed their marriage, even back then. If they knew that she'd now had a child by another man—well, there'd be nothing more to say.

The pencil was in her hand, but her mind had gone blank. In the end she wrote a simple note, telling him that she'd been seriously ill ever since their break-up, and hoping he'd come to Shanghai when this letter reached him. She gave her present address, but nothing further. She even pared her signature down to the last, single syllable: *Zhen*. He'd said that no one read his mail, but it was better to play it safe.

She sent it express to Nanking, but Shijun was away from home, still in Shanghai. Shijun's mother couldn't read, but she'd seen feminine handwriting on the post that came for her son, back when Shijun was staying at his father's other place and Manzhen was writing to him frequently. After she'd met Manzhen, it was easy to tell who had sent the letters. No letter of that sort for the past half-year at least, and now this one appeared—it was disconcerting. The wedding date was set; she wanted no interference with that, and this letter looked like trouble. After a moment's hesitation, she opened the envelope and got her daughter-in-law to read its contents aloud.

"This is rather strange," the younger woman said. "It looks as though they broke up, and now this girl is pretending to be ill, to get him to come and see her."

Mrs. Shen nodded.

The two of them talked it through and agreed that Shijun could not see that letter. They put a match to it then and there.

Meanwhile, Manzhen was counting the days since the letter had been sent. Even though they'd had a spat, he would come, she was sure, the moment the letter arrived. Three, four days, at most. But a week of days went by, each one filled, from dawn to dusk, with waiting, and still he didn't come—he didn't even send a reply. She wondered if he'd heard, somehow, about her misfortune. Maybe he didn't want to see her? If that was all his affection was worth, their relationship had been a complete waste of time. She lay on the bed with her eyes shut, but the tears streamed out, spreading a patch of sodden cold across her pillow. She turned the pillow over, only to find the other side tear-stained already.

Gradually it occurred to her that he might not have received the letter, that his family could have intercepted it. If so, there wasn't any point in writing again, since the letter would only be stolen again. Her best choice was to nurse herself back to health, then go to Nanking to find him. But she had no money with her—how frustrating! Here she was, eating at the Tsai family's table and occupying their only room, forcing her host out of his own home. It was too much to bear! Then she thought of the half-month's pay she hadn't claimed from the factory: that would help tide her over. She wrote a little memo and got Linsheng to deliver it for her. A clerk returned with him and paid out the wages she was owed. From him she also learned that her position as typist had been filled.

She rented out a little roof-top shed, above the top floor, and Linsheng set up a pallet-bed and other basic furnishings for her. He was still providing her meals. Manzhen tried to give him the money that remained after she'd paid the rent, to help cover the food costs, but he wouldn't take it. He said she could pay him later, after she'd found work. Jinfang had returned from the hospital and was resting at home. When Manzhen insisted that she take the money, Jinfang took matters into her own hands: she got Linsheng to buy a dress-length of cotton cloth and some lining, took the fabric to a tailor down the alley and told him to make a padded gown for Manzhen, who really had nothing to wear. Jinfang then forced Manzhen, despite her many objections, to keep the remaining bit of money.

Jinfang told her what had happened when Manlu returned with the chestnut cake only to find Manzhen gone. She didn't spend much time trying to find her sister, but simply took the baby home to Hongtsai. Manzhen thought the two of them must be feeling sheepish, unwilling to draw attention to themselves. Now that they had the child, they were willing to let her go.

Manzhen had a strong constitution, and she was young: she recovered fairly quickly. As soon as she was well, she went looking for Shuhui, hoping he could help her find a job. She also hoped she might happen to see Shijun, if he were still in Shanghai. She went to the Hsus' on a Saturday evening, thinking that would be the best time to catch Shuhui.

She went through the rear door into the apartment building and found his mother in the communal kitchen. "Hello, Auntie Hsu!" she said.

"Oh my goodness, it's Miss Gu—I haven't seen you in ages."

"Is Shuhui home?"

"Oh yes, he's here. You've come at the right time—he just got back from Nanking."

"Oh?" Manzhen was thinking that if Shuhui had gone to Nanking again, it must have been at Shijun's invitation. When she had climbed up two floors, someone was standing at the door, alerted by the sound of her footsteps in the stairwell. It was a young woman she'd never seen before, looking at her inquisitively. Manzhen thought maybe she'd gone to someone else's apartment by mistake. "Is Mr. Hsu in?" she asked.

Just then, Shuhui himself came to the door. "Oh! It's you!" he exclaimed. "Come in, come in! This is my younger sister."

Manzhen remembered that Shijun had once been a maths tutor to this girl—it made her head spin.

They went into the room and sat down.

"I was just thinking I'd go and look for you," Shuhui said, "and here you are."

His sister came in with the tea things, and Shuhui dropped the subject. Manzhen wondered if he'd heard about her big row with Shijun and wanted to help patch things up. It could even be that Shijun had asked him to be a go-between. She picked up her teacup, drank some tea and made small talk with Shuhui's sister. The girl stood there a while, smiling slightly, then left the room. Apparently she was at that awkward age.

"I'm heading off," Shuhui announced, and told her about his arrangements for going abroad. Manzhen was truly happy for him. But in all the details that came spilling out, not once did he mention Shijun. She found this rather strange. Then it felt as though the time for asking had somehow slipped past. She got embarrassed, which only made the question harder to ask. Could Shuhui be avoiding the subject because he knew they'd had a terrible fight? In that case, Shijun must have told him their relationship was over.

But Manzhen, even if she'd had far less to tell, would not have been inclined to divulge her feelings to Shuhui. She lifted the teacup to her lips and glanced around the room, looking for something to say. "This room looks different somehow."

"My sister's taken it over."

"Oh, that's it! It's neat and tidy now. It was such a mess when you two lived here!"

Saying "you two" was a nudge, a way to get him to talk about Shijun. But he didn't take the hint.

Manzhen asked him again when he planned to leave.

"Day after tomorrow, first thing in the morning."

"It's a pity I didn't come to see you before this. I wanted to ask you to help me find a job."

"What? Don't you have a job already? Did you leave the factory?"

"I was sick a long time, and they had to replace me."

"So that's why you look so thin!"

He asked her what sort of illness she'd had, and she rattled off the first thing that came to mind—typhoid fever. He said he'd heard of an opening at a certain foreign bank. He'd call someone on her behalf, and she should go to the bank and ask to see a Mr. Wu.

All this conversation, but not a word about Shijun. Finally, Manzhen asked him, her eyes lit up with a smile, "Have you been to Nanking lately?"

"How on earth did you know that?"

"Your mother told me, when I came in."

But Shuhui still did not say anything about Shijun. He struck a match, lit a cigarette and threw the match out of the window. Then he stood at the window and looked out, silently smoking his cigarette.

Manzhen couldn't bear it any longer. She went over to the window and stood next to him, resting her hands on the sill. "When you were in Nanking, did you see Shijun?"

"He's the one who asked me to go. He got married two days ago."

Manzhen gripped the windowsill with both hands, but it swayed beneath her. The stiff wooden frame was swirling about like an ocean wave. It was ungraspable.

Shuhui saw that she was shocked. "Oh, you hadn't heard? He married Miss Shi. You've met her, haven't you?"

"Yes, that time when you and I went to Nanking."

Manzhen naturally assumed that Shuhui's reluctance to discuss the topic was due to his awareness of her relationship with Shijun. She had no idea that he himself was plunged in gloom, because of Tsuizhi. She managed to stay on her feet, letting the conversation die out. "You must be very busy," she said, "since you're leaving so soon. I'd better go, and let you get back to your packing."

Shuhui wanted her to have dinner with him in a restaurant, but Manzhen dissuaded him. "I hadn't planned on throwing you a farewell party, and I don't want you to play host either, so let's just leave it that way."

Shuhui wanted to exchange contact information, but didn't know where he'd be living. All he could give her was the address of the American university.

As she walked out from Shuhui's place, the world around her seemed utterly changed. She'd been locked up in the Zhu house for almost a year, now free at last, only to find that the world outside had turned into a different place. Could Shijun really have got married to someone else *in less than a year?*

She walked along the lamplit streets a long way before realizing she could take a tram. Then she took the wrong tram, a line that ended on the Bund, without crossing Suzhou Creek. She had no choice but to get off there and continue on foot. It must have rained earlier—the ground was damp. Slowly she made her way towards the brightly lit steel bridge. Running alongside the bridge, on the ashen surface of the water, were the big black shadows cast by the struts. A flotilla of little boats bobbed underneath, and the long, dark shadows swept across their decks and sails. Not a gleam of light anywhere on that water. How deep was it? The flat, ash-brown skin of the water looked like concrete. It was hard to tell whether a person who jumped in would crack her head open, or sink and drown.

A heavy truck came lumbering across the bridge, shaking the road so hard the soles of her feet tingled. Manzhen stood with her back to the traffic, staring out across the water. The pain she was feeling was because of Shijun—no one, not even her own mother and sister, had hurt her this much. Back there at Shuhui's, when she heard what he had done, she had gone completely numb, like a patient pumped full of anaesthetic before surgery. The pain could not reach her then, but now she was slowly coming around. The suffering had begun.

The boats under the bridge were filled with darkness. No light anywhere—all the people on board must be asleep. It was getting late, and Jinfang had told her she was expected for dinner. It was her baby son's one-month birthday, and they were celebrating with a special meal. Manzhen thought of her own child, gone from her life. She didn't even know if he was still alive.

How she got through that night she could never tell. But since she was alive, she had to go on living, one day after another. She got a teaching job, in fairly short order. It didn't pay much, but it gave her a place to live. She moved out of Jinfang's alley and into the teachers' dormitory. She'd once worked as a tutor for the Yang family, and their two children had liked her a lot; they were the ones who found her the teaching job. Their understanding was that she'd been ill and had lost her position at the factory, but was staying on in Shanghai after her family's return to the countryside.

For the next year or so Manzhen spent her time mostly at the school. Even her visits to the Yang family were fairly rare. But one day she went to see them, and Mrs. Yang told her that her mother had come the day before, wanting to know her address. Mrs. Yang must have thought it strange that Manzhen's mother didn't know where to find her. She had given Mrs. Gu the school's address. Manzhen knew at once that trouble was coming.

It wasn't that she hadn't thought of her mother in all this while: she missed her, but still she didn't want to see her. When she left the Yang family that day, she was reluctant to return to her living quarters. But then she realized she couldn't avoid it: sooner or later, her mother would come to the school. Sure enough, when she got back, her mother was in the sitting room, waiting for her.

Mrs. Gu burst into tears the moment she saw her, but Manzhen met her with a distant hello. "You've lost weight," Mrs. Gu said, but Manzhen did not respond. She didn't even ask for the latest family news, or where they were living, because she knew they were all being supported by Manlu.

Mrs. Gu had to tell her stories without any input from her. "Your granny's been in good health these two years, stronger than ever. Your oldest brother's going to finish his studies this summer. I guess you haven't heard that we're in Suzhou now—"

"I only know that you moved out of our old neighborhood. I assumed it was my sister's idea. She thinks of everything." Manzhen couldn't hold back a sarcastic laugh.

Mrs. Gu sighed. "I know you won't like hearing me say you should go back, but really, your sister did not mean to hurt you. It was all Hongtsai's fault. Anyway, you've had the baby, and there's no reason why you should live alone in such misery."

Apparently she had become the object of her mother's pity, because she lived on her own, without family support; and the solution was to go back to the Zhu household, in the role of unofficial concubine.

Manzhen got so angry her face turned red. "Ma," she said, "don't talk like that to me. You'll make me lose my temper."

Mrs. Gu wiped away her tears. "I'm just trying to help you . . ."

"You say you're helping, but what you've done has only hurt me. I don't know what my sister said to you, to make you look the other way while they kept me locked up for months on end. They have evil in their hearts. I almost didn't make it, you know—it was their fault I ended up on death's doorstep, because they waited so long to take me to a hospital!"

"I knew you'd say I'm to blame—you've got such a hot temper. But to my old eyes, it still seems that you should marry Hongtsai. Your sister's being very generous, says she's willing to let you be the first, official wife. I think you're being entirely too stubborn. How are you going to manage, off on your own like this?" The sobs caught in her throat, and she burst out crying again.

At first, Manzhen kept quiet, but after a bit she said, rather impatiently, "Ma, stop that! What if someone sees you?"

Mrs. Gu controlled herself with great difficulty, and sat wiping her eyes and nose with a handkerchief. After a long while, she muttered, almost to herself, "He's such a smart little boy. He talks so well already, and he's good with people, always running after me and calling me Grandma. He was awfully thin at first, but now he's nice and round, with sweet white skin."

Manzhen still did not say anything. Then finally she said, "You can save your breath. No matter what you say, I'm not going back to them."

A bell rang, announcing the dinner hour. "You should go, Ma. It's getting late."

Mrs. Gu heaved a sigh, and got up from her seat. "You should think it over. I'll come back to see you again."

But in fact she did not reappear, probably because Manzhen had been so curt with her, stamping out the hopes she had been nursing. It looked as though she'd gone back to Suzhou. Manzhen asked herself if she had been overly brutal, but in the end she was sure that keeping up contact with her mother would only lead to trouble. Standing between her mother and herself, disrupting those ties, were Manlu and Hongtsai.

Time passed, and eventually the winter break came. The dormitory emptied out, except for Manzhen, who didn't have anywhere else to go. Since she was alone in the building, she moved into the best room, but it was supremely quiet. There's nothing lonelier than a school dormitory during the holidays.

One afternoon, when she had nothing to do, and it was too cold simply to sit around, she burrowed into her quilt and had a nap. A midday snooze in the summer is a simple, natural thing, but a winter nap invites grogginess. Pale yellow sunlight slanted downwards through the window. The flying shadow of a wind-tossed clothes line flicked across the room, like a sudden human presence at the door. Manzhen woke with a start, frightened.

Even after she'd woken up, her mind was muddled for a long while. Then she heard the dormitory attendant calling loudly, from the ground floor, "Teacher Gu, you've got family here to see you."

She thought it must be her mother, but judging from the footsteps on the stairs, a small crowd was on its way. "Why so many people?" she wondered. By the time she'd got a grip on herself, thrown on some clothes and climbed out of bed, they had arrived. Ah Bao and Amah Zhang were supporting Manlu; behind them was a nurse with a child in her arms. Ah Bao saluted her politely, but before Manzhen could reply her sister was being helped over to the bed and settled onto it, her back supported by a cushion improvised from a quickly folded quilt. Manlu was so thin her whole body seemed to have shrunk, but her silhouette was swollen, and she actually looked fat, because she was wrapped in so many layers of clothing. She had a camel-hair overcoat, and a woolen scarf wound around her head. The scarf covered her mouth, so that all that could be seen were half-shut eyes in a pale, clammy face. She sat on the bed, panting for breath. Ah Bao helped arrange her arms and legs, trying to make her more comfortable. "You three should go back to the car and wait for me," Manlu told them, her voice weak. "Leave the child here." Ah Bao put the boy on the bed, then went downstairs with the others.

The toddler was wearing a dark red outfit of plush velvet, perfectly new, as if he'd been specially dressed for the occasion—this visit to her. He'd even been dusted with face powder, with a red circle painted on each of his cheeks. He tottered around on the bed, babbling and tugging at Manlu, wanting her to look this way and that.

Manzhen stood at the window with her arms crossed, watching them.

"Sister," Manlu said, "you can see how sick I am. I don't think I can last more than a month or two."

Manzhen couldn't help smirking. "Don't put a hex on yourself."

Manlu fell silent. "Well, I can see why you don't believe me. But this time it's for real, and incurable—intestinal tuberculosis." She herself felt like the boy who cried wolf; when the wolf did come, no one believed him.

The air in the room was freezing cold, and when Manlu tried to speak it felt like walking barefoot through icy water. Still she had to try. "I've had a rough time of it, these past two years. Hongtsai goes out constantly, up to no good. He'd have sent me packing, long ago, if it weren't for this child. What kind of woman do you think will come in and rule this boy's life, after I'm dead? That's why I'm begging you to come back."

"Don't keep bombarding me with that nonsense."

"You don't believe me, but I am telling the truth. Hongtsai respects you—he thinks you're different from every other woman. If you tried, you could manage him."

"What is that man to me, that I would want to manage him?"

"Then let's not think about him—think of this child, and what *he'll* go through after I die. You've got to take care of him."

That stopped Manzhen in her tracks. "I'll get him out of there," she said at last.

"Impossible. Do you think Hongtsai would let you do that? If you take him to court, he'll spend every penny he's got fighting you. This is his one and only precious son—he won't let go of this boy."

"Yes, I suppose that's so."

"Of course it is. If there were any other solution, I wouldn't come to you like this: after I die, you can marry Hongtsai—"

"Stop right there! I'd rather die than marry him!"

But Manlu gathered up the boy, with much effort, and tried to thrust him into Manzhen's arms. "You can kick up as much of a fuss as you like, but in the end you have to think of the child. How can you be so hard-hearted?"

Manzhen did not want to hold the child, because she did not

want her sister to see her crying. But Manlu, wheezing hard, thrust the child towards her once more. Before Manzhen could respond, the child burst into tears and plunged back into Manlu's arms. "Ma! Ma!" he cried. Of course he thought Manlu was his mother, but at that moment, heedless of any logic, Manzhen's heart ached.

The child's display of affection stirred Manlu too, and all her sorrow came spilling out. "When I die," she sobbed to Manzhen, "I can walk away from everything, everything except this boy. I can't bear the thought of leaving him!" Her tears came in a flood, like water welling up from a spring.

Manzhen was almost as affected as she was, but when she saw her sister shuddering and sobbing in great gasps, something in her reacted. She hardened her heart and frowned with impatience. "How can you let yourself get so worked up? Time to go home, don't you think?"

She jumped up, ran down the stairs and got Ah Bao and Amah Zhang to bundle Manlu out of there. Manlu went off sobbing and crying, followed by the nurse with the child in her arms.

Alone in the room again, Manzhen straightened the rumpled quilts and sat on the edge of the bed, thinking. The revulsion she felt towards Hongtsai was so fierce, so instinctive, that just hearing his name was enough to set her off—which was why she'd rejected her sister's plea without a moment's deliberation. But after she'd calmed down and thought it over, it still felt like the right thing to do. Of course she loved her son—and now he was the only family she still had. If she had any means of getting him out of there, she'd raise him on her own; she had no qualms about this whatsoever. She was ready to endure all the opprobrium, all the social pressure meted out to single mothers. She'd do anything for her son—anything except marry Zhu Hongtsai.

Manlu would come again, she thought, or maybe send their mother, to keep pushing her to return. She'd better leave the school. She submitted her resignation, despite considerable protests, since her contract for the second term had been issued before the winter break. She found another position, this time as an accountant. She'd studied accountancy in school. After she'd got the job, she found a room for rent, in a property owned by a Mr. and Mrs. Guo.

One day, as she returned from work, she happened to see a young woman at the back entrance to the Guos' place. The woman had a small round face and dark complexion, rouge on her cheeks and hair pinned up high above her temples; her light linen dress had orange flowers on a white background. It was none other than Ah Bao. But how could they have tracked her down here? It gave Manzhen quite a shock. Ah Bao also seemed surprised. "Goodness!" she exclaimed. "It's Second Sister!"

Standing next to her was a man whom Manzhen recognized as a clerk from a nearby employment agency. Then she remembered that one of the maids who worked for the Guos had recently gone back to her home village, and the agency had sent someone new, on a trial basis. Evidently it hadn't been successful and they were looking again, which meant that Ah Bao was here after work, not because she'd been sent to find Manzhen. Nonetheless, Manzhen stayed cool towards a girl who, back when they were both at the Zhus', had been in league with her enemies. It's true that a maid cannot be entirely blamed for following the orders of her employers—after all, she depends on them for her livelihood—but even so, Manzhen felt a strong repugnance when she saw Ah Bao. She gave the girl a curt nod and walked straight past her towards the house. But Ah Bao ran after her.

"Did you hear, Second Sister? The mistress passed away."

The news was not unexpected, but still it took Manzhen by surprise. "What? When did that happen?"

Ah Bao clucked her tongue. "A week or two after she went to see you at your school." Her eyes reddened and filled with tears.

The maid was crying, but Manzhen looked at her unsympathetically. Her heart felt bare of emotion.

Ah Bao took out a handkerchief, dabbed at the corners of her eyes, then turned to the agency clerk. "Please go ahead without me. I have something to discuss with the people here."

Manzhen did not want to get into a conversation with her. "Go on in," she said. "I don't want to detain you."

Ah Bao could tell that Manzhen was being cold towards her, and thought it had to do with the ring. "Second Sister," she said, "I know you must blame me for not delivering the letter you gave me, but—well, there's more to it than you know. Do you know why they wouldn't let me go to your room after that?"

That was as far as she got. "Why are you even bringing this up?" Manzhen demanded, glowering at her.

Ah Bao shrank into silence, rubbing her hands over her crossed arms. After a long moment, she spoke again. "I don't work there anymore. It made me so mad—Second Sister, you haven't heard about this, but after the mistress died, Amah Zhou fed the master a lot of trumped-up lies about me. That Amah Zhou, she's a slick one, very good at wheedling. She got rid of the nanny, and now she's the one who looks after the child. When the master's around, she puts on a show, pretending to treat the boy nicely, but when the master's gone, she turns into an evil stepmother. The way she treated him—I couldn't bear to see it. That's why I left."

She was overflowing with self-righteousness. Manzhen believed about half of it, mainly the part about being pushed out by another maid. She clearly was worked up about something; she had a bellyful of grievances but no one to talk to. Manzhen had not invited her in, but she stayed where she was at the back door and prattled on. "The master's losing all his money, so his temper is worse than ever. He's almost wiped out, had to sell the house on Hongqiao Road. He moved into the city, over in Great Peace District. They used to say that Mistress Manlu was his good-luck charm. It must be true, because the minute she died, everything fell apart! He's feeling it now, I tell you. He stays at home, sad and lonely. No more running around—he got rid of all his other women. He's always looking at the mistress's portrait, and when he does, his eyes are full of tears."

When the talk turned to Hongtsai, Manzhen's manner grew even more impatient, as if she'd had enough of standing around waiting to go in. Ah Bao finally got the point, and changed tack. "Are you living here now, Second Young Lady?"

Manzhen gave her a cursory reply, and asked if she'd come looking for work.

"Yes. But they've already got a lot of staff, and the pay is low, so I don't want to work here. If any of your friends need a maid, would you be good enough to let me know? I'm at the employment agency just across the way."

Manzhen said she would.

A silence fell, and Manzhen wished Ah Bao would say more about the boy, how big he'd grown, how amusing he was—children can say such funny things, and ask such odd little questions, the sort of things that maids love to repeat. Which dialects had he picked up, she wondered. Was he healthy and strong? Did he have a nice personality? Ah Bao said nothing about him, and Manzhen, suddenly shy and tongue-tied, couldn't bring herself to ask.

"Well, I'd better go, Second Young Lady," Ah Bao said.

She left, and Manzhen went inside.

Ah Bao had said that the Zhus now lived in Great Peace District, which Manzhen traversed daily on her way to the tram stop. From that point on, she stuck to the main thoroughfare, even though it made the walk longer. She didn't want to take the risk, while cutting through the alleys, of running into Zhu Hongtsai. He had no power over her, but the mere thought of seeing him was repulsive.

On her way home from work one day, she found herself following a pair of primary-school boys. Whenever she saw a child, she guessed at its age and compared it to her son's, wondering if he had grown that tall yet. These two were older of course, maybe seven or eight, in brand-new blue gowns that cascaded over their padded clothes, giving each of them a nice big belly. They marched side by side like a pair of soldiers, swinging their abacuses up and down with each strutting step. The rattling clack-clack was like the beat of an army band. Sometimes an abacus rose up like a rifle-butt and tapped a shoulder smartly.

Manzhen could catch snatches of their discussion, which turned out to be not at all heroic. "Ma Zhenglin's father runs a bakery," said one. "Ma Zhenglin gets to eat bread every day." His voice was warm with envy.

Suddenly they cut across the main road, and into an alley in Great Peace District. Manzhen's heart stopped for a moment, even though she knew the neighborhood was filled with boys like these, and neither of them was her son. Her feet took her, of their own accord, towards the alley the boys had just entered. Her steps were hesitant, and by the time she made the turn, the boys were nowhere to be seen.

It was a dank, gray afternoon early in the spring. It's often like that, early in the year, before the first breath of warmth: there's an odor everywhere, and besides the clinging cold, there's an itch in the bones that feels greasy and grimy. It hadn't rained, and yet the street was beaded with moisture. Going down the alley, Manzhen saw, between the two rows of stone-clad houses, a pedlar with a pole across his shoulders who was selling chewy, fermented bean curd. He was halfway down the passage, hands on his hips, crying out his wares. A girl bought a stick of bean-curd squares and slathered hot sauce on them. Was that Beckon, Hongtsai's daughter by his first wife? Manzhen couldn't study the girl any further: her eyes were drawn to a little boy, three or four years old, who was standing next to Beckon. They had to be brother and sister, because their gowns were made of the same cloth, cotton with a purple floral pattern. Even though it was spring already, they were still wearing last year's cloth-soled shoes, but without any socks. The sight of those bare, red ankles in tired, black shoes sent a stab of sympathy through her heart. The boy's hair had grown long, down to his eyebrows; his face, though grubby, had a delicate charm.

Manzhen was too flustered to take a closer look. Her eyes went back to the girl, searching for something to confirm her hunch. It had been a long time since she'd seen Beckon, and then only once, but the image was clear in her mind. A child's looks usually change quite fast, but this thin, yellow-skinned girl didn't seem to have changed at all. She didn't even seem to have grown any taller—but that had to be an illusion, since her gown was too short, by several inches.

The girl stood beside the bean-curd pedlar, reaching into a little ceramic jar for hot sauce to spread on her snack. Hot sauce was free, which was probably why she slathered it like jam on bread, turning the bean curd bright red. The pedlar gave her a look, ready to say something, then changed his mind. Beckon had three squares of bean curd on one long stick, and ate them where she stood. Her little brother wanted some too; he stood on tiptoe and pawed at her clothes, craning up to get a bite. Even one bite, Manzhen thought, would scald his throat and bring tears to his eyes. She broke into a sweat just thinking of it, but the boy swallowed the morsel without batting an eyelid and went back for more. He got up on tiptoe again, chin raised high, and Beckon shared the treat out companionably, one bite for herself, the next bite for him. Manzhen had to smile, her son was so silly—but her eyes overflowed, even as she smiled.

She turned around smartly and plunged into an intersecting alley, flicking the tears away as she strode along. Suddenly she heard footsteps behind her. There was Beckon, running towards her in cloth shoes stretched loose with wear, the soles squeaking on the wet cement.

Oh no! Manzhen thought. She's recognized me. I didn't think she could. She only saw me the once, back when she was little. She turned around, and pretended to be scanning house numbers, looking for a certain address, all the while watching Beckon out of the corner of her eye. But Beckon stopped short, and stood looking at a house where a Buddhist mourning service was in progress: the strip of yellow paper over the gate had been ripped apart, and the paper funerary offerings were burning in the courtyard, flames rising high from the brazier. Beckon ate her bean-curd snacks and watched the people putting tinfoil money in the fire. She paid no attention to Manzhen. Manzhen finally relaxed and retraced her steps, walking calmly again.

A maid was with the boy now, a woman in her forties with small black eyes, tadpole-shaped, in a yellowish face. She had pulled out a little bench and was sitting at the back door, sorting vegetables. That's the Amah Zhou that Ah Bao described to me, Manzhen thought. Beckon scampered away when the amah appeared—to hide her snacks.

Manzhen walked slowly past them. Something in her face or

clothing must have caught the boy's eye. "Hello, Auntie!" he suddenly called out. Manzhen turned and smiled at him, and the boy went on calling to her, "Hello, Auntie, hello!"

The maid grumbled at him. "Won't greet people when you are asked to, won't keep quiet when you're not!"

Manzhen walked out of the alley, past a dozen shop-fronts, with her heart pounding. When she came to a display window, she smiled at her reflection. But she couldn't find anything special, something to catch a child's eye and make him call out to her. The boy's greeting still rang in her ears. She recalled each detail of his face. Back when his aunt had brought him to see her, he'd been too little to walk; he'd crawled across the bed like a sweet little animal. Now he was a person, with his own personality.

Walking in there and finding him like that—it was pure luck. And a journey she could not repeat. Nothing good could come of seeing him, it would only break her heart. But she did send money to her mother. It didn't look as though Hongtsai had much cash to spare for the support of his deceased concubine's mother. Manzhen did not, however, send her mother her address; she still didn't want her to come looking for her.

When summer rolled around, Manzhen remembered that her mother had said her brother Weimin would graduate then and could start earning money. But Manzhen didn't think that a young graduate, fresh out of college, could support the whole family. She sent them another sum. All her savings from the past two years of work—she sent it all to them.

One hot, humid evening, a heavy rain started to fall. The landlord's young maid ran out to the balcony to fetch the clothes she'd hung out to dry. The doorbell rang downstairs, repeatedly, and finally Manzhen went down and answered it. It was a young woman she'd not seen before, smiling at her rather uncertainly. "Could I use your phone, please?" she asked. "I live across the way, in No. 9."

The rain was pouring down hard, so Manzhen invited her in and said she'd get Mrs. Guo to come. She called out several times, to no avail, and the maid came down the stairs with her arms full of clothes and said, "The missus isn't in." So Manzhen led the woman into the hallway to use the phone. The visitor picked up the directory and started to look up a number; Manzhen turned on the light for her. Even with a rain jacket thrown over her shoulders, it was clear that she was expecting. Her long straight hair was tucked behind her ears, and she didn't look like a Shanghainese, though neither did she seem a small-town girl. Her face was pretty and refined, with smooth, small features in an oval shape. It took her a long time to find the phone number. She kept looking up at Manzhen with an apologetic smile, and filled in the time by asking for her name and where she was from. Her own surname was Zhang. When she heard that Manzhen was from Anhui Province, her ears perked up.

"Where in Anhui?"

"Liu An."

"Oh my goodness. I've just arrived from there."

"You're from Liu An too? But you don't have our local accent."

"I'm originally from Shanghai. My husband is from Liu An."

Manzhen took a moment to think, then said, "There's a Dr. Yujin Zhang in Liu An. Do you happen to know him?"

The woman blinked, then quietly said, "That's my husband."

"What a coincidence! That means you and I are relatives."

Mrs. Zhang gasped and smiled. "A coincidence indeed! Yujin came with me on this trip. I hope you can come and see us. We're staying at my mother's place."

Manzhen stepped away, into the back of the house, while Mrs. Zhang made her call, then came back to see her to the door. She wanted her visitor to stay till the weather cleared, but Mrs. Zhang had things to do. A relative was coming to take them to dinner—that was why she'd needed to borrow the phone, to ask Yujin to go directly to the restaurant, and meet them there.

After she'd left, Manzhen went back to her room. The rain kept coming in squalls, with no sign of letting up. If Yujin knew where she was living, he'd certainly come to see her, sometime in the next day or two. She was a little afraid of seeing him, since that would make her think of all the things that had happened since they parted ways. That nightmarish phase of her life bore no relation to her previous twenty-odd years, or to the Manzhen whom Yujin had known, back then. She very much needed to let it all out, by telling him about it. Otherwise, it would feel like a terrifying world hidden in her heart forever.

That night, her memories rose up in waves, making sleep impossible. Even though it had been so hot during the day, the windows had to stay shut because of the rain. She lay on her bed constantly fanning herself—and still broke out in a cold sweat. The doorbell rang, at nearly ten o'clock, and the maid who slept on the ground floor stumbled to the door. "Who is it?" Her voice was harsh and hollow. "What? What? Who are you looking for?"

Manzhen suddenly realized that Yujin had come. She clambered out of bed, flicked on the light, pulled on her clothes and ran downstairs. The maid didn't want to let a stranger into the house at that hour. But it was Yujin, standing at the back door in his raincoat, wiping his face with a handkerchief. The raindrops glimmered as they fell from his hair.

He nodded at her and smiled. "I've just returned to Shanghai, and heard you were living here."

A mix of emotions whirled up in her; fortunately she had her back to the light, so he couldn't see the tears glistening in her eyes. She turned around quickly and led him up the stairs, staying in front so her face was hidden. Once in her room, she busied herself with the bed-quilt, making it neat and tidy; she needed that moment to get her eyes steady.

Yujin came in and looked around. "Why are you here by yourself?" he asked. "Your grandmother, and all the others—are they OK?"

Manzhen answered him indirectly. "They're living in Suzhou now."

Yujin looked surprised, which was the very cue she needed for telling him the whole story. That's what she'd decided to do, once she'd realized that he'd ventured out in the rain, at night, the moment he'd heard where to find her. His friendship for her was clearly unchanged. But some thorny topics are easier to broach with a complete stranger, a sympathetic someone to whom you can bare your heart. It hadn't been like this, back in the hospital when she'd told Jinfang everything—faced now with her old friend Yujin, she didn't know where to begin.

So she changed the subject. "It was such a stroke of luck, running into your wife like that. When did you two come to Shanghai?"

"A few days ago. My wife's going to have surgery, and the hospitals where we live are not well equipped, so we came here."

Manzhen didn't ask why surgery was needed; she guessed it was the impending childbirth, and that they were expecting a difficult delivery.

"She's going into hospital tomorrow," he told her. "We're staying at her mother's place now."

He sat down, the rain dripping off his coat, which he still had not taken off. Given the lateness of the hour, he couldn't be planning to stay long. Manzhen poured him a cup of steaming water. "Were you at a dinner party just now?" she asked.

"Yes, at a Sichuanese restaurant. They're all on their way home, but I came by here first." Apparently he'd had some wine, for his face was bright red. It was hot and stuffy, sitting in that room with his raincoat on; he picked up a newspaper that was lying on the table and used it to fan himself. Manzhen peeled a piece of fruit for him, and opened the window halfway. Looking out of the window, she saw that the houses were dark, scarcely a light anywhere. Yujin's in-laws must be in bed by now. His wife might not mind if he stayed out a while, but eyebrows would be raised in her family. Manzhen told herself they'd meet again, one way or another; she should wait and tell him her story another time.

But from the moment he'd entered her room, Yujin had been wondering what was going on. Why was she living like this, all on her own, with her family off in Suzhou? Were they trying to save money? But where was Shijun? Why hadn't they got married yet?

He had to ask. "Does Shen Shijun come around a lot?"

"I haven't seen him in a long time. He went back to Nanking a couple of years ago."

"Really?"

Manzhen paused. "Later on, I heard that he got married."

Yujin was at a loss for words.

In the silence that fell, the sound of dripping water reached them. Raindrops were falling on some books that lay on a table near the window.

"Better close that window," Yujin said. He picked up a book and started to dry it with his handkerchief.

"Oh, please don't bother," Manzhen said. "It's so dusty, it'll get your handkerchief all dirty."

But Yujin went on wiping the book with great care; he was remembering the time when he stayed with her family, and the noise of the neighbor's radio kept him awake at night, and she lent him her books to read. If it hadn't been for Shen Shijun, things could have been so different for them . . .

Suddenly he started talking about his life now, to leave behind that train of thought. "A small-town clinic doesn't make much money. We have to buy supplies and equipment, so we keep costs down by using a tiny staff, and that means I'm very busy. Even though I'm a local, I don't have much of a social life. All that isolation was hard on Rongzhen, when she first arrived. She needed something to do, so she studied nursing, and now she helps me at the clinic. As long as you've got something to do, you won't be lonely."

Rongzhen—that must be his wife.

He himself felt he'd gone on too long. He rose to his feet. "I should go now."

Since it was so late, Manzhen didn't try to detain him. She saw him to the door. As they were going down the stairs, Yujin remembered something. "Last time I was here, I heard that your sister was ill. Is she better now?"

"She died, not too long ago," Manzhen answered softly.

Yujin was shocked. "I heard at one point that she had an intestinal tumor. Was that what caused her death?"

"Well, that time . . . that time it wasn't really so serious."

That was the time her sister had pretended to be ill and lured her in late at night. Manzhen paused, then continued: "I wasn't with her when she was dying—well, a lot of things have happened these past few years. When you have time, I'll tell you about it."

Yujin stood stock-still and looked at her, as if he wanted to hear everything, right then and there. But when he saw the weariness that had come over her face, he restrained himself, turned again and went down the stairs. She saw him to the back door.

Returning upstairs, she noticed, on the one padded chair her room contained, the damp patches left by his raincoat. Looking at those water marks, she fell into a daze of silent grief.

The rainstorm had come on suddenly—Yujin's wife had most likely brought his raincoat to him at the restaurant, since he wouldn't have needed it earlier in the day. They had a good marriage. The way he talked about her made that plain. And as for Shijun? Was his a happy marriage too? It had been so long since she'd thought of him. Surely, by now, her pain should have worn off. But that pain seemed to be the only living thing left in her body; it stayed fierce and fresh, not allowing her a moment's rest, once it had been aroused.

She emptied his teacup into the spittoon, then tipped the thermos to refill her own cup. The hot water sputtered out, splashing across her bare foot, but she was so numb she could scarcely feel it. It was like striking her foot with a hammer, but feeling no effects.

The rain fell through the night, not tapering off till dawn, at which point she finally fell asleep. Moments later, someone was tugging her awake. It was like that time in the hospital, when the nurse brought her son at dawn so she could feed him. She clutched him close, her head reeling, her heart swirling with joy and pain, as if he had been lost, then found again. Suddenly he went ice-cold—he was dead, his body stiff and straight. She held him even closer, burying his face in her breast, terrified that others would discover this death. Which they did: that yellow-faced Amah Zhou came and grabbed the boy from her arms, rolled him up in a burial mat and took him away. But the dead child was struggling inside the mat. "Auntie! Auntie!" he called out. His cries grew louder and louder, till Manzhen broke out in a cold sweat and awoke to find it was day, with the bright, blank light streaming in through her window.

The dream, to her, was simply strange. The pain that awakened when she thought of the past, and Shijun, had fed her yearning for her son, but she didn't see that, nor that these pieces had been woven together to make this dream.

Sleep would not come again, so she got up. She was far ahead of her usual schedule today. She left the house before seven, a full two hours before she was due at the office. As she slowly walked down the main road, she suddenly decided to look for her son. It wasn't a decision, actually. It was a recognition of her own true intention, the reason why she'd got up and out of the house so early.

It didn't take her long to reach Great Peace District. She could see, in the distance, a line of people filing out of the cross-alley towards which she was headed. Two were carrying, on their shoulders, a small coffin. Behind them came a maid—could it really be that Amah Zhou? Manzhen's vision went black and she crumpled against the alley wall. Then, pulling herself together, she tried to get a better look. Amah Zhou, with a banana-leaf fan on her head, to shade herself from the sun, was twitching and grimacing: apparently she'd just finished breakfast and was cleaning the loose bits from her teeth. Manzhen's eyes registered that scene with perfect clarity, even though her mind was misted over with confusion. She felt as though she'd fallen, again, into a nightmare.

The coffin passed in front of her. She wanted to ask Amah Zhou who had died, but Amah Zhou wouldn't know who was asking. As she stood there hesitating, the little troupe went down the alley. A new plan came to mind, and she headed back towards the Great Peace gateway with a firm stride. The Zhus' house was the fourth one in, she recalled. The maid who answered the doorbell had served in the family for many years. Her name was Amah Zhang. "Second Sister!" she exclaimed, staring in surprise at Manzhen.

"How is the boy?" Manzhen asked, cutting through any small talk.

"A bit better today."

So he was still alive. The knot in her chest loosened and her feet came back down to the ground, but it was like a high-speed descent in a lift: it left her dizzy. She leaned on the door frame for a moment, then walked straight in. "Where is he? I need to see him."

It looked as though Manzhen, having heard that her son was sick, had come to check on him. Amah Zhang led her in. This stone-front house was single-story; from the back door, they passed through the kitchen and into the parlor. The French doors to the parlor were shut tight, and a bed had been set up in the darkened room. The boy lay there, sleeping. His face was flushed, his sleep restless, and when Manzhen felt his forehead, it almost burned her hand. Amah Zhang had said he was "better today," but clearly this was smooth-tongued servant-talk.

"Has a doctor been to see him?" Manzhen asked quietly.

"Yes. He said the boy caught it from his sister, and that the two of them should sleep in separate rooms."

"So it's something infectious. Do you know what it is?"

"Scarlet fever, he called it. It was terrible, what happened to Beckon. And then, last night, she died. It was so sad."

Manzhen finally understood that the coffin she had seen was Beckon's.

She examined the boy's face, but didn't see any red spots. Then again, she had heard that scarlet fever did not always cause a rash. He was tossing back and forth in obvious discomfort, constantly shifting his position. She took his hand. So hot and dry—it made her realize how cold her hand had become.

Amah Zhang brought her tea. "Do you know if the doctor will come today?" Manzhen asked.

"I haven't heard. The master went out early today."

Manzhen ground her teeth. How she hated him—this man who would not let this child out of his control, and yet would not take care of him. She could not allow this boy to suffer Beckon's fate, sent to the grave through mere carelessness. Suddenly she was on her feet and heading for the door. "I'll be back in a moment," she said, and hurried out. She had decided to fetch Yujin and ask him to confirm the diagnosis. The doctors consulted by the Zhu family did not inspire much confidence.

Since it was still quite early, Yujin was probably at home, at his in-laws'. She jumped into a pedicab, rushed back to her own street, and went to the house diagonally across from hers. Yujin, who was on the upper-floor balcony, saw her ringing the doorbell; he came out to greet her just as she was asking the servant if the doctor was at home. "Won't you come in?" he asked.

"I'm afraid not," she said, forcing a smile. "Are you busy right now?"

Her face told him something was wrong. "What's the matter? Are you sick?"

"It's not me. My sister's boy is terribly sick. It might be scarlet fever. Could you come and see him?"

"Yes. I'll come right now." He went in, picked up a jacket and his bag, and headed out with her. They went to Great Peace District by pedicab.

Yujin had heard that Manlu married well. That was what her grandmother had said, telling him how rich she was, in the house they had built on Hongqiao Road. Finding her family now in a small, dark house was quite a surprise. He also had thought he would meet her husband, but the master of the house did not appear; a maid had to play host instead. He saw Manlu's portrait in its frame the moment he entered the parlor: it was hanging right in front of him. Manzhen had not noticed it. On both of her trips to this house, her mind had been a blur, her attention focused only on the child.

The photo must have been taken several years before Manlu died. She was looking at the viewer from the corner of her eyes, one hand raised to her cheek, sporting a big, shiny diamond ring. The aging flirt—it was a jarring effect, and it made him quite sad. Memories of their last meeting came back to him. Maybe he should not have been so unsympathetic to her. It brought him real pain, when he thought back on it.

This boy was her son, so naturally he was very concerned. The diagnosis, he agreed, was scarlet fever.

"Should he go to a hospital?" Manzhen asked.

Doctors usually recommend a stay in hospital, but after seeing the signs of hardship in the Zhu household, Yujin felt he should be sensitive to their financial situation. "Hospitals can be quite expensive," he said. "If there's someone at home who can nurse him carefully, that would be just as good."

Manzhen had been thinking that if the boy were in a hospital it would be easier for her to take care of him, but the fees were beyond her means, and Hongtsai was not likely to cough up the money. So, no hospital. She asked Amah Zhang to get the prescription that the other doctor had written and show it to Yujin, who said it was the right medicine.

Manzhen saw Yujin out to the main street, and got the prescription filled in a pharmacy at the head of the alleyway. While there, she telephoned her office and asked for a half-day's leave from work.

The boy was now waking up a bit, and kept staring at her with bright, shining eyes. The moment she turned her back, he whispered, "Amah Zhang, who is that?"

Amah Zhang hesitated, then smiled. "She's your . . . Second Auntie." She stole a glance at Manzhen, unsure of whether she had given the right answer.

Manzhen went on swirling the medicine in its bottle, then got a spoon and coaxed some into the boy. "Here, drink this up and you'll feel better." Then she asked Amah Zhang what the boy's name was.

"Rongbao. I feel so sorry for him. The mistress always made so much of him, but now that Amah Zhou—" She broke off and looked around the room. Then, speaking now in a hushed voice, she continued: "Amah Zhou is a heartless woman. The master dotes on the boy, but he is a man and doesn't see half of what goes on. She used to beat Beckon, that poor child, and though she doesn't dare abuse this precious one in broad daylight, once they're out of sight, she finds ways to make him suffer. But please don't tell anyone I told you this. If she finds out, I'll be out on the street. Ah Bao tussled with her, and Amah Zhou got rid of Ah Bao. Well, Ah Bao did do something wrong—a lot of valuables in her charge went missing, after the mistress died. Amah Zhou wasn't in on it, so she got mad, went to the master, and ratted on Ah Bao."

This long recital of household squabbles could mean only that Amah Zhang thought Manzhen had patched things up with Hongtsai and would return to serve as mistress of the house. That's why Amah Zhang wanted to tell her all of this, while Amah Zhou was out of the house. For Manzhen, this was very disturbing. She didn't want to hear this scurrilous talk, didn't want to be in this situation at all, but she also couldn't see a way out, at least not at this moment.

Someone was rapping on the back door. Was it Hongtsai? Manzhen couldn't help feeling nervous, though she had known all along that he might appear—after all, this was his home. Amah Zhang answered the door. There were scratchy whispers in the kitchen and she returned with Amah Zhou, who had come back from the pauper's graveyard, where Beckon's coffin was now buried. Even though she'd never met Manzhen, Amah Zhou knew something about her, along with the fact that her deceased mistress was not Rongbao's birth-mother. Manzhen's sudden appearance threw her into a state of apprehensive flattery. It was "Second Miss" this, and "Second Miss" that, her glowering mug pasted over with gleaming smiles as she danced attendance—a sight to make one shudder. But Manzhen was careful not to react: if this amah got offended, she could turn around and take it out on the boy. The amah too was being wary: she was afraid her misdeeds would come to Manzhen's attention, through Amah Zhang telling tales. She usually treated the scruffy old woman like dirt, but today those gray hairs inspired sudden reverence. "Grandma Zhang," as she now called the elder maid, got whisked off to the kitchen so the two of them could make something nice for Second Miss to eat.

Manzhen, however, was getting ready to go. Her plan was to set out a few essential tasks for Amah Zhang, then come back in the afternoon. But just then, Rongbao spoke up, asking for his sister. It was the first time he had addressed Manzhen directly, and she had no answer for him. After a long pause, she finally said, in a low tone, "Sister is sleeping. You should get some rest."

When she thought of Beckon's death, a rush of cold fear enveloped her heart. Prompted by this primal instinct, she promised herself that if he made it through this crisis, she would never leave him. And yet she knew full well it could not be arranged. Rongbao was fiddling with the woven-grass mat on his bed, poking his finger into a hole and gradually making it bigger. Manzhen took both of his hands in her own. "Stop that now," she said gently. Two tears fell, making a soft plop on the mat.

Hongtsai's voice suddenly rose at the back entrance. "Has the doctor been yet?" he asked, the moment he came in through the door.

"No," said Amah Zhang. "But Second Young Lady is here."

A long silence fell when he heard this. So long a silence that Manzhen knew that he was standing at the entrance to the parlor, had been standing there for many minutes. She did not move a muscle, but her face grew taut, her gaze cold and stony.

She did not turn to look at him, but finally he lumbered into view. He looked a shambles, face unwashed, beard unshaved, his hard, sharp features covered with a shiny layer of greasy sweat. He was wearing an old lined gown of muddy orange silk and an old straw hat, also a muddy orange, which he didn't take off, apparently because he was too distracted. He made his way to the head of Rongbao's bed and rubbed the boy's cheeks. "Are you feeling better today?" he murmured. "Why hasn't the doctor come yet?"

Manzhen said nothing.

Hongtsai coughed and went on. "It's such a relief to have you here, Second Sister. What a time I've had of it, these past two years. Bad luck everywhere. When Beckon got sick, it didn't seem all that serious. By the time I saw that it was, and hurried to get her treated, which cost a pretty penny indeed, it was too late. The boy caught it from her, and this time I knew we had to get it treated right away. I've been out since early this morning, trying to rustle up the necessary funds." He heaved a weary sigh. "I never thought things could get this bad!"

Half the reason his investments had failed was his deep-rooted belief in Manlu's ability to bring good luck to her husband. He'd never have admitted, back then, that she had a role in his success, but in fact he was swayed by that old fortune-teller. Several deals went bad for him, right after she died, and that only made him more apprehensive. Business investing is basically a form of gambling: once he lost his nerve, he lost everything—which only strengthened his belief that Manlu had been his good-luck charm.

Amah Zhou brought him a hot washcloth to wipe his face. Without registering what he was doing, he rubbed his hands with the cloth, over and over again. Amah Zhou gave up and left him to it. A long moment passed, then suddenly he burst out, "I feel so guilty when I think of her." He turned his back to Manzhen and stood gazing at Manlu's portrait, using the cloth to wipe his nose. It was clear that he was crying.

The sun was shining directly on the portrait. The reflection was so strong that the picture itself could not be seen—only the layer of dust on the glass. Manzhen stared blankly at the photograph. Her sister was dead, and in the years that had passed since her death, her own feelings had also subsided. That tangle of rage and resentment had turned into thin, trailing wisps of dust.

"I feel so guilty now," Hongtsai said again. "I made things hard for her, even after she got ill. Maybe that's what led to her death. Second Sister, it really was all my fault. You shouldn't hold it against her."

Greed was the motivation behind his confession, but Manzhen did not see this. His self-accusation made her think that he had some kind of conscience after all. Her experience of the world was still not deep enough to help her see that cruelty and cowardice go hand in hand; and that those who, when they're riding high, transgress flagrantly are later crushed by the slightest touch of hardship, at which they pull long, sad faces. A small streak of sympathy leavened her loathing: she had no intention of heeding his wishes, but neither did she want to add to his suffering.

Hongtsai stole a glance at her face. "Second Sister," he stammered, "for the child's sake . . . his sake at least . . . stay here a few days and help him get well. I'll go and stay with a friend." Even as he spoke, he was heading out of the door, as if afraid she would refuse. Reaching into his pocket, he took out a wad of notes and gave it to Amah Zhang. "Give this to Second Mistress, so she can pay the doctor when he comes. I'll be at the Wangs', or with Mr. Yen. If something comes up, you can telephone me there." He hurried out of the door like an escapee.

Manzhen believed him, when he said he'd stay away. Manlu had told her many times that Hongtsai held her in the highest respect, that he put her in a class by herself, different from every other woman. He'd been out of his mind when he committed that crime, but even that was because his love for her was so terribly strong. This kind of reasoning is easy for a woman—any woman—to believe. When Manlu said all this, it didn't seem to make the slightest impression on Manzhen. But in the end, the elder sister had not wasted her breath.

Manzhen stayed at Hongtsai's house that night, watching over the child from dusk to dawn. The following day she had to go to work, and when she got back to the house she found that Hongtsai had returned and then departed again. That made her feel more secure: she could devote herself to caring for the child without worrying about its father. She had planned to ask Yujin to come again, but then remembered that he was very busy. Hadn't he said that his wife was being admitted to hospital? It must be today or tomorrow that the operation was to be performed. She'd been so distraught she'd forgotten all about it when she had brought him to the house. She didn't really need to ask him to come again. The other doctor would do as well.

Yujin himself was concerned about the child, and that very night he went to Manzhen's place to get the latest news on the boy's progress. Her landlord told him that Manzhen had not come back to the house. Yujin knew they had another doctor on the case, and with Manzhen taking charge of things, there really was nothing to worry about. So he let the matter drop.

Yujin's room at his in-laws' had a window that faced Manzhen's. He often found himself looking that way. Her windows stayed shut, even though the weather was hot. There was no one in that room. Two towels could be seen through the glass—a pink one draped on the back of a chair and a white one hanging on the clothes line. Their position did not change. The sun blasted down from morning to night—surely those towels were more than dry. They hung there for two weeks, baked stiff, all the color faded away. Yujin did not think it strange that Manzhen was staying at the Zhus' all this while. They needed someone to nurse the child. Manlu had died, and if the boy's father did not have an education, he probably spent all day scraping a living, so he wouldn't be available. Manzhen had always been the helpful, responsible type; doubtless, she'd answered the call of duty, and gone off to nurse the sick boy.

The days kept slipping by. Yujin's wife had her operation, and now they had a baby daughter. The new mother had been recuperating in the hospital, but it was almost time to return to the countryside. Manzhen still had not come back. Yujin thought of going to her sister's house to say goodbye, but he didn't know the family well; showing up on their doorstep seemed awkward. He kept putting it off.

Then one day, glancing across the way, he suddenly realized that the two towels had been moved, apparently washed and hung out again. She must have come back, he thought. He went downstairs straight away, and crossed the street to her door.

He'd been there twice before, so her landlord recognized him and let him find his own way to her room. Manzhen was dusting and sweeping; she'd been gone so long that the dust had grown thick everywhere. Yujin knocked on the open door and smiled at her. When she looked up and saw him, a shadow seemed to flit across her face, as if she didn't want him to come in, but Yujin thought he must have imagined that.

He stepped in, still smiling. "Haven't seen you in a long time. Has the boy recovered?"

"Yes, he has. And I haven't come to congratulate you yet. Is your wife out of the hospital? Is it a boy, or a girl?"

"A girl. Rongzhen got out of the hospital a week ago. We're going home tomorrow."

"Oh! Leaving already?" She wiped off a chair and invited him to sit down.

"Yes, we're set to go tomorrow. It's hard to say when we'll meet again, so I wanted to be sure to find you today, hoping we could catch up a bit." He had come because her tone, when she had said she had something to tell him, suggested some hidden trouble. But Manzhen, at this point, regretted those words. She didn't want to go through all that, now that she'd decided to become Hongtsai's wife.

The table was already clean, but she kept rubbing at it with the cloth, back and forth, mechanically. After a long while, she went to the window and shook the dust out. It was an old piece of pink gauze, once a headband, now a dusting cloth. She flung it up and down, using both hands, and the pink gauze floated softly in the breeze-filled light. It was a beautiful afternoon.

She hadn't said anything all this while, so Yujin prompted her. "Didn't you say you had something to tell me?"

"Yes, but then I realized I don't want to talk about it after all."

Yujin thought she was afraid of stirring up some sorrow. He paused a moment, then said gently, "Maybe talking about it will help you feel better."

Manzhen still said nothing. Yujin thought hard. "You seem unhappy, not the way you used to be." It was a simple comment, but the voice that uttered it was warm with feeling.

A shudder of alarm ran through her. He had seen, in just one glance, the inner collapse that all those layers of stress had wrought in her. And here she'd thought she was managing to appear calm and collected. A smile played across her face as she looked at him and asked, "So you think I've changed that much, got old maybe?"

He hesitated, then said, "You still look the same, but something seems . . ." She had always seemed to him marvelously cheerful, yet steely with determination; when she was supporting her whole family, she stayed relaxed and composed, as if she had all the strength she needed, and plenty to spare. But now she seemed dispirited, even shaky. The ordinary pressures of life could not have caused a change as deep as this—it had to be Shijun. Something must have happened, something that ended their marriage plans. She didn't want to tell him about it, and of course he wouldn't press her for details.

"After I go back, will you keep in touch by letter?" His voice was warm with concern. "To tell you the truth, I'm a bit uneasy about how you're doing." His kindness only increased her pain. She could not keep the tears from streaming down her face. He stopped speaking, when he saw that. He smiled at her and said, "I shouldn't have said that. I'm sorry."

"No, I do want to tell you—" The words came bursting from her. But then her voice caught, and she stopped.

She didn't know where to begin. The expression on his face, all that readiness to hear her out, threw her into disarray. Again the words came blurting out: "That boy you saw is not my sister's—"

He was horror-struck. She turned away, her face now calm and hard.

If the boy is hers, he was thinking, that means she gave birth in secret—then gave him to her sister to bring up? Is Shijun the father? Or was it someone else? Was that why Shijun left her? Even he could not believe the thoughts now racing through his mind.

Manzhen started again, still in snatches, this time picking up from the point at which he had come to her house to deliver the wedding invitation. That was the night that she and her mother went to her sister's, to help her while she was ill. Manzhen did her best not to cast blame on her sister; Yujin had once been close to Manlu, and she didn't want to harm his fond feelings for her. Besides, Manlu was now in the grave. But try as she might to cover up for her sister, the fact was that, through all those long months of her captivity, Manlu had simply stood aside, not lifting a finger.

Yujin was shocked to the core. He couldn't understand how Manlu could have been involved in such an evil scheme. He didn't know her husband, who apparently was a complete scoundrel, but Manlu . . . he thought back to the time when he'd first met her, a girl of sixteen, after which they'd got engaged, till she broke it off so she could work as a taxi-dancer, to support her family. The Manlu he knew was a good, pure-hearted person. She did seem to have grown coarser, that last time he saw her, but not through any fault of her own: he'd always believed she had a good heart. How could she have been so cruel to her own sister?

Manzhen went on with her tale. She told him about the narrow escape from the hospital, after she'd given birth, then about her mother finding out where she was living and trying to persuade her to go back to Hongtsai. Mrs. Gu, it seemed to Yujin, had taken leave of her senses; he was so angry that words failed him. Then Manzhen told him how her sister, now very ill, had sought her out and begged her, for the sake of the child, to marry Hongtsai, but she had refused. Her voice, when she told him this part, grew husky and low, because even though she had refused then, she was about to do what her dead sister had asked of her. It wasn't right, she knew. Her mind was filled with contradictory thoughts, and she yearned to talk it through with him, but she didn't have the courage. She felt utterly ashamed of herself, especially in front of Yujin.

She had tried, out of consideration for Yujin's feelings, to lighten the load of blame that would otherwise fall on her sister, thereby increasing the guilt laid at Hongtsai's feet, making him into an utter monster; she could not now suddenly turn around now and say she was going to marry him—the words simply would not come out. She knew full well that even if she had put him in a better light, by describing him as a man easily swayed by others, Yujin would still not approve. A marriage so flawed as this could never be approved of by anyone who was looking out for her interests, anyone who was a true friend of hers.

So when she got to the part where her sister died, she ended her tale. Yujin sat with his arms folded and his eyelids half-closed, saying not a word. He could think of no way to comfort her. But her tale wasn't finished—Yujin suddenly recalled that when she went to the Zhu household to take care of the sick boy, she stayed a long time, which probably meant that she and Hongtsai had reached an understanding of some kind. Otherwise, she wouldn't have stayed on, for all those many days. Could she have so altered her original intention that she planned now to sacrifice her own happiness for the sake of her son, by marrying Hongtsai? He even wondered if she were already cohabiting with him. No, that couldn't be, she wasn't that kind, he was wrong to think her capable of anything like that.

Having thought all this through, he finally spoke, his tone grave and thoughtful. "You've done the right thing, and your sister's idea makes no sense. Entering that kind of forced marriage would be like entering the grave, ending your life." He kept on in this vein, in a manner and to a degree she had never seen in him before. He was of the opinion that conjugal life depends on the happiness of both spouses, and that if one of them is suffering, the other cannot be happy. In fact, there wasn't much need for him to say this, since she'd already considered anything he could say, with even greater depth and thoroughness. For instance, even though one could say that Hongtsai, assuming he did love her, would not love her for long, because of the sort of man he was, there was more to it than that.

She had believed that Shijun truly loved her, and that his love was the lasting kind, but it had turned out otherwise. That was why she had no concrete faith in anything now; the world and everything in it was a vague blur. The one real thing for her was her son. Having hauled him back from the brink of death, she could not cast him to the winds again.

She herself was suspended in limbo: where she went was of no consequence, made no difference to her. It was about the same as being dead already.

"All you have to do is get a good grip on yourself," Yujin said. "You've got a bright future ahead of you."

He meant to be encouraging, but his words caused her such pain and sorrow that the tears started flowing again. What was the use of crying like this, in front of him? Yujin had moved on with his life, and she ought not to burden him thus. She rose abruptly to her feet and said with a smile, "Look how silly I'm being, telling you all this nonsense, without even offering you a cup of tea."

She had two glasses perched on top of the cupboard, but when she held one to the light she found it was covered with dust, from long disuse. She busied herself with cleaning the glasses and pulling out the tea, leaving Yujin in stunned silence. This sudden burst of hostessing seemed to come from an unwillingness to continue their talk. But then, as he thought about it further, he felt that his warnings and advice were empty consolation; his concern and care were of no use to her. After a long moment of silence, he said, "Don't worry about the tea. It's time for me to go."

Manzhen did not try to persuade him to stay. She picked up the other tea glass, blew the dust off it, then rubbed it with a cloth. Yujin stood up to go, but first took a notebook from his pocket, ripped out a page, then leaned over the table, wrote out his address and gave it to her.

"I've got your address already," she said.

"Your house number here is fourteen, isn't it?" he asked. He wrote it in his notebook.

Manzhen was thinking ahead to the time when she'd leave this house and his letters wouldn't reach her, but she didn't say anything.

She had no strength for that conversation. He'd find out, eventually. Someone would tell him that she'd married Hongtsai, and he'd wonder why he'd ever thought so highly of her, why he'd wasted his time on such a disappointing person.

She went down the stairs with him, seeing him to the door. "When are you two leaving tomorrow?" she asked, as they were saying goodbye.

"Early in the morning."

Manzhen went back upstairs and stood at her window watching Yujin, who was standing at the back door of his in-laws' house. Apparently he'd rung the bell and was waiting for someone to come. He saw her too, then smiled and raised a hand high in the air, as if he were waving to her. Manzhen smiled back and nodded in reply, then stepped back quickly to hide her streaming tears. She stood at the table, sobbing hard, and picked up something to wipe her eyes. When she realized it was the cleaning cloth, she threw it back. The old pink cloth slid slowly off the table, and onto the floor.

15

The Battle of Shanghai began in mid-August,* and the fighting was intense for three months: the wealthier inhabitants fled in a panic, heading inland to escape. Manzhen's mother was in Suzhou, and people there were equally alarmed. Mrs. Gu wasn't wealthy, but she was caught up in the agitation—that bee-swarm of people rushing up the Yangzi River, towards the interior—and she fled to her old home town, Liu An in Anhui Province. Granny had already passed away. Mrs. Gu, almost sixty years old by this time, had spent several decades as daughter-in-law to Granny, and though she'd sometimes complained behind Granny's back, the many hardships they'd endured together had made them life companions. When the older woman died, Mrs. Gu was left all by herself, her children having moved out of the house. One daughter was in Suzhou, training to be a nurse, and the two youngest children were in college, supported by their older brother Weimin. He was married now, and had a teaching job in Shanghai.

The Gu family had a two-room, baked-clay house on the out-skirts of Liu An, built as the lodgings for the grave-keeper; Mrs. Gu reclaimed it now for her own use. Yujin came to see her soon after she'd arrived, hoping to hear news of Manzhen. The letters he'd sent had all been returned by the postal service. Judging from what he knew of the quarrel between Manzhen and the Zhu household, it looked as though Mrs. Gu had repeatedly made a sacrificial pawn of her daughter, and had even condoned the long imprisonment

---

* On 13 August 1937. Chinese forces based in Shanghai were attempting a valiant but ultimately unsuccessful counter-offensive against the Japanese.

inflicted on her. Maybe she'd felt forced into it; maybe she'd been played for a fool; either way, Mrs. Gu had sold off her own daughter, and he could not summon much affection for her. His manner reflected his change of heart, whereas Mrs. Gu was as happy as if he were an old friend re-encountered in a new place: she was delighted to see him. They chatted for a while, and Yujin asked where Manzhen was.

"She's still in Shanghai, married now . . . you heard, didn't you, that Manlu died? Well, Manzhen got married to Hongtsai."

She was glossing over the facts, acting as if Manzhen's having married her brother-in-law was a completely ordinary occurrence, never once suspecting that Yujin knew the awful parts of the story. Still, it was a topic that made her uneasy, a blot on her family's honor; she left it at that, and changed the subject.

Although this didn't come as a complete surprise to Yujin, still it was highly disturbing. His heart was full of pity for Manzhen. Mrs. Gu was eager to continue the conversation, but he stopped responding to her; he said he had to go and left.

It was only that once that he came to see her. He didn't visit her that next New Year's, or on any of the other holidays, to offer her the compliments of the season. Mrs. Gu was incensed. Look at him, so high and mighty! she thought to herself. Who would have imagined he'd turn so haughty? He used to stay with us when he came to Shanghai, but now he sees me sunk in poverty and doesn't want to admit we're related.

The battle zone was coming closer. Mrs. Gu couldn't work out what to do. She thought she might go to Shanghai, but traveling was dangerous and she was a solitary, elderly person with no one to help her along the way. By the time she'd made up her mind, that plan was impossible.

Shanghai, by this time, had fallen to the enemy. The newspapers there reported the fall of Liu An, but since it was in such a small district, details were scant and nothing further was announced. In Shanghai, Manzhen and her brothers Weimin and Jiemin were naturally quite worried about their mother's safety. Weimin received a letter from her, but it had been posted before Liu An surrendered, and thus told them nothing about her current situation. Still, he had to pass the letter around so everyone could see it. He gave it to Jiemin and asked him to take it to Manzhen. Jiemin had a job in a bank; he'd left college after only one year of study and started working. Whenever he came to the house, his nephew Rongbao, who was very fond of him, stuck close to him. It was a hot day, and Jiemin was wearing a white undershirt and khaki shorts. He came in and sat down, and Rongbao, who was nestling up against Manzhen, suddenly turned to her. "Ma."

"Yes?" his mother said, but the boy didn't answer.

A few minutes later, he finally leaned in towards her ear and whispered, "Ma, Uncle has a scar on his leg."

Manzhen looked at Jiemin's knee and had to laugh. "That scar's got bigger. It's grown right along with you."

Jiemin looked down at his knee and rubbed it. "It's from that time I was learning to ride a bike and fell off it," he said and grinned. Then his expression changed, his mind preoccupied with something. Manzhen asked if he was busy at work, and he gave a cursory reply, but then suddenly he made a fist and pounded his leg. "Oh! I've got something to tell you, and I almost forgot. You'll never guess who I ran into the other day—Shen Shijun." The mention of that bicycle-riding lesson, when he was being coached by Shijun, had reminded him of this. The blank look on his sister's face made him think she hadn't understood, and needed more explanation. "*Shen Shijun.* He opened an account at the bank, and I remembered his name when I saw his business card. I didn't say anything special to him, and of course he didn't recognize me—how old was I, the last time he saw me?" He pointed at Rongbao. "About his age, I guess!"

Manzhen laughed too. She wanted to ask him what Shijun looked like now, but before she could get the words out, Jiemin reached into his pocket and pulled out their mother's letter, then handed it to her. He went on to tell her he was being transferred to a different branch of the bank, starting next month. The conversation had moved on, and Manzhen couldn't find a way to bring it back to Shijun. There really was no need for embarrassment: there was surely nothing significant in asking about a long-ago boyfriend. She was over thirty, with a son who was half-grown already: from her younger brother's perspective, she must seem a woman well past her youth. But precisely because it would seem that way to him, she couldn't reveal to him those long-burning embers of emotion: it would be too embarrassing.

She read her mother's letter, but there wasn't much she could say in response to it. She and her brother tried to comfort one another, but in their hearts they both knew that if tragedy struck their mother, they'd all blame themselves for not insisting that she come to Shanghai earlier. Jiemin had nothing to offer her; he lived in the dormitory provided by his employer, and had nothing that he could call his own. Weimin was in a cramped set of rooms, along with his mother-in-law. His wife was an only child, and when he married her he'd agreed to support his mother-in-law in her old age, and that she would live with them. Things were different for Manzhen: she had the means to invite her mother to live with her. Businessmen were the only ones making money in the occupied areas, and in the past two years Hongtsai's situation had turned around completely. He'd built a new house, two rooms on the main floor, two rooms above, so there was plenty of space for Mrs. Gu. But Manzhen was not keen. She didn't see much of her brothers, didn't see much of anyone: all she wanted to do was hide in a dark cave. She saw herself as sullied.

Hongtsai was very disappointed in her. He'd yearned for her for years on end, back when he thought she was unattainable; and after he'd landed her, his shock and amazement were so great he couldn't believe she actually was in his possession. But after they were married, the passage of time took the luster away, and he started to feel cheated. It was like a bowl of vegetarian prawns: they look like prawns, but they're made of potato, and taste like wood pulp, no flavor at all. But at least she was attractive, or so he thought at first, taking some satisfaction in the status he got from having a wife with her looks. For a time he'd insisted she make the social rounds with him, but she'd let herself go, and now was no match for his friends' wives. She made no effort to look pretty; her skin had yellowed and she had a sickly air, her clothes were always out of fashion, and she never had anything to say. Sometimes she seemed not to hear when others spoke to her, and her gaze was vacant. This utter transformation, after he'd finally made her his own, was beyond his comprehension: it made him frustrated and angry. He was therefore constantly quarreling with her. But no matter how fierce the verbal attack, Manzhen would not bring up the past, or how loath she had been to marry him. Thinking about it only increased her pain, so she mentally shunned the whole topic; since she never brought it up, he gradually forgot it had happened. Once a couple has married, everything in their past becomes insignificant. Which of them was the pursuer, which the pursued, gives way to a new dynamic: the loser is the one who fails to fight back. Hongtsai found fault with her day in and day out, and Manzhen barely responded. She felt she was lying in a muddy hole, covered in filth from head to toe. What was the point of keeping score, in a situation like that? Nothing made any difference, one way or the other.

It had been about two weeks since the fall of Liu An and communications with the town were intermittent, which meant it had to be chaos there. Manzhen wanted to wire some money to her mother, and the first step was to ask her brother if that could be done, but she didn't want to discuss it over the phone. She had to go and see him at the bank and give him the money directly, in the hope that he could get it through. It was a small branch office, with an upper-story dormitory for the staff, who came and went through the rear door. Manzhen purposely waited till the bank was closed for the day, because Jiemin had told her that Shijun had an account there and she didn't want to run into him. He was the one who ought to feel guilty, but with the passage of time she'd lost sight of that and felt only that her life now was a source of deep shame—she couldn't even face herself. There may have been an edge of animosity too. She did not want his sympathy.

The weather had been hot for several days running, the last blast of early autumn heat, but temperatures had dropped this evening. Manzhen seldom went out, and in any case would not take the pedicab kept at their house for Hongtsai's use. She took the tram. When she'd reached her stop and was walking down the street in the dusky light, she felt the coolness of the breeze and knew it must be raining somewhere nearby. Shijun had come to mind several times recently, along with memories of her youth. In those days she'd gone out to tutor her students every evening, and Shijun went with her, the two of them walking down the street just like this. Those two young people seemed to be right next to her—she could reach out and touch them, as if the breeze lifting the hems of their clothing were the same breeze brushing now against her body. One moment they seemed to be right at her elbow, but then a whole mountain towered between them, there in that little gap.

The bank where Jiemin worked faced onto the main street, and the back entrance led into an alley. Manzhen studied the street numbers on the buildings she passed, looking for No. 509. When she came to the alley entrance she found a shop with a pink neon sign hung high in the air, casting a soft light over the passageway. Someone was walking towards her out of the alley, and though she couldn't see clearly in the reddish glow, her heart caught in her throat. Maybe she'd noticed something familiar in his gait . . . but a full decade had passed since she'd last seen Shijun, so if she hadn't been thinking of him just then, she never would have recognized him so quickly. She whipped around to face the shop window. It was unlikely that he had spotted her. He had no reason to think she might be here, no reason to look closely when he passed a woman on the street. Manzhen had not anticipated his coming to the bank this late. Precisely because it was late, he'd gone around to the rear door, looking for the clerk who usually helped him. This explanation occurred to Manzhen only later on; at the time she was too alarmed to think at all. Her only thought was an overwhelming desire *not* to see him. Ducking her head, she turned and walked westwards along the street. Apparently he had turned in the same direction; she could hear footsteps behind her, and thought they must be his. Even though she still believed he hadn't noticed her, the feeling of panic was rising. Not a single pedicab in sight. A show had just ended at a nearby theater, and all the pedicabs in the area were gathered there. Precisely because the audience was leaving, there was a steady line of automobile traffic on the street, leaving no gaps through which she could squeeze. The person behind her was walking faster, had even started running. Now she panicked completely. A bus lumbered past her, heading towards a stop, and she also started to run, hoping to catch it. She'd taken no more than a few steps when Shijun overtook her, and kept going. He wasn't chasing her; he was trying to catch the bus.

Manzhen stood still. Now that the danger was past, she had to look again and make sure it was Shijun. The whole thing was so dreamlike she couldn't quite believe it was happening. There were a couple of shoe shops along the street, each with a brightly lit window, lights so bright they shone out to the edge of the pavement. She would have been able to see what Shijun was wearing, what his face looked like. Even though it would be only a quick glimpse, she probably would have been able to tell whether he'd put on weight, or grown thin, whether he looked prosperous, or had fallen on hard times. But Manzhen could not take any of this in. She got no clear impression at all, because the moment she could tell it was him, she lost her bearings. Her heart started pounding, a flood of conflicting emotions surged within her, and her whole body seemed to be buffeted by waves at sea.

As she stood there staring at him, the bus drove away, leaving Shijun still standing on the pavement. The bus was too full, he couldn't get on, so he was waiting for the next one. It would come from the east, so naturally he turned around and looked back that way, straight at Manzhen—as she immediately saw. If she whirled around suddenly, he'd surely notice her. No time for any further thought: she stepped into the road, aiming to get across it. By this time the steady line of snaking traffic had eased a little, but at that moment a lorry came speeding down the street: the white glare of its headlights blinded her, making the truck's front huge and concave, like the mouth of a black cavern hurtling towards her. She wasn't quite sure what happened next, but she heard a long, sharp scream as the lorry braked, and a stream of curses from the driver. Her legs were trembling so hard she could barely walk, but somehow she scurried to the other side. She'd gone only a short distance when a pedicab came by and she clambered in. The cab took her down one street, then another, and still the pounding in her chest did not stop.

Perhaps it was only the undoing that follows a big shock, but tears poured from her eyes like water from a bubbling spring. It would have been better to have been crushed to death by that truck. She wished she could die. It had started to rain, big drops falling on her, but she didn't ask the driver to stop and put the canopy up. When she got home, she went upstairs to the bedroom. The windows were sealed tight because of the rain, and the room was too warm. Leaving the lamps off, she lay flat on her back on the bed. The only light in the dusk-dark room was a faint gleam caught in the wardrobe-door mirror. Some of the furniture had been bought when she and Hongtsai got married, some had been added later. The room's gloomy stillness made the furniture seem tightly packed together; it was all so dark and close she could scarcely breathe. This was the grave she had dug and in which she lay buried alive. She rolled over, onto her chest, racked with sobs.

Suddenly a light was switched on. Hongtsai had come home. Manzhen turned to face the wall. It was unusual for him to be home so early. He was hardly ever there at dinnertime, and Manzhen didn't ask him to explain. She knew he was womanizing again, and it was only the rain that had brought him home at this hour. He walked over to the bed, sat down and put on his house slippers. "What's the matter? Why are you lying here?" he asked, reaching over to give her knees a pinch. For some reason, he was feeling affectionate towards her today. When that happened, her own repugnance surged up with such force that it took all her strength away, leaving no energy for anything else. She lay there silently, not moving a muscle. The room was too hot for Hongtsai, so after he'd changed his shoes he went down to the living room, in search of a fan.

Even though the bedroom windows were closed, Manzhen could hear, from where she lay on the bed, a radio in another house on the lane. It was a tune played on a four-stringed lute, with a middle-aged crooner singing in a soft, smooth, almost feminine voice; the words themselves were indistinct. The pluck-pluck of the lute sounded like falling rain; listening to it through a window, with the pattering rain, made it even sadder, more lonely.

The weather turned cold the next day, the rain having passed. Manzhen, still intent on wiring money to her mother, was planning to telephone Jiemin and ask him to come and see her after he got off work; but then she got a call from Weimin, who told her their mother had arrived in Shanghai and was now at his place. Manzhen went to see her, right away.

Traveling to Shanghai had been arduous indeed. Mrs. Gu had started out in a one-wheeled pushcart, but when the man pushing the barrow was conscripted by an army unit, she'd had to continue on foot for miles and miles, till finally she reached a railway line. She'd been chilled to the bone on the train, and clearly she was feeling the cold weather today: she had a bad cough and a hoarse voice. But she'd had to keep talking from the moment she arrived in Shanghai. Weimin wasn't at home at first, so she told the story of her travels to his wife and mother-in-law, then repeated it when he arrived. Weimin phoned Jiemin, who came over, and she told him, then went through the whole thing a fourth time after Manzhen arrived. Liu An had fallen to the Japanese but was then retaken by the Chinese—a development not reported by newspapers in occupied Shanghai. The violent to-and-fro of two armies had reduced Mrs. Gu's little house, outside the city wall, to a heap of rubble. She'd had to seek refuge inside the city wall, in a cousin's uncle's house. There was the usual carnage and mayhem when the Japanese broke into the city, but the two of them, old people without livestock or anything of value, were left mostly unscathed. The enemy had held Liu An for only ten days when the Chinese recaptured it. The moment the fighting stopped, she seized the opportunity to flee to Shanghai. Quite a few people in Liu An had the same idea. They found someone who knew the way, and he led them to Shanghai.

She'd located Weimin's place, but his quarters were a single room with a partitioned-off sleeping area for Mrs. Tao, his mother-in-law. When Mrs. Tao saw that Weimin's own mother had nowhere to live, she felt embarrassed, as if she were taking something not rightfully hers. She poured herself into a warm welcome for Mrs. Gu, outdoing her own daughter in this regard, yet at the same time anxious neither to overstep her own role as a guest in this household, nor to shower Mrs. Gu with so much attention that she felt uncomfortable. It was a difficult balancing-act. Mrs. Gu knew only that Mrs. Tao was behaving rather oddly, warm and kind one moment, then cold and distant the next. Wanzhu, Weimin's wife, was being entirely polite, of course, but Mrs. Gu could see that the two women were afraid she'd have to move in with them.

After Weimin came home, he and his mother had a good talk. He didn't want to plead poverty the moment she got to Shanghai, but once they started talking there was no way to avoid the issue. Teachers had always been badly paid, and now that prices were rising, he was feeling the pinch. Wanzhu spoke up at that point, saying she wanted to work and help out with the household expenses.

"It's hard to find a wage-paying job," her husband said. "The only people in Shanghai making money these days are businessmen and investors. We've got plenty of nouveaux riches."

Mrs. Tao said nothing about her daughter's proposal, thus making clear her position on the matter. Whether Wanzhu worked or not was beside the point; there wasn't any job she could get that would solve their financial problems. But there was something Weimin could do. His sister was rich, Zhu Hongtsai was raking in the cash, they'd be fully able to take Mrs. Gu in—and they were all in the same family, weren't they? Why shouldn't *he* take care of Mrs. Gu? Having held this opinion for a long time, Mrs. Tao tended to have a resentful, cross attitude towards Manzhen.

Manzhen arrived, and they all chatted together for some time. Manzhen could tell that her mother and Mrs. Tao were not getting along. Two older women, each with her own fixed habits, couldn't share a home comfortably, and in any case the room clearly was too small. Manzhen had no choice but to say her mother should come to her house.

"That's a good idea," her brother said. "You've got more space, and that'll make it easier for Ma to rest."

So Mrs. Gu went back with Manzhen. Hongtsai wasn't in when they arrived.

"What kind of trading is he doing now?" Mrs. Gu asked her daughter. "Is it going well?"

"I can't stomach anything he and his cronies are doing these days. Hoarding rice, or medicine maybe, to drive up the price. It's always something unconscionable like that."

Mrs. Gu had not realized that her daughter's attitude was unchanged, that the mere mention of Hongtsai's name was enough to set her off. She tried to laugh it off. "Well, that's how the world is these days—no way to get around it!"

Manzhen said nothing. Mrs. Gu had noticed that she seemed dispirited, her face dark and sullen. "Are you feeling all right?" she asked, with a frown. "Goodness! You were always working so hard, wearing yourself out from dawn to dusk! The strain didn't show then, but it's all caught up with you now."

Manzhen did not argue with her. The whole topic of work was a sore point: she and Hongtsai had agreed that she'd keep her job after they married, he being so ready, at that point, to accommodate her; but he'd never liked the arrangement and kept nagging at her to quit. They'd fought endlessly over this. Finally, out of sheer exhaustion, she'd left her job.

"When we were at your brother's place," Mrs. Gu said, "your sister-in-law talked about getting a job to help with their expenses. They were pleading poverty, just to put me off—after all, he's got enough to support his mother-in-law, hasn't he? I suppose raising a son is useless after all." She heaved an angry sigh.

When Rongbao came home from school, Mrs. Gu tugged at him and asked, with a smile, "Ah! Who am I, can you tell? Do you remember who I am?" Then, turning to Manzhen, she said, "Do you know who he looks like? The older he gets, the more he looks like his grandfather."

"Like Dad?" Manzhen was puzzled. The father she remembered had a sweeping mustache and a thin, sharp face, but her mother remembered him differently; her mind held on to the image of a young man, and kept finding it again in her loved ones' faces. Her daughter had to smile.

Manzhen sent a maid out to buy some snacks. "No need to make a fuss on my account," her mother said. "I don't want anything to eat, but I would like to lie down for a bit."

"It must have been a tiring trip," Manzhen said.

"Yes, I'm quite worn out."

Manzhen took her upstairs, where a bed was already made up for her. Mrs. Gu lay down and Manzhen sat next to the bed, keeping her company, since her mother had started talking again about her experiences in the war zone. She'd not yet mentioned Yujin, and Manzhen was anxious to hear his news.

"I was really worried when I heard that the fighting had reached Liu An, since you were there all by yourself, but then I remembered Yujin was around and might be able to help you."

"He was no help at all!" her mother huffed. "He only came to see me once, the whole time I was in Liu An." Suddenly she remembered something and sat up in bed. "Oh, did you hear?" Her voice had turned soft. "His wife's dead, and he was captured."

"What? How could—"

Mrs. Gu started her tale right from the beginning, dwelling on the falling-out she'd had with Yujin, which nearly drove Manzhen mad with impatience. With mind-numbing thoroughness, she gave every detail of his not coming to see her, and her not going to see him. "I didn't bring this up at your brother's, because I don't want the Tao family thinking our relatives don't respect us.

"Well, in any case, when the fighting came closer, and I was outside the town wall, all on my own, not even then did he come to see how I was coping. Then, when the Japanese entered the town, they grabbed him, and assaulted the nurses in the clinic, one after the other. They say his wife was violated too, and that's how she lost her life. Oh, dear, when I heard that . . . He didn't have time to spare for me, this poor old aunt of his, but I've known him since he was a boy! I didn't get to know his wife at all, but to think of her dying like that—how tragic! I don't know what happened to him after he was captured. The town was in total chaos when I left, and I heard that the hospital equipment had all been taken away. That's probably what the invaders were after—Yujin's medical equipment."

Manzhen was stunned. "Tomorrow," she said sadly, "I'll go to see Yujin's parents-in-law. Maybe they'll know more."

"His wife's family? I heard Yujin say they'd gone to the interior. Didn't a lot of people leave Shanghai when the fighting broke out?"

Manzhen fell silent again. Yujin was the only one who'd ever shown real concern for her; and now, likely as not, he had left this world. As she sat there stunned, Mrs. Gu leaned in close and ran her hand over Manzhen's face, then her own. Her brows were knit, but she said not a word, and lay down again.

"Are you OK, Ma? Have you got a temperature?"

"Uh-huh."

"Should I get a doctor?"

"No, don't bother. It's something I caught while traveling. Some medicinal tea will cure it."

Manzhen got out a tea packet and asked a maid to prepare it, then told Rongbao to play downstairs so his grandmother could rest.

Rongbao went off by himself to the living room, and started making paper airplanes. His uncle Jiemin, that last time he'd dropped in, had taught the boy to make planes that flew a long way. He folded and launched several at once, then ran around chasing them, laughing and panting as he squatted to pick them up. Hongtsai came in just then. Rongbao briefly acknowledged his father, then stood up and left the room. That made Hongtsai angry.

"What are you doing, running off the minute you see me? You don't have permission to leave!"

His feelings were hurt because it seemed that, ever since the boy's mother had moved in, he'd had eyes for her only. Rongbao hid behind the sofa, and Hongtsai hauled him out. "Why do you turn into a frightened ghost, the minute you see me? What's this all about? Tell me!"

Rongbao burst out crying.

"What are you crying for?" Hongtsai growled. "I haven't hit you! But I will, if you keep this up—"

When Manzhen heard her son crying, she rushed downstairs: here was Hongtsai beating the boy the moment he entered the house. "What are you doing?" She pulled him away from the boy. "This is senseless!"

Hongtsai, his face livid, turned on her: "He's my son, and I'll beat him if I please! He *is* my son, isn't he?"

Manzhen was enraged, ready to hit him, but she would not argue with him. Instead she yanked at the boy with all her might, pulling him away from Hongtsai.

"Who's turning him against me?" Hongtsai snarled, as he landed a few parting blows. "Why does he act like I'm the enemy, the minute he sees me?"

A maid came running into the room, ready to smooth things over. She led the weeping boy away. "Don't cry," she said, trying to distract him. "Let's go and see Grandma Gu!"

Hongtsai blinked when he heard that. "What did she say? Grandma Gu is here?" He looked at Manzhen, but she gave him the cold silent treatment, and went upstairs without a word.

It was left to the maid to explain that Mrs. Gu had arrived that day and was now upstairs. When Hongtsai heard they had a guest from distant parts, he straightened his collar, smoothed his sleeves and mounted the stairs in a dignified manner.

Hearing Mrs. Gu coughing, he went to the back bedroom and found her alone there. "Ma," he greeted her. Mrs. Gu sat up and started a conversation, in the course of which she once again recounted her escape and long journey to the city. She also asked how business was faring, and Hongtsai said that times were hard and costs high, with no way to get ahead. But he was the sort of man who, when he talked like this, didn't want others to think he was truly poor, so he'd turn around and mention some huge sum he'd thrown away, without a thought, on a meal with four of his friends in a swanky restaurant.

Manzhen did not come in. A maid brought a bowl of medicinal tea, and Hongtsai asked if Mrs. Gu was feeling unwell. "When you've rested a couple of days and are feeling better, I'll take you to a show," he said. "There's lots of entertainment in Shanghai, more going on than ever before."

Another maid came in, letting them know dinner was ready. A table had been set on the first floor so that Mrs. Gu wouldn't have to go downstairs. They'd made rice porridge for her, but Mrs. Gu said she couldn't eat a thing. That meant it was the usual family meal, just the two of them and the boy. Rongbao's tears had been dried by his mother, but his eyelids were red and puffy. The three of them sat around the square table, the scene so silent their chewing seemed loud; there was a dark cloud looming right over their heads.

"What awful food!" Hongtsai suddenly said. "What kind of cooking is this?"

Manzhen said nothing.

A moment later, he complained again. "There's nothing here that's fit to eat!"

Manzhen went on ignoring him. The fish soup was out of Rongbao's reach, so he stood up and leaned across the table with his chopsticks to take some fish. Hongtsai struck out, clamping his chopsticks around the boy's and knocking them out of his hand. "What kind of manners is that!" he scolded.

Rongbao's chopsticks landed on the table, his tears on the tablecloth. Manzhen knew that Hongtsai was trying to upset her, and the best way to hurt her was through her son. She stayed silent and expressionless, and went on eating her dinner. Even though he was sobbing away, Rongbao picked up his chopsticks. He was used to scenes like this. He lifted his bowl, bringing it close to his mouth, and scooped the rice in. There was a big morsel of fish, from the fleshy part of the belly where there aren't any bones, that Manzhen had slipped into his bowl. He'd almost stopped crying now, but when he saw what she'd done, his tears flowed again.

If things went on in this way, Manzhen feared her child would develop a stomach disorder. Nearly every meal they shared turned out like this. It was too much to take. Hongtsai himself couldn't bear the pressure; he wanted a quick exit from the table. He still had half a bowl of rice, but he gulped it down as fast as he could. That meant tilting his head back, raising the bowl till it covered his face and hurriedly scraping food into his mouth, the chopsticks knocking on the porcelain like rapid raindrops. It was his usual way, when rushing to finish a meal. He had lots of little habits like that, like clearing his nose by pressing a finger to one nostril and blowing the mucus down and out through the other, with a quick snort. It shouldn't have mattered, it wasn't a particularly bad habit. But Manzhen herself had developed a habit that wasn't good at all: when he made one of his little habitual gestures, a spasm of revulsion flitted across her face. She could feel the twitch, uncontrollable, under her eyes.

Hongtsai's chopsticks were still scuttling against his bowl. Manzhen put her own bowl down, stood up and went to the back bedroom. Mrs. Gu heard her coming in and pretended to be asleep. She could hear, from this room, everything that went on at the dinner table, and though there hadn't been much talk, the heavy, stiff silence told her that this was not a one-off tiff. In a house where fighting is continuous, a guest is sure to feel awkward and de trop. Hongtsai had welcomed her nicely thus far, but Mrs. Gu knew that a relative often seems "lovely from a distance, unlovely up close." If she stayed, there could be a complete change in his attitude. It looked as though she'd better go back to her son's. Even with his mother-in-law there, with all of them putting on a brave face while inwardly complaining, an aggravating situation indeed, she'd still feel more entitled to live there. It would set her heart at ease.

Mrs. Gu therefore decided to return to Weimin's place as soon as she felt better. But her ill health lingered, and she was laid up for a week. There was not a single day on which Manzhen made an effort to avoid an argument with her husband, but Mrs. Gu didn't dare intervene; she simply pretended not to hear. She would have liked to take her daughter aside and urge her to adopt a different approach; she had a cartload of motherly advice to hand on, with lots of tricks for managing a husband. But speaking her mind to Manzhen proved impossible. She could see that there were now distinct limits to her daughter's affections, that she was being dutiful and nothing more.

Mrs. Gu's health eventually improved a little: she could get up and move around, but her appetite was poor and she still felt weak and shaky. Manzhen said it was time to consult a doctor. Mrs. Gu resisted at first, because she didn't think seeing a doctor would do any good, but then Manzhen told her that Hongtsai was on excellent terms with a Dr. Wei. A doctor who was also a personal friend was more reliable, Mrs. Gu thought; he'd pay closer attention to her case. That afternoon she went with Manzhen to his office. It was in a tall building with a crowd of pedicabs at the front entrance, the drivers loitering there till their clients returned. Manzhen spotted their own driver, Chun Yuan, standing with the others, but he froze when he saw her and said nothing. Manzhen at first thought it odd, then guessed he was working on the side, taking other customers out; that would explain his embarrassment on seeing her. Paying him no further attention, she led her mother into the building and they took the lift up.

Business was good at Dr. Wei's, and the waiting room was full. Manzhen filled out the registration form and found a seat for her mother near the window. She herself stood with her back to it. In front of her was a couch on which two people only, a man and a girl, were sitting, with plenty of room between them, but that wasn't a seat that she, or another woman in her place, would be inclined to take. The girl looked about twelve years old, with a long, narrow face and ivory skin. She seemed both delicate and scrawny. She was passing the time by slowly twirling a man's felt hat, around and around, on her chest. The expression on her face was gentle. Her father's hat, apparently. The man at the other end of the couch, reading the paper, must be her father. Manzhen let her gaze rest on the pair. Their familial bond seemed so strong.

The man was hidden behind his newspaper, revealing only his socks, shoes, and trousers. Which seemed familiar. Suddenly, Manzhen felt cold all over. Those were Hongtsai's clothes, the ones he'd put on that morning before leaving the house. Was he here as a patient, or for some other reason? He must be bringing this girl to the doctor. Could she be his daughter? No wonder Chun Yuan was startled when he ran into her at the entrance. Hongtsai must have seen them walk in, and was screening his face with the newspaper, hiding from her and her mother. Manzhen had no intention of poking a hole in his cover. Why make a scene, with all these people here? And her mother too. She didn't want her to get caught in the middle of a mess like this. It would only lead to more trouble.

The window offered a sweeping view of the streets below. "Ma," said Manzhen, pointing towards the window, "come and see—there's the place where we used to live, behind that church steeple. Do you see it?"

Mrs. Gu stood next to her, the two of them leaning in to the window as they peered out, Manzhen pointing out places to her while also watching, from the corner of her eye, the man with the paper stand up and walk towards the door. She took a quick glance behind her, and the man spun around, hands clasped behind his back as he stared up at the doctor's medical license mounted on the wall. She could tell, without any doubt now: it was Hongtsai.

Hongtsai stared up at the glass-framed certificate, whose surface was darkened by shadow, thus creating a mirror in which he could follow the movements of the two people behind him. Manzhen turned away again and joined her mother at the window, peering at the street scene below. Once he'd confirmed that they were looking the other way, Hongtsai quickly stepped towards the door.

But at that moment Mrs. Gu turned around, squeezing her eyes shut. "Goodness! Makes me dizzy to look down like that." She left the window and returned to her seat, catching a glimpse of Hongtsai's back as he rushed away, but not particularly noticing him.

The girl, though, stood up and called out, "Dad, where are you going?"

The roomful of bored patients, having nothing else to do, responded as if on cue, all of them turning to look at Hongtsai. Mrs. Gu gasped. "Is that Hongtsai?" she asked her daughter.

Hongtsai knew he couldn't dodge away now: he had to come towards them, beaming a smile. "Oh, *you're* here!"

Mrs. Gu had heard the girl calling him her dad. She was stiff with surprise; clearly, something was awry. Manzhen wasn't responding either.

At first, Hongtsai froze, but then he came up with something.

"This is my goddaughter, her father is Old He." He looked towards Manzhen, smiling. "I told you about that, didn't I? Old He insisted I take her as my goddaughter."

Everyone in the room, including the girl, was staring at them.

"Her family knows I'm friends with Dr. Wei, and wanted me to bring her to see him. She's got stomach trouble of some sort. Why did you come? Is it because of Ma?" He bobbed his head up and down, his voice turning deep and solemn. "Yes, Ma, you really should see Dr. Wei. He is an excellent doctor." He was panicking, and had to say something.

"Manzhen insisted I come," Mrs. Gu said in a subdued tone. "I'm fine, really."

The door to the consulting room opened and a patient emerged, followed by a nurse. "Mr. Zhu," she called.

"Well, time for me to go in," Hongtsai said. He took with him the girl, who was dragging her feet, reluctant to see the doctor. She hung on to Hongtsai's hat, hugging it for support as he pulled her by the hand. She took two steps, then turned and looked at a woman behind her. "Mummy, you come too!"

The woman was sitting next to the sofa where they had just been, her head also buried in a newspaper. When the child called out, she had to put the paper down and join them. Hongtsai, looking quite embarrassed, couldn't come up with any sort of explanation right then and there. Cringing, he led the woman and child into the examining room.

Mrs. Gu made a grumbling sound and threw a sharp glance at Manzhen. Manzhen walked over to the empty sofa and sat down, then invited her mother to join her. Her mother sat stiffly at her side, saying nothing. Manzhen picked up a newspaper and started to read. She wasn't pretending to be calm. Discovering that her husband was having an affair did not perturb her in the least. The pain of their relationship had so exhausted her, she had no feelings left that could be provoked. Her only reaction was to wonder if he had a son by this other woman. If so, she might be able to take Rongbao and bring him up on her own, if she and Hongtsai got divorced. She'd been wanting a divorce for a long time now.

Mr. Gu fidgeted with the registration card, stealing glances at Manzhen and coughing softly. Manzhen was making plans. After she'd taken her mother home, she'd make a visit to the Yang family. She'd stopped seeing people in the past few years and had lost touch with most of her friends, but the Yang children she'd once tutored, a boy and a girl, maintained warm ties with her. The boy had graduated from college already, and was working for a lawyer. She'd ask him to arrange an appointment with the lawyer. Better to go through someone she knew, to minimize the risk of being overcharged.

The white door leading to the doctor's room was shut tight, with no one emerging for a long time. Dr. Wei was probably being unusually thorough, as a sign of his friendship for Hongtsai; the other patients could wait while they chatted. Finally, the door opened and the three of them came out in a single file. Manzhen and her mother got a good look at the woman, who was at least thirty years old, with a long face shaped like a date pit, bewitching little eyes, and bright red rouge sweeping up to her temples. She was wearing a black wool cloak, but her feet were clad in black slippers edged with white satin and embroidered with curly white chrysanthemums.

Hongtsai was following her, then pushed in front to make the introductions. "This is Mrs. He, this is my mother-in-law, and this is my wife." Mrs. He did not step closer, but smiled and nodded from a distance, first at them and then at Hongtsai. Then she led the child away. Hongtsai sat down next to Mrs. Gu and started chatting with her. He stayed by her side throughout the consultation with the doctor, then all the way home. All that caution came from his worry that Manzhen might make a scene in the doctor's office; once he'd made sure she wouldn't do that, he would feel much less stressed. Any fuss she might raise later on would be easy to handle. But his attitude towards her was inconsistent: one minute he'd be doing everything in his power to demean her; the next moment, he'd be terror-struck by her mere presence.

He gave Manzhen and her mother his own pedicab, and hired another from the street for himself. Mrs. Gu was afraid of riding in a pedicab, so Chun Yuan pedaled slowly, gradually slipping behind. Mrs. Gu wanted to discuss the woman they'd seen, but refrained for fear of Chun Yuan overhearing. Manzhen directed him to a pharmacy, where they bought the pills prescribed by the doctor, and after that they went home.

Hongtsai had arrived already, and was sitting in the living room reading a newspaper. The outing had used up all of Mrs. Gu's energy; she went upstairs and lay on the bed in her street clothes, then pulled out the medicine. When Manzhen went past the door, she called her in and asked for help reading the label. Manzhen picked it up to take a closer look, but Mrs. Gu, having craned her head up from the pillow and checked to make sure no one could overhear, took the opportunity to say, "What was that all about? That woman, I mean."

Manzhen smiled lightly. "Must be a woman he's keeping, judging from the way he's slinking around."

Mrs. Gu sighed. "So—the reason he picks fights with you is this other woman he's got? I've tried to tell you, and I don't mean to criticize, but you put too much focus on the child, leaving the father out in the cold. Don't you see what a man like that wants? You've got to flatter him a little, make him feel he's important."

Manzhen kept her head bent over the medicine label. Mrs. Gu was puzzled by her daughter's silence. Manzhen would fight with Hongtsai over the tiniest things, and now that she had something big to hold against him, a grievance not to be lightly forgiven, she took it entirely in her stride, or so it seemed. What a mixed-up child she was—as a mother, Mrs. Gu knew her duty was to smooth out the rough spots in her daughter's marriage, not stir up trouble, but her daughter's strange behavior made her restless with worry.

And Manzhen was so careless when it came to money. She never laid aside a little something for her own needs. Any income Hongtsai brought in, according to her, was tainted, and she wouldn't involve herself in any part of the family's finances. Mrs. Gu felt this to be extremely unwise. After a moment's silence, she took up this tack.

"I know you don't like hearing me say this, but the things I've been seeing make me worry, for your sake. I think you should take this chance, now, when he's willing to give you some money, and build up an emergency fund. The two of you fight so much—a small reserve would be good, in case things get so bad he refuses to pay the household expenses. I'm not sure what you'd think about that." A feeling of loneliness swept over her: her children were generally unwilling to share their thoughts with her. She heaved another sigh. "Goodness me! Hearing the two of you fight every day—it's hard to bear."

Manzhen rolled her eyes towards her mother. "Yes, I know it's hard for you. After you're feeling better, maybe you should stay with Weimin for a few days. It'll be quieter there."

Mrs. Gu was dumbstruck. She'd never imagined her own daughter would show her the door. "Maybe that would be better," she said. But further reflection convinced her that Manzhen was laying the groundwork for a showdown when she'd make Hongtsai give up the other woman. Manzhen wouldn't want her mother around for a big row like that, she'd want her well out of the way. Mrs. Gu considered it all carefully, and new worries arose. "I have to say, and I'll say it again," she admonished her daughter, "be careful when you argue with him. Don't be too hard on him. You saw how big that child is— he's been with that woman a long time already. Looks like it started even before you two got married. She won't be easy to get rid of."

Manzhen nodded slightly. Mrs. Gu would have continued, but a woman could be heard calling from downstairs, "Second Sister?"

That stopped her. "Who is it?" she asked her daughter, who didn't know either, but then Manzhen saw her sister-in-law coming upstairs to join them. Manzhen offered Wanzhu a seat.

"Weimin's here too," Wanzhu said. "Ma, are you feeling any better?"

Hongtsai appeared, bringing Weimin upstairs with him. He was being especially gracious to his in-laws today. "How nice that all three of you are here! Let's get Jiemin to come over, and all play mahjong."

Mrs. Gu was in no mood for a party, but when she saw Manzhen taking everything in her stride, perfectly calm and forbearing, she had to play along too. The maids set up a mahjong table, and Weimin and his wife, plus Hongtsai, started playing rounds with Mrs. Gu.

Jiemin came over, and he and Manzhen sat to one side, chatting. Jiemin asked where Rongbao was, and the boy was brought out; but with his father there, Rongbao was like a mouse hiding from a cat. He stood back as far as he could, and barely replied when Jiemin spoke to him.

Mrs. Gu turned and smiled at him. "What's the matter? Don't you like your uncle today?" As soon as no one was looking, the boy slipped away.

Jiemin crossed the room and stood behind his mother's seat, watching her play. The lamp above the mahjong table shone brightly on the players' faces. As Manzhen gazed at the circle of people seated in the light, a strange feeling came over her: it was as if she were looking at them across a great distance; even the sound of their laughter and chatter seemed faint and indistinct.

There was no one in her family with whom she could share the thoughts taking shape in her mind. No point in even considering telling her mother. It all had to be kept from her, or she'd burst into a panic and try with all her might to oppose it. As for her brothers, even though they'd never liked Hongtsai and hadn't approved of her marriage to him, now that she'd been married so long, they'd disapprove again of her plans to divorce him. A woman in her situation, past thirty years of age, wouldn't get any support for her bid to get a divorce if the husband wasn't flagrantly mistreating her, or failing to provide for the family. It didn't matter if he had another woman on the side, as long as he didn't make it too obvious and rub their faces in it. She was supposed to put up with it, simply to preserve appearances. Even a friend who wanted to help would quickly find, upon asking around, that no one thought she had proper grounds for a divorce. Manzhen could be sure that if Weimin asked his mother-in-law what she thought, she'd say his sister had taken leave of her senses. Manzhen knew that in a little while now, after the proceedings had begun, she'd probably have to stay with Weimin for a bit, and there'd she be, living cheek by jowl with Mrs. Tao and her own mother. She had to smile, when she thought of that.

Hongtsai was keeping one eye on Manzhen while he played his hand. To his surprise, she seemed to be in good spirits, with a liveliness in her face quite unlike the downcast expression she usually wore. Apparently her suspicions had not been aroused, or if they had been, she'd decided to overlook the whole thing, without kicking up any fuss. That was a huge relief to him. He told the others he'd have to go out for a while, because he had another engagement. He got Jiemin to take his place at the mahjong table and went off in his pedicab.

Manzhen thought it through. If Hongtsai really had been invited out for a meal, Chun Yuan would be back at the house fairly soon to get his own dinner. Masters, as a rule, gave their drivers a meal allowance when they went out to eat, but a driver usually rode home nonetheless and had his dinner there, so he could save that extra bit of cash. Manzhen told the maid she had an errand for Chun Yuan, something she wanted him to buy, and to let her know as soon as he came back.

The meal they'd ordered from a nearby restaurant arrived and they ate between rounds of mahjong. Manzhen went upstairs by herself and unlocked a cupboard. She was counting out notes, from her own small supply of cash, when Chun Yuan appeared. He stood in the doorway, but Manzhen called him into the room and handed him a roll of notes. "This is from my mother," she said with a smile. Chun Yuan saw the thick roll of large-denomination notes and knew it was the biggest tip he'd ever been given. Not something he'd expected from the old lady, who looked so unassuming and countrified. A big grin broke out across his face. "Oh my, thank you, Mrs. Gu!" But he knew the money had to come from Manzhen herself, probably because she'd seen the master and that woman at the doctor's office today, all very suspicious. When it came to a master's whereabouts, a driver was always the best source of information, and evidently she wanted to question him.

His conjecture was correct, for after checking that no one was in the hallway, though she already knew the maids were eating their own meal downstairs, then closing the door as an extra precaution, Manzhen started on him with her questions. She acted as if she knew the main part already, and only wanted to know where the woman lived.

Chun Yuan feigned ignorance at first. He said he'd never seen her till today, that she met Hongtsai at a corner near the police station, then rode with him to the doctor's office. When she and the girl came out of the doctor's, they hired another cab and went off on their own.

His smooth evasion made Manzhen smile. "I know the master told you to keep quiet. But I promise no harm will come to you for telling me." She added a few notes to the roll. Her manner with the servants was consistently polite, but there was always the risk of being fired if she were offended. And Chun Yuan knew she would keep her word, and that his own role in this would not be revealed to Hongtsai. So he dropped his guard, and told her the woman's address, plus everything he knew about her. The woman had been the mistress of Mr. He, a friend of Hongtsai's, so Hongtsai wasn't lying when he introduced her as Mrs. He. Hongtsai met her when Mr. He enlisted him to work out a separation agreement, and from there he went on to take his friend's place, and set up his own residence with her. It had been going on for almost two years now. "She has a daughter from a previous relationship," Chun Yuan said, "the same girl who went to the doctor today."

The girl wasn't Hongtsai's daughter, after all. That surprised Manzhen. She'd been struck by the way the girl clutched his hat, as if it were a source of comfort. The girl felt close to Hongtsai and evidently was responding to paternal love. He must be showing her some affection, and on a regular basis. He too was unhappy in the home they'd made, and went off to find the comforts of family life elsewhere, with a child not his own. A sad, hard smile played across Manzhen's lips as she considered the joke that life was playing on her.

These past few years had been terribly hard on her, just as she had foreseen. But there hadn't been any pleasure for him either. If she was doing this for her son's sake, then all she really was doing was dragging him into misery too. Her self-sacrificing plan sprang from a suicidal impulse. If she had done that—killed herself—it would have ended there. Life can indeed be worse than death, because it unfolds in twists and turns; and her life had grown worse. It was even more awful now than anything she'd been able, back then, to imagine.

She was alone in the room, leaning on a corner of the table, staring into space. Chun Yuan had gone downstairs. The rustling click of mahjong tiles drifted up from the floor below. The room was completely quiet, save for the hum of the faintly green fluorescent light.

The greatest difficulty was still her son. Even though Hongtsai ill-treated Rongbao on a daily basis, he'd still refuse to let her take him away. That would be the case even if the boy were not his father's only son; a man with that kind of temperament, even if he had three or four sons, would not willingly give up a single iota of his own flesh and blood. Now, however, Hongtsai had given her good legal grounds for divorce. She could seize the evidence of his affair and use it to press her point. The law should be on her side; it even should give her custody of their child. But if he poured money into the case, the outcome would be uncertain. It all came down to money. She slapped her palm with the thin leather strap she'd used to tie up her little stock of cash, then slapped it again; the third time she struck too hard and stung her palm.

There could hardly be a worse time to look for a job. All the legitimate businesses had closed up shop, due to the Japanese occupation. Everywhere they were letting people go, not hiring anyone new. And she wasn't so young anymore. Did she have enough energy to start out again, forging a new path in the working world?

Once she got through the hard times immediately ahead, she could manage the years after that; she still had enough self-confidence for that. The urgent question was where to get the money that she needed now. Going to court would cost a lot. If there really were no other way, she could take the child and flee into another part of the city. Maybe she should start by hiding Rongbao in some secret location; otherwise, Hongtsai might, by some devious means, prevent her from claiming custody of him.

Suddenly she thought of Jinfang and her family. She could send Rongbao to live with them—it was the perfect hiding place. Hongtsai had no idea that she had such a close friend. She hadn't been in touch with Jinfang for several years, couldn't even be sure where she lived now. She'd not visited her since she'd got married; she'd been too embarrassed to tell her friend she'd gone back on her decision so completely, after taking such pains to evade Hongtsai. Looking back now, all she saw was the huge mistake she had made. The first mistake was Hongtsai's. But she shouldn't have married him afterwards. That was *her* big mistake.

16

The world works in ways likely to take many by surprise. Shijun's sister-in-law had been utterly bent on fixing him up with Tsuizhi, but once it was accomplished and the bride moved in, the two women could not get along. Tsuizhi was still childish in many ways, and her older sister-in-law could be thin-skinned, even though they'd been kin to each other even before entering the Shen family as daughters-in-law. Perhaps they were simply too close, but whatever the cause, they were constantly at odds. It started from the favoritism shown by Shijun's mother. As the saying goes, even a new wooden bucket smells good for days. A new face has to get more attention, and since Mrs. Shen already doted on her son Shijun, she naturally leaned towards his side of the family, even though the conflicts had nothing to do with him per se.

Discontent grew within the family. Tsuizhi suggested to Shijun that the household be divided up as soon as possible, so they wouldn't seem to be making life miserable for a widow and father-less child. After a lengthy period of consideration, the division was achieved. The leather-goods shop was sold off. Vim and his mother got their own place, and Shijun found a job at a foreign-owned engineering firm in Shanghai. His mother and wife moved with him.

Mrs. Shen couldn't get used to her new life there, and without their common foe, the elder daughter-in-law, she and Tsuizhi gradually fell into discord. Mrs. Shen felt that Tsuizhi didn't take proper care of her son, and even pushed him around, and that Shijun was far too lenient with her. She couldn't refrain from coming between them, now and then, and giving Tsuizhi a piece of her mind. Her advanced matronly status notwithstanding, she'd take the route well known to women and decamp, in a huff, back to her own family. She'd stay at her brother's a few days, till Shijun had to go in person to fetch her. She wanted to move back to Nanking, but feared the derision of her elder daughter-in-law, who surely would say she'd been kicked out by the very household she'd helped set up, the same branch of the family at which she'd thrown so many favors.

In the end, Mrs. Shen did return to Nanking, taking two servants to live with her in a new house. Shijun made frequent trips to visit her. Then Tsuizhi had a baby, and the three of them made a visit together. It was a grandson, and Mrs. Shen was overjoyed. She and Tsuizhi got along much better now. A second trip to Grandma's followed soon thereafter.

There are women who grow even more beautiful after they've had a child, and Tsuizhi was one of them: when she filled out, this only accentuated her curves. She had a second child, a girl. Even though these were years full of change, her heart remained calm, unperturbed. It was as if the worst that could befall her, in this, the young-wife phase of her life, was to find a worm in some piece of fruit she was eating.

The war had ended by this time, and Shuhui was coming back to China from America. Shijun went to the airport to meet him, and Tsuizhi went too. They arrived before Shuhui's family and found the airport, as usual, nearly deserted. It looked like a department store during the war years, with empty counters and shiny, bare, lino-tile floors. When the loudspeaker boomed into life, it clearly had no connection to the sweet-faced girl, wearing a uniform, who held a microphone in her hand. The sound could not be coming from her. It boomed out from somewhere else entirely, which was a bit alarming.

The two of them wandered around. "Shuhui's been gone so long," Shijun mused, "he must have got married by now."

A long silence fell before Tsuizhi responded. "If he'd got married, wouldn't he have mentioned it in his letters?"

"But he's always been a joker. Maybe he's planning to surprise us."

Tsuizhi turned away. "What's the point of speculating?" she asked crossly. "We'll know soon enough, once he's here!"

Shijun was in such high spirits that he didn't register her irritation and he went on merrily: "If he hasn't married, we can find someone for him!"

Tsuizhi's temper flared when she heard that, but she bit it back, and turned sarcastic instead. "Shuhui's a grown man, isn't he? Do you really think he'll require your assistance, if he wants to get married?"

A long silence ensued. When next she spoke, her tone was much more friendly. "We should throw a party for him. We could get the Yuan family to lend us their cook, and give him a nice dinner."

"Oh goodness—that chef commands really high fees. And Shuhui isn't some grand stranger. Why put on such a show?"

"But he's your close friend and you haven't seen him in years. I can't believe you're being so tight-fisted."

"No, that's not it. If we throw him a dinner at our house we'll be swamped with people. Let's invite him out instead. It'll be just us, and we can have a really proper talk together."

The anger that Tsuizhi had just repressed rose up fast and hard. "OK, have it your way," she said loudly. "I don't care if you take him out or not, but don't get red-faced at me, and claim that I'm the one at fault!"

Shijun, who hadn't been red-faced in the least, now got so angry that the blood did indeed rise to his cheeks. "You're the one whose face is red," he retorted, "why are you saying this to me?"

Tsuizhi was about to respond when Shijun spotted Mrs. Hsu in the distance. He started waving at her and Tsuizhi realized this must be Shuhui's mother. Silently putting their differences aside, they rushed forward together, faces wreathed in smiles, to greet Mrs. Hsu.

During the Japanese invasion, Mr. Hsu had gone to the interior capital at Chongqing, and he hadn't yet been sent back to Shanghai. Mrs. Hsu had gone instead to her old home town in the countryside. She'd made this trip into Shanghai only to meet her son, and was staying temporarily with her daughter's family. Shijun had wanted to bring her with them to the airport, but she'd told him to go ahead because she'd be coming with her son-in-law and his family. Introductions were made all around—and a good thing too, since Shijun would not have recognized this young wife, in her twenties, as Shuhui's younger sister.

They stood together chatting. "Is Shuhui married?" Shijun asked. "Has he said anything about it in his letters to you?"

"Married, then divorced," Mrs. Hsu said lightly. "It all happened a few years ago, but he never told us the details."

A silence fell over the group. "That's how it is in America," Shuhui's sister said.

"Was she an American?" Shijun asked softly.

Mrs. Hsu laughed. "A Chinese."

Surely I would have heard about a Chinese woman who got divorced while living abroad, Shijun thought. But then again, communications during the war had been greatly disrupted. Or maybe it was a different situation—a young lady born overseas, perhaps? An Americanized Chinese?"

He didn't ask, but Mrs. Hsu had guessed his question. "She was studying abroad, like Shuhui."

"She's the daughter of Ji Fangsen," said Shuhui's sister's mother-in-law.

Shijun didn't know who Ji Fangsen was, but from the sound of it, he was either rich or famous. Another silence fell.

"I never thought he'd be gone this long," Shijun said. "It's been ten whole years."

"No, nor did we," Mrs. Hsu said. "The war came, and he couldn't get back."

"We've really been looking forward to his return," Shuhui's sister said, "and yet Dad can't be here. It's terrible, really."

"Have you received any letters from your father lately?" Shijun asked.

"He's still waiting for a place on a riverboat," Mrs. Hsu said. "We're hoping he can make it back in time for New Year's."

Time passed quickly as they talked, and the plane arrived on schedule. They were jammed together in the waiting area, pushed up against the waist-high chain-link barrier. Then they saw Shuhui, suitcase in hand, raincoat slung across his shoulders, emerging from the crowd. Airports are like that: a temporal and spatial meeting-point, yet so banal one has to grin in disappointment, and pleasure too. Shuhui was as handsome as ever, but a mother's eye sees only one thing. "He's got thin," she said to her daughter. "Don't you see how thin he's become?"

A moment later, they had him in their midst. Shuhui shook hands warmly with Shijun, and of course did the same with Tsuizhi. He shifted to a more Chinese style when greeting his family. It was the first time that he'd met his sister's husband.

Tsuizhi was unusually taciturn, but this was only to be expected. She'd never met Mrs. Hsu before, and here they were right in the middle of another family's gathering.

"Have you eaten?" Shuhui's sister asked.

"Yes, on the plane."

"Let's go to our place," Shijun said, picking up the suitcase.

"It's hard to find lodgings in Shanghai," Mrs. Hsu explained, "so I thought we'd work on that after you got here. I was going to get a hotel room for you, but Shijun said you should stay with him."

The other matron, Shuhui's sister's mother-in-law, had a different idea. "Come and stay with us a few days. We're so glad you're here. It'll be crowded, but the more the merrier."

"You live on Baker Road, don't you?" Shijun asked. "That's very close to us. It'd be easy for him to spend time at your place while staying with us."

"Do come and stay with us," Tsuizhi added.

After all this coaxing, Shuhui accepted the offer.

They called two taxicabs, filled them up completely, and headed home. The first stop was on Baker Road, where Shuhui's sister's in-laws wanted them all to come in, then join them at a restaurant for a welcome-home party. Shijun and Tsuizhi had another engagement, and didn't go in, guessing of course that mother and son, so long parted, would have much to discuss. The plan was therefore modified: Shuhui would spend one night at his sister's family's, then move to their place the next day. "OK then, we'll head back now," Tsuizhi said to Shuhui. "But be sure to come to us tomorrow."

They got back home, which was not a big house, but still large enough to have a bit of lawn out front for the dog, since Tsuizhi always liked having one. It was a play area for their children too: the boy was called Beibei, so after his sister was born, he became Big Bei and she Little Bei. The children were home from school already, and Little Bei was in the living room eating a piece of bread. Crumbs were scattered across the floor, attracting ants. Little Bei knelt down to observe them, and when her father came into the room, she called out to him, "Daddy, Daddy! Come and see the ants, they're forming work teams!"

Shijun knelt down beside her. "Why are they doing that?" he asked.

"They're fetching grain, stocking up the larder."

"Really, stocking up just like we do?"

Tsuizhi came in and scolded Little Bei. "What are you doing? Why aren't you eating at the table, instead of on the floor? It's so dirty!"

"Come and see, Mum—they're stocking up on grain."

Tsuizhi turned to Shijun. "You're joining in with her. Why do you encourage this nonsense, instead of setting her straight?"

"What she says is interesting, I think."

"But you make so much of her, and that turns me into the enemy. Then the children both like you, and don't like me! Just look at this floor—once the ants have been in once, they'll come again, and when people come to the house, what will they think? It's impossible to keep this room clean."

She was, at that moment, clearing out the study, turning it into a guest room for Shuhui. The servants were waxing the floor. The whole house was in an uproar, and the dog got excited too, trailing after people as he skittered across the newly waxed floor, tripping them up, nearly making them fall over.

That reminded Tsuizhi. "The dog might bite a stranger," she said. "Let's make sure he's tied up in the storage room tomorrow."

Tsuizhi had never before been willing to admit that her dog bit people. Shijun's nephew Vim had come to Shanghai the year before to take his university entrance exam and stayed at their place. The dog bit him, but Tsuizhi made it out to be his fault: she said he'd shown too much fear, and if he hadn't run away, the dog never would have bitten him. Her sudden readiness to tie up the dog seemed to all who heard it a great departure from the norm.

Little Bei and the dog followed Shijun up the stairs. When they passed the storage room, Shijun saw his own books and papers from the study piled in stacks on the floor. "What's this? Why are my books on the floor?"

The dog was gnawing at them already, tearing to shreds an engineering journal to which he'd subscribed for many years. "Oi! Stop chewing that!" Shijun yelled.

"Stop chewing that!" Little Bei echoed. She picked up a book and threw it at the dog, but missed. The book flew off somewhere. She grabbed another, bigger book with both hands and was about to throw it when Shijun came over and pulled it away from her.

"What on earth are you doing?" he scolded.

Little Bei started crying. Her tears were partly for effect, because she'd heard her mother coming up the stairs. The children knew that even though their mother blamed their father for being too lenient, the minute he did discipline them, she'd come running to shield the child.

Tsuizhi had by now reached the storage room, and when she saw Little Bei crying hard and struggling with Shijun over a book, she frowned at him. "Look at you! Acting like a child yourself—if she wants to play with the book, why not let her? Instead, you make her cry!"

Little Bei howled all the harder.

That left Shijun to thrust hurriedly a stack of journals into a trunk.

Tsuizhi knit her brow. "You two made such a racket, I can't recall why I came up here . . . Oh, now I remember. Why don't you buy a bottle of good Scotch? Johnny Walker, Black Label."

"I don't think Shuhui cares for fancy foreign booze. Don't we still have a few bottles of perfectly good green plum wine? He'll like that. It'll be a nice change for him."

"He doesn't like Chinese alcohol."

"What? After all the years I've known him, don't you think I'd know what he likes?"

It made him laugh, the way she wanted to tell him what Shuhui liked, and didn't like. She'd seen him, what, maybe twice?

"Don't you remember?" he went on. "When we got married he drank a lot—and wasn't it all Chinese?"

She hadn't expected him to bring up their wedding day. The memory came back in a rush—how Shuhui, already three sheets to the wind, had held her hand on the wedding dais, gripping it with deep emotion. The memory came with pain and a surge of strong feeling. She'd always had a hunch that his departure for foreign shores had been provoked by something, a something connected to her.

She said absolutely nothing, turned on her heel and left. Shijun threw books together at random and went downstairs but saw no sign of Tsuizhi. "Where is she?" he asked the maid.

"She went out to buy some alcohol."

He frowned; a woman who wants to show off cannot be stopped. Of course he could see what she was after. Shuhui was his best friend, and she wanted to make a good impression. What she didn't see was that Shuhui was such a good friend that none of this was needed.

He went into the study to check on things. They had finished waxing the floor, but the furniture was still piled up in one corner. The tidying-up was only half done, everything was still in disarray, and she'd gone running off, leaving it all behind. She'd been gone a long time, night was falling, and they had an eight o'clock dinner engagement that Tsuizhi had made some time earlier. Shijun kept looking at the clock, and when the maid brought the evening paper, he told her to put the study furniture back into place. But she insisted on waiting till Tsuizhi returned to direct the task.

Finally, she came back with lots of packages, big and small, carried into the house by the pedicab driver. She'd got the whisky, a set of whisky glasses, two bouquets of flowers, an Irish-linen tablecloth, two tins of Italian coffee and a trendy new coffee-maker.

"You were gone so long," Shijun said, "I thought you'd forgotten our date at the Yuans'."

"I had practically forgotten it. Is there still time to call and cancel?"

"I wouldn't mind canceling—but they'd think we'd stood them up."

"What time is it? Have to call early if you want to cancel. I think it's too late. Oh, and I forgot to buy some good cigarettes. I had to get some smoked ham, ran all the way over to the racetrack district where there's a shop that makes it right. It's no use sending a servant to get it, I had to go myself."

"I've been wanting some ham myself, these past few days."

Tsuizhi looked at him in surprise. "You like smoked ham?" she asked in disbelief. "Why have I never heard you say so?"

"But I've told you countless times. Whenever I say I'd like some ham, you tell me you'd have to go all the way to the racetrack district and pick it out yourself. Which has never happened, so I haven't had any ham."

Tsuizhi made no reply. She was busy arranging the flowers in vases, which she then placed in each of the rooms—living room, dining room, study. When she got to the study, she cried out. "Oh dear! Why is this room such a mess? You just sit and do nothing. Why didn't you tell them to put the furniture back? Nanny Li! Amah Tao! What useless people—everything goes to pieces if I'm not here!" She carried the vase back into the living room and looked at the walls. "I wish I'd thought to get those paintings out of storage and hung up here."

"I think you should hurry up and get ready to go out."

"There you are, pushing me to get ready, and you haven't budged an inch."

"I won't need five minutes."

Tsuizhi finally started getting ready. She went into the bathroom, then back to the bedroom to change her clothes. Shijun was searching the dresser drawers. "Where's Amah Li? I can't find a single undershirt."

"I sent her to buy cigarettes. You can keep that same shirt. She's washing the others, and hasn't ironed them yet."

"Not even one?"

"As if she didn't have enough to do already! She's no longer young, you know."

"I cannot understand why all our help is old or sick or lame. Not a single one of them is of any use to us."

"There are capable people out there, of course. Mrs. Yuan recommended someone to us, a girl she said was sharp and quick, but we don't host mahjong parties so there aren't extra tips, and the girl wouldn't come to us. Where did you put the aspirin?"

"I haven't seen it."

Tsuizhi went to the head of the stairs. "Amah Tao! Amah Tao! Bring me that medicine, the pills we gave Big Bei last time he had a cold."

"Why do you need aspirin?" Shijun asked. "Do you have a headache?"

"You put it in the flower-vase water, to make the flowers last longer."

"Is it really so urgent? Do you have to do this now?"

"By the time we get back, it'll be too late."

She'd got her hair half done when Amah Tao brought the pills. She ran downstairs in her slippers and went from vase to vase, slipping an aspirin into each one.

Shijun looked at this watch. "It's five past eight. Can you hurry up, please?"

"I'll be ready in a moment. Tell Amah Tao to get us a cab."

Several minutes later, Shijun called up to her from the lower floor, "The cab is ready. Are you?"

"Stop nagging. I can't think straight when you do that. Did you take the key off the dresser?"

"I don't have it."

"I saw you pick it up! You must have put it in your pocket."

Shijun had to rummage through all his pockets, turning them inside out. Tsuizhi had by then found the key. Lips pursed, she unlocked the jewelery case, took out some pieces and put them on.

When she was finally coming down, she called out from the stairs, "Amah Tao! If anyone calls, give them the phone number of the Yuan household. Got it? If you need help, ask Amah Li. Keep an eye on the children. When Amah Li brings them home, tell them it's time for bed."

She got into the pedicab, then called out again, "Amah Tao! Don't forget to feed the dog!"

They sat side by side in the cab, and had just got comfortably settled when she turned to him. "Oh, dear—run back in for me, will you? There's a makeup mirror in the second drawer of the dresser. I need you to get it for me. Not the big one—the one with the suede-leather case."

"I'll need the key."

Wordlessly, Tsuizhi took the key from her handbag and gave it to him. He too said nothing, but climbed out of the cab, crossed the garden, went up the stairs, got the mirror from the dresser and handed it to her, along with the key. After she'd put it into her handbag, she said, "It's all because you were rushing me. A person can't think when someone's rushing her."

The party at the Yuans' was in full swing by the time they got there. Their host, Yuan Sihua, and his wife, Penny, came forward to shake hands with them. Penny was the "top hostess" in their social circle, a gorgeous woman with elegant manners, willowy and tall, with thin, arched eyebrows and a long, oval face, perfectly powdered and rouged. She spoke in a high, thin voice that for some reason rose a whole octave when she spoke English, like an opera singer moving into falsetto. "It's been such a long time," she warbled at Shijun. "How have you been lately? Busy? Do you play *bridge*?"

"Yes, but not too well."

"You're just being modest, I'm sure. But one does have to be clever to play *bridge*." A wide smile stretched across her face. "Some people never quite get the hang of it."

She'd never thought that Shijun amounted to much. This was the longest she'd ever spoken to him. He was a good enough fellow but so run-of-the-mill, without a single distinguishing feature. He hadn't done well, either: he hadn't made any money, and Tsuizhi's own money was practically gone now, used up on household expenses. She thought it quite unfair on Tsuizhi.

Some time later, in the midst of a different conversation, Penny smiled and said, "Tsuizhi's a lucky woman. Shijun never loses his temper, and he never goes behind her back, or out on the town." She gestured with her chin. "But take our own Mr. Yuan here—the money he spends! It's all those social obligations, too many temptations to resist. All that going out—it's terrible, really." Her tone made it clear that a mild-mannered, law-abiding husband like Shijun was in fact contemptible. Her own husband was a robust philanderer, as everyone knew. This was the only category in which Tsuizhi trumped her. But since she was so used to winning, she had to find a way to turn defeat into victory.

It wasn't a large party: there were enough guests to fill one big table only. Penny had put her child at the table with them, along with the child's nanny. A child had to have a nanny, and if possible a nurse, ready to give the adults any injections they needed. It was all the rage in the moneyed class; a family without a nurse was falling behind. This nanny was also a nurse, so everyone, servants and masters alike, addressed her as "Miss Yang," even though she was not a young woman. Nor was she good-looking; it was hard to say where Penny had managed to find such a person. But she had to be like that, in a house where the master had such a roving eye.

Shijun was seated next to a Mrs. Li. "These crabs," she informed him, "are from Yangzheng Lake. The Yuans had them specially delivered the other day."

"The other day?"

"Alive, of course," she harrumphed. "Packed in buckets of lake water, along with the lake grasses."

"Went to a lot of trouble, didn't they?" He'd met Mrs. Li several times and never had anything to say to her. He remembered hearing that her husband owned Orchid Soap, the advertisements for which could be seen everywhere. "Isn't your husband involved with Orchid Soap products?" he asked.

Mrs. Li laughed oddly. "Oh, he has a lot of businesses." She turned away and started talking to someone else.

They played bridge after dinner, and Shijun was forced to take a hand. Tsuizhi didn't know how to play. It was after midnight when they finally left.

"What did Mrs. Li say to you during dinner?" Tsuizhi asked as they rode home in the pedicab.

"Mrs. Li?" he said vaguely. "Nothing. We talked about the crabs."

"No, you said something that made her laugh oddly. What was it?"

"Oh. It was about soap. Orchid Soap. I heard that it's her old man's business."

"Oh, so that's it. I knew something was wrong. There's a dance-hall girl who used to go by the stage name of Foxy Essence. Old Man Li started touting her around, and now everyone calls her Claire Essence, because that's the name of the Orchid Soap Company's latest product."

"Who can keep up with their goings-on!"

"But whatever were you thinking? Asking her, just like that, if her husband's involved with soap products!"

"Why were you listening in on my conversations with other people? Next time, please don't bother!"

"I was worried you'd offend someone."

Shijun couldn't help but remember how Manzhen had said he had a way with words. Maybe she hadn't been entirely objective, given her fondness for him then. But he couldn't believe that things had got to the point where people worried in case he said the wrong thing.

It had been many years since he'd thought of Manzhen, but Shuhui's return had reminded him of their times together.

"Penny's got beautiful skin," Tsuizhi said.

"She's supposed to be pretty, but I don't see why."

"I know you don't like her. But then, by and large, you don't like women."

He disliked all her women friends, and paid no attention to the women around him. At least one could say his affections were undivided. But Tsuizhi always felt he was going through the motions with her. She attributed it to a lukewarm temperament, intrinsic to him. Shijun was of the same opinion. But now he wondered if he had untapped reserves within him. How else could he have been so enamored of Manzhen? Maybe a love like that came to a person only once in a lifetime? Once was enough, maybe.

"Shijun," Tsuizhi called to him a second time. He hadn't heard her, the first time. It made her a little afraid. "Goodness! Are you all right? What on earth are you thinking about over there?"

"Well, um . . . I'm over here thinking about my life."

"What?" she said, half angry and half amused. "What's got into you today? Are you angry about something?"

"No, of course not."

"You should be, you know. So don't pretend you're not. As if I couldn't read you like a book."

Is that so? Shijun thought to himself.

They got home. Shijun paid the cab driver and Tsuizhi rang the doorbell. A sleepy-eyed Amah Li came out to open the door. She yawned and stretched, then went back to bed. Tsuizhi headed up the stairs, then turned to Shijun. "Eh—do you smell it? I think it's gas."

Shijun stood sniffing the air. "No, I don't smell anything."

Their kitchen had a gas stove, and they'd installed a gas oven too. "I don't trust that Amah Li," Tsuizhi said, "she still doesn't know how to use that oven. I think she didn't turn it off properly."

They went upstairs together, Shijun still not saying a word. Tsuizhi thought his behavior rather odd, and it worried her. When they reached the landing, she laid her head on his shoulder. "Shijun," she murmured.

He embraced her, his mind elsewhere. "Hmm. Now I smell it."

"Smell what?"

"Gas."

Tsuizhi's heart sank. "Well, go and have a look," she said mildly, after a moment's pause. "And let the dog out while you're at it. Don't you hear him whining? Amah Li must have forgotten to do it."

Shijun checked the kitchen carefully. The oven controls were turned off tight, but there could be a leak in the pipes. He'd have to call the gas company in the morning. He took the dog with him through the front door, leaving it unlatched, and walked into the darkness of the garden. Insects chirped in the grass, which was heavy with dew. A cool breeze brushed across his face. The traces of alcohol vanished and his mind grew clear.

A lamp was on in their upstairs bedroom, and in the window he could see Tsuizhi's outline as she moved about. Once, when she got angry with him, she said she didn't know why they'd got married in the first place. Neither did he. He remembered he was in great pain then, over Manzhen, and his father's having just passed away. Seeking distraction, he'd gone to Amy's to play tennis, all summer long, practically every day. There was a Miss Ding who played too, and thinking about it now he realized he could have married her. Or any of the girls in their circle, several of whom he'd seen quite regularly back then. He could have married any of them. Some small shift of events might easily have led to his not marrying Tsuizhi. Rather funny, when he thought about it.

They'd first met at her brother's wedding, back when they were little. She carried the bride's train, he was the ring bearer. He took a strong dislike to that little girl in the bride's party, and she looked down on him because her family looked down on his. But now she'd say, as he'd often heard, "It was so romantic, the way we first met." It was a regular refrain of hers.

He brought the dog back in, shut the front door and tied the dog up in the kitchen. The book over which Little Bei had wrestled with him had tumbled down the stairs, and he picked it up, then returned it to the storage room. The books were piled up so haphazardly that he had to straighten them a little. He picked up one volume, brushed the dust off the cover and saw that it was a collection of modern fiction, an old one he'd tried, repeatedly, to find. If they hadn't cleared out the study for Shuhui, he'd never have come across it. He leafed through the pages and found an envelope inserted between them. It was folded in half, and the paper had yellowed. An old letter from Manzhen. He'd got rid of her letters and photographs a long time ago; they only made him feel worse. This was the only one left, the letter he couldn't bear to destroy. He slumped down and started to read. It must have been written back when his father was sick and he'd rushed to Nanking. It said:

Dear Shijun,

It's night, and everyone is asleep. The only sound is the chirping of the crickets my brothers are keeping. The weather's got colder, and you left in such a hurry I'm afraid you didn't take any winter clothing. I know you let these things pass you right by, and never think to wear warm clothing. I don't know why I'm worrying about it either, it seems so fussy of me. It's just that I keep turning anything I see, anything I hear, into a reason to think of you.

I went to Shuhui's yesterday, though I knew he wouldn't be at home, to see his parents. You've lived with them a long while, and I thought maybe I'd hear something about you. His mother told me lots of things I didn't know. She said you used to be even thinner, and told me stories from your student days. It made me feel better. After you'd left, I started to feel afraid, for no particular reason. Shijun, I want you to know there's someone in this world who's yours always. Please know that, forever and wherever. Yours, always.

Reading over that last line, he could almost hear her speaking to him. Her voice came to him clearly, across those long, long years. Could she still be waiting for me? he wondered.

There was a postscript: "All that was written last night, not quite consciously—" The letter broke off suddenly, half the page still blank, with no date or signature. Now he remembered that day he'd returned from Nanking. He'd gone to her office and found her writing him a letter. That's why it was unfinished. It all came back to him, clear as day—every little detail of their time together. How long ago, exactly, had they first met? Working it out, he realized it had been fourteen years since then. Fourteen years!

17

"Shijun!"

He looked up. There was Tsuizhi, shock on her face, standing in the doorway in her dressing gown.

"What are you doing here? Don't you think it's time for bed?"

"I'm coming."

He rose unsteadily, his legs now numb, stuffed the envelope between the pages, then closed the book and put it back.

"Do you know what time it is? Almost three o'clock!"

"No need to get up early—it's Sunday."

"Didn't you say you'd take Shuhui out for the day? Can't start out too late in the morning. The alarm is set for ten o'clock."

Shijun made no reply. Tsuizhi was a bit apprehensive, thinking he might have found her efforts on Shuhui's behalf suspiciously excessive. That would explain why he was acting so strangely.

He woke twice in the night and had to get up before the alarm went off. It must have been the crab meat, upsetting his stomach. He sat with Shuhui at the lunch table, but soup was all that he could manage. A friend he'd not seen in years, and when they were finally reunited, the two of them so close and yet such strangers to each other, it was hard to find the right tone, neither too intimate nor too casual. It was a strange thing, this groping towards each other in the dark, but that didn't mean it lacked real pleasure.

The three of them sat together chatting, which reminded him of Manzhen. They had always been a threesome, he and Shuhui; always the two of them plus a woman. He wondered if Shuhui had the same feeling.

After they'd eaten, Tsuizhi went to make the coffee, since the servants had never used an espresso pot. Shuhui was telling Shijun about life in America. Work had been plentiful during the war, and salaries were high.

"You've really gone up in the world," Shijun said. "Now I'm sorry I didn't go with you. It's just as you said—all we're doing here is treading water."

"That's all one can do, anywhere. The main thing is to be happy while you're at it."

"Our life here is monotonous, I suppose. But taken as a whole, it's got something to it. Even if it's only watching the children grow up. That's about as much as one can expect from life, eh?"

Shuhui gave him a hard look and seemed ready to say something further, but didn't. Tsuizhi came in with the coffee, ending that line of the conversation.

Shuhui went out after the meal, to see a friend. It was an old colleague from the factory, and they chatted about the people they'd known there. Shuhui's friend told him Manzhen had come back, about a year ago, looking for work, so now he had her address. It was his impression that she'd got married, then divorced. Shuhui copied down the address. His friend having other things to do, they went their separate ways after agreeing to get together again. Shuhui then decided, on the spur of the moment, to look up Manzhen. Her place was on a secluded street, so quiet it hardly seemed a part of Shanghai. He entered the little cobblestone alley, lined with stone-clad residences, and found a wooden gate at the alley's end, behind which stood a large well. It was evening now, and a maid was at the well, scrubbing a bucket with a bristle-brush. The recessed compound, shaded from the sun, was filled with flower pots. There was even a peach tree supported by bamboo stilts, and evergreen bonsai.

There were several families living at this address, and a large, fat woman who looked like the one in charge was in the courtyard doing laundry, slapping soapy clothes on a table shoved up against the wall.

"Excuse me. Does a Miss Gu live there?"

The woman stood up straight, looked him over carefully, then called out to the maid, "Miss Gu hasn't returned yet, has she? Her door is still locked."

Shuhui mulled over his options, then tore a page from a notebook and wrote out his name, along with the telephone number at his sister's place. "Please give this to her when she comes back," he said to the woman, then walked off at a good clip.

Half an hour later, his sister's phone rang. Her mother-in-law picked it up and answered courteously. "He's gone to a friend's house. Their phone number is seven-two-zero-seven-five. Try to reach him there."

Tsuizhi picked up Manzhen's next call. "Mr. Hsu has gone out," she said. "What's your family name, please? Uh-huh. And your number? Three-five-one-seven-four. Sure. You're most welcome."

Shijun had spent most of the day in bed, feeling quite unwell. Tsuizhi put the phone back on the hook and came up the stairs. "Miss Gu just called, looking for Shuhui. I wonder who she is? Could it be that female colleague you and Shuhui brought with you to Nanking, all those years ago?"

"A lot of married women still use their own family names," Shijun mused, "and it would be especially likely when she's contacting a former colleague."

"Your mother, back then, said she was Shuhui's girlfriend, and Yipeng said she was yours. What nonsense you all talked!" She laughed.

Shijun said nothing.

A brief silence fell.

"Did Shuhui tell you anything about his divorce?" she asked.

"When could I have asked him about that? We've scarcely had a moment to talk privately."

"Ah, so that's it—the nosy wife, of course. When he gets back I'll leave you to your own devices, and you can discuss whatever you like."

A short while later, Shuhui returned. When he came upstairs to see Shijun, Tsuizhi was gone.

"Did Tsuizhi tell you that someone called Miss Gu telephoned, looking for you?" asked Shijun.

"It has to be Manzhen. I went to see her, but she wasn't in."

"I didn't know she was in Shanghai."

"You haven't seen her in the past few years?"

"No."

"I heard she got married, then divorced. Like me."

It was the perfect opening for Shijun to ask about his friend's divorce. But a welter of mixed-up feelings blocked any further thoughts about Shuhui. She and Yujin were divorced? How could that be? And why? Surely it wasn't anything related to him. And even if it were, what then? What options did he have, at this point?

Seeing how the mention of Manzhen had bothered Shijun, Shuhui changed the subject. Then Tsuizhi came in and asked Shijun if he was feeling better.

"I'm not fit for anything at all today. You'll have to take Shuhui out to dinner on your own."

"Oh, can't we eat here?" Shuhui asked.

"No, no. You haven't seen Shanghai in such a long time. Go out and see the city."

"That's a good idea," Tsuizhi put in. "Nothing is ready for dinner here. We were planning to go out."

"No need for anything fancy," Shuhui said. "Let's not go out. I've been running around all afternoon. Better to stay in and take it easy."

But they overruled his objections, and Tsuizhi got so busy deciding on the restaurant, and whether to make a reservation, that Shijun had to push her to get changed. Shuhui had no choice but to go downstairs and wait for her.

Tsuizhi sat at the mirror fixing her hair while Shijun lay on the bed watching her. She sometimes wore her hair up, sometimes let it down; she'd curl it under, then turn the curl out. So many different styles, over the years. Today she was piling it high on her head, which brought out the lovely roundness of her face. Normally, when Shijun had to wait while she got dressed before an evening out, it drove him crazy with impatience. But because he wasn't going with her, he had the leisure needed for detached observation. She really had not aged, looked younger than ever today, and the sparkle in her eyes, that edge of excitement, made her look like a young girl going out on a date. She put on a cheongsam of dark green silk covered with large green peonies.

"You look beautiful."

His words surprised her, and made her happy. "Oh, not really. Look how old I'm getting."

The children came back from seeing a film, and Little Bei stood by her mother's dressing-table, watching her put on her makeup. Big Bei said he'd never take his sister to the pictures again. She got frightened and, right at the most exciting part, had to be taken to the toilet. He was such a quiet little fellow when he was home, hardly ever laughed or smiled. Shijun wondered, as if he himself had never been that age, what was in the head of a nine-year-old boy. To the best of his recollection, he was well behaved by then, nothing like this little rascal.

Tsuizhi left, and the children went to have their dinner. Now that he had a moment to himself, his mind flew to the things he'd just learned about Manzhen. His heart gave a great thump when it occurred to him that . . . but Shuhui had doubtless torn off the sheet with the number Tsuizhi had taken down on the pad by the phone. He'd been leaning back in bed, in his dressing gown, but the moment this idea came to him, he leaped up and ran downstairs. On the top page of the little notebook he saw, written in a hurried scrawl, "Gu 35174." Shuhui must have copied the number into his address book, while he was waiting for Tsuizhi to come down. He'd probably already returned her call. Her voice had been here—this very evening, in his own hallway—twice in two hours. He almost could see her smiling at him in the lamplight. Why not call her? Old friends, hadn't seen each other in years, he'd be remiss if he didn't. She hadn't known, on the first call, that this was his house; Shuhui must have told her when he called back. It would be rude not to follow up and call her himself. If he didn't call, she'd think he'd objected to her having called his home. The past was the past, no need to keep thrashing it out, or even to mention it at all. They were well past their youth now, able to put it all in perspective—they could have a casual conversation. Manzhen had always been easy to talk to, and here he was, alone in the house, no Tsuizhi to eavesdrop on him. Tsuizhi wouldn't listen when he was speaking to her, but the minute he was talking to someone else, she was all ears. But precisely because that was the case, and the occasion so perfect, he felt a bit ashamed of himself.

As he was hesitating, he heard Amah Li calling out, "Oh, you've come downstairs, Mr. Shen! Would you like to eat down here? I was just bringing something up to you. Mrs. Shen told me to heat up some soup, and there's also some rice porridge with side dishes."

"We want rice porridge too!" the children shouted. "Dad, come and eat with us!"

Shijun copied the phone number, then sat with them at the table and heard all about the film they'd just seen. He stayed downstairs after the meal, reading the evening paper. He was feeling better now, and wished he had tried to make that dinner outing with Shuhui. Perhaps because he hadn't made the call to Manzhen, a sense of loneliness crept over him. He hoped they'd be back early. He'd not had a chance to have a proper talk with Shuhui; maybe they could have a good late-night chat. It was almost ten now and the children were in bed. Perhaps his wife and friend had gone on somewhere after dinner. He'd heard Tsuizhi talking about some nightclub that put on a great show.

He waited and waited, but when Amah Li told him someone had come to the door, it turned out to be his sister-in-law. Vim was at university in Shanghai, and his mother didn't like his being in the city by himself, so she'd moved there too. She rarely came over, since she and Tsuizhi didn't get along; the dog-bite episode had only made things worse.

But Shijun could guess her reason for coming tonight. Something to do with her son, of course. This boy Vim was apparently not making much progress. He did sloppy work at college, went out every night to have a good time. All this could be traced, of course, to the myopic indulgence of his mother. He'd come to see Shijun recently, decked out like a character in a martial arts novel, and looking to borrow some money. His mother, who'd not known about the transaction then, had probably found out and was coming to pay off the debt.

But Shijun's conjectures were wrong. His sister-in-law had been invited out that evening, to a meal in a restaurant, and happened to see Tsuizhi. Her dinner party was being held upstairs, while Tsuizhi and Shuhui were in a booth on the main floor. Shijun's sister-in-law had walked right past them and seen Tsuizhi wiping tears from her eyes. She recognized Shuhui, but Shuhui didn't recognize her, due to the degree to which she had aged, over the many years since they'd first met. Her clothing and hairstyle made her look like an old lady. Tsuizhi had not noticed her, no doubt because her entire attention was focused on Shuhui, though neither of them was speaking. The sister-in-law hadn't stopped to greet them, but went straight up to her gathering. Afterwards, on her way out, she saw that they'd already left. The whole thing bothered her so much that she came straight to Shijun's place, to give him a full report. She'd made a major discovery, and wouldn't conceal it even though Tsuizhi was a blood relative; she came in with a sense of her own virtuous willingness to ignore her family's interests, not as someone who delighted in the misfortune of others. The first thing she noticed, of course, was that Tsuizhi was not home yet.

"How did you get left alone at home?" was her opening question.

Shijun told her he hadn't been feeling well and so hadn't gone out.

They exchanged news and greetings and talked about Vim. Shijun got the impression she didn't know about her son's wild behavior and felt he had an obligation to tell her. Otherwise, he'd be the one at fault, for having lent the boy money behind his mother's back. But news of this sort was not easy to break. It might look as though he were asking her to repay the debt. His sister-in-law was highly protective of her son, who according to her was an exceptionally gifted, promising lad. It was impossible to say anything bad about him to her.

When she saw Shijun swallowing hard, as if he had something on his mind but couldn't get it out, his sister-in-law thought he must be struggling with feelings too difficult to discuss. She and Tsuizhi were blood relatives, cousins from the same family. He must want to complain, to someone in her family, about his wife's terrible misdeeds.

"Is there something you want to say? You can tell me, it's all right."

"No, it's nothing—"

"Is it Tsuizhi?" she broke in, before he could finish his sentence. "What she's doing is so wrong, such a slap in the face to you, sitting in a restaurant with another man, openly crying—I wouldn't have barged in like this, if it weren't that she's gone too far. It doesn't matter if *I* see her like that, but what about everyone else in that restaurant?"

Shijun had no idea what she was on about. "Are you talking about this evening?" he finally asked. "She took Shuhui out for dinner."

"Yes, I knew who it was," his sister-in-law said calmly. "Isn't he the one who used to come to Nanking, and stay at our house? But he didn't recognize me."

"He's just returned from overseas, he arrived yesterday. We had plans to go out together, but then I got sick and Tsuizhi took him out for dinner."

"Going out for fun is all very well and good, but what does it mean when they sit face to face, tears streaming down their cheeks?"

"I'm afraid your eyes must be playing tricks on you. It's not possible. Shuhui is my best friend, and Tsuizhi is at most a bit tetchy. Nothing worse than that, I assure you!" He laughed.

"Well, that *is* wonderful! You believe her, which is all that matters."

Seeing how irate she'd become, Shijun decided it wasn't the right time to tell her about Vim's misdoings. It would only look like a tit-for-tat, if he took that up after she'd told him that Tsuizhi was misbehaving. It would only stoke her anger. So he dropped that topic, and found something else to say. Her fury never did abate, and she left soon thereafter.

After she was gone, Shijun could only shake his head and sigh. This constant scaremongering of hers seemed to him obsessive. It was because she'd been widowed as a young woman; truly she was a casualty of an antiquated moral system.

Tsuizhi came back, alone, a bit after eleven.

"Where's Shuhui?" he asked.

"He went to his sister's place, said he promised her mother-in-law he'd be back tonight."

Shijun was very disappointed when he learned they'd made the rounds of several clubs and seen some stage shows. Tsuizhi, for her part, was sorry to hear he'd sat downstairs all evening waiting for them.

"You should go to bed," she urged.

"I'm fine now. I can go out tomorrow."

"Then you should get up early. All the more reason to get a good rest."

"I've already slept a whole day. Lying in bed now just makes me restless."

She'd heard that her cousin had come by and asked about what, but Shijun didn't give her the details; the two of them were already at such odds, no point in making it worse. He didn't take seriously this business about her crying in public, but knew she'd be angry if he mentioned it. Her face bore no trace of tears, no sign of unhappiness.

She urged him again to go to bed. Making a special effort to be good to him, she even went to the storage room and got him a book to help him relax. She brought a cup of tea and tossed the book towards him, onto the bed. The envelope that had been stuck into the book fell onto the floor. Shijun hurriedly kicked it under the bed, but Tsuizhi, still being helpful, had already bent down to pick it up for him. Her glance fell on it, accidentally.

"Give it here," Shijun said. "Nothing worth looking at." He reached over to take it from her.

But Tsuizhi wouldn't let go and a look of surprise spread across her face as she opened the envelope. "Oh! *A love letter!* What's this all about? Who wrote this to you?"

"It's from a long time ago. Give it back!"

Tsuizhi held the letter high in the air and read aloud, "'You left in such a hurry I'm afraid you didn't take any winter clothing. I know you let these things pass you right by, and never think to wear warm clothing. I don't know why I'm worrying about it either—'" Tsuizhi stopped at that point, snickering.

"Give it to me."

She tightened her throat and continued reading in the high, nasal tone of a stage actress: "'It's just that I keep turning anything I see, anything I hear, into a reason to think of you.'" She turned and smiled at him. "My, oh my! Who would have guessed you could cast a spell like this?" She went on: "'I went to Shuhui's yesterday, though I knew he wouldn't be at home, to see his parents. You've lived with them a long while—.' Oh!" She looked over at him. "I know. It's that Miss Gu, the one who wore an old sheepskin coat when she came to Nanking. Supposed to be Shuhui's girlfriend, but I didn't believe it."

"Why is that? Not pretty enough? Not trendy enough?"

"Goodness, goodness—an insult to one you hold dear? Look how angry you're getting!" Resuming her pose as a stage actress, she warbled in a high-pitched voice, "'Shijun, I want you to know there's someone in this world who's always yours. Please know that, forever and wherever. Yours, always—' What's this? Is she *still* waiting for you?"

Shijun could bear it no longer. "Give it to me!" he yelled, grabbing at the letter.

She didn't let go and the two of them scuffled, Shijun almost striking her. With a loud cry, Tsuizhi suddenly let go and gave him a fierce glare. "OK, OK, take it, why don't you? Who wants to read your sordid letters anyway!" Holding her bosom high, she stalked out of the room.

Shijun tightened his grip on the wadded-up letter and thrust it into his pocket. He was beside himself. He put on his street clothes and went downstairs. Tsuizhi was sitting on the sofa, beading a purse. "Oh—where are you going at this time of night?" she asked calmly.

All the fight had gone out of her voice, but Shijun, ignoring her, headed through the door.

Their little street was plunged in darkness, but when he got to some larger roads the neon lighting gradually increased. He went into a pharmacy to use the public telephone. He didn't have Manzhen's address, only her number. A man answered, and when Shijun asked for Miss Gu, he was asked to wait. The wait was long. Shijun guessed that Manzhen had no phone of her own, and this phone was somewhere nearby, a noisy place, so probably in a shop of some kind. He could hear a child crying in the background. It made him think of his own children, and his reckless intention of seeing this through began to falter. Nothing could come of this, why was he doing it? Wouldn't he be dragging her, once again, into his family's long-running quarrels? How could he treat her like that? Through the receiver he heard the sound of a car horn; the faint, far-away *honk-honk* had a dream-like quality.

He wished he hadn't made the call, but just as he was about to hang up a woman's voice came through.

"Hello?" she said. "We're calling her. Please wait a moment."

He wanted to tell them not to bother, but of course the woman was gone already. He put the receiver back, gently. She would come to the phone for nothing, but it was better this way.

He left the pharmacy and walked down the street. It was midnight or so, the streets were practically empty. Probably because he'd spent all day in bed, he felt light, as if he were floating, till a few minutes' walk used up all his energy; still, he wasn't the least interested in going home. He regretted making her come to the phone for nothing; he'd walk the streets too, to make it up to her. The early autumn wind blew across his face. The air, at long last, was cool: it felt like a blind man's fingers touching him to find out how much he had aged, whether he had changed. Change in her wasn't something he'd ever imagined.

Amah Li knew he'd left the house—she'd gone to bed after Tsuizhi returned, then heard what sounded like quarreling, and confirmation in the form of high-heeled shoes coming down the stairs. Not wanting to miss this, she'd found something to do in the kitchen, which allowed her to see a fully dressed Shijun, ready to go out, also coming downstairs. Strange, and stranger. He'd not got dressed all day; where was he going, fully clothed, at this hour? Tsuizhi asked and, for the first time ever, got the silent treatment. But Amah Li could tell, clear as day, that this was the consequence of the news brought by his sister-in-law that very evening—every syllable of which the old servant had overheard. She may have been growing slow and hard of hearing, but when it came to eavesdropping, she was second to none. Shijun's sister-in-law had told him his wife was involved with Mr. Hsu; Shijun had defended his wife and dismissed the report, but only in order to protect his self-respect, for he'd waited till the bearer of the accusation left, then picked a fight with Tsuizhi when she returned, on some other subject entirely. It all made sense. Amah Li just had to look in on Tsuizhi; once she realized that Tsuizhi didn't know what had been said against her, only that her sister-in-law had stopped by for a visit, out came the whole tale, this time from Amah Li.

When Shijun came home, he found Tsuizhi sitting in bed, still working on the beaded purse, her face very calm. He undid his tie. "There's nothing to get worked up about," he said, speaking slowly for emphasis. "There's no affair going on. Anyway it was all a long time ago."

Tsuizhi flew into a temper. "What do you mean? What affair? What are you talking about?"

Shijun paused. "I'm talking about the letter."

She gave him a long look. "Oh! The letter! I've forgotten about that already."

He was clueless, her tone implied, still worrying about that, as if a letter written a dozen years ago could have any significance.

"Everything's fine then." He let it go at that.

When he saw Shuhui the next day, he'd ask him about chances of going to America. The situation was highly fluid, he did realize that, and he'd already wasted a lot of time. Shuhui himself was unsure as to whether he'd go back overseas; he was going north first. Maybe he could look up there for some opening that would suit his old friend. It would be good to get a job in the north, get a change of scenery, live apart from Tsuizhi for a while, though he wouldn't mention this last part to Shuhui, at least not for the time being.

But, as it turned out, Shuhui didn't come over for several days running, didn't even telephone. Shijun started to wonder if Tsuizhi had offended him. He didn't want to ask her, not in the midst of their spat. In the end he phoned Shuhui himself and found his friend up to his ears in activity: plans had changed, and he was leaving for the north in just a few days, might even be going all the way up to the northeast. He had no time to talk then but agreed to come over for dinner on Friday.

On Friday afternoon, Shijun started thinking about the difficulty of talking when Tsuizhi was around. Maybe he'd go to Shuhui's sister's in-laws', invite him out to a café, then bring him back to the house. No point in phoning first, since he was often out; the best thing was to go there directly from his office, hoping to catch him. Shuhui's sister's family lived on a little street behind the stadium. It was a central location, easy to get to, but the building was old: the trellises that ran over the courtyard were filled with ivy whose shiny leaves reflected, quite distinctly, the young, blue-green bamboo screening the windows. The cement pavement had been dampened by a light rain, and just outside the building's back door a woman crouched over a brazier, fanning it: he could see the flames. Shijun looked around till he found the right building-unit, then asked, at the kitchen entrance, if Mr. Hsu was in. A kitchen maid called out loudly, "Mistress! Someone's here to see your brother!"

Shuhui's sister came out with a child in her arms, greeted him, then led him a long way into the apartment. She stopped at the doorway to a room and called in softly, "Ma, Mr. Shen is here." Something in her manner was odd, and he noticed a stiffness in her smile, as if she were feeling uncertain. Apparently he'd come at an awkward moment. "If Shuhui's not here, I'll come another day to see Mrs. Hsu," he offered.

But Mrs. Hsu had already risen to her feet and was crossing the floor to welcome him. Her daughter stepped aside so Shijun could enter the room, and that's when he saw that they had another guest, a woman. The room was long and narrow, with hardly any sunlight, and it wasn't yet time to turn on the evening lamps. Before he could really make out that it was Manzhen, he heard a great thud, the rush of blood in a body some distance from his own; the sound rose and fell like a wave, all before he could grasp that these were his own senses, rising in excitement. The eyes of those already in the room were accustomed to the dim light, not blinded as he was, coming in from the outside. She would have seen him at once, and in any case had heard them announce his arrival.

The house had the old-style, raised thresholds, half a foot high. Focused on crossing it, one foot on either side, he didn't hear something Mrs. Hsu said, but Manzhen he heard clearly: "Oh, Shijun's here!" Her voice was bright with happiness.

Everyone's voices were unusually high, but not loud, like tinkling chatter some distance away: there was a time lag before he grasped what they were saying.

"Now everyone's here," Mrs. Hsu was saying, "except for Shuhui. He left already."

"That's my fault," Manzhen said. "We planned to meet at four, but I was delayed, and he couldn't wait any longer."

Mrs. Hsu was being perfectly natural, but talking a lot, filling up the silences before they had a chance to grow. She ran through all the reasons why Shuhui was so busy, then switched to Shuhui's sister. How old had she been, Mrs. Hsu wondered, back when Shijun was her maths tutor? Now she was a mother, had children of her own. And Manzhen—how long since they'd seen her? They added it up, but Mrs. Hsu didn't ask how long it had been since Manzhen and Shijun had seen each other. Shuhui was coming to his house tonight for dinner, which Mrs. Hsu surely knew, but that topic didn't come up either. She was avoiding any mention of his family. So she spoke of her own husband instead.

After a while, Manzhen said she had to go.

"I need to leave too," Shijun said. "I'll come back another time to see you, Mrs. Hsu."

Shuhui's sister led them through the house, all the way out to the rear door. She'd known, back when she was a child, that they were sweethearts, and now she watched them walking side by side.

All the times he'd dreamed of seeing her again—it was happening now, but was utterly unlike anything he'd imagined. A feeling he could not describe, his mind blank, his heart dazed. As they walked down the long hallway, the whole world seemed to have changed: it had grown tiny and distant, like something seen through a telescope the wrong way around. He was surprised to find that the sky was still bright. Manzhen was looking quite gaunt, but fortunately her squarish face would keep its shape no matter how thin she grew. Also helpful was the fact that her appearance had changed somewhat; otherwise, he'd be dreaming again.

"So here we are," she was saying. "How long has it been?"

"I had no idea that you were in Shanghai."

"I thought you were in Nanking."

Their words were swallowed by the stillness around them, and they fell silent again.

They came out onto the main street, and he still hadn't asked where she was going, hadn't invited her to have dinner with him. He didn't want to risk getting into a pedicab, in case the spell broke and she said she had to go. So they walked and walked, till they saw in the distance the neon sign of a restaurant.

"Let's go in there. We can talk over dinner," Shijun proposed.

As he had feared, she smiled and said, "I'm afraid I've got things to do, and I have to get home. You should come another time to see Shuhui."

"Then let's just sit for a bit. We don't have to eat."

She didn't answer. They kept walking and when they got to the restaurant, they turned and went in. It was a small place, noisy and crowded, since it was now the dinner hour. Shijun suddenly recalled that Shuhui was coming to his house. He'd probably arrived by now. They sat down in a booth and ordered some food.

"I have to make a quick call. Don't run off," he said with a smile. "I'd spot you."

The phone was in the entryway, or he really would not have

taken the chance. He dialed the number, looking all the while at Manzhen, there in the yellow light. Tsuizhi's voice seemed to come from another world. The little kitchen window framed a piece of the limitless street and amplified the whir of vehicles passing by. The green neon tubes hanging in the main window spelled out the name of the restaurant, but he couldn't make the words out in reverse. He couldn't even tell what language it was, what country he was in.

He was speaking now. "Is Shuhui there yet? I won't be back for dinner. You two go ahead. Get him to stay for a bit, and I'll be there after I've eaten."

He'd never before backed out like this, inviting someone over then breaking the date at the last minute. He could explain it all to Shuhui later on, but he was expecting a loud protest from Tsuizhi. He was prepared to hang up immediately, both to avoid an argument and prevent any of it from reaching Manzhen's ears. But Tsuizhi didn't argue, she didn't even ask where he was or what he was doing. It was almost as if she'd been expecting his call.

When he hung up, he noticed that a private room was available. He went back to Manzhen and suggested that they move into the quieter area. The waiter heard them, transferred their teacups and place settings, then pulled the white door-curtain closed behind them. Manzhen saw a round table, already perfectly set, and a coat rack in the corner. She took off her coat and hung it up. There had been a time, back when he was seeing her home from the office on a regular basis, that her family had played along, by staying out of the room when they arrived. After she'd taken off her coat, he used to kiss her. And now? Did she remember that? She had to remember. He should say something, but nothing came to him. He hoped she would speak, but she didn't. They stood there, facing one another. Maybe she wanted him to kiss her. But if he did, what then? He'd spent days wondering whether to seek her out, and decided not to. What, if anything, had changed since then? Fundamental truth is unyielding, like a mountain. He felt a pricking in his eyes as the tears came, and his throat was full. He stared hard at her. Her lips were trembling.

"Shijun." Her voice shook too.

He said nothing, waiting for her to continue, his throat so tight he couldn't speak.

A long moment passed. "Shijun, we can't go back."

He knew it was true, but the words shook him to the core. Her head was already on his shoulder. She was in his arms.

She stepped back finally, to get a good look at him, then kissed his face, the warm hollow below his ear. She stepped back again and another pause fell.

"Are you happily married, Shijun?"

What is "happily married"? he wondered. It depends on how you define it. She shouldn't be asking him that. He couldn't brush it off, the way he would if the question came from any of his other, ordinary friends. His heart was broken with pain—why couldn't he tell her that? Because a gentleman doesn't discuss one woman's faults with another? Or was it masculine pride, unwillingness to admit he'd made a mistake? Maybe he was simply protecting Tsuizhi? Love is not passion, perhaps. Not yearning either, but the experience of time, the part of life that accumulates over the months and years.

Long minutes had passed as he thought about this. If he didn't say something soon, the silence would speak for itself. "It's your happiness that I care about."

He saw his mistake the moment the words were out of his mouth, the way they turned his silence into the answer. In his despair, he held her tight, and she returned the embrace, stroking his face with her hand. He took her hand and was about to kiss it when he saw a deep scar that hadn't been there before. "What happened here?"

To his bewilderment, her face suddenly turned emotionless, and she gazed at her hand without answering. The glass had cut her there. That day at her sister's when she'd screamed and no one responded, then she'd broken the window and sliced open her hand. She'd always imagined, back then, that she'd see Shijun again, and tell him what happened. How many times she had told him, in her dreams. And always she was awakened by her own tears. Now that it was real, and she was telling him, her voice was level and calm, because it had all happened such a long time ago.

They were sitting down now, since the waiter might walk in at any moment. Shijun was stunned, his face empty of emotion, deathly pale. That such a thing could happen—he was horrified. And the worst part was that he couldn't do anything about it. There was no way now to rise to her defense, no way to go back and save her.

Manzhen spoke without looking at him, in the only way she could get the words out. When she told him about escaping from the Zhus', then going back later to marry Hongtsai, she started speaking faster and faster. Then she told him about the divorce, the ordeal that had been, and how she'd finally been awarded custody of her son, whom she was now bringing up on her own. She'd borrowed huge amounts of money for the court case.

"How are you managing now? Do you have enough money?"

"I'm fine now. All the loans have been repaid."

"Where is that man now?"

"Why even ask? It's all finished now. I made my mistake too. I can hardly believe how foolish I was. I feel so sorry whenever I think of it."

Her marriage to Hongtsai, she meant. Shijun knew she must have heard, right at that point, that he'd got married and been gripped by an urge towards self-destruction.

"I think you must have felt . . . that I'd abandoned you."

Manzhen turned away quickly. She was crying, he knew.

There was nothing he could say for a long while. Finally, in a low voice, he said, "I went to your sister's. She returned your ring to me and said you'd married Yujin."

That took Manzhen by surprise. "What? She said *that*?"

Shijun told her how events had unfurled from his perspective, how her mother had told him she'd gone to the Zhu house to recuperate after an illness, and when he went looking for her, was told she wasn't there, which he interpreted to mean she didn't want to see him. He'd written to her from Nanking, received no reply, and when he again went looking for her, her mother had moved the family out of Shanghai. When he went to her sister's, he was told she'd got married. It had never occurred to him that her own sister would stoop so low, and he'd already heard, from other sources, that Yujin was in Shanghai to get married.

"He did get married then."

"Where is he now?"

"In the interior. During the Japanese invasion, their army dragged him off, after killing his wife. Later, after he was released, he went to Chongqing."

After he'd recovered a little from that news, Shijun asked, "How is he doing now? Have you heard from him?"

"A relative bumped into him in Guiyang a couple of years ago, and then we got in touch by letter. He helped me with the loans."

That was to be expected, given the warmth of Yujin's affection for her. Shijun hesitated, then had to ask, trying to make it sound natural, "Has he remarried?"

"Him?" She looked at Shijun and laughed. "Both of us are used to being on our own."

Shame crept over Shijun. Now it looked as though he'd been hoping to pass his dilemma over to Yujin. In fact, he was ready to toss everything aside and restore to Manzhen whatever was in his power, after all she'd been through. He held her hand in his on the table, paused a moment, then said with a smile, "But at least we're together now. Everything else can be sorted out. We can recover whatever has been lost: I'm sure of it. Please just leave everything to me—"

Manzhen broke in before he had finished, pain written across her face. "Don't talk like that, will you?" she said softly. "Seeing you today is already . . . more than I can bear!"

Tears were streaming down her cheeks, and she bent down to wipe them away.

She'd seen it clearly all along. It was as she said: they couldn't go back. Now he understood why he'd felt trapped in a daze today. He'd been fighting against time. Their last parting had been so sudden, so unexpected, they'd not had a chance to say goodbye. When they walked out of this room today, they'd be saying goodbye forever. It was completely clear, like death.

While the two of them in the restaurant were saying their final adieux, the pair back at the house were embroiled in a similar ordeal. The moment Tsuizhi hung up the phone and said Shijun would not be home for dinner, awkwardness filled the room. Since Shuhui seemed not to want to discuss it, Tsuizhi went off to instruct the servants regarding dinner. The children had eaten already. Amah Li saw what was going on and didn't come into the dining room to wait on them. Even Amah Tao had disappeared. Dull though they seemed, these old servants knew what to do without being told. Shuhui had tossed down a few drinks before he came, probably in self-defense, nervous about having dinner with his old friend and the friend's wife. It was even worse now that Shijun had left the two of them alone.

They drummed up a bit of small talk over dinner, without dispelling that sense of having nothing to say. Tsuizhi thought carefully, then said, in a light, even tone, "I know you're afraid I'll bring it up again."

He'd got angry, that evening when they went to dinner and she opened up to him. Surely she knew that in their situation his only option was to take her to bed, which he couldn't do, given his friendship with Shijun. That left her free to speak without fear of the consequences. Women do like to talk. Men aren't interested in all that love talk, except when they're very young.

He'd got angry because he was sorely tempted. He'd stayed away a few days, then wanted to come back, feeling he'd been unjust. He gazed at her, slightly drunk, then stood up and went to her, smiling tenderly as he stroked her hair. Tsuizhi sat still, not moving an inch. She looked straight ahead, her face a mask; although she did not look at him, she clearly was feeling serene and sad. Shuhui kept stroking her hair, a little smile showing in his eyes.

"My wife, Yigui, was like you in many ways, but not nearly so good. Or maybe it's just that I was too young to appreciate her."

He told her about his marriage. His attitude had been all wrong.

He couldn't have told anyone then that his actions arose from pure spite. The way Tsuizhi's mother had treated him that day, in that one brief meeting, many years before and a world and an ocean away—he knew she'd never hear how he'd paid her back, and yet he did it. He didn't elaborate, but it was all very clear to Tsuizhi—the young lady who was richer, and more popular, than she was.

Yigui was afraid of childbirth, and therefore its precondition, and they fought endlessly over this. He had a decent income, but living costs in America are high, so of course there wasn't enough money to keep her satisfied. He wouldn't allow her to spend her own money, wanted her to make do on a tighter budget. If she used her own money, the day would come when she looked down on him, unconsciously at least. They kept quarreling over money, till she was constantly on edge and he got so annoyed that he turned his back on her. He made a mistake, she found out and asked for a divorce. He didn't quibble, didn't want anyone to say he was angling for alimony.

The mistake to which he referred, though he hadn't made it explicit, had to be a woman. That sort of thing was all too common, in America during the war. He'd married late, doubtless had affairs before, but Tsuizhi was his lifelong passion, the woman he knew best, and for whom he'd yearned the longest. They looked at each other in the lamplight, the night breeze blowing the light yellow woolen curtain like a girl's skirt billowing in the wind, puffed up high then swinging to the side, about to drop down again, but then not quite. Beyond the window, the night was pitch-black. That long skirt swirling about in the air almost blew back into the room, then stopped at the window. Watching it made them feel they'd missed out on something, and life was passing them by.

"I think"—Tsuizhi was suddenly smiling at him—"that you'll soon marry again."

"Oh?"

"And your wife will be young and pretty and—"

Shuhui finished the thought for her: "*Rich.*"

They both laughed.

"So you think it's a vicious circle?" she asked.

"I'd say it's your doing, entirely. I'll keep going on like this, till I'm so old nobody wants me."

As she laughed, Tsuizhi felt a twinge of lonely triumph and satisfaction.

ALSO BY

Eileen Chang

LUST, CAUTION
The Story

In the midst of the Japanese occupation of China and Hong Kong, two lives become intertwined: Wang Chia-chih, a young student active in the resistance, and Mr. Yee, a powerful political figure who works for the Japanese occupational government. As these two move deftly between Shanghai's tea parties and secret interrogations, they become embroiled in the complicated politics of wartime—and in a mutual attraction that may be more than what they expected. Written in lush, lavish prose, and with the tension of a political thriller, *Lust, Caution* brings 1940s Shanghai artfully to life even as it limns the erotic pulse of a doomed love affair.

Fiction

ANCHOR BOOKS
Available wherever books are sold.
www.anchorbooks.com

CHINA IN TEN WORDS
by Yu Hua
translated by Allan H. Barr

Framed by ten phrases common in the Chinese vernacular, *China in Ten Words* uses personal stories and astute analysis to reveal, as never before, the world's most populous yet oft-misunderstood nation. In "Disparity," for example, Yu Hua illustrates the expanding gaps that separate citizens of the country. In "Copycat," he depicts the escalating trend of piracy and imitation as a creative new form of revolutionary action. And in "Bamboozle," he describes the increasingly brazen practices of trickery, fraud, and chicanery that are, he suggests, becoming a way of life at every level of society. Witty, insightful, and courageous, this is a refreshingly candid vision of the "Chinese miracle" and all of its consequences.

Current Affairs/China

I AM CHINA
by Xiaolu Guo

London translator Iona Kirkpatrick is at work on a new project: a collection of letters and diaries by a Chinese punk guitarist named Kublai Jian. As she translates the handwritten pages, a story of romance and revolution emerges between Jian, who believes there is no art without political commitment, and Mu, a poet whom he loves as fiercely as his ideals. As Iona charts the course of their twenty-year relationship from its beginnings at Beijing University to Jian's defiant march in the Jasmine Revolution, her empty life takes on an urgent purpose: to bring Jian and Mu together again before it's too late.

Fiction

THE GOOD WOMEN OF CHINA
Hidden Voices
by Xinran

When Deng Xiaoping's efforts to "open up" China took root in the late 1980s, Xinran recognized an invaluable opportunity. As an employee for the state radio system, she had long wanted to help improve the lives of Chinese women. But when she was given clearance to host a radio call-in show, she barely anticipated the enthusiasm it would quickly generate. Operating within the constraints imposed by government censors, "Words on the Night Breeze" sparked a tremendous outpouring, and the hours of tape on her answering machines were soon filled every night. Whether angry or muted, posing questions or simply relating experiences, these anonymous women bore witness to decades of civil strife, and of halting attempts at self-understanding in a painfully restrictive society. In this collection, by turns heartrending and inspiring, Xinran brings us the stories that affected her most, and offers a graphically detailed, altogether unprecedented work of oral history.

Current Affairs/Women's Studies

ANCHOR BOOKS
Available wherever books are sold.
www.anchorbooks.com